MICHAEL MARSHALL

THE INTRUDERS

"A brilliant new tale of paranoid suspense."
Newark Star-Ledger

"[A] novel that defies classification . . . Michael Marshall's book will satisfy those who have a deep affection for *The X-Files, Invasion of the Body Snatchers,* and other entertainment platforms that delve into conspiracy theories and unexplained phenomena. In addition to its intriguing characters . . . **readers are rewarded with a well-constructed, terrifying story line** that makes many other novels, of any genre, feel like Novel Writing 101."
USA Today

"Mr. Marshall recalls Stephen King's ability to set a story in the world of the commonplace, then suddenly jolt it into a more hellish realm. He also has some of Mr. King's ability to rivet attention with **eerie surprises**. It's not necessary to believe this book's spooky, underlying premise to be caught up in the **campfire-tale power** of its action."
New York Times

"The pacing is excellent, the plotting brisk, and the protagonist . . . is laced with believability . . . **An outstanding story."**
Baltimore Sun

"Complex and creepy . . . Your eyes will go wide and you'll shift in your chair and you'll say to yourself: This guy is good. Marshall knows how to create real suspense, how to dole it out slowly and catch you off guard. . . . A story that will not let you go."

Arizona Republic

"A bucket full of twists and turns beyond expectation. . . . *The Intruders* might turn out to be **one of the five best books I've read this year.** . . . A powerful writer . . . It's easy to become attached to Marshall's fully drawn characters."

The Olympian (WA)

"[Marshall] is one of those writers who can propel readers along with an inventive plot, then stop them cold with a brilliant descriptive line that demands repeated reading. He is **a master of the thriller laced with the supernatural**, writing with the rocketing pace of the conspiracy unveiled. His most recent novel displays his great strengths as a writer: a compelling plot, characters who are completely believable and unforgettable, and sharp, smart insights into the nature of modern life."

New Orleans Times-Picayune

"A fluid blend of crime and horror . . . dovetailing two genres so neatly as to earn M. Night Shyamalan's respect. . . . Marshall ratchets up the paranoia."

New York Daily News

"Michael Marshall delivers plenty of deep-seated fear in *The Intruders*. The resolution will have readers looking over their shoulders."

South Florida Sun-Sentinel

"A novel that keeps the reader off-kilter . . . **Brilliant** . . . Marshall expertly builds on an escalating fear that infuses the story at every turn. . . . *The Intruders'* **originality and suspense** keep the story fresh."

Detroit Free Press

"You'll love this. . . . **A good, taut thriller,** with lots of action and a very gripping ending. Marshall takes the reader with him on the investigation with a great deal of guile and style."

The Guardian (London)

"Marshall outdoes his own high standards with this **potent blend of suspense, paranoia, and just plain creepiness**. . . . Marshall ingeniously threads these strands together into a provocative and supremely intelligent thriller that reads like a cross between Andrew Klavan and Philip K. Dick."

Publishers Weekly (*Starred Review*)

"[Marshall] keeps readers guessing with twisting plot . . . **Adrenaline-paced . . . Addictive."**

Cleveland Plain Dealer

"A smart and engaging conspiracy thriller . . . that's anything but predictable."

Sunday Telegraph Magazine (Australia)

"The suspense kills . . . Marshall knows how to pull you into his net, hold you encased, and then throw a one-two punch when you're looking the other way. *The Intruders* is **fast, original, and thoroughly engrossing.**"

Madison County Herald (MS)

By Michael Marshall

THE INTRUDERS
THE BLOOD OF ANGELS
THE UPRIGHT MAN
THE STRAW MEN

Coming Soon in Hardcover

BAD THINGS

MICHAEL MARSHALL

THE INTRUDERS

HARPER
An Imprint of HarperCollins*Publishers*

This book was originally published in hardcover August 2007 by William Morrow, an Imprint of HarperCollins Publishers.

HARPER

An Imprint of HarperCollins*Publishers*
10 East 53rd Street
New York, New York 10022-5299

ISBN 978-0-06-123503-0

First Harper paperback printing: January 2009
First William Morrow hardcover printing: August 2007

Printed in the United States of America

Visit Harper paperbacks on the World Wide Web at
www.harpercollins.com

10 9 8 7 6 5 4 3 2 1

For Nathaniel
—I did it

Acknowledgments

A huge thank-you to my editors, Jane Johnson and Carolyn Marino, for their help in making this book a book; also to Sarah Hodgson, Lisa Gallagher, Lynn Grady, and Amanda Ridout; to Jonny Geller and Ralph Vicinanza for advocacy and advice; to Sara Broecker and Jon Digby for research; to Ariel for the web; to Stephen Jones, Adam Simon, David Smith (and The Junction) for support—and to Andreia "Peppa" Passos for so much else. Mad props as always to my ho, Paula, and to the shortie, N8. Y'all be clutch.

How can we be sure we are not imposters?

–Jacques Lacan

The Four Fundamental Concepts of Psychoanalysis

Prologue

Thump, thump, thump. You could hear it halfway up the street. It was bizarre that the neighbors didn't complain. Or do so more often and more stridently. Gina sure as hell would—especially if the music sucked this bad. She knew she ought to go upstairs as soon as she got indoors, yell at Josh to turn it down. She also knew he'd look at her in that way teenagers have, like they're wondering who you are and what gives you the right to bother them and what the hell happened in your life to make you so boring and old. He was a good son at heart, though, and so he'd roll his eyes and nudge the stereo down a notch, and then over the next half hour the volume would creep up until it was even louder than before.

Usually Bill was around to get into it with him—if he wasn't hidden in his basement, tinkering—but tonight he was out with a couple of faculty colleagues. That was good, partly so he could get the bowling out of his system without involving Gina, who couldn't stand the dumb sport, and also because he went out very seldom. They usually managed to grab a meal somewhere once every couple weeks, just the two of them, but most evenings this year had seen him disappearing downstairs after dinner, wrench in hand and a pleasurably preoccupied look on his face. For a while he'd generated his own strange noises down there, low booming sounds you felt in the pit of your stomach, but thankfully that had stopped. It was healthy for a guy to get out of the house now and then, hang with other guys—even if Pete Chen and Gerry Johnson were two of the geekiest dudes Gina had met in her entire *life,* and she found it impossible to imagine them cutting loose at bowling or drinking or indeed anything at all that didn't involve UNIX and/or a soldering iron. It also gave Gina a little time to herself, which—no matter how much you love your husband—is a nice thing once in a while. Her plan was a couple hours in front of the tube with *her* choice of show—screw the documentary channels. In preparation she'd gone to the big deli on Broadway, picked up groceries for the week and a handful of deluxe nibbles for right now.

As she opened the door to the house and stepped into a zone of even higher volume, she wondered if Josh ever considered that his vanilla mom might have rocked out on her own account, back in the day. That before she'd fallen in love with a young physics lecturer named Bill Anderson and settled down to a life of happy domesticity, she'd done plenty time in the grungier venues of Seattle-Tacoma and its environs, had been no stranger to high volume, cheap beer, and waking up with a head that felt like someone had gone at it with hammers. That she'd bounced sweatily to Pearl Jam and Ideal Mausoleum and even Nirvana—back when they were local unknowns and sharp and hungry instead of hollow-faced and dying—most memorably on a summer night when she'd puked while crowd surfing, been dropped on her head, and still got lucky in the soaking and dope-reeking restrooms with some guy she'd never met before and never saw again.

Probably not. She smiled to herself.

Just went to show kids didn't know everything, huh?

An hour later she'd had enough. The thumping was okay while she was just watching with half an eye—and the volume had actually dropped for a while, which maybe suggested he was doing some homework, and that was a relief—but it had started ratcheting up again, and in ten minutes there was a rerun of a *West Wing* episode she'd never seen before. You needed a clear head and peace and quiet to follow what the hell was going on with those guys, they talked so fast. Plus, Jesus, it was half past nine and getting beyond a joke.

She tried hollering up at the ceiling (Josh's bedroom was directly overhead) but received no indication she'd been heard. So she sighed, put her depleted plate of goodies on the coffee table, and hoisted herself off the couch. Trudged upstairs, feeling as if she were pushing against a wall of noise, and banged on his door.

After a fairly short time, it was opened by some skinny guy with extraordinary hair. For a split second, Gina didn't even recognize him. She wasn't looking at a boy anymore, nothing like, and Gina realized suddenly that she and Bill were sharing their house with a young man.

"Honey," she said, "I don't want to cramp your style, but do you have anything that's more like actual music, if you're going to play it that loud?"

"Huh?"

"Turn it down."

He grinned lopsidedly and walked into the room to jack the volume back. He actually cut it in half, which emboldened Gina to take a step into his room. It struck her that it had been a while since she'd been there when he was also present. In years past she and Bill had spent hours sitting on the floor here together, watching their toddler careering around on wobbly legs and bringing them random objects with a triumphant "Gah!," thinking how magical it all was, then later tucking him in and reading a story, or two, or three; then perched on the bed in the early years of homework and puzzling out math problems.

At some point in the last year, the rules had changed. It was a solo mission now when she came in to fix the bed or sweep up piles of T-shirts. She was in and out quickly, too, remembering her own youth well enough to respect her child's space.

She saw that, among the chaos of clothing and CD cases and pieces of at least one dismembered computer, there was evidence of homework being tackled.

"How's it going?"

He shrugged. Shrugging was the lingua franca. She remembered that, too. "Okay," he added.

"Good. Who's that you're listening to anyway?"

Josh blushed faintly, as if his mom had asked who this Connie Lingus was, that everyone was talking about.

"Stu Rezni," he said diffidently. "He—"

"Used to hit sticks for Fallow. I know. I saw him at the Astoria. Before they knocked it down. He was so wasted he fell off his stool."

She was gratified to see her son's eyebrows shoot up. She tried not to smile.

"Can you keep the volume sane for a while, honey? There's a show I want to watch. Plus, people are staggering up the street with bleeding ears, and you know what that does to property values."

"Sure," he said with a genuine smile. "Sorry."

"No problem," she said, thinking, *I hope he's going to be okay*. He was a nice boy, polite, a slacker who still got (most of) his chores done eventually. She hoped without a trace of egotism that he'd taken on enough of her, too, along with the big old helping of Bill he'd absorbed. This young man already spent a lot of time alone, and he seldom seemed more content than when taking something apart or putting it back together. That was cool, of course, but she hoped it wouldn't be too long before she saw evidence of his first hangover. Man cannot live by coding skills alone, not even in these strange days.

"Later," she said, hoping it didn't sound too lame.

The doorbell rang.

* * *

As she hurried downstairs, she heard the volume drop a little further and smiled. She still had this expression on her face when she opened the front door.

It was dark outside, the streetlamps at the corner spreading orange light over the fallen leaves on the lawn and sidewalk. A strong breeze rustled those still left on the trees, sending a few to spiral down and around the crossroads where the two residential streets met.

A figure was standing a couple of yards back from the door. It was tall, wearing a long, dark coat.

"Yes?" Gina said.

She flipped the porch light on. It showed a man in his mid-fifties, with short, dark hair, sallow skin in flat planes around his face. His eyes seemed dark, too, almost black. They gave no impression of depth, as if they had been painted on his head from the outside.

"I'm looking for William Anderson," he said.

"He's not here right now. Who are you?"

"Agent Shepherd, FBI," the man said, and then paused, for a deep cough. "Mind if I come inside?"

Gina did mind, but he just stepped up onto the porch and walked right past her and into the house.

"Hold on a second there, buster," she said, leaving the door open and following him. "Can I see some ID?"

The man pulled out a wallet and flipped it open at her without bothering to look in her direction. Instead he panned his gaze methodically around the room, then up at the ceiling.

"What's this about?" Gina asked. She'd seen the three big letters clearly enough, but the idea of having a real live fed in the house didn't even slightly compute.

"I need to talk to your husband," the man said. His matter-of-factness made the situation seem even more absurd.

Gina put her hands on her hips. This was her house, after all. “Well, he’s out, like I said.”

The man turned toward her. His eyes, which had appeared flat and dead before, slowly seemed to be coming alive.

“You did, and I heard you. I want to know *where* he is. And I need to take a look around your house.”

“The hell you do,” Gina said. “I don’t know what you think you’re doing here, but—”

His hand came up so fast she didn’t even see it. The first she knew was when it was clamped around the bottom of her face, holding her jaw like a claw.

She was too shocked to make a sound as he began to pull her slowly toward him. But then she started to shout, substituting volume for the articulation denied her by being unable to move the lower half of her mouth.

“Where is it?” he asked. Matter-of-fact had become almost bored.

Gina had no clue what he was talking about. She tried to yank away, hitting at him with her fists, kicking out, jerking her head back and forth. He put up with this for about one second and then whipped his other hand around to smack her across the side of her head. Her ears rang like a dropped hubcap and she nearly fell, but he held her up, wrenching her jaw to the side in the process, making it feel like it was going to pop out.

“I’m going to find it anyway,” he said, and now she knew she could feel something tearing at the side of her head. “But you can save us both some time and trouble. Where is it? Where does he work?”

“I . . . don’t . . .”

“Mom?”

Gina and the man turned together, to see Josh at the bottom of the stairs. Her son blinked, a deep frown spreading across his face.

“Let go of my mom.”

Gina tried to tell Josh to get back upstairs, to just run, but it came out as desperate, breathless grunts. The man stuck his other hand in the pocket of his coat, started taking something out.

Josh hit the ground running and launched himself across the living room. *"Let go of my—"*

Gina just had time to realize she'd gotten it wrong before, that her son wasn't a man after all, that he was just a little boy, stretched taller and thinner but still so young, when the man shot him in the face.

She screamed then, or tried to, and the tall man swore quietly and dragged her with him as he walked over to the front door and pushed it shut.

Then he pulled her back into the room where her son lay on the floor, one arm and one leg moving in twitches. Her head felt like it was full of bright light, stuttering with shock. Then he punched her precisely on the jaw, and she didn't know where she was.

A second or several minutes passed.

At length she was aware again, sprawled on the floor, half propped against the couch she'd been curled up in ten minutes before. The plate of food lay upside down within arm's reach. Her jaw was hanging loose, and she couldn't seem to move it. It felt as if someone had pushed long, thick nails into both of her ears.

The man in the coat was squatted down next to Josh, whose right arm was still moving, lazily smearing its way through the pool of blood seeping from his head.

The smell of gasoline reached Gina's face. The man finished squirting something from a small metal can all over her son, then dropped it on him and stood up.

He looked down at Gina.

"Last chance," he said. His forehead was beaded with sweat, though the house was not warm. In one hand he held a cigarette lighter. In the other he held his gun. "Where is it?"

As he flicked on the lighter, holding it over Josh and looking her in the eyes, Gina knew that—whatever this was—it wasn't a last chance to live.

Part I

The greatest hazard of all, losing one's self, can occur very quietly in the world, as if it were nothing at all. No other loss can occur so quietly; any other loss—an arm, a leg, five dollars, a wife, etc.—is sure to be noticed.

—Søren Kierkegaard
The Sickness Unto Death

chapter ONE

There was this girl I knew back in high school. Her name was Donna, and even that was wrong about her, as if she'd been mislabeled at birth. She wasn't a Donna. Not in real terms. She made you realize there must be an underlying rhythm to the universe, and you knew this purely because she wasn't hitting it. She walked a little too quickly. She turned her head a little too slowly. It was like she was dubbed onto reality a beat out of sync. She was one of those kids you saw at a distance, toting a pile of books, standing diffidently with people you didn't realize were even at the school. She had friends, she did okay in class, she wasn't a total loser, and she wasn't dumb. She was just kind of hard to see.

Like all schools we had a pecking order of looks, but Donna somehow wasn't on the same scale. Her skin was pale and her features fine-boned and evenly spaced, fault-less except for a crescent scar to the side of her right eye, legacy of some toddling collision with a table. The eyes themselves were inky gray and very clear, and on the rare occasions when you got to look into them, you received a vivid sense she was real after all—which only made you wonder what you thought she was the rest of the time. She was a little skinny, maybe, but otherwise slightly cute in every way except that she somehow just . . . wasn't. It was as if she released no pheromones, or they operated on an inaudible wavelength, broadcasting their signal to sexual radios either out of date or not yet invented.

I found her attractive nonetheless, though I was never really sure why. So I noticed when it looked like she was hanging out with—or in the vicinity of—a guy named Gary Fisher. Fisher was one of the kids who strode the halls as if accompanied by fanfare, the group that makes anyone who's been through the American school system instantly wary of egalitarian philosophies later in life. He played football with conspicuous success. He was on the starting basketball lineup, played significant tennis, too. He was good-looking, naturally: When God confers control of sports spheres, he tends to wrap it in a prettier package, too. Fisher wasn't like the actors you see in teen movies now, impossibly handsome and free of facial blemish, but he looked *right,* back in the days when the rest of us stared dismally in the mirror every morning and wondered what had gone wrong and whether it would get better—or even worse.

He was also, oddly, not too much of an asshole. I knew him a little from track, where I had a minor talent for hurling things a long way. I'd gathered from the jock grapevine that a realignment had taken place among the ruling classes, principally that Gary's girl, Nicole, was now going with one of his friends instead, in what appeared to be an amicable transfer of chattels. You didn't have to be too keen an observer of the social scene to perceive a degree of interest in taking her place—but the truly weird thing was that Donna seemed to believe herself in the running. It was as if she had received intelligence from somewhere that the caste system was illusory and you actually *could* fit a square peg in a round hole. She couldn't sit at the same table at lunch, of course, but would wind up at one nearby, close to Gary's line of sight. She would engineer "accidental" bumps in the corridor but manage nothing more than nervous laughs. I even saw her a couple of Fridays out at Radical Bob's, a burger/pizza place where people tended to start the weekend. She would stop by whatever table Fisher was sitting at and deliver some remark about a class or assignment, which would fall to the floor like a brick. Then she would wander off, a little too slowly now, as if hoping to be called back. This never happened. Other than being mildly perplexed, I doubt Fisher had the slightest clue what was going on. After a couple weeks, a deal was done in some gilded back room—or the backseat of a gilded car, more likely—and one morning Gary was to be found in the company of Courtney Willis, textbook hot blonde. Life went on.

For most of us.

Two days later Donna was found in the bathtub at her parents' home. Her wrists had been cut with determination and only one testing slash on the forearm. The adult consensus, which I overheard more than once, was that it could not have been a fast way to go—despite a last-ditch attempt to hasten progress by pushing a pair of nail scissors deep into her right eye socket, as if that crescent scar had been some kind of omen. There was a handwritten letter to Gary Fisher on the floor, the words blurred by water that had spilled over the edges of the tub. Lots of people later claimed to have seen the letter, or a photocopy, or overheard someone saying what was in it. But, as far as I know, none of this was true.

News spread fast. People went through the motions, and there were outbreaks of crying and prayer, but I don't think any of us were shaken to our core. Personally, I was not surprised or even particularly sorry. That sounds callous, but the truth was, it felt like it made sense. Donna was a weird chick.

A strange girl, a dumb death. End of story.

Or so it seemed to most of us. Gary Fisher's reaction was different, and at the time it was the most surprising thing I had ever seen. Everything was new and strange back then, events backlit by the foreshortened perspective of a fledgling life. The guy who did something halfway cool one time became our very own Clint Eastwood. A party that happened a year before could take on the status of legend, generating nicknames that would last a lifetime. And when someone went tearing out into the farther reaches of left field, it tended to stick in your mind.

On the following Monday, we heard that Fisher had quit the team. *All* the teams. He stood there and let the coaches bawl him out, then just walked away. Maybe these days you'd get some kind of slacker kudos for that kind of shit. Not in the 1980s, and not in the town where I grew up. It was so out there it was disturbing—the Alpha Teenager Who Resigned. Fisher became the guy you'd see wandering across the campus in transit between the library and class, as if he'd slipped into Donna's slot. And he worked. Hard. Over the next months, he hauled his grade-point average up, first a little, then a lot. He went from being a C student—and some of *those* had been massaged through sports prowess—to B's and some regular A's. Maybe he was getting parent-funded extra tutoring after school, but actually I doubt it. I think he just jumped tracks, decided to be some other guy. By the end you hardly ever saw him except in class. The masses dealt with him warily. No one wanted to get too close, in case the madness was catching.

I did see him this one afternoon, though. I'd been out training for our last-ever track meet and stayed on after the rest of the team left. Theoretically I was practicing the javelin, but really I just liked being there when no one else was around. I'd spent a lot of hours running that track, and it had started to dawn on me that the end was coming and some things were happening for the last time. As I pounded up the approach, back and forth, refining my run-up, I saw a guy walking from the far end. Finally I realized it was Gary Fisher.

He wandered the periphery, not headed anywhere in particular. He'd been one of our star sprinters before he quit, and maybe he was there for the same kind of reason that I was. He wound up a few yards away and watched for a little while. Eventually he spoke.

"How's it going?"

"Okay," I said. "Not going to win, though."

"How's that?"

I explained that a guy from another school had recently revealed himself not only to be good at throwing but to care about it also. After easy wins had stopped being a given, my interest had waned. I didn't put it in those terms, but that was the bottom line.

He shrugged. "Never know. Could be Friday's going to be your day. Be cool to go out on a win."

For a moment then, I found I *did* care. Maybe I *could* do it, this last time. Fisher stood a bit longer, looking across the track, as if hearing the beat of feet in races gone by.

"She was provisional," I said suddenly.

It was like he hadn't heard me. Then he slowly turned his head. "What's that?"

"Donna," I said. "She never really . . . locked in, you know? Like she was just renting space."

He frowned. I kept going.

"It was like . . . like she knew it might just not work out, you know? Like she came into the world aware that happy-ever-after was a long shot. So she put all her chips on one bet to win. Came in red instead of black, so she just walked away from the table."

I hadn't rehearsed any of this, but when I'd said it, I felt proud. It meant something profound, or sounded like it might—which is plenty good enough when you're eighteen.

Fisher looked at the ground for a minute and then seemed to nod faintly. "Thanks."

I nodded back, all out of words, and went thudding down the track to hurl my spear. Maybe I was showing off, hoping to impress the Gary Fisher of eight months before. Either way I pulled my arm over far too fast, reopened an old split on the tip of my middle finger, and wound up not making the last meet after all.

The end of school came and went. Like everyone else, I was too busy rushing through celebrated rites of passage to pay much attention to people I didn't really know. Tests, dances, everything hurried as our childhoods started to run out of gas. Then—bang: out into the real world, which has a way of feeling like that supertest you never got around to studying for. It still feels that way to me sometimes. I don't think I heard Fisher's name mentioned once during the summer, and then I left town to go to college. I thought about him every now and then over the next couple years, but eventually he dropped out of my head along with all the other things that had no relevance to my life.

And so I was not really prepared for the experience of meeting him again, nearly twenty years later, when he turned up at the door of my house and started talking as if no time had passed at all.

I was at my desk. I was trying to work, though a time-management study would probably have suggested that my job consisted of staring out the window, with only occasional and apparently random glances at a computer screen. The house was very quiet, and when the phone rang, it jerked me back in my chair.

I reached out, surprised that Amy was calling the landline rather than my cell, but not thinking much more about it than that. Being on the phone to my wife meant a break from work. Then I could make more coffee. Go have a cigarette on the deck. Time would pass. Tomorrow would come.

"Hey, babe," I said. "How stands the corporate struggle?"

"Is this Jack? Jack Whalen?"

It was a man's voice. "Yes," I said, sitting up and paying more attention. "Who's this?"

"Hang on to your hat, my friend. It's Gary Fisher."

The name sent up a flag right away, but it took another second to haul it back through the years. Names from the past are like streets you haven't driven in a while. You have to remember where they go.

"You still there?"

"Yes," I said. "Just surprised. Gary Fisher? Really?"

"It's my name," the guy said, and laughed. "I wouldn't lie about something like that."

"I guess not," I said. I had question marks right across the dial. "How did you get my number?"

"A contact in L.A. I tried calling last night."

"Right," I said, remembering a couple of hang-ups on the machine. "You didn't leave a message."

"Thought it might come across kind of weird, getting in touch after nearly twenty years."

"A little," I admitted. I found it hard to imagine that Fisher and I had anything to discuss unless he was running the class reunion, which seemed unlikely in the extreme. "So what can I do for you, Gary?"

"It's more what I might be able to do for you," he said. "Or maybe both of us. Look—where is it you live, exactly? I'm in Seattle for a few days. Thought it might be cool to meet up, talk about old times."

"Place called Birch Crossing. Hour and a half inland. Plus, my wife's got the car," I added. Amy has claimed that if you could get enough unsociable people together in a room to vote, they'd make me their king. She's probably right. Since my book came out, I'd been contacted by a few other people from the past, though none as far back as Fisher. I hadn't bothered to reply to their e-mails, forwarded via the publisher. Okay, so we used to know each other. What's your point?

"I've got a day to kill," Fished persisted. "Had a string of meetings canceled."

"You don't want to just tell me on the phone?"

"Would be a long call. Seriously, you'd be doing me a favor, Jack. I'm going nuts in this hotel, and if I walk round Pike Place Market one more time, I'm going to wind up with a big dead fish I don't need."

I thought about it. Curiosity struck a deal with the desire not to work, the terms brokered by a small part of my soul for which—absurdly—Gary Fisher's name evidently still held something of a charge.

"Well, okay," I said. "Why not?"

He arrived a little after two. I'd achieved nothing in the meantime. Even a call to Amy's cell phone for a hey-how-are-you had dead-ended in her answering service. I was becalmed in the kitchen thinking vaguely about lunch when I heard someone pulling into the drive.

I walked up the polished wood steps and opened the front door to see a black Lexus where our SUV usually sat—a vehicle that was currently in Seattle, with my wife. The car door opened and some mid-thirties guy got out. He came crunching over the gravel.

"Jack Whalen," he said, breath clouding around his face. "So you grew up. How did that happen?"

"Beats me," I said. "Did everything I could to avoid it."

I made coffee, and we took it down into the living room. He looked around for a few moments, checking out the view of the wooded valley through the big plate-glass windows, then turned to me.

"So," he said, "still got that good throwing arm?"

"Don't know," I said. "Don't get much occasion to throw stuff these days."

"You should. It's very liberating. I try to throw something at least once a week."

He grinned, and for a moment he looked pretty much how I remembered him, albeit better dressed. He reached a hand across the coffee table. I shook it.

"Looking good, Jack."

"You, too."

He was. You can tell men in good condition just from how they sit in a chair. There's a confidence in their poise, a sense that sitting is not a relief but merely one of the many positions in which their body is at ease. Gary looked trim and fit. His hair was well cut and not gray, and he had the skin that healthy eating and nonsmoking deliver to those with the patience to endure that type of lifestyle. His face had matured into that of a youthful senator from somewhere unimportant, the kind who might have a shot at vice president someday, and his eyes were clear and blue. The only thing I had over him was that the lines around my mouth and eyes were less pronounced, which surprised me.

He was silent for a few moments, undoubtedly making a similar assessment. Meeting a contemporary after a long time personifies the passage of time in a serious and irrevocable way.

"I read your book," he said, confirming what I'd suspected.

"So you're the one."

"Really? Didn't do so well? I'm surprised."

"It did okay," I admitted. "Better than. Problem is, I'm not sure there's another."

He shrugged. "Everyone thinks you've got to do things over and over. Nail your colors to the mast, make it who you are. Maybe one was all you had."

"Could be."

"You couldn't go back to the police force?" He saw the way I looked at him. "You thank the LAPD in the acknowledgments, Jack."

Slightly against my will, I smiled back. Fisher still had that effect. "No. I'm done there. So how do you earn a buck these days?"

"Corporate law. I'm a partner in a firm back east."

Him being an attorney figured, but it didn't give me a lot to work with. We knocked sentences back and forth for a little while, mentioning people and places we'd once known, but it didn't catch fire. It's one thing if you've kept in touch over the years, lit beacons to steer you across the seas of time. Otherwise it seems strange, being confronted with this impostor who happens to have the same name as a kid you once knew. Though Fisher had referred to old times, we didn't really have any, unless pounding around the same track counted, or a shared ability to remember the menu at Radical Bob's. A lot had happened to me since then, probably to him, too. It was evident that neither of us counted classmates as friends or retained ties to the town where we'd grown up. The kids we'd once been now seemed imaginary, a genesis myth to explain how we'd used up our first twenty years.

"So," I said, swallowing the rest of my coffee, "what did you want to talk to me about?"

He smiled. "You're done with the small talk?"

"Never really been a core skill."

"I remember. What makes you think I've got something to say?"

"You said you did. Plus, until you got my new number, you evidently thought I still lived in L.A. That's *not* a couple hours' drive from Seattle. So you started looking for me for some other reason."

He nodded, as if pleased. "How'd you find this place anyway? Birch Crossing? Is it even on maps?"

"Amy did. We'd talked about getting out of L.A. I had, at least. She got this new job. It meant we could basically be anywhere as long as she could get to an airport once in a while. She found this place online or somewhere, came and checked it out. I took her word for it."

"Liking it?"

"Sure," I said.

"Kind of a change from Los Angeles, though."

"That was partly the point."

"Any kids?"

"No."

"I got a couple. Five and two years old. You should try it. They change your life, dude."

"So I hear. Where are you based these days?"

"Evanston. Though I work in downtown Chicago. Which brings me to it, I guess."

He stared at his hands for a moment, and then started talking in earnest.

chapter TWO

"Here's what I know," he said. "Three weeks ago two people were murdered in Seattle. A woman and her son, killed in their own home. The police were called after a neighbor noticed smoke and came outside to see flames in the house. When the police get in, they find Gina Anderson, thirty-seven, lying in the living room. Someone had dislocated her jaw and broken her neck. On the other side of the room was Joshua Anderson. He'd been shot in the head and then set on fire. According to the fire department, that wasn't what burned the house, though: The flames had only just reached that room when they arrived. The main blaze had been set in the basement, where the woman's husband, Bill Anderson, had a workshop. From the debris it looked like someone had trashed the place, emptied out a bunch of filing cabinets full of notes and papers, and put a match to it all. I don't know how well you know Seattle, but this is up in the Broadway area, overlooking downtown. The houses are close to each other, bungalows, two-story, mainly wooden construction. If the fire had really gotten going, it wouldn't have taken much to jump to the ones around it and wipe out the whole block."

"So where's the husband?" I asked.

"No one knows. In the early part of the evening, he was

out with two male friends. He's a lecturer at the community college, about a half mile away. They have a semiregular night out, every six weeks. These guys confirm that Anderson was with them until a quarter after ten. They split up outside a bar, went their separate ways. Nobody's seen Anderson since."

"How are the police handling it?"

"Nobody saw anyone come or go from the house during the evening. The prevailing assumption is Anderson is the suspect, and they're not looking anywhere else. Problem is working out why he'd do this. His colleagues say he seemed distracted, and they and others claim he'd been that way for a few weeks, maybe a month or more. But no one's got anything on problems he might have had, there's no talk of another woman or anything along those lines. Lecturers don't make a whole lot of cash, and Gina Anderson wasn't earning, but there's no evidence of a drastic need for money. There's a life insurance policy on the wife, but it's hardly worth getting out of bed for, never mind killing someone."

"The husband did it," I said. "They always do. Except when it's the wives."

Fisher shook his head. "I don't think so. According to the neighbors, everything was fine. Their son liked his music a little loud, but otherwise all was good. No arguments, no atmosphere."

"Bad families are like the minds of functioning alcoholics. You have to live inside to have the first clue what's going on."

"So how do you read it?"

"Could be one of any number of scenarios. Maybe Bill was laying into Gina that night over something you and I will never understand. Son hears the noise, comes down, yells at Dad to stop. Dad won't. Son's been seeing this all his life, tonight he's not taking it anymore. He goes to the closet and gets his father's gun. Comes back and says he means it—stop beating up on Mom. They fight, Dad grabs hold of the gun, or it goes off accidentally, whatever. Son gets shot.

Wife's screaming the place down, his son's lying on the floor, Anderson knows he's not walking away from this. So he sets a fire in the part of the house that's known to be his domain to make it look like an intruder, then makes sure there's no witnesses to tell the story another way. Right now he's on the other side of the country and drunk and practically out of his mind with remorse, or else halfway to convincing himself they brought it on themselves. He'll either commit suicide within the week or get caught in eighteen months living quietly with a waitress in North Carolina."

Fisher was silent for a moment. "That works, I guess," he said. "But I don't believe it. Three reasons. First is that Anderson is the nerds' poster nerd, a hundred and twenty pounds soaking wet. He doesn't present as someone who could physically dominate two other people."

"Body weight is irrelevant," I said. "Domination is mental. Always."

"Which also doesn't sound like Anderson, but I'll let that pass. The second reason is there's a witness who claims to have seen someone who looked like Anderson entering the street at around twenty to eleven. No one's paying much attention to this woman, because she's old and nuts and loaded to her back teeth with lithium, but she claims she saw him get far enough down the road to see his house, then turn and run away."

"Not someone you're going to put on the stand," I said. "And even if she *did* see him, it could be Anderson setting up an alibi. What else you got?"

"Just this: Joshua Anderson died from the burn injuries in the end, but he was already leaving the world thanks to the gunshot wound to the face. But no bullet was found at the scene. The pathology report suggests it got trapped in the skull, bounced around, never made it out the other side. There's no exit wound. But there *are* indications of subsequent trauma from a sharp instrument. So the person who killed him then stuck a knife in the mess and dug out the shell, while the kid's clothes were on fire. That doesn't sound to me like something a physics lecturer could do. To his son." He sat back in his chair. "Especially when he didn't own a gun in the first place."

I shrugged. "Sure," I admitted. "There's loose ends. There always are. But the smart money stays on the husband. What's your interest in this anyhow?"

"It relates to an estate we're handling back home," he said. "I can't get into it more than that right now."

For just a moment, Fisher seemed evasive, but the details of his professional life were not my concern.

"So why are you telling me about it?"

"I want your help."

"With what?"

"Isn't it obvious?"

I shook my head. "Not really."

"It would benefit me, benefit us, to find out what actually took place that night."

"The police are on it, aren't they?"

"The cops are all about proving that Anderson murdered his wife and son, and I don't think that's what happened."

I smiled. "So I gather. But that doesn't mean you're right. And I still don't get why you're here."

"You're a cop."

"No. I *was* a cop."

"Same thing. You have investigative experience."

"For once your research fails you, Gary. I was with Patrol Division all the way. A street grunt."

"Not *formal* experience, no. I know you never made detective. I also know you never even applied."

I looked hard at him. "Gary, if you're going to tell me you somehow got access to my personnel files, then . . ."

"I didn't need to, Jack. You're a smart guy. You wanted to make detective, you would have. You didn't, so I figure you didn't try."

"I'm not very susceptible to flattery," I said.

He smiled. "I know that, too. And I remember that you

would rather not try than try and fail, and maybe that's the real reason you spent nearly a decade on the streets."

It had been awhile since someone had spoken to me this way. He saw it in my face.

"Look," he said, holding up his hands. "This isn't coming out right. I'm sorry. What happened to the Andersons isn't actually a huge deal to me. It's just a little weird and might make my life simpler if I could get it unraveled. I read your book. It seemed to me you might be interested. That's all."

"I appreciate the thought," I said. "But that feels like another life now. Plus, I was on the job in L.A., not Seattle. I don't know the city, and I don't know the people. I couldn't do much more than you, and I can do a lot less than the cops. If you genuinely think there's a problem with the way they're investigating this, it's them you should be talking to."

"I tried," he said. "They think the same as you."

"So probably that's the way it is. A sad story. The end."

Fisher nodded slowly, his eyes on the view outside the window. The light was beginning to turn, the sky heading toward a more leaden gray. "Looks like heavy weather. I should probably be heading back. I don't want to be driving over that mountain in the dark."

"I'm sorry," I said, standing. "After that drive I guess you were hoping for more."

"I wanted an opinion, and I got one. Too bad it wasn't the one I was looking for."

"Could have gotten you this far on the phone." I smiled. "Like I said."

"Yeah, I know. But hey—been good to see you after all this time. To catch up. Let's keep in touch."

I said yes it had, and yes we should, and that was that. We small-talked a bit longer, and then I walked him to the door and watched as he drove away.

I stayed outside for a few moments after he'd gone, though it was cold. I felt a little as if a bigger kid had come up to me on the playground and asked if I wanted to join his game, and I'd said no out of pride. Growing older, it appears, does not mean growing up.

I went back indoors and returned to my desk. There I wasted probably the last straightforward afternoon of my life gazing out the window, waiting vaguely for time to pass.

Sometimes I wonder what would have happened if I'd been working harder that morning, let the machine take Fisher's call. Even if he'd left a message, I'd have been unlikely to get around to calling him back. Most of the time, I don't think this would have made any difference. I believe that this thing was heading toward me regardless, on the horizon, inevitable. I'd like to claim I had no warning, that it came from nowhere out of a clear blue sky. It wouldn't be true. The signs and causes were there. At times in the last nine months, perhaps the last few years, I had noticed little differences. I'd tried to ignore them, to keep going, and so when it happened, it was like falling off a log, a sturdy trunk that had been floating down the same river for many years, to discover there'd never been any water supporting me after all and I was suddenly flat on my back in a strange land I didn't recognize: a dusty plain where there were no trees, no mountains, no landmarks of any kind, no way of telling how I might have gotten there from wherever I had been before.

The fall must have been coming for a while, gathering pace below the threshold of discernible change. At least since the afternoon on the deck of the new house, probably for months or even years before that. But digging up the roots of chaos is like saying it's not the moment the car hits you that's important, or the split second when you step off the curb without looking. You can argue that as soon as you stopped checking when you crossed the street, that's when the trouble really began. The moment of impact is what you remember, however. That breathless instant of screech and thud, the second when the car hits and all other futures are canceled.

The beat in time when it suddenly becomes clear that something in your world is badly wrong.

chapter THREE

A beach on the Pacific coast, a seemingly endless stretch of sand: almost white by day but now turning sallow gray and matte in the fading light. The afternoon's few footprints have been washed away, in one of nature's many patient acts of erasure. In summer, kids from inland spend the weekends here, gleaming in the sun of uncomplicated youth and pumping default-value music out of baby speakers. They are almost never picked off by sharpshooters, sadly, but go on to have happy and unfulfilled lives making too much noise all over the planet. On a Thursday a long way out of season, the beach is left undisturbed except for the busy teams of sandpipers who skitter up and down at the waterline, legs scissoring like those of cheerful mechanical toys. They have concluded the day's business and flown to bed, leaving the beach quiet and still.

Half a mile up the coast is the small and exclusive seaside town of Cannon Beach, with its short run of discreet hotels, but here most of the buildings are modest vacation homes, none more than two stories high and each a decent distance from its neighbor. Some are squat white oblongs in need of replastering, others more adventurous arrangements of wooden octagonal structures. All have weathered walkways leading over the scrubby dune, down to the sand. It is

November now, and almost all these buildings are dark, the smell of suntan lotion and candle wax sealed in to await future vacations, to welcome parents who each time glumly spy a little more silver in these unfamiliar mirrors and children who stand a little taller and a little farther from the adults who were once the center of their lives.

There has been no precipitation for two days—very rare for Oregon at this time of year—but this evening a thick knot of cloud is coalescing out to sea, like a drop of ink spreading in water. It will take an hour or two to make landfall, where it will turn the shadows a rich blue-black and strip the air with relentless rain.

In the meantime a girl is sitting on the sand, down at the tide line.

Her watch said it was twenty-five minutes before six, which was okay. When it was fifteen minutes before six, she had to go home—well, not home exactly, but the cottage. Dad always called it the beach house, but Mom always said the cottage, and since Dad was not here, it was obviously the cottage this time. Dad's not being here made a number of other differences, one of which Madison was currently considering.

When they came to spend a week at the beach, most days were exactly the same. They would drive up to Cannon Beach, have a look around the galleries (once), get groceries from the market (twice), and see if there was maybe something cool in Geppetto's Toy Shoppe (as often as Madison would make it happen; three times was the record). Otherwise they just lived on the sand. They got up early and walked along the beach, then back again. The day was spent sitting and swimming and playing—with a break midday in the cottage for sandwiches and to cool down—and then around five o'clock a long walk again, in the opposite direction from the one in the morning. The early walk was just for waking up, filling sleepy heads with light. At the end of the afternoon, it was all about shells—and sand dollars in particular. Though it was Mom who liked them the most (she had saved all the ones they'd ever found, in a cigar box back home), the three of them looked together, a family with one ambulatory goal. After the walk, everyone showered, and there were nachos and bean dip and frosted glasses of Tropical Punch Kool-Aid in the beach house, and then they'd drive out for dinner to Pacific Cowgirls in Cannon Beach, which had fishermen's nets on the walls and breaded shrimp with cocktail sauce and waiters who called you ma'am even if you were small.

But when Madison and her mom had arrived yesterday, they'd been sailing under different colors. It was the wrong time of year, and cold. They unpacked in silence and dutifully walked up the beach a little way, but though her mother's eyes appeared to be on the tide line, Madison didn't see her bend down once, even for a quartz pebble that was flushed rose pink at one end, something she'd normally have had like a shot. When they got back, Maddy managed to find some Kool-Aid from last time in the cupboard but her mom had not remembered to buy Doritos or anything else. Madison had started to protest but saw how slowly her mom was moving, and so she stopped. Cowgirls was closed for winter renovations, so they went somewhere else and sat by a window in a big empty room overlooking a dark sea under flat clouds. She had spaghetti, which was okay, but not what you had at the beach.

That morning it had started out freezing, and they'd barely walked at all. Mom spent the morning near the bottom of the walkway over the dunes, huddled in a blanket, wearing dark glasses and holding a book. Midafternoon she went back inside, telling Madison it was all right for her to stay out but she had to remain within forty yards of the cottage.

This was okay for a while, even kind of fun to have the beach to herself. She didn't go into the sea. Though she'd enjoyed this in the past, for the last couple of years she had found herself slightly wary of large bodies of water, even when it wasn't this cold. She built and refined a castle instead, which was fun. She dug as deep a hole as she could.

But when it got close to five o'clock, her feet started itching. She stood up, sat down. Played a little longer, though the game was getting old. It was bad enough skipping the walk in the morning, but not doing it now was really weird. The walking was important. It must be. Or why else did they always do it?

In the end she walked down to the surf alone and stood irresolute for a few moments. The beach remained deserted in both directions, the sky low and heavy and gray and the air getting cool. She waited as the first strong breeze came running ahead of the storm, worrying at the leg of her shorts and buzzing it against her leg. She waited, looking up at the dunes at the point where they hid the cottage, just over the other side.

Her mother did not appear.

She started slowly. She walked forty yards to the right, using the length of a big stride as a rough guide. It felt strange. She immediately turned around and walked back to where she'd started, and then another forty yards. This double length almost felt like walking, nearly reached the point where you forgot you were supposed to be going anywhere—because you weren't—and instead it became just the wet rustle of waves in your ears and the blur of your feet swishing in and out of view as your eyes picked over shapes and colors between the curling water and the hard, wet sand.

And so she did it again, and again. Kept doing it until the two turning points were just like odd, curved steps. Trying to make the waves sound like they always had. Trying not to imagine where they would eat tonight, and how little they would talk. Trying not to . . .

Then she stopped. Slowly she bent down, hand outstretched. She picked something out of the collage of seaweed, driftwood fragments, battered homes of dead sea dwellers. Held it up to her face, scarcely believing.

She had found an almost-complete sand dollar.

It was small, admittedly, not much bigger than a quarter. It had a couple of dings around the edges. It was a dirtier gray than most, and stained green on one side. But it would count. Would have counted, that is, if things were counting as normal. Things were not.

What should have been a moment of jubilation felt heavy and dull. She realized that the thing she held in her hand might as well be as big as a dinner plate and have no chips in it at all. It could be dry, sandy-golden, and perfect like the ones you saw for sale in stores. It wouldn't matter.

Madison sat down suddenly and stared at the flat shell in her hand. She made a gentle fist around it, then looked out at the sea.

She was still sitting there ten minutes later when she heard a noise. A *whapping* sound, as if a large bird were flying up the tide line toward her, long black wings slowly beating. Madison turned her head.

A man was standing on the beach.

He was about thirty feet away. He was tall, and the noise was the sound of his black coat flapping in the cold winds from a storm now boiling across the sky like a purple-black second sea. The man was motionless, hands pushed deep into the pockets of his coat. What low light made its way through the cloud was behind him, and you could not see his face. Madison knew immediately that the man was looking at her, however. Why else would he be standing there, like a scarecrow made of shadows, dressed not for the beach but for church or the cemetery?

She glanced casually back over her shoulder, logging her position in relation to the cottage's walkway. It was not directly behind, but it was close enough. She could get there quickly. Maybe that would be a good idea, especially as the big hand was at quarter to.

But instead she turned back and once more looked out at

the dark and choppy ocean. It was a bad decision, partly caused by something as simple as the lack of a congratulatory clap on the shoulder when she'd found what she held in her hand, but she made the call, and in the end no one else was to blame.

The man waited a moment and then headed toward her. He walked in a straight line, seemingly unbothered by the water that hissed around his shoes, up and back. He crunched as he came. He was not looking for shells and did not care what happened to them.

Madison realized she'd been dumb. She should have moved right away, when she had a bigger advantage. Just got up, walked home. Now she'd have to rely on surprise, on the fact that the man was probably assuming that if she hadn't run before, she wouldn't now. Madison decided she would wait until the man got a little closer and then suddenly bolt, moving as fast as she could and shouting loud. Mom would have the door open. She might even be on her way out right now, looking to see why Maddy was not yet back. She should be—she was officially late. But Madison knew in her heart that her mother might just be sitting in her chair instead, shoulders rounded and bent, looking down at her hands the way she had after they came back from the restaurant the night before.

And so she got ready, making sure her heels were well planted in the hard sand, that her legs were tensed like springs, ready to push off with everything she had.

The man stopped.

Madison had intended to keep looking out at the waves until the last second, as if she wasn't even aware of the man's presence, but instead found herself turning her head a little to check what was going on.

The man had came to a halt earlier than Madison expected, still about twenty feet away. Now she could see his face, she could tell he was way older than her dad, maybe even past Uncle Brian's age, which was fifty. Uncle Brian was always smiling, though, as if he were trying to remember a joke he'd heard at the office and was sure you were going to enjoy. This man did not look like that.

"I've got something for you," he said. His voice was dry and quiet, but it carried.

Madison hurriedly looked away, heart thumping. Unthinkingly protecting the flat shell still in her left hand, she braced her right palm, too, into the sand now, ready to push off against it, hard.

"But first I need to know something," he said.

Madison realized she had to reach maximum speed immediately. Uncle Brian was fat and looked like he couldn't run at all. This man was different that way, too. She took a deep breath. Decided to do it on three. One . . .

"Look at me, girl."

Two . . .

Then suddenly the man was between Madison and the dunes. He moved so quickly that Madison barely saw it happen.

"You'll like it," he said, as if he had done nothing at all. "I promise. You want it. But first you have to answer my question. Okay?"

His voice sounded wetter now, and Madison realized dismally just how stupid she'd been, understood why moms and dads said children had to be back at certain times, and to not stray too far, and not talk to strangers, and so many other things. Parents weren't just being mean or difficult or boring, it turned out. They were trying to prevent what was about to happen.

She looked up at the man's face, nodded. She didn't know what else to do and hoped it might help. The man smiled. He had a spray of small, dark moles across one cheek. His teeth were stained and uneven.

"Good," he said. He took another step toward her, and now his hands were out of his coat pockets. His fingers were long and pale.

Madison heard the word "Three . . ." in her head, but it was too quiet and she didn't believe in it. Her arm and legs were no longer like springs. They felt like rubber. She couldn't even tell if they were still tensed.

The man was too close now. He smelled damp. There was a strange light in his eyes, as if he'd found something he'd been looking for for a long time.

He squatted down close to her, and the smell suddenly got worse, an earthy odor on his breath, a smell that spoke of parts of the body normally kept hidden.

"Can you keep a secret?" he said.

chapter FOUR

I got home around a quarter after nine in the evening. Apart from picking up milk and coffee, the trip had been make-work: Amy kept the cupboards well stocked. I'd walked into town from the house, which took twenty minutes. It was a pleasant stroll, and I'd have done it that way even if the car hadn't been unavailable. I sat outside the coffee place and nursed an Americano while leafing through the local paper, learning several things: The trajectories of two cars had intersected a few nights before—nobody was hurt, not even a little bit; some local big shot got reelected to the school board for the twelfth straight year, which seemed borderline obsessional; and the Cascades Gallery needed a mature person to help sell paintings and sculptures of eagles and bears and Indian braves. Experience unnecessary, but candidates were instructed to bring a willingness to follow a dream. That didn't sound like me, even if the writing project remained stalled. I hoped the gallery did find someone, however, and that the lucky winner was sufficiently mature. I hated to think of limited-edition art prints being sold in a juvenile manner.

I prowled the aisles of Sam's Market for longer than necessary, picking items up and putting them back. Found a couple things too outré to have shown up on more enlightened shopping agendas, chiefly beers, and at the checkout I added a paperback Stephen King. I'd read it before, but most of my books were still in storage down in L.A., plus it was right there in front of me, in a rickety rack full of secondhand Dan Brown and triple-named romantic women done up in lurid gilt.

Back in the lot, I loaded the bag into my backpack and stood irresolute. A pickup truck sat ticking in the silence. I'd seen the owner inside, a local with craggy features and moss in his ears, and he'd ignored me in the way newcomers deserved. I'd made a point of saying hi, just to mess with his head. A couple emerged from Laverne's Rib across the street, rolling as if on the deck of a ship. Laverne's prided itself on the magnitude of its portions. The couple looked like they'd known this ahead of time. A tired-looking woman pushed a stroller past the market with the air of someone not engaged in the activity for the sheer fun of it, and her baby fought the night with everything it had, principally sound. The woman saw me looking and muttered, "Ten months," as if that explained everything. I looked away from her awkwardly.

Down the road a stoplight blinked.

I still wasn't hungry. Didn't want to go drink a beer somewhere public. I could walk up the street, see if the little bookstore was still open. It wasn't likely, and I now had a novel to read, which was what ultimately took the wind out of the night's sails. The expedition was over, run aground on an impulse purchase.

So now what? Pick your own adventure.

In the end I walked back the way I'd come, past the hundred yards of stores that constituted Birch Crossing. Most were single-story and wood-fronted, a dentist, hair salon, and drugstore interspersing places of more transitory appeal, including the Cascades Gallery itself, from which Amy had already acquired two aimlessly competent paintings of the generic West. The blocks were rooted by stolid brick structures built when the town's frock-coated boosters believed it would amount to more than it had. One of these held Laverne's, another was a bank no longer locally owned, and the last offered the opportunity to buy decoratively battered bits of furniture. Amy had availed herself of these wares, too, an example of which currently served as my desk. The street trailed off into a small gas station that had been tricked out long ago to look like a mountain chalet, and finally the local sheriff's office, set back from the road. I had to fight an impulse to look at this as I passed, and I wondered how long it would take before some part of me got the message.

I crossed the empty two-lane highway before taking the last left in town. This led into the woods, the fences sparsely punctuated with heavy-duty mailboxes and gates leading to houses down long driveways. After ten minutes I reached the box labeled JACK AND AMY WHALEN. Rather than open the gate, I vaulted over it, as I had on the way out. I forgot to compensate for the weight in the backpack and almost reached the other side face-first. I'd started exercising again recently, taking runs through the National Forest land that started at the boundary of our property. Now that the initial aches had worn off, I felt better than in awhile, but my body wasn't ready to forget that it was a year since I'd been truly fit. Though there was no one to see, I still felt like an ass and swore briskly at the gate for fucking me around. My father used to claim that inanimate objects hate us and plot our downfall behind our backs. He was probably right.

I walked up the rutted path toward the place a rental agreement said was now home. It was colder again, and I wondered if tonight was going to be when the snows finally dropped. I wondered also—not for the first time—how we were going to get in and out when that happened. The locals referred to snow without starry-eyed romanticism. They talked about it like death or taxes. The Realtor had breezily said something about a snowmobile being advisable in the deepest months. We didn't have a snowmobile. Weren't going to be getting one either. Nowhere in my life plans was there a slot for ownership of a snowmobile. Instead I was laying in reserves of cigarettes, canned chili, and sauerkraut. Always have had a thing for sauerkraut, not sure why.

The drive curved down into a hollow before climbing back up along the ridge. About a half mile from the road, it widened into the parking area. From this side the house wasn't much to look at, a single-story band of weathered cedar shingles largely obscured in summer by trees. It had been that way in the photo I'd seen on the Internet, and it looked rustic and cute. In winter and real life, it looked like a nuclear bunker caught between the legs of dead spiders. It was only when you got inside that you realized you'd entered at the top of two and a half levels, and there was double-height glass along most of the north face of the building, where the hillside dropped away sharply. In daylight this gave a view across a forest valley that climbed up to the Wenatchee Mountains, segueing into the Cascades and from there eventually to Canada. As Gary Fisher had found, you tended to just look at it for a while. From the deck you could also see a pond, about 150 yards in diameter, which lay within the property's four-acre boundary. In the afternoons birds of prey floated across the valley like distant leaves.

I unloaded the backpack's contents into their predetermined spots in the kitchen. The answering machine was on the far end of the counter. The light was flashing.

"About time," I said, the first words the house had heard since Fisher left.

But it wasn't. Two people had called, or one person twice, but left no message. I sent beats of ill-will to the perpetrator/s and another to myself for not getting caller ID working yet. The box claimed it was possible, but the manual had been translated from Japanese by a halfwit prairie dog. Just changing the outgoing message had required technical support from NASA. I knew the caller/s couldn't have been Amy, who knew how much nonmessages piss me off and would at least have intoned "No message, master" in a gravelly tone.

I got out my cell and pressed her speed-dial number, hooking it under my ear while I got a beer from the fridge.

After five rings I was diverted to the answering service yet again. Her business voice warmly thanked whomever for calling and promised she'd get back to them. I left a message asking her to do just that. Again.

"Soon would be nice," I muttered when the phone had been replaced in my pocket.

I took the drink through to my study. As the person earning actual money, Amy had a grander lair on the floor below. Mine had nothing in it but a file box of reference material, the expensively distressed table from the store in town, and a cheaply distressed chair I'd found in the garage. The only thing on the table was my laptop. It was not dusty because I made a point of wiping it with my sleeve every morning. It was not nailed shut because we didn't have any nails. I dimmed the lights and sat. When I opened the lid, the machine sprang to life, not learning from experience. It presented me with a word-processing document in which not many words had yet been processed. This was partly because of the panoramic view of bitterbrush and Douglas firs from the window, which I'd found myself able to stare at for hours. When the snows did come, I knew I might just as well leave the computer shut. It was harder to be distracted in the room at night, however, because aside from a few branches picked out by the light from the window, you couldn't see anything at all. So maybe now my fingers and mind would unlock and start working together. Maybe I'd think of something to say and fall into it for a while.

Maybe I'd be able to ignore the fact that after only a month I was bored out of my tiny mind.

I was sitting at the table because two years ago I wrote a book about certain places in L.A. I say "wrote," but mainly it was photographs, and even that word stretches the truth. I took the pictures with the camera in my cell phone: One day I happened to be somewhere with my phone in my hand, and I clicked a picture. When I transferred it to the computer later, I saw that it was actually okay. The technical quality was so low that you could see through the image to the place, caught in a moment, blurred and ephemeral. After that it became a habit, and when I had enough, I threw them into a document, jotting a comment about each. Over time these annotations grew until there was a page or two of text accompanying each photograph, sometimes more. Amy came in one evening when I was doing this, asked to read it. I let her. I felt no anxiety while it was in her hands, knowing she would be kind, and had only mild interest in what she'd say. A couple days later, she handed me the name and phone number of someone who worked at an art-house publisher. I laughed hard, but she said try it, and so I mailed the file to this guy without thinking much more about it.

Three weeks after that, he called me one afternoon and offered me twenty thousand dollars. Mainly out of bafflement, I said sure, knock yourself out. Amy squealed when she heard, and she took me out to dinner.

It was published eight months later, a square hardcover with a grainy photograph of a nondescript Santa Monica house on the front. It looked to me like the kind of book you had to be out of your mind to even pick up, let alone buy, but the *L.A. Times* noticed it, and it got a couple other good reviews, and, weirdly, it became something that sold a little, for a while.

The world rolled on, and so did we. Stuff happened. I quit my job, we moved. If I was anything now, I was the guy who'd written that book. Which meant, presumably, I now needed to become a guy who'd written some *other* book. Nothing had come to mind. It kept continuing to fail to come to mind, with a steady resolve that suggested not coming to mind was what it was all about, that failing to come to mind was its chief skill and purpose in life.

A couple hours later I was in the living room. I'd drunk more beer, but this hadn't seemed to help. I was adrift in the middle of the couch, mired in the restless fugue state characteristic of those who've failed to conjure something out of thin air. I knew I should unpack the box of Web "research" I'd halfheartedly accumulated. But I also knew if I hit the clippings and nothing shook out of it, then walking back into town and buying some good, long nails would move up to Plan A. The laptop had done me little deliberate harm. I wasn't ready to kill it yet.

I took an unearned work's-done cigarette from the pack on the table and headed out to the deck. I stopped smoking indoors the year Amy and I got married. She'd tolerated it at first because she'd done a little tobacco herself, back in the day and long before I'd known her, but had taken to using air-freshening devices and raising an eyebrow whenever I lit up. Subtly, and sweetly, and for my own good. I didn't especially mind the new regime. I could smoke all I wanted at work, and now houseguests couldn't accuse me of attempted manslaughter by secondhand smoke, and it just made life easier all around.

I leaned against the rail. The world was silent but for the confidential whispering of trees. The sky was clear and cold above, and midnight blue. I could smell firs and faint wood smoke from a distant hearth fire—likely our neighbors, the Zimmermans. It was good here, I knew that. We had a fancy house. The landscape was rugged, and not much had changed for it in a long time. Birch Crossing was real without being an ass about it: Pickups and SUVs were equally represented, and you could buy a very fancy spatula if you wanted. The Zimmermans were a five-minute drive away, but we'd already had dinner at their house twice. They were a couple of retired history professors from Berkeley, and conversation had not exactly flowed the first time, but the gift of a single-malt on our second visit had oiled the wheels. Both were sprightly for people in their early seventies—Bobbi filled the CD player with everything from Mozart to Sparklehorse, and Ben's black hair was barely flecked with gray. He and I now chatted affably enough on the street when we met, though I suspected that his wife had the measure of me.

And yet a week ago, I'd been standing right there on the deck when something had happened.

I was watching Amy through the glass doors as she chopped vegetables and supervised a saucepan on the stove. I could smell simmering plum tomatoes and capers and oregano. It was only midafternoon, and there was enough light to appreciate both the view and the house's good side. Instead of being in the office until after nine, my wife was at her kitchen counter happily making mud pies, and she remained appealing from both left and right and front and back, too. I'd even gotten an idea down that morning, and halfway believed I might produce another book about something or other. The spheres were in alignment, and nine-tenths of the world's population would have traded places with me in a heartbeat.

Yet for a moment it was as if a cloud drifted across the world. At first I wasn't sure what I was feeling. Then I realized I had no idea where I was. Not just the name of the town—I couldn't even remember what *state* I was in. I couldn't recall what had happened to me, or when, had no idea of how I'd gotten to this place and time. The house looked unfamiliar, the trees as if they'd been slipped into position when I wasn't looking. The woman on the other side of the big window was a stranger to me, her movements foreign and unexpected.

Who was she? Why was she standing in there holding a knife? And why was she looking at it as if she couldn't remember what it was for? The feeling was too pervasive to be described as panic, but I felt the hairs on the back of my neck rise. I blinked, looking around, trying to lock into something tangible. It wasn't a reaction to the newness of the environment. I've traveled a lot, and I'd been sick to death of L.A. I was tired because I hadn't been sleeping well, but it wasn't that either, or the usual shadows that came to haunt me. It was not about regrets or guilt. It wasn't specific.

Everything was wrong. With everything.

Then the cloud passed. It was gone, just like that. Amy looked up and winked at me through the glass, unquestionably the woman I loved. I smiled back, turned to the mountains to finish my smoke. The forest looked the way I had come to expect. Everything was okay again.

Dinner was good, and I listened while Amy went over the structure of her new job. She's in advertising. Maybe you're familiar with it. It's a profession that seeks to make people spend money so that folks they don't know can buy an even bigger house. In this way it's somewhat like organized crime, except the hours are longer. I said this to Amy once, suggesting they should tell clients to dispense with ads and demographics and encourage people to buy their wares through direct threats against their person and/or property. She asked me never to say this in front of her colleagues in case they took it seriously.

The revised basis of her employment was important to us because her new position as roving creative director across her company's empire—with offices in Seattle, Portland, San Francisco, and back down in L.A.—was what had enabled us to get out of L.A. It was a big change for her, a California girl born and bred, who'd liked being close to the family who still lived in the city where she was born. She had painted her willingness to move as related to the sizable hike in salary, but she'd never really been obsessed with money. I believed instead that she'd done it mainly for my sake, to let me get out of the city, and over dessert I told her I was grateful.

She rolled her eyes and told me not to be a dork, but she accepted the kiss I offered in thanks. And the ones that came afterward.

When I'd finished my cigarette, I pulled the phone out of my pocket to check the time. It was half past eleven. Amy's job involved many client dinners, especially now, and it was possible she hadn't even gotten back to her hotel yet. I knew she'd pick up her messages as soon as she could. But I hadn't heard from her all day, and at that moment I really wanted to.

I was about to try her number again when the phone chirped into life on its own. The words AMY'S CELL popped up on the screen. I smiled, pleased at the coincidence, and put the phone up to my ear.

"Hey," I said. "Busy, busy?"

But the person on the other end was not my wife.

chapter FIVE

"Who is this, please?"

The voice was male, rough, loud. Coming from Amy's number, it was about as wrong as could be.

"It's Jack," I said. It sounded dumb. "Who—"

"Is this home?"

"What? Who are you?"

The voice said something that might have been a name but sounded more like a random collection of syllables.

"What?" I repeated. He said it again. Could have been Polish, Russian, Martian. Could have been a coughing fit. There was a lot of noise in the background. Traffic, presumably.

"Is this home?" he barked again.

"What do you mean? What are you doing with—"

The guy had one question, and he was going to keep asking it. "This is number says 'Home'?"

A light went on in my head. "Yes," I said, finally getting what he was driving at. "This is the number listed as 'Home.' It's my wife's phone. But where's—"

"Find in cab," the man said.

"Okay. I understand. *When* did you find it?"

"Fifteen minutes. I call when I get good signal. Phones here not always so good."

"It belongs to a woman," I said, loudly and clearly. "Short blond hair, probably wearing a business suit. Have you just driven someone like that?"

"All day," he said. "All day women like this."

"This *evening*?"

"Maybe. Is she there, please? I speak her?"

"No, I'm not in Seattle," I said. "*She* is, and you are, but I am not."

"Oh, okay. So . . . I don't know. What you want me?"

"Wait a minute," I said. "Stay on the line."

I quickly walked downstairs and into Amy's study. Stuck dead center to the flat screen of her computer was a Post-it note with a hotel name written on it. The Malo, that was it.

All I could hear through the phone was a distant siren. I waited for it to fade.

"The Hotel Malo," I said. "Do you know it?"

"Of course," he said. "Downtown."

"Can you take it there? Can you take the phone to the hotel and hand it in at reception?"

"Is long way," the man said.

"I'm sure. But take it to reception and get them to call the lady down. Her name is Amy Whalen. You got that?"

He said something that sounded very slightly like Amy's name. I repeated it another few times and spelled it twice. "Take it there, okay? She'll pay you. I'll call her, tell her you're coming. Yes? Take it to the hotel."

"Okay," he said. "Twenty dollar."

My heart was still thudding after he'd hung up. At least I knew the score. No reply to my last message because Amy hadn't heard it, which gave me a time before which she had to have lost the phone. When had that been? Around nine, I thought. Or could be she'd lost it earlier in the day and chosen to wait until she got back to the hotel to fill me in. Either way, she needed a heads-up to deal with this guy, assuming he was on the level. When phones are stolen, the thieves will sometimes call a home number, pretending to be a helpful citizen, in the hope of reassuring the owner that the phone isn't lost. That way the victim will hold off getting the phone killed at the provider, leaving the perpetrator free to use the hell out of it until the agreed handover time, when he just drops it in the trash. If this guy was using that scam, there wasn't a lot I could do about it—I wasn't going to cancel Amy's phone without talking to her first. The hotel's number wasn't on the note, unsurprisingly—we always communicated via cell when she was out of the house, which is how come mine was down as "Home" in her contacts list.

Ten seconds on the Internet tracked down the Hotel Malo. I called the number and withstood the receptionist's mandatory welcoming message, which included highlights of the day's restaurant specials. When he was done, I asked to be put through to Amy Whalen. A faint background rattle of someone typing. Then: "I can't do that, sir."

"She's not back yet?" I checked the clock. Nearly midnight. Kind of late, however important the client. "Okay. Put me through to voice mail."

"No, sir, I meant I have no one here under that name."

I opened my mouth. Shut it again. Had I gotten the dates wrong? "What time did she check out?"

More tapping. When the man spoke again, he sounded circumspect. "I have no record of a reservation being made under that name, sir."

"For today?"

"For the past week."

"She's been in town two days," I said patiently. "She arrived Tuesday. She's in town until Friday morning. Tomorrow."

The guy said nothing.

"Could you try 'Amy Dyer'?"

I spelled "Dyer" for him. This had been her name before we married, and it was credible that someone in her office might have made a booking for her in that name seven years later. Just about credible.

Tapping. "No, sir. No Dyer."

"Try Kerry, Crane & Hardy. That's a company name."

Tapping. "Nothing for that either, sir."

"She never checked in?"

"Can I help you with anything else this evening?"

I couldn't think of anything else to ask. The guy waited a beat, told me the hotel group's Web URL, and cut the connection.

I took the Post-it from the screen. Amy's handwriting is extremely legible. You can make out what it says from low-lying space orbits. It said Hotel Malo.

I dialed the hotel again and got put through to reservations. I rechecked all three names. At the last minute, I remembered to get myself transferred back to the front desk, this time reaching a woman. I told her that someone would be bringing in a cell phone, asked if she'd hold it under my name. I gave her my credit-card number against twenty bucks to pay the driver.

Then I went back on the Web. Did searches for hotels in downtown, for anything similar to "Malo." I found a Hotel Monaco, only a few streets away. Their Web site suggested that it was exactly the kind of place Amy hung her coat on trips: funky decor; restaurant specializing in Pan-Cajun this, that, and the other; complimentary goldfish in the rooms. Whatever the fuck that meant.

I looked at her note again. It could *just* about be "Monaco," if written in a hurry or while having an embolism. It might even be she'd misheard the name when being told where she'd been booked and written it down wrong for me. Mal-o/Monac-o. Maybe.

I called the Monaco front desk and got someone human and responsive. She was able to quickly and regretfully establish that my wife was not, and had never been, resident in the hotel. I thanked her and put the phone down. I did this calmly, as if what I'd done made the slightest sense. As if I could really have misread the note or Amy misheard something from an assistant and as a result happened to name a hotel that actually existed, only a couple of streets away in the same town.

I stood up. I rubbed my hands together, cracked my knuckles. The house felt large around me. There was a sudden clatter from the floor above, as the fridge dropped a new load of ice into the tray.

I am not an especially imaginative man. The flashes of intuition I've experienced in my life usually have a basis in something obvious, even if only in retrospect. But right then I felt untethered, unguarded, as when I'd stood out on the deck a week before. It was after midnight now. I'd last spoken to my wife around eleven the previous evening. A shorthand debrief between two people who've loved each other for a while. Your day, my day; errand reminders; kiss kiss, good night. I'd idly pictured her sitting Indian style on a turned-down bed, a pot of coffee by her side or on its way, her expensive and doubtless too-tight business shoes kicked halfway across the floor of her room, in this Hotel Malo.

Except she hadn't been there.

I put my hand on the mouse to her computer. Hesitated, then found her personal-organizer software and double-clicked it. It felt like an intrusion, but I needed to check. The diary window popped up on the screen. A bar across four days said "Seattle." The space in between was peppered with meetings, plus a clutch of client breakfasts, lunches, and dinners. Except for this evening. Tonight had been clear from six-thirty.

So why no earlier call?

There *had* been a couple of attempts at contact via the house phone. But she always called the cell. She knew I was supposed to be at home working but also that my desk and I acted like magnets with the same charge, and it was highly possible I would be elsewhere. And she *always* left a message. Amy had strong views on hotels. Maybe she got to the Malo and didn't like it, checked herself in somewhere else.

Didn't mention it because it was trivia and didn't affect our communication. Back-to-back meetings, then had herself booked into this week's most fashionable Seattle eatery, table for one, briefings and demographics to read while she ate—leave calling Jack until she gets back to the room. Her phone slips out in the cab on the way there. She runs into someone from work, stays for an extra glass of wine. Would be getting back to the hotel round about now, reaching into her bag . . . and thinking, *Shit?*

Yeah, maybe.

I looked around her desk again. Other people's working spaces are like the ruins of lost civilizations. It's impossible to understand why they'd have that thing there, put the other here. Even with Amy's, which is blisteringly neat and looks like an office-supplies serving suggestion. The desk looked as it always did, in I'll-be-back-later mode. Except that her PDA was sitting in its dock. Amy was the only person I knew who actually used an organizer instead of merely owning one. She kept lists and her diary on it, maintained addresses, took notes, referred to it twenty times a day. She always toted it with her on business.

But there it was. I lifted it out, turned it on. A mirror of the diary I'd seen on the main computer. To-do lists. Slogans-in-progress. I put it back. So she elected to take one less piece of equipment on the road this time. Rock and roll. Amy had her systems. In her world there was a place for everything and everything stayed in its place, if it knew what was good for it.

And yet tonight she was not in her allotted space.

So now what? Her phone was taken care of. I'd run down every available route for trying to talk to her and hit dead ends. It all probably meant nothing. My rational mind was braced for an incoming phone call, a tired/apologetic Amy with a complex tale of screwed hotel bookings and phone-loss woe. I could almost hear how shrill the ring would sound and was halfway to deciding to go have a cigarette on the deck while I waited. Either that or just go to bed.

Instead I found myself in the living room, standing in front of the big windows, hands down by my sides. Minutes passed, and I did not move. The house was quiet around me, so silent in the continued absence of a phone call, that after a time the background rustle of moving blood in my ears began to seem very loud, appeared to swell until it sounded like the tires of a car on a wet road, still some distance away, but coming closer.

I could not shake off the ridiculous idea that something had happened to my wife. That she might be in danger. As I stared past my reflection in the plate glass, out toward the dark shapes against the blue-black sky, I began to feel dimly certain that this unknown car was heading inexorably toward me.

That I had always been its target, and now the time had come. That this was the night when the car hit.

chapter SIX

Oz Turner sat in the seat he'd preselected, wall side of the booth nearest the door. This position was obscured from most of Blizzard Mary's other patrons by the coatrack. It gave him a good view onto the parking lot, cars and pickups whose sole shared characteristic was that of not looking too new. He'd been to the bar twice the day before, in preparation. Office workers at lunch, young moms sharing salads. Late at night the clientele switched to lone men interspersed with middle-aged couples drinking steadily in silences companionable or otherwise. Meanwhile their vehicles waited outside, like old dogs, pale and ghostly in the dark. Beyond the lot was the little town of Hanley. A few streets away, through the small and prettified knot of the old quarter, was a wide, flat watercourse. Either the Mississippi itself or the Black River. Oz wasn't sure. He didn't really care.

He was nursing a beer to hold his place. He'd ordered one of the specials, too, but barely touched the gluey Buffalo wings. This was only partly due to nervousness. Over the last year, his habits had changed. He'd once been something of a gourmand, in his own way: a connoisseur of quantity. He made his coffee with three big spoonfuls of Maxwell House. He took his meals supersized. He'd enjoyed the tastes of these things, of course, but also responded to the comfort of sheer bulk. He no longer found solace there. After a time the waitress came and took his plate, and he felt no sense of loss.

He checked his watch again. Well after midnight. The bar was dim but for lamps and neon beer advertisements. The television was on low. There were only ten, fifteen people left. Oz was going to give the guy another quarter hour, then go.

As he was telling himself this, a car pulled into the lot outside.

The man who entered the bar wore old denim and a battered Raiders jacket. He had the air of a person who spent his days on the wide, flat plains, near farm machinery. The Raiders didn't hail from anywhere near here, of course, but geography has become malleable now. It could also, Oz realized, be intended as a signal. To him. He turned to the window and watched the man's reflection in the glass.

He went up to the counter, got a beer, exchanged the pleasantries required to pass as no one in particular. Then he came straight over toward the booth. He had evidently used the mirrors behind the bar to scope the room, so he could look like he was coming to meet a friend, not searching for a stranger.

Oz turned from the window as the man slid into the opposite side of the booth. "Mr. Jones?"

The man nodded, looking Oz over. Oz knew what he was seeing. A man who looked ten years older than he should. Gray stubble over the dry jowls of someone who used to carry an extra sixty pounds. A thick coat that looked like it doubled as the bed blanket of a large dog.

"Glad you agreed to meet in person," the man said. "A little surprised, too."

"Two guys in a bar," Oz said, "they're the only people ever have to know. E-mails, anyone can find out what was said. Even after both of you are dead."

The man nodded appreciatively. "'They' want to find you, they gonna."

Oz knew this only too well, having been attacked by "them" a year before. He still wasn't sure who "they" were. He'd managed to fix the damage they'd tried to cause before it became insurmountable, but he still felt he had to leave town. He'd kept moving ever since, leaving behind a job on a small local newspaper and the few people he'd called friends. Joining the undertow. It was better that way.

Jones didn't know about this, of course. He was referring instead to the fact that every e-mail you send, every message you post, every file you download is logged on a server somewhere. Machines see nothing, understand less, but their memories are perfect. There is no anonymity on the Internet, and sooner or later a lot of solid citizens were going to discover that e-mails to lovers were not private, nor were hours spent bathed in the light of other people's nakedness. That people were watching you, all the time. That the Web was not some huge sand pit. It was quicksand. It could swallow you up.

"So how come Hanley?" the man asked, looking around. A couple in the next booth were conducting a vague, whispered fight, bitter sentences that bore no relevance to what the other had just said. "I know Wisconsin, some. Never even heard of this town."

"It's where I am right now," Oz said. "That's all. How did you get my e-mail address?"

"Heard your podcast. Made us want to talk to you. Did a little digging, took a chance. No big deal."

Oz nodded. Once upon a time, he'd had a little late-night radio show, back east. That stopped when he left town, of course. But in the last couple of months, he'd started recording snippets onto his laptop, uploading them onto the Web, started spreading the word again. There were others like him, doing the same thing. "It concerns me that you were able to find my e-mail address."

"Should worry you even more if I couldn't. Otherwise I'd just be an amateur, right?"

"And what did you want to say to me?"

"You first," Jones said. "What you said in the 'cast was pretty oblique. I threw you a couple bones in my e-mail, hinted what we know. Let's hear you talk now."

Oz had thought about ways of communicating the bottom line while remaining circumspect. He took a sip of his beer, then set it back on the table and looked the man in the eye.

"The Neanderthals had flutes," he said. "Why?"

The man shrugged. "To play tunes."

"That just rephrases the question. Why did they believe it important to be able to replicate certain sounds, when just getting enough to eat was hard labor?"

"Why indeed."

"Because sound is important in ways we've forgotten. For millions of years, it couldn't be recorded. Now it can, so we concentrate on the types with obvious *meaning*. But music is a side alley. Even speech isn't important. Every other species on the planet gets by with chirps and barks—how come we need thousands of words?"

"Because our universe is more complex than a dog's."

"But that's *because* of speech, not the other way around. Our world is full of talking, radio, television, everybody chattering, so loud all the time that we forget why control of sound was originally important to us."

"Which was?"

"Speech developed from prehistoric religious ritual, grew out of chanted sounds. The question is why we were doing this back then. Who we were trying to talk to."

The man had begun to smile faintly.

"Also why, when you look at European Stone Age monuments, it's clear that sound was a major design factor. New Grange. Carnac. Stonehenge itself—the outside faces of the uprights are rough, but the interiors are smooth. To channel sound. Certain *frequencies* of sound."

"Long time ago, Oz. Who knows what those guys were up to? Why should we care?"

"Read the *Syntagma Musicum,* Praetorius's ancient catalog of musical instruments. Back in the sixteenth century, all the major cathedral organs in Europe had thirty-two-foot organ pipes, monsters that produce infrasound, sounds too low for the human ear to even *hear.* Why—if not for some other effect these frequencies have? Why *did* people feel so different in church, so connected with something beyond? And why do so many alternative therapies now center on vibration, which is just another way of quantifying sound?"

"Tell me," Jones said quietly.

"Because the walls-of-Jericho story is about sound breaking down not literal walls but *figurative* ones," Oz said. "The walls between this place and another. Sound isn't just about hearing. It's about *seeing* things, too."

The man nodded slowly, and in acquiescence. "I hear you, my friend, if you'll excuse the pun. I hear you loud and clear."

Oz sat back. "That enough?"

"For now. We're on the same page, that's for sure. I'm curious. Where did *you* first hear about this?"

"Met a guy at a conference a couple years ago. A small convention of the anomalous, down in Texas."

"WeirdCon?"

"Right. We kept in touch. He had some ideas, started working on them in his spare time. He was building something. We e-mailed once in a while, I shared my research on prehistorical parallels with him. Then, nearly a month ago, he dropped off the face. Haven't heard from him since."

"Probably he's fine," the man said. "People get spooked, lay low for a while. You two ever discuss this in a public forum?"

"Hell no. Always private."

"You never e-mail anyone else about it yourself?"

"Nope."

"Never know when 'they' might be listening, right?"

This was both a joke and not a joke, and Oz grunted. Among people trying to find the truth, the concept of "them" was complicated. You knew "they" were out there, of course—it was the only way to make sense of all the unexplained things in the world—but you understood that talking about "them" made you sound like a kook. So you put air quotes around it. Someone said *THEM* with double underlining and a big, bold typeface, and you knew he was either faking it or a nut. You heard those little ironical quote marks, however . . . chances were the guy was okay.

"Isn't that the truth," Oz said, playing along. "You just never know. Even if 'they' don't actually exist."

The man smiled. "I'm going to talk to my friends, see about getting us all together. Glad we met, Oz. Been waiting a long time to connect with someone like you."

"Me, too," Oz said, for a moment feeling very alone.

"We'll hook up soon. Take care of yourself in the meantime," Jones said, and left.

Oz watched the man get back into his car, drive out of the lot, and take the turn toward the freeway. Then he slowly finished his beer. He did not hurry, for once. He was feeling almost as if he were just sitting in a bar, rather than hiding there. The people at the counter were talking, laughing. The arguing couple were now chewing face across their table, the woman's hand hooked meatily around the man's neck. Oz wished them well.

When he eventually stepped outside, it was cold and windy, the streets deserted. People with normal lives were home asleep. Oz was going to join them now. Home for the time being was an anonymous motel on the edge of town, but any kind of home is better than none.

As he walked, he considered the man he'd just met, what he represented. There were countless groups interested in the underbelly, in finding the hidden truths. JFK obsessives who met once a month to pore over autopsy shots. Online

9/11 nuts with their trajectory-modeling software, Priory of Sion wannabes, Holocaust revisionists—circle jerks for everything that might or might not ever have been true. Jones's people sounded very different, or Oz would not have agreed to make contact in the first place. A tight, focused group of men and women who studied the facts without previous agenda, who met in secret, who weren't too close to one particular issue to miss a glimpse of the whole. This was what Oz needed. People with rigor. People with dedication.

Just some fucking people, bottom line.

Maybe, after his time in the wilderness, things were going to start turning around. Oz picked up the pace a little, idly wondering if his motel had a snack machine.

It did not, and the soda machine didn't work. After establishing these facts and becoming resigned to them, Oz let himself into his room, first noting that the strip of Scotch tape he'd laid across the bottom of the door had not been disturbed.

Once inside, he stood irresolute. It was late. He should go to bed. Get on the road early. Keep on the move. But he still felt hopped up from the meeting and knew that if he laid his head down, it would get locked in a long spiral that would leave him exhausted and headachy in the morning.

He turned instead to the ancient console television next to the room's shabby desk. The huge screen warmed slowly, to reveal a rerun of a show so old Oz barely remembered it. Perfect. A little background noise, the kind that creeps inside your head and tells you everything's all right. Comfort sound.

There was a knock on the door.

Oz turned fast, heart beating hard.

The television wasn't on loud enough to provoke a complaint. It was hard to imagine why else someone should be outside. The bedside clock said it was 2:33 A.M.

The knock came again, more quietly this time.

Oz knew that the flickering of the television screen would be visible around the edges of the curtains. He went and stood behind the door. This was the moment he'd feared, the prospect that kept him awake at night, and he realized suddenly that he'd never really come up with a *plan* for when it came to pass. So much for the Lone Horseman of the Unknown.

"Mr. Turner? It's Mr. Jones."

The person outside had spoken very quietly. Oz stared at the door for a moment, put his ear closer. "What?"

"Could you let me in?"

Oz hesitated, undid the lock. Opened the door a crack, to see Jones standing shivering outside.

"What the hell do you want?"

Jones kept well back from the door, didn't crowd him. "I got a few miles down the road and realized there were a couple things I forgot to say. I turned around, saw you walking through town, followed you back here."

Oz let the man into the hotel room, annoyed at how careless he'd been to allow someone to spot him on the street.

"You scared the fucking life out of me, man," he said, closing the door and locking it. "Jesus."

"I know. I'm sorry, really. It's just that I came all this way. And, you know, I think meeting up was kind of a big deal for both of us. The start of something bigger."

"You could say that."

"Right. So I just wanted to make sure we got everything said."

Oz relaxed a little. "So what was it?"

The man looked sheepish. "First thing . . . well, it's embarrassing. It's just that Jones isn't my real name."

"Okay," Oz said, confused. He'd already assumed that the other guy might have given a false one. "No big deal."

"I know. Just . . . you were going to find out later, and I didn't want you to think I'd been jerking you around."

"That's okay," Oz said, disarmed, wondering if he should offer the guy a drink and realizing he didn't have anything.

The motel wasn't the type that supplied coffeemaking facilities. It was barely the type that supplied clean towels. "So—what is it? Your name."

The man moved slightly, so he was farther from the door.

"It's Shepherd," he said.

Oz held his gaze, noticing for the first time how dark the man's eyes were. "Well, mine really *is* Oz Turner. So now we're straight on nomenclature. What was the other thing?"

"Just this," the man said. He pushed Oz in the chest.

Oz was caught off guard. He couldn't maintain his balance against the calm, firm shove, especially when the man slipped his right foot behind one of Oz's. His arms pinwheeled, but he toppled straight over backward, catching his head hard against the television.

He was stunned and barely had time to slur a questioning syllable before the man quickly bent down over him. He grabbed handfuls of Oz's coat, careful not to touch flesh, and yanked him halfway back to standing.

"What?" Oz managed. His right eye was blinking hard. He felt weak. He realized that the man was wearing gloves. "What are you . . ."

The man put his face up close. "Just so you know," he said, " 'They' *do* exist. They send their regards."

Then he dropped him, twisting Oz's shoulder forward just as he let go. Oz's head hit the side of the television again, at a bad sideways angle this time, and there was a muffled click.

Shepherd sat on the end of the bed and waited for the man's gasps to subside, watching the television with half an eye. He couldn't remember the name of the show, but he knew that just about everyone on it was long dead. Ghosts of light, playing to a dying man. Almost funny.

When he was satisfied that Turner was done, he took a fifth of vodka out of his pocket and tipped most of it into Oz's mouth. A little over his hands, some on his coat. He left the bottle on the floor, where it might have fallen. A diligent coroner could question either stomach contents or blood-alcohol level within the body, but Shepherd doubted it would come to that. Not here in the sticks. Not when Turner looked so much like a man who had this kind of end coming to him sooner or later.

It took Shepherd less than three minutes to find where the man had hidden his laptop and notebook. He replaced these with further empty vodka bottles. He shut the room door quietly behind him as he left and then took only another minute to find the backup disk duct-taped under the dashboard of Oz's car in the lot outside. All three would be destroyed before daybreak.

And that, he believed, was that.

When Shepherd got into his own vehicle, he realized his cell phone was ringing. He reached quickly under the seat for it, but he'd missed the call.

He checked the log. He didn't recognize the number, but he did know the area code, and he swore.

A 503 prefix. Oregon. Cannon Beach.

He slammed the door and drove fast out of the lot.

chapter SEVEN

If you lay still, really still, you could hear the waves. That was one of the best things about the cottage, Madison thought. When you went to bed, assuming the television in the main room wasn't on—it usually wasn't, because time at the beach was for reading and thinking, Dad said, instead of watching the same old (rude word)—you could lie there and hear the ocean. You had to tune yourself first. The dune was in the way, and depending on the tides the water could be quite a distance down the beach. You had to let your breathing settle, lie flat and very still on your back with both ears open, and just wait . . . and gradually you would begin to hear the distant rustle and thump that said tonight you were sleeping near the edge of the world. And you certainly would sleep, as the waves seemed to get closer and closer, tugging gently at your feet, pulling you into friendly warmth and darkness and rest.

If you woke up in the night, you heard them, too. It was even better then, as they were the only sound anywhere. Back in Portland there was always other noise—cars, dogs, people walking by. Not here. Sometimes the waves would be very quiet, barely audible above the ringing of your ears, but if there was heavy weather, they could sound very loud. Madison could remember one time being really scared in the night when there had been a storm and it sounded like the waves were chaotic right into the next room. They hadn't been, of course, and Dad said the dune would protect them and they never would, so now when she heard them in the night, she enjoyed it, feeling adventurous and safe, knowing that there was a vigorous, crashing universe out there but that it could never harm her.

So when Madison realized that she was awake, the first thing she noticed was the waves. Then that it was raining, and beginning to rain harder, drumming onto the roof of the cottage. The storm she'd seen heading down the beach earlier had arrived. Tomorrow the sand would be pocked and gray and probably strewn with seaweed. It got thrown up onto the beach in bad weather, and it felt weird and squishy underfoot. Assuming they even went for a walk tomorrow at all, which—

Suddenly she sat up.

She stayed absolutely still for a moment, staring straight ahead. The rain on the roof above her was so loud it sounded like hail. Madison looked at her bedside table. The clock said 1:12. So why was she awake? Sometimes she had to go to the bathroom. She didn't now, though, and usually when she woke in the night, it was a vague and fuzzy kind of awake. Now she felt like she'd never been asleep. Ever. There was a question going around in her head, urgently.

What was she doing here?

Next to the clock was a small, round shape. She picked it up. A sand dollar, small. She remembered finding it that afternoon, but that felt like it was something that had happened a while ago, like last time they'd come here, or the summer before. She brought it up to her nose and sniffed. It still smelled like the sea.

She could remember being on the beach as the storm headed south toward her. Sitting there knowing she'd have to go in the cottage soon. Then . . . she just couldn't quite . . .

It was like sometimes when you were in the car on a long drive and suddenly you realized that a chunk of time had passed. One minute you were twenty minutes from home, and then suddenly you were pulling into the driveway. It wasn't like you'd been asleep, more like you hadn't been paying attention, daydreaming, and the world had gone on regardless. The world, including your own body. You must have been awake, because you'd done stuff, but it had happened without your thinking or noticing. Like putting a car on cruise, as Daddy did on the freeway. Then, boom—you reached an interchange and there you were, noticing things again, taking back control.

Though . . . now she *could* remember being in the cottage afterward. When she'd come in from the beach, Mom had been sitting in her chair without a book and without the TV on. Doing that looking-at-her-hands thing. She said hi when Madison came in, but nothing else—which was weird, because Maddy was late. At least a half hour. In fact . . . now she even remembered looking at the clock in the kitchen and realizing it was seven o'clock—which was a *whole hour* later than she was supposed to come back.

She'd taken a shower to get the sand off, and when she came out, Mom said she didn't feel like going out to eat tonight and what did Madison think about calling for pizza? Madison thought this was a world-class idea, because Mario's in Cannon Beach did what her dad called "real serious pies," and you could only get them here because they weren't a chain. It was strange that Mom was suggesting it, because her usual position was that Mario's put too much cheese on and not all the toppings were certified organic or GM-free, but, whatever. "Yes, please" was the answer whichever way you cut it.

But then Mom couldn't find the menu, and she was going to call directory assistance, and it grew later and later, and after a while Madison got the idea that pizza wasn't going to happen after all. She found a box of soup mix in the cupboard and made that instead. Her mother didn't want any. Madison didn't either, but she made herself eat about half and then spent a while reading one of her history books. She liked history, enjoyed knowing about how things had been in years gone by.

Then she'd gone to bed. Got into her jammies and climbed in. Then she must have fallen asleep.

And now she had woken up.

Madison opened her hand and looked at the sand dollar again. She could remember bending down to pick it up. She could remember sitting with it. So how come she couldn't remember what had happened right after that? Sand dollars were big news. Surely she would have come running in right away to show her mom, maybe thinking it might cheer her up? Why couldn't she remember doing that?

Madison lay back, pulling the covers up under her chin. Her memory was good. She performed well in tests at school and triumphantly took on all comers at Remember, Remember and Snap—Uncle Brian said she could win a Remember, Remember World Series, if there was one. But now it was like the world was a big television, showing two shows at once—or as if the signal had gotten confused and the screen was showing one thing but the sound was from another movie altogether. And even though she'd mainly sorted out the question of what she was doing here, it didn't seem to answer anything. She was here because it was the beach house, and she was here with her mom, and it was night so she was in bed.

But was that what she'd actually meant?

She was breathing a little quickly now, as if expecting bad news or hearing a sound that meant that somewhere something bad was coming toward her. Something felt wrong and crooked and out of kilter.

And . . . hadn't there been a man?

Hadn't he given her something she had put in the drawer of the bedside table? A card, like one of Dad's business cards but very plain and white?

No. Absolutely not.

There had been no man. She was sure of that. So there could be no card. She did not need to check.

But she did, and she found that there was in fact such a card in the drawer. It had a name printed on it and a phone number added in ballpoint. There was a design drawn on the other side. The symbol looked as if someone had drawn a number 9, then rotated the card a little and drawn another 9 and kept doing that until they came back around to where they'd started.

Barely aware that she was doing it, Madison reached to the phone on the bedside table and dialed the number. It rang and rang, sounding as if it was trying to connect to the other side of the moon. Nobody answered, and she put the phone down.

She forced herself to lie back in bed. To try to listen beyond the rain, to focus on the sound of the waves, behind this temporary storm: to find the reassuring sound of crashing water, drawing its line at the end of the world. She kept her eyes closed and listened, waiting for the tide to pull her back into the dark. Tomorrow she would wake and everything would feel normal. She was just tired, and half asleep. Everything was okay. Everything was just like always.

And there had been no man.

When Alison O'Donnell woke at 2:37, it was the sound of rain she first noticed, but she knew that this had not been what had woken her. She pulled the covers back and swung her legs out of bed. Grabbed her robe from the end and pulled it on. She was foggy with bad sleep and mechanical dreams, but a mother's feet operate outside her own control. Doesn't matter how tired you are, how worn, how much your body and brain want to climb into bed again and stay there for a week, a month, maybe even the rest of your life. There are sounds that speak to the back brain and countermand your own desires.

The discomfort of your young is one of them.

She padded out of her room and into the hallway. Through the window she glimpsed trees pulled back and forth in high winds, white lines of water speeding across the glass. There was a sudden gust, and rain hit the window like a handful of stones.

Then she heard the noise again.

She shuffled down to the door at the end of the hall. It was slightly ajar. She gently opened it a little farther and looked inside.

Madison was in bed, but the covers had been thrown down to her waist. Alison's daughter was moving, slowly, her head turning from side to side. Her eyes were closed, but she was making a low, moaning sound.

Alison walked into the room. She knew this sound well. Her daughter had started having nightmares a little before the age of three, and for a few years they were pretty bad. It got to the point where Maddy had been afraid to go to bed, convinced that whatever she saw there—she could never remember, when she woke up, what it was—would come for her again, that the feeling of constriction and suffocation would descend upon her again. A year or so ago, they had just petered out, become a thing of the past. But now here was that noise again.

Alison wasn't sure what to do. They'd never found a successful approach. You could wake her, but often it took a long time for her to find sleep again, and sometimes the nightmare would simply return immediately.

Suddenly Madison's back arched, the movement startling Alison. She'd not seen that before. Her daughter let out a long, rasping sound . . . and then slowly deflated. Her head turned, quickly, but then she sighed. Her lips moved a little, but no sound came out. And then she was still. And not moaning anymore.

Alison waited a few minutes more, until she was sure her daughter was sleeping soundly. She carefully reached out and pulled the covers back over her. Stood for an additional moment, looking down at Madison's sleeping face.

Make the most of it, kiddo, she found herself thinking. *A nightmare is just a nightmare. You don't know anything about real sadness yet.*

As she turned away, she noticed something on the floor, lying on the bare wood just on the other side of the old rug that went under the bed.

She bent down and discovered that it was a sand dollar. It was small, gray. It had been broken in half.

She picked up one of the pieces. Where had it come from? Had Madison found it that afternoon? If so, why hadn't she *said*? There was a reward. . . .

Abruptly Alison realized why her daughter hadn't said anything, and she felt toxically ashamed. The piece Alison held in her hands was firm. Snapping the shell in half must have taken effort and been deliberate.

She dropped the fragment to the floor and left the room, pulling the door almost closed behind her. Then she went back to her own bed and lay there for a long time, staring up at the ceiling and listening to the rain.

chapter EIGHT

I got to the Hotel Malo just before 10:00 A.M. I'd been awake since before 6:00 but realized I could not call Amy's office for several hours. So I put myself into movement instead. Seven was the earliest I could arrive at the Zimmermans' and borrow a car without looking too strange. Inspired by Fisher's visit the day before, I told them I'd gotten a call from an old friend and was heading to the city for lunch. Bobbi looked at me a beat longer than necessary. Ben got straight to explaining how steering wheels worked.

I headed west on 90, joining 5 as the rush hour was starting in earnest, and fought my way off at James Street. Familiar territory so far, the route we'd taken when we came to spend a day in the city a week after we moved up north. Amy had showed me a couple of major draws like the Pike Place Market and the Space Needle, but she was more familiar with the city's boardrooms than its tourist attractions. The sky was low and an unrelenting gray. It had been that way the previous time, too. I eventually spiraled onto Sixth Avenue, a wide downtown canyon with tall concrete buildings on either side, lined with small and well-behaved trees bearing little yellow lights.

I pulled up outside the Malo, joining the back of a line of black town cars. The hotel had an awning of red and ocher stripes. A guy in a coat and hat tried to take my car someplace, but I convinced him not to. The lobby was done in limestone and rich fabrics, a big fireplace on one side. The luggage trolleys were of distressed brass, and the bellhops were demure. Something unobtrusive and New Age floated discreetly from hidden speakers, like the smell of vanilla cookies almost ready to come out of the oven.

The woman behind the desk was the one I'd spoken to a little after midnight. I was surprised to find that she did have an envelope for me, and a receipt for my twenty bucks. Also that she'd had the initiative to get the driver to write down his name—which is more than I'd done—together with the company he worked for. His first name was Georj, the second a collection of crunchy syllables from not-around-here. The company was Red Cabs. She relayed this information in a way that implied that guests at her hotel usually employed more upscale or funkier means of transport, like native bearers or cold-fusion hoverboards. I got her to check a final time for a reservation, implying that I was a colleague who believed that my assistant had made one and that he was going to catch seven shades of hell if he had not. No record, still.

"Can you do me another favor?" I asked, having also planned this on the journey. "I'm *sure* we've booked her in here before. Can you check back a few months?"

She tapped and squinted at the screen for a minute, nodded, then tapped again.

"Okay," she said, pressing her finger on the screen. "Ms. Whalen *did* stay with us three months ago, two nights. And before that I have a reservation back in January. Three nights that time. You want me to go farther?"

I said no and went back outside. Walked up to the corner, where I was beyond the influence of the doorman and his familiars, who remained eager that I do the right thing with my car. I still wasn't sure if I was overreacting, and I knew from experience that I have a tendency to stomp on the gas pedal when sitting and waiting would be the more considered option. But now I knew that Amy *had* stayed in this hotel before, and that changed things. Not because it confirmed she'd been in Seattle on those occasions—I knew that—but because it meant she was familiar with the Malo and it was unlikely that she'd have turned up and rejected it this time. I knew from their Web site that the hotel had vacancies for this week. So it wasn't a screwed-up booking either.

I went over to the doorman, gave him some money, and told him I'd be right back. I zigzagged the few blocks to the Hotel Monaco on Fourth Avenue. Amy would have liked this place, too—God would have liked it—but a quick conversation confirmed that neither of them had stayed there in the recent past.

The hotel had always been a dead end. It was time to forget about it. Time to forget about the whole thing, probably. I'd made the decision to come to the city around one o'clock the previous night, telling myself it was to do Amy the favor of retrieving her phone. A hundred-plus miles is not a huge deal in the Pacific Northwest. But it wasn't just that, of course. Amy had made business trips six, seven times a year ever since I'd known her. We had a standard operating procedure. We didn't go for whole days without being in contact, however brief. But . . . bottom line, she hadn't been staying in the hotel she'd used before. That was all I had, and in the light of day it didn't amount to a whole lot. I felt embarrassed for being there and was not entirely inclined to dismiss the voice in my head that claimed it was merely an excuse for leaving my desk for the day.

When I got back to the Malo, I went inside and perched on a chair by the big window. I opened the envelope and got out Amy's phone. It was easy to recognize, though I noticed she'd changed the picture she used as her background. It was a standard cell phone and no more: In an uncharacteristically anticorporate stand, she'd resisted getting sucked into BlackBerry hell. I pressed the green button. The list of outgoing calls showed one to my cell at the top—from cab guy late last night—preceded by names and numbers I didn't recognize, until it showed an incoming from me the afternoon before last.

I switched to her contacts list and scrolled through it, searching for Kerry, Crane & Hardy, Seattle. It wasn't there, of course. She'd know these people by first name and direct line, rather than hacking her way in through the general switchboard.

I noticed that the battery indicator was flashing about two seconds before the cell went dead.

Using my own, I called directory assistance and got a number for KC&H. I punched in the number and heard a perky voice sing out the familiar three letters. I asked to talk with someone who worked with Amy Whalen. I figured I'd find some underling who knew Amy's schedule, come up with a time and place to meet her. She might even be right there in the office. I could take her to lunch.

The phone went quiet for a while, and then I was talking to someone's assistant. She worked for a person named Todd and confirmed he'd be the guy to talk to, but was in a meeting right now. I was told he'd phone me just as soon as he possibly could, if not sooner.

Then I called Red Cabs and tried to learn how to get in contact with Georj Unpronounceable. He was off duty, and the dispatcher was cagey but claimed he'd tell the guy to get in touch with me when he came back to work. I ended the call knowing that it would never happen.

So I left the hotel and walked across the street to a Seattle's Best. I sat at a table outside there with a big, strong coffee, smoking and watching the rain and waiting for someone—anyone—to call me back.

By half past eleven, I was cold and getting pissed. The ten bucks I'd left with the Malo's doorman had worn off, and he'd gotten uptight about the car's continued presence outside the hotel. The Zimmermans' second-best SUV did not make a great advertisement for the establishment. For any establishment, actually. Retired professors apparently don't care a great deal about mud and dents, and the faded antiwar stickers in the back window were large and strident. Finally the guy in the hat crossed the street to come give me grief, and I agreed to move along.

I drove around the block until I found an underground lot. When I reemerged, I spent a couple of minutes with a downtown map I'd scored from the Malo reception. It was optimized toward shopping and eating opportunities, and it took me a while to locate the agency's street. It wasn't where I expected either. I'd assumed that the agency would be located a zillion floors up in one of the corporate behemoths that surrounded me. Instead it seemed to be in a narrow street near the marketplace.

I walked down a couple of vertiginous blocks until I found the big Public Market Center sign, then asked directions from a guy running a newsstand. He directed me down a side street that went under the main market and swerved sharply and steeply left. A sign confirmed that this was Post Alley. It looked more like a locale for loading and unloading fish and/or selling drugs. After a hundred yards, it suddenly segued into a section remade in 1990s postmodernist, with hanging baskets with a sushi restaurant and a little deli with a row of people sitting in the window eating identical salads. Soon I saw a restrained sign hanging from a picturesque wooden beam and knew I was in the right place.

I walked in, deciding how to play this. Our working lives had always been very separate. I'd gotten to know Amy's assistant in L.A. a little from crisis phone calls and occasional flying visits to the house, but she'd left to have a baby a couple of months before Amy realigned her working conditions. I'd heard colleagues' names mentioned, some enough to vaguely remember. I was pretty sure a Todd was among them. Could be this one, could be some other. There was probably some law that said a Todd had to be working in every advertising agency in the country. The whole deal would have been easier to handle on the phone—I could pretend I was still back out in the sticks and trying to casually get in touch with her—but I was tired of waiting for a return call.

Reception was an existential statement, and they'd spent a lot of money on it, mainly in an attempt to make it look like they hadn't, which is presumably the kind of thing that impresses the hell out of other advertising folk. Each chair cost far more than the woman behind the desk earned in a month, but she didn't seem put out by this. She was all in black and willowy and big-eyed—yet also possessed of a fierce intelligence, you could just tell—and came across like a girl who inhabited the best of all possible worlds and was anxious to spread the joy around.

I asked for Todd and in return was asked if I was expected.

"Oh no," I said, shrugging in what I hoped was a charming way. I didn't have much practice. "Just here on the off chance."

She beamed, as if this were simply the *best* possible way of stopping by, and got on the phone. She nodded vigorously at the end of her conversation, so I assumed that either I was good to go or she had mildly lost her mind.

Five minutes later someone eerily identical appeared from behind a frosted-glass door at the end of the room. She beckoned, and I got up and followed her into the offices beyond. This woman evidently inhabited only the third- or fourth-best of all worlds and was not disposed to mirth or unnecessary chatter, though I did learn that her name was Bianca. We took an elevator up two floors and then marched along a corridor with glass walls, past funky little rooms in which pairs of short-haired people were working so hard and creatively it made me want to set off a fire alarm, preferably by starting an actual fire.

At the end she opened a door and ushered me through.

"Todd Crane," she announced.

Ah, I thought, only at that moment realizing I was about

to talk to a third of the people who made up the company name.

I found myself in an austere space with big windows on two sides, giving a wide view of Elliott Bay and the piers. The remaining walls were covered with framed certificates and awards and huge and celebratory product shots, including a few campaigns I knew Amy had been involved with. In the middle of the room, there was a desk big enough to play basketball on. A trim man in his early fifties was coming out from behind it. Chinos, well-pressed lilac shirt. Hair once black now streaked with flecks of gray, bone structure so blandly handsome he could have been cast in a television spot for just about anything good and wholesome and reasonably expensive.

"Hey," he said, extending his hand. "I'm Todd Crane."

I'll just bet you are, I thought, as I shook it. *And I don't like you.*

He was smooth, though. I guess half his job was making strangers feel at home. There was a framed photograph on one corner of his desk, a studio portrait showing Crane with his arm around a glossy woman, flanked by three daughters of widely spaced ages. Curiously, it was angled not toward his chair but out into the room, as if it were another credential, like the certificates on the walls. There was a retro radio on the floor in the corner of the room, too, 1970s era, presumably another character statement.

"So, Jack," he said, leaning back. "Great to finally put a face to the name after all this time. I'm amazed it never happened before."

"Didn't get out of L.A. often," I said. "Until we moved."

"So what brings you to the city today? You're in books now, right?"

"I have a meeting. Plus, Amy managed to leave her cell phone in a cab yesterday. So I thought I'd kill two birds with one stone, get the phone to her right away. She must be in withdrawal by now."

Todd laughed. Ha, ha, ha. The beats were separate, as if

the sequence had been composed, practiced, and perfected in private many, many years before.

Then he paused, as if waiting for me to say something else. I thought that was weird. I had been expecting him to be the one to start volunteering information.

"So," I said eventually. "What's the best way for me to do that?"

"Well, I don't know," Crane said. He looked confused.

"I assumed someone here would have her diary."

"Well, not really," he said, folding his arms and pursing his lips. "Amy's our roving troubleshooter now. As you know, of course. Finger in a lot of pies. A global view. Strategic. But fundamentally she still reports to the L.A. office. They'd be the people who'd—"

He stopped, as if he'd just put things together in his head. Looked at me carefully.

"Uh, Amy's not in Seattle this week, Jack," he said. "At least not with us."

I was as fast as I could be, but my mouth must still have been hanging open for a second. Maybe two.

"I know that," I said, smiling broadly. "She's visiting friends. I just wondered whether she was expected to touch base at any point. As she's here anyway."

Todd shook his head slowly. "Not that I know of. But maybe, you know? Have you tried her hotel? We always book people in the Malo. Or is she staying with her . . . friends?"

"I left a message for her there already. Just wanted to get this phone back to her as quick as I can."

"Understand that." Todd nodded, all smiles again. "Lost without them these days, right? Wish I could help you more, Jack. She stops by, I'll tell her you're on the hunt. You want to give me your number?"

"I left it already," I said.

"That's right, sorry. Hell of a morning. Clients. Can't live with them, not recommended business practice to shoot them in the head. Or so they say."

He clapped me on the shoulder and walked me out back along the corridor, filling the journey with praise of Amy and a sustained meditation on how her new position was going to shake things up for the company, and in a good way. It was not difficult to imagine him greeting his wife and kids in a similar manner every morning, a goals-and-achievements spiel capped with assurances of his best attention at all times, CC'd to his personal assistant.

He left me at the door, and I walked across reception alone. I turned my head just before stepping back out into the world. It seemed to me that there might be someone standing behind the frosted-glass door watching me leave, but I couldn't be sure.

I walked down the alley slowly. I hadn't brought Amy's organizer, but I remembered the contents. Three days full of meetings. Sure, I hadn't read the details, and they could theoretically have been in L.A., San Francisco, or Portland—the last only a three-hour drive away—but I didn't believe for a moment that I'd confused the city. Plus, I had her phone in my pocket, found here in this city last night. Amy had come here and until the night before last had been in contact as usual. Now she was nowhere to be found. The hotel was a blank. The people at her job didn't know where she was—or said they didn't.

And neither did I.

Post Alley deposited me in a stubby dead end, over which the beginnings of an elevated street set off toward the bay before banking sharply left to join the Alaskan Viaduct above. The concrete supports had been covered in graffiti, over what looked like many years. REV9 and LATER and BACK AGAIN, it said, among other things. While my eyes were wandering over this, I felt a sudden itch in my shoulder blades.

I turned, slowly, as if that were simply what I was doing next. A few people were walking back and forth at the end of the road, going about their business in the shadow of the elevated highway, getting in or out of cars, moving stuff here and there. Beyond that there was a wide road and a couple of piers, and then the flicker of light hitting water out on Elliott Bay.

No one was looking in my direction. Everyone was in motion, walking or driving. Traffic rumbled over the elevated highway above, sending deep vibrations through the buildings and sidewalks around me, until the whole city almost seemed to be singing one long, low note.

chapter NINE

I found a bar downtown. I scored a table by the window and ordered a pot of coffee—employing the last of my charm to get the waitress to let me use an outlet behind the bar to plug in a power adapter I'd bought on the way for Amy's phone. While I waited for the coffee, I watched people at the other tables. Bars used to be a place where you came to get away from the outside world. That was the point. Now everyone seemed to be sucking free Wi-Fi or talking on cell phones.

Nobody did anything interesting enough to distract me from the interlocking dialogues in my head. The fact that Amy wasn't in town on Kerry, Crane & Hardy business could be explained. I knew that. I was calm. It was still possible there was nothing strange going on here except inside my own head, and it reminded me of a time a year or so before, when Amy went through a period of talking in her sleep. At first it was just a mumbling, and you couldn't really make out anything. After a while it got stronger, words and sections of sentences. It would wake me up, night after night. It began to screw with both our sleep patterns. She tried adjusting her diet and caffeine intake and spending even longer in the gym on the way to work, but nothing helped. Then it just stopped, though it was a couple of weeks before I started sleeping soundly again. In the meantime I had plenty of time to lie in the dark and wonder what made the brain do such a thing, how it must be organized so that when all the conscious functions had apparently checked out, some part was still verbalizing about something. How was it doing that, and why? Who was it talking to?

That's what it felt as if my brain was doing right now. The part under my conscious control was sticking fingers in dikes and providing rational explanations. It was doing good work, suggesting that Amy might indeed be here on the quiet in the hope of bringing clients to KC&H as a lock, stock, and barrel triumph that couldn't be group-owned. She lived and breathed office politics. Could even be that was what she'd been trying to explain the evening when I didn't listen properly.

But meanwhile other bits of my head were running scattershot in all directions. Deep inside each of us is a part that mistrusts order and craves the relief of seeing the world shatter into the chaos it believes lies underneath all along. Or perhaps that's just me.

When Amy's phone had enough charge, I retrieved it from behind the bar. Sitting with it in my hands felt strange. This was the only device through which I could talk to my wife: but it was currently with me and thus made her feel even farther away. We have evolved now, gained a sixth sense through the invention of e-mail and cell phones—an awareness of the utterances and circumstances of people who are not present. When this sense is taken away, you feel panicked, struck blind. I had a sudden idea and called the phone back at the house, but it rang and rang before switching to the machine. I left a message saying where I was and why, just in case Amy got home ahead of me. It should have felt like a good, sensible thing to do. Instead it was as if another road had just been washed away in the rain.

Amy's phone was a different brand from mine, and the keys were a lot smaller. As a result my first brush with the interface put me in the music-player section by mistake. There were eight MP3 tracks listed, which surprised me. Like any other occupant of the twenty-first century who wasn't Amish, Amy owned an iPod, a dedicated digital music player. She wasn't going to be using her phone for music, but while I could imagine that a device might come with a couple of songs preloaded, eight seemed like a lot. Seven of the tracks were simply numbered Track 1 to Track 7, the other a long string of digits. I tried Track 1. Tinny music came out of the earpiece, old jazz, one of those crackly 1920s guys. Very much not Amy's kind of thing—she'd gone on record more than once as hating jazz, or basically anything that predated Blondie. I tried another track, then one more, with similar results. It was like holding the world's smallest speakeasy.

I took another scroll through the contacts section, this time looking not for Kerry, Crane & Hardy but for anything else that stuck out. I didn't see anything to make me linger. I didn't recognize all the names, but I was never going to. Your partner's workplace is like another country. You'll always be a stranger there.

So I headed to the SMS section. Amy had picked up the joy of SMS messaging from the younger dudes in the agency, and she and I now exchanged texts regularly—when I knew she'd be in a meeting or when she wanted to convey information that didn't need my attention right away. Usually just to say hi. Sure enough, there were four from me there, going back a few months. A couple from her sister, Natalie, who lived down in Santa Monica, in the house where she and Amy had been born and had grown up.

And eleven from somebody else.

The messages from Natalie and me had our names attached. These others didn't, just a phone number. It was the same number each time.

I selected the earliest. It was blank. An SMS communication had been sent and received, but there was no text in it at all. The next was the same, and the next. Why would you keep sending texts without anything in them? Because you were incompetent maybe, but by the third or fourth you'd think anyone could have gotten the hang of it. I kept scrolling. I'd grown so used to the single line of nothing in each message that when the sixth contained something else, it took me by surprise. It didn't make much sense either.

yes

No period, even. The next few messages were blank again. Then I got to the final one.

A rose by ny othr name wll sml as sweet . . .
:-D

I put the phone on the table and poured another cup of coffee. Eleven messages was a lot, even if most of them had nothing to say. Besides, Amy wasn't the type to let her phone be clogged with other people's Luddite errors. She was not sentimental. I'd already noted she'd only kept the texts from me that contained information of long-term use. A few thinking-of-you ones I'd sent a couple of days before, and which she'd replied to, had already been erased. The couple from Natalie looked like they'd been saved because they were especially annoying and could be used later as evidence against her.

So why keep someone else's blanks? And under what circumstances would you receive this many messages from someone and yet not have that person's name in your list of contacts? The others came up as "Home"—my phone—and "Natalie." These just listed the number. If you're that regularly in contact, why not go to the minuscule trouble of entering the person's name into your phone book? Unless it's something you don't want found?

I flipped over to the made/received calls log. The number didn't appear anywhere on it. Communication from this source evidently came only in the form of text, or at least no call had come from it in the last month.

This gave me an idea, and I went back to the first SMS message and found that it had been sent a little over three months previously. There'd been a month gap between the first and the second. Then another two weeks. Then they'd started coming more frequently. The one saying "yes" had been sent six days before. And the one about roses had arrived just yesterday, late in the afternoon. Amy had seen this message—she must have; otherwise it would still have been filed under "Unread." Then, sometime in the next few hours, she had lost the phone, during the course of an evening her schedule listed as blank.

Then she had, so far as I could tell, lost herself.

I navigated sideways from received messages into the section recording texts that Amy had sent. The list there was very short. A couple of replies to her sister and to me. And one other. It had been sent two minutes after the last message to her and consisted of the following:

Bell 9. Will b waitng, whenever yr redE, 2dy, nxt wk, nxt year xoxox

The waitress swung by at that moment to see if I wanted fresh coffee. I said no. I asked for beer.

One thing my father was always good at was answering questions. He didn't have infinite patience in other directions, but if you asked him something—how the moon was created, why cats slept all the time, why that man over there had only one arm—he'd always give you a grown-up answer, except for this one occasion. I was about twelve. I'd heard an older kid at school being pretentious and been somewhat impressed and came home and asked my dad what was the meaning of life, thinking it made me sound at *least* sixteen. He seemed unaccountably annoyed and said it was a dumb question. I didn't understand. "Say you come back to your house one afternoon," he said, "and there's someone at your table, eating your food. You don't ask him, 'What the hell are you doing, sitting there, eating my dinner?'—because he could simply say he was hungry. Which is an answer to what you asked him, sure enough. But not to your *real* question, which is 'What the hell are you doing in my house?' "

I still didn't get it, but I found I remembered this from time to time when I was older. It probably made me a slightly better cop, less prone to ask witnesses my questions instead of just letting them tell me what they knew. I remembered it again as I sat there in the bar in Seattle and started my first beer.

My head felt heavy and cold, and I was coming to suspect that the day was not going to end well. I realized that maybe I had to stop asking where Amy *was* and start thinking about *why*.

chapter TEN

Meanwhile a girl was standing in an airport concourse. A big clock suspended from the ceiling said it was twenty-four minutes to four. As she watched, the last number changed, going from 16:36 to 16:37. She kept watching until it flipped to 16:39. She liked the 9. She didn't know why it should seem compelling, but it did. A recorded voice kept telling people not to smoke, which Madison suspected must be annoying for them.

Madison was not sure where she was going next. She had not, for a couple of minutes, been sure where she was right at this moment. She recognized it now. It was the Portland airport, of course. She'd been here several times in the past, most recently when they went to visit Mom's mom down in Florida in the spring. Madison could remember browsing around the little Powell's bookstore and drinking a juice at the café where you could watch planes landing and taking off. Mom had been nervous about flying, and Dad had joked and made her feel better about it. There had been more joking in those days. A lot more.

But today? Madison remembered early talk of a trip up to the grocery store in Cannon Beach that morning, discussion that hadn't come to anything. Then a little time on the beach. It had been cold and windy. There had been no walk. A quiet and skimpy lunch, in the cottage. Mom stayed indoors afterward, so Madison went back out to hang on the beach by herself.

After that . . . there was this *gap.* Like when she'd woken last night and couldn't remember the time on the beach. It was like there was a cloud in the way.

Mom wasn't here at the airport with her, that was clear. Mom wouldn't have walked off and left her by herself. Madison was wearing her new coat, too, she realized. That was also strange. She wouldn't have gone out to the beach in her new coat. She would have worn her *old* coat, because it didn't matter if that got sand on it. So she must have gone into the cottage after the beach, to change, and snuck back out.

Then what? How had she gotten from there to Portland? Maddy knew the word her Uncle Brian would use for this: perplexing. In every other way, she felt fine. Just like normal. So what was the deal with the blank spot? And what was she supposed to do now?

She realized that the hand in her pocket was holding something. She pulled it out. A notebook. It was small, bound in stained brown leather, and looked old. She opened it. The pages were covered in handwriting. The first line said:

In the beginning there was Death.

It was written in a pen that smudged occasionally, in an ink that was a kind of red-brown. There were drawings in the book, too, maps and diagrams, lists of names. One of the diagrams looked exactly like the drawing on the back of the business card she also had in her possession, the interlinked nines. Even the handwriting looked the same. Slipped in the front of the notebook was a long piece of paper. It was a United Airlines ticket.

Wow—how had she bought *that*?

These questions didn't make her feel scared. Not quite. For the time being, there was something dreamlike about her situation. Maybe all that mattered was going where she needed to go, and she could worry about everything else later. Yes. That sounded good. Easier.

Madison blinked, and by the time her eyelids had flipped back up, she had largely stopped worrying about trivia like how she'd traveled the fifty miles from Cannon Beach to the Portland airport, or how she'd purchased an airline ticket costing over a hundred dollars, or why she was alone.

Instead she turned to look at the departures information, to find out where it was she needed to go.

As far as Jim Morgan was concerned, there was a simple secret to life, and it was something he'd learned from his uncle Clive. His father's cadaverous brother spent his entire working days in security at the Ready Ship dispatch warehouse over in Tigard. Checked trucks as they came in, checked them as they went out. He'd done this five days a week for over thirty years. Jim's dad never hid the fact that as a (junior) executive in a bank, he considered himself many steps up the ladder compared with his older sibling—but the curious thing was that while his father spent his life moaning and feeling put-upon, Uncle Clive seemed utterly content with his lot.

One evening when Jim was thirteen, his uncle had spent an entire Sunday dinner talking about his job. This was not the first time—and Jim's father and mother weren't subtle about rolling their eyes—but on this occasion their son listened. He listened to information about schedules and shipping targets. He listened to discussion of procedures. He came to understand that every day, between the hours of eight and four, getting in and out of the Ready Ship warehouse was like shoving a fat camel through the eye of a needle. Uncle Clive was that needle. Didn't matter who you were or what you were carrying, how late or urgent your shipment or how many times he'd seen your face before. You showed your badge or pass or letter. You were polite.

You dealt with Uncle Clive in the proper manner. Otherwise you didn't get past—or at least not without a protracted exchange involving two-way radios and head shaking, from which you would limp away feeling like an ass. Which you were. The rules were simple. You showed your pass. It was the law. You couldn't get this through your head, it wasn't Uncle Clive's fault.

Fifteen years later Jim had taken this to heart. You could do things the hard way or the right way, and it was always someone's god- or government-given job to make sure you did like you'd been told. There was something else to be learned from this, a way of living your life. You took your pleasures where you could, and you made sure you were king of your own domain. Amen.

Jim's domain was the Portland airport security line. He ran a tight ship. People stood where and how they were supposed to stand, or they faced Jim's wrath—he had no problem with stopping the checking process and walking slowly down the line of fretful travelers to tell the assholes at the back to keep the line straight. Jim had a system at the front, too. The person he was dealing with was allowed to approach. All others (including that person's spouse, business partner, mother, or spirit guide) stood the hell back at the yellow line and waited their turn. Failure to comply would cause Jim to again stop what he was doing and step forward to explain it at uncomfortable length. He actually *did* have all day to spend on the matter, or at least a set of three two-hour shifts. The people in line weren't on the side of the troublemaker at the front. They wanted to get on with their journey, buy a magazine, take a dump. Anyone obstructing these goals became an enemy of the people. Jim's philosophy was "divide and rule," or it would have been if he'd ever thought to articulate it. He didn't have to. It wasn't his job to explain things. His way was just the way it was.

At 16:48 all was well in Jim's world. He had his line moving in a well-ordered manner. It was neither too long (making Jim look inefficient) nor too short (suggesting he was insufficiently thorough, which would be far worse), and it was very straight. Jim nodded curtly at an octogenarian from Nebraska who—he was now confident—was unlikely to be carrying a cigarette lighter, handgun, or atomic weapon, and waved her on to the X-ray machine. Then he took his own good time about turning back to the line.

A little girl was standing there. About nine, ten maybe, long hair. She seemed to be alone.

Jim cupped his hand, indicated she should come forward. She did so. He raised his head, the signal for "turn over your documentation and make sure it's in the right (though unspecified) order, or I'm going to make you feel like a dork in front of everyone."

"Hello," she said, smiling up at him. It was a nice smile, the kind that guaranteed second or third visits to toy shops, the smile of a little girl who had always been pretty good at getting people to do what she wanted.

Jim did not return it. Security was not a smiling matter. "Ticket."

She handed it to him promptly. He looked it over for his standard period, three times longer than was necessary. With his eyes firmly on the self-explanatory piece of paper, he demanded, "Accompanying adult?"

"Excuse me?"

He looked up slowly. "Where is she? Or he?"

"What?" she said. She looked confused.

Jim prepared to deliver one of the stock phrases to deal with diversions from set procedure. His versions were famously brisk. But this was just a kid. The two guys behind her in line were now taking a mild interest in the proceedings. Jim couldn't just chew her out.

He smiled inexpertly. "You need an accompanying adult to get you to departure," he said. "It's the law."

"Really?" she said. "Are you sure?"

"Uh-huh. 'Unaccompanied minors must be brought to the gate by a parent or responsible adult,'" he added, quoting, "'who must remain at the airport until the child boards and the airplane departs the gate.' You need all this arranged and booked ahead of time, too. You can't just turn up at the gate and fly, kid."

"But . . . I'm going to visit my aunt," the girl said, sounding slightly panicky. "She's waiting for me. She's going to be worried."

"Well, maybe your momma should have made sure you—"

"Please? I do have someone with me. They . . . had to go outside to smoke. They'll be here in a minute, really."

Jim shook his head. "Even if I let you through here, which I ain't gonna, they'll check again at the gate. You're not getting near that plane without an adult."

The girl's smile slowly faded.

"Sorry, kid," Jim said, making what was for him quite an effort to hide the fact that he was not.

She looked up at him for a moment. "Watch your back," she said softly. Then she ducked under the rope and walked away across the concourse, where she was quickly lost among the other evening travelers.

Openmouthed, Jim watched her go. When it came to kids, he was phoning it in from the land of Who Gives a Shit, from a really bad connection. But . . . shouldn't he maybe go after her? Check that she really was here with someone?

On the other hand, the line was getting long, and some of the people in it looked bad-tempered, and, if the truth be told, Jim just didn't really care. All he wanted was to close out his shift, get home, and drink a series of beers while watching the tube, then get on the Net and find some porn. There was that, plus . . .

Of course it was absurd, just a little a girl using a phrase picked up from a movie. But there'd been something in her tone that made him think if she'd been a couple feet taller, he would have taken the threat seriously. Even from a woman. He didn't want to have to explain this to anyone. So he went to the next person in line, who turned out to be

French, so, .while he had identification, it wasn't *American* identification, which mandated Jim to stare even longer and harder than usual at his documents and to look up at the guy's face in a suspicious and "Don't think we've forgotten about you punking out over Iraq" kind of way. By the end of this, he was King of the Line again.

He didn't think about the little girl until the detectives turned up the next day, and it wasn't until he realized he'd missed the opportunity to prevent a nine-year-old girl from vanishing into thin air that he understood there were smaller holes than he'd ever realized, and he was about to spend a while being pulled back and forth through one of them.

Meanwhile Madison had made her way back outside the airport building and was standing forlornly on the sidewalk.

Now what?

Frowning, trying to remember why she'd been so convinced she had to fly when getting a cab to the house and her father would make the most sense, Madison noticed a guy standing ten feet away having a cigarette. He was looking at her as if he were wondering what she was doing here by herself. He seemed like a nice man and the kind who might ask her if she was okay, and Madison wasn't sure what the answer to that was. She wasn't sure she trusted herself to speak either; she'd been almost rude to the man in the airport, which was not like her *at all.* Maddy was very polite, always, especially to grown-ups.

She crossed the street quickly and went into the multistory parking lot, as if that's where she'd been going all along. Seeing the smoking man stirred a memory from the blank period earlier in the day. Another man had looked at her, she thought, after she had . . . of *course.*

That's how she'd gotten to the city.

By bus, duh. She'd arrived at the Greyhound station on NW Sixth Avenue. Then she'd walked for a long time, she remembered, looking for an address. It was in a place she knew, but somehow she didn't know where that place actually *was*. The area wasn't very nice. A lot of the storefronts were boarded over and had letters above them that didn't make words in English. There were cardboard boxes all over and the smell of rotting fruit in gutters. The parked cars looked old. It had been different also from the parts of Portland that Madison knew in that it seemed to be a place where only men lived. Men, standing in dirty grocery stores. Men leaning in doorways, by themselves or with someone just like them, not talking to each other but watching everyone who went past. Men, on street corners, shivering. There were white men and black men and Asian men, but they all looked more or less the same and like they all knew about the same things. Maybe this was what her mom meant when she said the color of someone's skin made no difference. At some point there'd been a man in particular, two men, in fact. They had a dog on a chain. They'd come toward her purposefully, looking all around as they got closer, but then their dog suddenly started going nuts and they crossed the street instead.

Did she find the place she was looking for? She still couldn't remember that part. But she knew she didn't have the small notebook when she left the house that morning. So maybe that's where it had come from. Good. Call that squared away. She got to Portland by bus.

Once she'd filled in every one of these little gaps, everything would be back to normal.

Inside the parking lot, it was dark and cool. People walked back and forth with suitcases that made clackety sounds. Cars pulled out of spaces and went swishing out onto the road. Big white and yellow and red buses with sliding doors and hotel names on them let people off or picked them up. It was a place full of people who didn't know each other. That was good. Madison decided she would find somewhere she could sit and think in quiet. She walked down the center of one of the aisles. Everyone was talking or laughing or paying cabdrivers or keeping track of their own children. It was like they couldn't see her at all. This reminded her of something, though she couldn't remember what.

She was approaching a car that was parked halfway along the aisle, when she found herself slowing down. The car was yellow, and the driver's-side door was open. She diverted her course to the other side of the aisle.

As she passed the car, she glanced across. A man was sitting inside. He was pretty old and had gray hair. His hands were on the steering wheel, though the engine was not running. He was staring through the windshield and looked like he'd been there a while. Madison was wondering what the man was looking at, when he seemed to wake up. He turned his head and saw her. She had time to notice that there was something weird about his face, and then he backed out of the space like he was in a car chase. He went screeching out of the lot before she really had time to absorb what was happening.

But now the last gap was filling, like water running back up through the drain into a bathtub. Something about when she was walking through town . . . a Chinese woman. Yes. She had given Madison the notebook. After she left the woman's house and was walking again, a man had pulled over to the curb, offered her a lift in his car. Maddy had lived all her life with very clear instructions about not getting into the cars of strangers, and yet that's what she'd done. The man had been very nice to her at first; he just happened to be heading to the airport, and he'd be happy to help out. Then he became nervous and like a little boy and kept laughing even though neither of them had said anything funny. He said stuff about how pretty she looked, which she liked when Dad said it but not when this man did.

Then they'd been together at the airline ticket desk, and she'd pretended he was her daddy, and he had bought the ticket with money she'd given him. But after that he'd wanted to come out here to the parking lot and had tried to get her to get into the car with him again. He said he'd done what she wanted, and now she had to be nice, too. He put his hand on her arm.

She still could not remember what happened then, but when he'd looked at her before driving away, the thing she remembered about his face was that there'd been a long scratch on it. Madison knew she hadn't gotten back into his car. Instead she had run back into the terminal, and tried to fly.

She pulled the ticket out of her pocket. She had never been to Seattle. Why did she want to go now? She didn't know. She did want to, though, and right away. Being kept away from Seattle felt bad. She would have to find—as Dad sometimes said, when on the phone to office people—"some other more workable solution."

Belatedly realizing that her coat felt bulky in the chest, she put her hand in the inside pocket. It came out holding an envelope. It was dusty. Inside were hundred-dollar bills. A *lot* of them. They couldn't be Mom's—she had credit cards. At the bottom of the envelope was a small metal ring, with two keys on it.

Madison put the envelope back into her pocket, mentally filing it among the things to be thought about later. She was smart. Everybody said so. She would get to the bottom of this.

Now, in the meantime, back in the parking garage, she noticed a woman standing a few cars down, loading a small suitcase into the back of her car. Madison walked toward her and stopped a few feet away.

The woman turned. She was younger than Madison's mom. "Hello," she said. "What's your name?"

"Madison. What's yours?"

The woman said her name was Karen. She was nice, and friendly, and within a couple of minutes Madison began to believe she had found a more workable solution.

* * *

When Karen drove the car out of the lot, Madison was sitting in the passenger seat. The woman seemed disconcerted by all the road choices, as Maddy's mom sometimes did, and so, to let her get on with it without an audience, Madison reached into her pocket and pulled out the notebook once more.

She opened it to the first page and read what came after the first line:

And the people looked, and they saw that Death sucked, but they assumed this is what God wanted—because our God was a harsh god, and hated us. They believed Death to be His final punishment, at the end of our short spans of bloody sorrow: that He drops us on this dark and brutal plane to scurry from cold shelter to poor food and back, in endless rain, all the while bowed under the knowledge that at some time, at any time, a heel dipped in gore could drop like thunder and smear us broken across stony ground. We see the people we love taken from us, turned sick and rotten in front of our eyes, and we eat and fuck and dream our febrile lives away, because we understand that this will be our fate, too—and that afterward comes an eternity lying silent and blind in a dark, soft cloud: this prospect sugared only by the lies we learned to tell ourselves as soon as we could speak, the promise of an imprisoned life everlasting, in the lofty attic of Heaven, or the basement corridors of Hell.

But, and here you must listen . . .

The lie is not quite a lie.

These places do exist, but close by. People realized this slowly, started to make plans. Some did. The very few. Those who possessed the will and strength of purpose. The self-chosen ones. Those who learned that the doors to prisons could be unlocked in the night, that we could venture back.

And who in time came to realize that they could inhabit the daylight hours, too, become the householder once again.

People like us.

People like you, my dear.

"What's that you're reading?" the woman asked as she turned with evident relief onto a big road.

"I have no idea," Madison said.

chapter ELEVEN

The bar I'd been in had been okay but staid, and after a while they put the game on and everyone watched with the sound off. Not my kind of place. So I migrated to somewhere along the street called Tillie's, which was more scuffed up and played loud rock and roll. That didn't mean it was a great environment for me to be in, however. The good and bad thing about bars and alcohol is that they blur social bonds. Sometimes this can be a plus—a lonely person finding solace in the company of strangers, the temporary tribal warmth of sitting around the same campfire. But it can also be that one individual begins to seem as relevant as the next, that the person you love is suddenly too annoying to bear and complete unknowns become your best friends. As a result you end up having conversations you probably shouldn't. I do anyhow. I'd been talking to one guy in particular, and the discussion was going downhill. This person had shadows under his eyes, his hair needed a trim, and his jacket was decent but looked like something he'd bought during better times and now inhabited in the way polite men of reduced circumstances spend winter afternoons sitting on benches in well-tended parks.

"Jack Whalen," I repeated, loudly, leaning forward to get

right in his face. "You might have to order it or get it off Amazon, but it exists."

The guy did not seem impressed. If anything, he looked like he thought I was even more of an asshole than before. Evidently he hadn't heard me correctly. Or hadn't understood. His eyes said he was as drunk as I was. That was pretty drunk. I opened my mouth to start snarling in earnest but noticed something in his eyes that stopped me in my tracks. I realized it wasn't just contempt I was dealing with, but a kind of weary hate.

There was a sound behind me, and I straightened up.

A guy in a pale gray suit strolled into the john with his hands already at his fly, barely getting to a urinal before pissing like a racehorse.

"Whoa!" he hooted, turning to grin at me, obviously impressed with his own voiding skills.

"Right," I said. It felt weak, but I'm not sure what else I could have contributed. I dried my hands primly on my pants and stumbled back out of the restroom, feeling cold along the back of my neck.

The music in the bar sounded flat and old now, and the room was brighter than I remembered. And yes of course I had sort of known I was in the men's room, talking to myself in the mirror over the sinks. It's happened before, when I've been exceptionally fried. I glance at my face, and for a moment the reflection there looks like a complete stranger. At first the encounter is convivial, but sometimes it gets personal, a "pull your socks up, shithead" routine. This time I knew that for a second I'd really forgotten I was talking to myself. That could not be good. Not when it was only eight in the evening and I could see no likelihood I'd be going home anytime soon.

Or tonight, for that matter. I suddenly remembered I was a hundred miles from where I lived. That I'd told the Zimmermans I'd be back hours before now. That I was long past driving and had nowhere to stay, and that I'd still had no contact with my wife, whose cell phone contained messages I did not like the look of.

Then I remembered I'd been thinking these things on the way to the restroom and had made no progress toward resolving them then either.

I was relieved to see I had most of a Mack & Jack's left, and I tried to lock back into the scene. One of the waitresses was pretty cute. She was slim and good-natured, with carefully unkempt hair, and wore her apron well. My appreciation of her was generic, like that of a woman registering a pair of nice shoes she neither wants, needs, nor can afford. Other patrons were more directly appreciative. Half an hour earlier, one guy had hoisted himself off his stool and gone regretfully into the night. I'd overheard the waitress saying good-bye as he went, adding, "You *do* have rights as a father, you know."

Right, I'd thought, *but do you* really *not get that he was recounting his problems with his bitch ex-wife, dwelling on how much he loves his kids, in expectation not of useful legal advice but rather in the vague hope of getting into your pants?* The more I drank, you see, the wiser I was becoming. It is often that way with me.

That guy's spot had been taken by a young semi-couple. The girl had dressed nicely and applied makeup with enthusiasm and yet remained irrevocably homely. Her stubbled companion had good cheekbones and olive skin and was dressed in denim and a battered red leather jacket, with sideburns that came to a sharp point. He was wearing a red bandanna, too. I'd hated him on sight, naturally.

"I could never be angry with you," the girl was saying. He nodded with the randomness that comes from possessing a significantly lower comprehension of the language than you've led everyone to believe.

The conversation meandered on, the girl doing all the

talking, the guy occasionally speaking with a clumsy deliberation that conferred half-assed profundity to gnomic gems along the lines of "Yes, I think that is so." The fact that he was harmless and possibly even almost charming simply made him all the more punchable. The girl leaned toward him often and covertly moved her stool a couple of inches his way. He endured this stoically, and suddenly I understood their situation as if I were perched outside their reality and watching it critically, some drunken god assigned to monitor their progress. In the end I was leaning so far in their direction that she noticed and turned to look at me.

And then suddenly I was talking.

"Honey," I said, "I'm going to save you time and unhappiness here. What young Carlos is trying to say—without actually saying it—is that he's enjoyed screwing you the last several weeks but is now going back to Europe, where he will return to screwing somebody else, probably the hometown girl whose letters he's been stashing under the bed all the while he's been here."

The girl blinked.

I shrugged. "How can this surprise you? Check out the fucking sideburns. Bottom line is, Pedro here is not a poet or bullfighter. He'll spend his glory years driving a delivery truck for his uncle's restaurant, sleeping around while he's still got it, and then getting exponentially fatter and more baggy-eyed. Accept that this guy's memory is who you're going to be unfaithful with for the rest of your life, and go back to Plan A and find yourself some nice local M.B.A. with a commitment to shaving and regular gym attendance."

Both were looking at me by now, him with utter incomprehension, smiling a little, thinking how friendly these Americans were—they just strike up conversations in bars, it's so great. The girl blinked twice more, however, and I realized I still hadn't nailed it.

"Though, actually . . ." I said as it dawned on me, "he *hasn't* been screwing you, right? But he's going home tomorrow, and so you hope tonight's going to be the night. Sorry, honey. Not going to happen. You've really just been friends all this time—except that he has, in some amphibian way, always known that you wanted it."

The girl was staring at me now, her mouth wide. I shook my head slowly, sharing her pain, compassionate for her essence and being in a moment of bonding with her flawed and yet honest human soul.

And then she hit me in the face with an ashtray.

I left Tillie's under something of a cloud. I tried explaining myself to the waitress but was hampered by the nosebleed, and she got a huge black guy from the kitchen to motivate me the hell out of their bar. He was good. I felt very motivated.

I made it out onto the sidewalk largely unassisted, to be confronted with traffic and steady drizzle. I wandered up and down Fourth for a while, smoking heroically and snarling at trees. I had already called the house three more times and received no answer. I knew I had gotten drunk to avoid thinking clearly about what these things implied, but this knowledge didn't help. I still didn't want to think about it. I couldn't find anywhere else apart from the Malo and another hotel's lounge bar, and I sensed I wouldn't be welcome there either. So I took a right down a street called Madison, thinking I'd head toward the waterfront. I discovered that Madison is not a street but a mountainside. I was okay for a couple of blocks, but when I got to Second Avenue and looked down the next stretch, I seriously considered just staying where I was and waiting until someone opened a bar nearby. I decided that this would somehow be a sign of weakness, however—being a man is riddled with that kind of bullshit—and persisted on my way. They'd replaced the concrete paving alongside the Federal Building with serrated bricks, which helped a little, but after a few steps I simply lost my footing. I crashed onto my elbow and ass and slid ten feet down the street, clanging resoundingly into a garbage can.

As I hauled myself back up, I was passed by a middle-aged couple methodically trekking in the other direction, bundled up in identical fleeces.

"Slippery, huh," one of them said. They looked like a double-headed grub.

"Fuck off," I replied. At the junction with First, I found a minimart and lurched in to buy more cigarettes. The Chinese woman behind the counter looked like she didn't want to get involved, but I gave her The Look and she did what I wanted. I bought a bottle of water, too, and used my reflection in the beverage cooler to make sure my face was clean of blood. Afterward I stood outside on the corner and spotted the glow of a bar on the other side. I limped over. It was a nice place, loosely attached to yet another hotel but dark enough inside that the welt on my cheek wouldn't be immediately obvious.

I ordered a glass of weaker light beer and sat in the corner, out of danger's way. That was the idea, at any rate. If I'd still been in active charge of the evening, I'd have realized that any beer was a bad idea now, or any bar. The problem is that the guy who means me the most harm seems to live inside my own head.

The first thing I did was check Amy's phone to make sure it hadn't been smashed to pieces. Luckily, it seemed fine. The shock of my collision with the ground seemed to have sobered me up a little, too, unless I'd merely entered that Indian summer of clarity you get when your nervous system is warning it's about to wash its hands of you and is giving you *one last chance* to get the hell home before it pulls the plug and drops you bonelessly to the floor.

Since I had made no progress with a positive explanation for Amy's collection of text messages, I went back to one of them. I'd realized earlier in the afternoon that there was a direct approach to finding out whom they were from. I hadn't wanted to go that far then, and I hadn't been drunk. Now I was.

I hit the green button and called the number.

After a few seconds of silence, I got an out-of-service recording. I cut the connection, feeling relieved and disturbed. Where the hell *was* Amy? Was she okay? If so, why didn't she call? How much longer should I leave it before going to the cops? I knew their likely response to a man with as little evidence as I had, but I was worried about her. The only other avenue I could think of was trying to find our car. I could try to check all the downtown parking lots, which would be a long-shot endeavor, but I suddenly found the idea compelling. At least I'd be *doing* something, the kind of legwork that had to lead somewhere. At the moment it was pouring rain outside. But maybe when it slacked off . . .

In the meantime I called home yet again. Still no reply, and it was now well after nine. I did the math and worked out that it had been about forty-six hours since we'd last spoken, a record in seven years. This forced me to believe that something *was* wrong and simultaneously made me want to believe it wasn't—like seeing the doctor wince on reading your blood tests, even though you've spent the last six months wanting to know why you feel like shit.

As a distraction I went back to the phone to see if there was anything else I could find. The picture section had four files. Over the last year, Amy had developed a weird resistance to photographs. She dealt with them all day at work, of course, glistening product shots and endless casting pictures, but didn't like being in them or seem to have much enthusiasm for taking them of anyone else. The first picture was the one she had previously used as the general wallpaper on her phone. It showed the two of us, heads together, laughing. I'd taken it with my phone a year and a half ago, at the end of the Santa Monica Pier. It was a good picture, and I didn't like the fact that she'd evidently stopped using it. The next two were called Photo–76.jpg and Photo–113.jpg.

Both were dark and grainy, and on such a small screen I couldn't make anything out. The final picture was lighter, and while it still looked as if it had been taken in twilight, its subject was more evident. A man's head and shoulders, shot from a distance of about six feet away. His face was shadowed. He wasn't looking at the camera but turned away, as if unaware he was being photographed. This picture didn't seem to have a title as much as an attached message:

> **Confirmed. Apologies for quality. You'll be happy, though.**

The number it had come from was not the same as that on the text messages. I laid the phone back on the table and took a swallow of beer. Going back to drinking Mack & Jack's was beginning to seem like a good idea. I knew it wasn't. I also knew that wasn't likely to stop me. When the drinks waitress came into view, I looked up at her but then turned back as I heard my phone ring.

I didn't recognize the number. "Hello?" I said. "Is that you?"

It wasn't Amy. It was the cabdriver.

chapter TWELVE

He arrived twenty minutes later. Too-blue jeans, a new three-quarter-length leather jacket. Short hair, sturdy and anonymous bone structure. I'd started to see guys like this arriving in L.A. a year or two before we left. The work-horses of the new millennium, young men who would stack shelves, sell contraband on street corners, toil like dogs in regular modes of employment or smack heads in the dead of night, all with a steady, glacial determination that seemed to elude the local populace.

And, of course, drive cabs. I indicated who I was with an upward nod. He came over and sat on the opposite side of the table, glanced at my beer.

"You want one?"

"Please," he said.

"But you're working, right?"

He just looked at me. I held my hand up, got us both a drink. The waitress was fast and had them back by the time I'd lit another cigarette.

When Georj had taken a long swallow, he nodded. "Good," he said. "So?"

"Thanks for taking the phone to the hotel."

He shrugged. "Thank you for the money. I think probably it not be there. So?"

"I just wanted to see if you remembered anything else."

He glanced at his hands like someone used to not remembering things and not remembering them on demand. "I drive all day. All over. They get in, they get out."

I clicked a couple buttons on my cell phone, held it up to him across the table. "That's her," I said.

He leaned forward, peered at the picture on the screen. It was the one that Amy had been using as her background until recently.

"She's my wife," I said. "That's me there with her, right? I'm not a cop. I'm just trying to find her."

He took the phone from me, angled it against the dim light. "Okay," he said finally. "I remember."

My heart started beating faster, but I had many years' experience of this kind of inquiry. "She's pretty tall," I said. "Around five ten?"

He shook his head immediately. "Then not her. Woman I think of, more like five feet and a half feet."

"Good," I said. "That's her."

He looked at me, raised an eyebrow sardonically. "Not a cop, right. I not Russian either. I from Disney World."

"You got me. I was once a cop. I'm guessing you're someone who's used to talking to the police, too. So let's not jerk each other around. When did you see her?"

He considered. "Early in the night. Pick up downtown. Drop in Belltown somewhere, I think."

I shook my head, not knowing where he was talking about. He pointed right. "Up, past fish market. She tip too much, is how I remember."

Score two for recognizable characteristics. "You recall anything else?"

"Not so much." He took a cigarette from my pack, lit it. "It was rain. I watch the road. They talk. I—"

"Wait a minute. *They?*"

"Her, a man."

My stomach felt sour. "What did the man look like?"

"Suit, I think. Dark hair. I don't remember."

"Did they get in the car together?"

"Yes."

"And then what?"

"I don't know. Just talk, you know."

"What were they talking about?"

"How do I know? I have radio playing."

"Come on, Georj. Did they look serious? Were they laughing? What?"

I realized he was staring at me and that my volume level was getting out of control. Took a breath.

"Okay," I said quietly. "I'm sorry. You picked two people up. Drove them someplace, up in Belltown, wherever. She pays, you drive away. That's it?"

He swallowed the rest of his beer. He was ready to leave. In desperation I took Amy's phone from the table. Found the final picture. Passed it over to him.

"Could that have been the man?"

He looked at it for barely a second, shook his head, stood up. "I don't know. Bad picture. Maybe. Maybe not."

"Okay," I said. "Thank you. You got a job to go on to?"

He hesitated. "No."

"You do now."

I walked behind him into the drizzle. I didn't even know if the Malo would have any rooms, or if they'd rent one this late to someone like me. But I knew that being in a public place would not be good for me, and the Malo was the last known address I had for Amy, however spurious that had turned out to be.

The driver took a right off First, walking ahead. Why hadn't he parked directly outside the bar?

"Why didn't you park directly outside the bar?" I asked truculently. I had begun to slur my words, just a little, and the boundary between the inside and the outside of my head was starting to fade.

"In case police," he said patiently, not bothering to turn around. "They see from bar to car, not so good."

I followed him around a couple more corners and suddenly realized we weren't far from the end of Post Alley. This made me think of Todd Crane. Who had dark hair. Who was the kind of guy who wore suits. He'd seemed convincing in his ignorance of Amy's whereabouts.

But . . .

We turned into another side street, narrow and cobbled, lined with the backs of old warehouses, a red cab parked on one side. Georj was twenty or thirty feet ahead of me now, and as he stopped to get his keys out, I saw something.

A couple of figures were approaching from the deep shadows farther up the alley. They were too far away to see clearly at first, but both wore dark clothing and were headed purposefully toward the cab.

"Georj," I said.

He looked around at me, confused, saw I had started to run. He turned to look back the other way and froze.

The figures were running now, too. Both heading in my direction, evidently having realized I was going to be their first cause of trouble. The men's faces were pale and calm. One was tall, blond; the other shorter, with red hair. Out of long habit, I reached to my belt, but there was nothing there.

I met the first man with my right elbow held up high and rigid, ducking low to catch him at the base of the throat. He flipped over backward onto the wet sidewalk, crashing down hard. Georj and the other guy had a hold of each other already—and before I could get to him, the stranger had whipped his forehead down to butt Georj in the middle of his face. Georj fell back, sliding down the side of the cab.

I felt a hand grab me on the right shoulder and dropped low again as I turned hard left, the opposite to what most people would do. By the time I'd twisted quickly around, the guy was pulled off balance, and I planted my fist hard into his side. Our faces were close enough for his coughed exhale to spatter over my face.

I slammed my kneecap into the side of his thigh just above the knee, trapping the nerve, and felt him drop again as the other assailant stopped hitting Georj and grabbed me around the throat with both hands.

He was stronger and more focused than the other guy and slung me back against the hood of the car. I bounced off it awkwardly and slid to crash onto the cobbles—but he stepped in toward me too fast.

I kicked my leg in a wide, low arc, catching him around the back of the calf. He stumbled, dropping enough that I could meet his face with my shoulder as I came back up. He went over on his side, and I lowered my foot hard onto the fingers of his right hand.

The other guy was reaching into his coat now, and I turned toward him, wanting him to put himself in a position where it had to play out. I don't think I even remembered I didn't have a weapon of my own. I don't believe I was thinking at all. I had just become the man who was doing this thing, powered by anger, fueled by the need to hurt someone for the sudden and inexplicable hole in the center of my life.

"No," the guy I'd taken down said, but not to me.

The other man hesitated. Took his hand back out of his coat. Then the two of them ran quickly and quietly up the street.

Georj was crouched by the side of his cab, hands over his face. I squatted in front of him, panting hard, and pried his hands away. There was a lot of blood under his nose, down his chin, over his jacket. Before he could stop me, I felt on either side of his nose. He swore hard, tried to shove my hand away.

"You're okay," I said. "It's not broken."

I stood up. Looked back up the street. The two men had disappeared. "Who were they?"

"*What?*" The driver was standing now, sorting through his keys with trembling hands. He was looking at me like I was something that had just crawled in out of the bay, some animal with dripping teeth.

"You heard. Who were they?"

He shook his head, as if in disbelief.

"What the fuck is your problem?" I said, grabbing the door as he climbed into the car. "I just saved your ass. Who were those men?"

"How you think I know?"

"Oh, come on," I said. "They didn't get you this time, but they're going to come back. You play dumb and—"

"*I don't know!*" he shouted. "I am not criminal. Not here, not *there*. I have degree in biochemistry."

"But—"

"You right, wise guy. I do spend time talk to police. My sister was journalist in St. Petersburg. Was murdered three year ago. *That's* how I talk them." He stabbed a finger up at my face. "What about you, huh? What *you* do?"

He spit at my feet, slammed the door, and drove away.

I was left standing in the middle of the alley. It suddenly seemed very quiet, the city silent but for the distant honks and sirens of life going on elsewhere. I did not feel like myself, and my fists hurt.

I turned and looked back up the street.

chapter THIRTEEN

Alison was in the kitchen, leaning against the counter, supported on both hands. The light outside the window was gray-blue, an unwelcome dawn. She knew she had to turn, to look at her husband. She knew they had to say more things to each other, although she'd said everything she could think of, and she believed Simon knew that. Even though her head felt like it was about to split down the middle, she knew she had to turn around. How do you look anyone in the eye on a day like this?

It doesn't matter. You have to do it anyway.

She turned. Her husband was sitting at the table. He was exhausted and horror-struck but bright and alert and can-do. She recognized the look. It was how he appeared when he knew something had to be done but had no idea what it was. It was a signal of readiness. A way of saying, "I know I'm not doing anything, but look—I'm ready to." He glanced up, a question on his face.

"No," she said. "Nothing else." Her voice was hoarse. That would be the talking, and yesterday's screaming. The screaming when she'd gone out onto the beach, then back and all through the house, and out the front into the yard between the cottage and the highway, and over to the other side of the road, and then straight through the house again and out over the dune to the windy beach. When she'd gotten to the beach again, she realized they hadn't walked in the morning and hoped maybe her daughter had taken it upon herself to do the walk alone. Alison had run a long, long way up the sand, far past the point the family had ever been before. Then she'd returned, past the cottage and at least as far in the opposite direction. Nothing, nobody, no sign.

She came back into the house, tried to regain a little calm, to think positive. Waited what felt like an hour but had barely been fifteen minutes. Then went out onto the beach once more, up and down, trying to search properly, to stop herself from panicking again.

Finally she went to ask the neighbors if they'd noticed a little girl. On one side was an ancient couple who'd been there since the Jurassic period but whom the O'Donnells barely knew. Neither looked as if they'd be guaranteed to notice a tactical missile strike on their house. The other side was a small four-unit condo, empty for the winter. The caretakers had seen nothing and didn't hesitate to suggest that Alison should have been keeping a better eye herself. Alison knew that. Suddenly she knew that. The fog she'd been in for the last few days, for months, had instantly dissipated. She knew what she should have been paying attention to, and she knew she had not been, and she knew now what the cost could be.

She had gone into the house and waited in the kitchen, walking back and forth between the window that looked toward the beach and the one that looked over the front yard. Then she went out, jumped into the car, and drove the half mile to Cannon Beach. She looked in all the stores and cafés, in the toy store, asking if anyone had seen a little girl. She drove home and went onto the beach a final time, running and calling and screaming her daughter's name. Madison was a strong swimmer. Alison didn't believe she'd have just walked into the sea and been carried away. It was something she probably *could* believe if she put her mind to it, but she wasn't going to do that, not yet. By now the light had almost gone, and she knew that running and screaming were going to solve nothing.

So then the talking. The phone call to the police.

And then to Simon.

"You last saw her—"

"Simon, I told you this."

"I know. But I've had no sleep, and I got here at three o'clock in the morning, and I'm really not—"

"About midday," Alison said. It came out as a croak. "She'd been out on the beach. She came back in and said she was going to read awhile. She went into her room. I was sitting in the chair. I . . . I must have fallen asleep. When I woke up, I went to see if she wanted to go for a walk, but . . ."

Simon nodded. He put his hands together on the table and looked at the wall again. He knew that his wife had opinions on the way he sat sometimes, that she seemed to feel she could read things into it. Things that reflected badly on him, naturally. In actuality he was sitting in this way, and holding his hands together, to make sure he didn't get up and hit the woman he'd been married to for twelve years. This had never happened in the past. He'd never come even remotely close—not even after he started to think . . . Whatever, that wasn't the issue now. But if she was responsible for his baby being lost, then . . . Of course it would still never happen. It did not help. It was not his way. He was not that kind of man.

He grasped his hands together more tightly.

This was the first time they'd been alone together since he arrived. She'd called him after the police. He had absolutely no problem with that. He wished she'd called them before running helter-skelter all over the place yesterday afternoon, that she'd called them the *instant* she'd discovered that Madison was neither in her room nor visible on the beach, but nothing could be done about that now. He'd gotten into the car immediately, broken every speed limit on the journey along 26 from Portland, and arrived to find four cops from the local sheriff's department already present. They'd asked Alison a lot of questions. They asked Simon some, too, even though it was the middle of the night and he'd obviously just arrived. They wanted to know if "everything was all right at home"—as if Maddy could possibly have just run away by herself. Then most of them had gone to join the others who were out searching. There are words that you don't want to have any bearing on your life. "Searching" is one of them. Especially in conjunction with your only child.

Since then, as night finally crawled toward dawn, the cops had been in and out and back and forth. In the yard. On the beach. They came and asked more questions, usually a couple at a time. There was generally at least one around. But for the moment it was just the two of them. Simon and his ever-loving wife.

A wife who had turned away again now, to the window that looked out across the yard to the road. Maybe she thought that keeping watch was going to make everything better, that she'd suddenly glimpse Maddy strolling up the highway carrying groceries (Simon had already noticed that food and drink were notable by their absence). That this would instantly make everything okay. That she—

"Someone's coming," she said.

There were footsteps up the front stairs, then a knock at the door. Simon answered it. A man was standing outside. He was tall and wore a dark coat. His face was serious, the planes of it flat, the skin sallow.

"Yes?" Simon said. His heart was thudding badly.

"May I come in?"

"Who are you?"

"My name is Shepherd," the man said.

Alison had come to stand behind Simon. "Are you with the police?"

"No, ma'am. I'm Federal Agent Shepherd, from the Portland office."

He flashed his card, and they stepped aside. The man walked into the center of the kitchen, looked around. "Your daughter is missing," he said flatly.

Alison started to say yes but suddenly began crying. None of the cops had put it this bluntly. She kept trying to speak but couldn't get anything out beyond whispers. Simon took her hand, which only made her feel worse. Meanwhile the man waited. He made no attempt to make her feel better, or at ease. If anything, he gave the impression he found her tiresome.

"When was the last time you saw her?"

"Early afternoon yesterday," Simon said.

The man looked at him. "You were here?"

"No, but—"

"Then please let Mrs. O'Donnell answer."

This was enough to stop the tears. "My husband knows what I know," Alison said.

The man nodded. "Which is not a great deal. She just walked out of here? Disappeared?"

"I was asleep. . . ."

"You have no idea where she might have gone? No friends in the area, no relatives nearby, no particular place she liked to go to be alone?"

"We always spent all our time here together. As a family."

She glanced at Simon and was glad to see he looked taken aback, too. It wasn't just her imagination. The agent's tone seemed odd, angry for nonobvious reasons.

"She's right," Simon said. "We don't really know anyone else here. We just come and—"

"Has Madison ever met Nick Golson?"

Alison froze.

Simon frowned. The name meant nothing. "Who?"

"The man your wife nearly had an affair with."

Simon's face drained of color. He turned and walked out of the cottage. Alison heard his steps thudding down the stairs to the yard.

Finally, unbelievably, things had gotten even worse.

"I never . . . How do you know about that?" she managed to ask. "How long have you . . . why have you . . . ?"

The man kept looking at her until she stopped. "Has he? Ever met him?"

Alison shook her head vehemently.

"Does Golson know you have a daughter? Did he ever show any interest in her?"

"Of course not. I mean, he knew she exists, but . . . What does this have to do with anything?"

"Hopefully nothing, and I have no interest in your life except as it pertains to Madison's safety," the man said. He pulled out a business card. It was pure white and had nothing on it except the name Richard Shepherd. A phone number had been written on the back. "If she returns, call me from your cell phone. If you think of *anywhere* she might have gone, call me—on your cell phone. Do it immediately. Understand?"

He didn't wait for an answer. He just left.

Alison stood adrift in the middle of a room in which she had cooked, laughed, even made love, back in the day. It needed redecorating. Funny what it took to make you realize that. She watched as the tall man walked quickly down the path and got into an anonymous sedan parked on the road. He drove off fast.

Then she pulled her gaze back to look at her husband, sitting on the grass to one side of the yard, his head in his hands. And she wondered, idly, whether it might not be simpler just to kill herself.

Twenty minutes later two of the local cops came into the house. It was obvious before they spoke that they had found nothing. Alison told them about the FBI agent. The policemen seemed confused. The Bureau had been alerted, of course, but no one was expected until eight or nine at the earliest. They questioned her closely on the man who had come into her kitchen, finally establishing that he had shown no formal identification. The cops said this was very unusual. Alison showed them the card the man had left. They tried calling the number. There was no reply.

The cops started moving quickly then, getting a description of the car she'd seen, and of the man himself, and began jabbering to people on their radios.

Alison left them to it and walked down the stairs to talk to her husband. When she got out to the yard, she found he was no longer there. She hurried over to the road and saw a figure about a hundred yards along it, walking toward Cannon Beach. She started to walk more quickly.

And then she started to run.

chapter FOURTEEN

The first thing I saw was a big man looming over me. I was freezing, and my head felt like it was broken, but even so I could tell that there was something extremely wrong with this person. His proportions were badly odd. His features were too strong and skewed, and the texture of his skin was ragged and worn, even in this early, low light. He was also, I finally realized, really, really huge.

And made of wood.

I sat up quickly. My brain followed later. I found I was huddled against the back of a building, partly covered in leaves. There were a couple of boarded-up windows and doors with rusty locks, the disused backs of shops on the other side. In front lay a small park. There were bushes and trees, at least, though the ground was paved in granite cobblestones. The buildings on the other side were made of dark stone, a uniform three stories high. A couple of other guys reclined on benches, most under dismantled cardboard boxes. More professional about their situation than I was, in other words.

The thing I'd seen when I first opened my eyes was a totem pole, or something like it. Big and wooden and primitive, certainly. There were several more dotted around, including one that looked like a pair of misshapen monsters wrestling, or about to wring each other's necks. The site collided heavily with dreams I must have been having, full of darkness and violence, of shouts in rooms where the air was dead. With looking for my father in the house where I grew up and not being able to find him.

My watch said it was ten past six in the morning. I was surprised I still had it. I hurriedly checked and discovered I also retained my phone, Amy's phone, and my wallet. Either the local thieves weren't up to much or they just hadn't wanted to get close to me. My face and hands hurt, but the physical discomfort was nothing compared to how I felt emotionally and spiritually. I assumed I must still be in Seattle, but otherwise the map was blank. I'm not a heavy drinker, most of the time. I don't find myself in these kinds of situations, and I have neither the skills nor the experience to deal with them. I felt sick and afraid. I stood up, hoping this would help.

"Sir, are you okay?"

I turned sluggishly to see a guy with a bicycle was standing six feet away. "Is this Seattle?"

"Occidental Park, sir," the guy said, coming closer. He was wearing a white cycling helmet, and his jacket was white, too. Everything about him was clean and upstanding—and white. He was like me with the word "not" in front.

"Which is in Seattle, right?" I asked doggedly, and immediately regretted it. While obviously not an actual cop, it was clear the bike guy occupied some kind of semiofficial law-and-order capacity. Could you be arrested in this town just for being an asshole?

"Yes, sir. You're a couple of blocks from Pioneer Square, if that means anything."

It did. I was actually only about five minutes' walk from where I could last recall being. "Look, I'm fine. Had a couple drinks too many, that's all."

He nodded, politely avoiding loading the action with too much *No shit*.

"Are you hurt?" He was looking at my face.

"Slipped on a steep sidewalk, banged myself up some."

"You lost anything overnight?"

I went through my pockets again, for his benefit. "Everything's present and accounted for," I said, hoping the choice of words would signal I was a stranger to this kind of situation. In fact it just made me look worse, like a half-senile old woman talking incessantly to prove she's not half senile.

"Do you have somewhere to stay?"

"Got a car. Will be driving home. Today."

"Wouldn't be in any hurry," he said. "And some breakfast would be a good idea."

He got back on his bike and pedaled off.

I walked out of the park. A single block got me to First, a right and another couple hundred yards to Pioneer Square. This is a small triangle rather than an actual square, with First on one edge, Yesler on another, the third arm cobbled over along with the rest of the "square." None of the sides is as much as fifty yards long. It has a paved area with a seating area protected by Victorian-style ironwork, trees, a drinking fountain with an Indian's head on it, and a totem pole, this one a taller and a more explicable straight-up-and-down affair.

I stood outside the Starbucks across the way, which wasn't yet open, and looked at the trees. There were people out sweeping the streets. One raised an eyebrow as he passed and paused, as if offering me the opportunity to be gathered up into his pile of detritus and cleaned up out of public sight. It was quite amusing, but I could have done without it. I still felt physically desperate, but I was no longer in the location where I'd woken up, and so I could start pretending that it hadn't really happened. The closing stages of the previous evening were opaque, the parts after the fight, but now that I could see it across the square, I distantly remembered being in a bar there called Doc Maynard's, perched belligerently on a stool in a dark and crowded room, knowing I was far past the point of recovery and deciding I might as well follow the road and see where it led. Very wise. I wished I could go back and stand next to this other self and punch him in the mouth. *It ends with you waking in a park!* I would have shouted. *How fucking cool is that?*

I decided to take the advice of the man in white and get some breakfast, specifically the kind that is hot and wet and comes in cups. If I was going to do what I guessed I now had to do, then not smelling too obviously of alcohol would be better. I lit a cigarette to gird my soul for the long, cold hack up to Pike Place Market, the one place presumably doing business at this hour. My head hurt in three ways. I had localized but significant pains in my back, neck, and right hand. My mouth felt like a seabed that had been drained after years of environmental disaster had rendered it ecologically dead.

But none of these was the real problem.

The problem was that over the last six months I had come to be concerned that my wife's feelings toward me had changed, and that yesterday I'd started to wonder if she might be actually having an affair. And that if either was true, I didn't know what I was going to do.

About her or about myself.

I sat in a waiting room for forty minutes reading grim posters and moving my feet occasionally to let people walk past. Some of them were sad, some of them were angry, some were shouting, some looked like they'd never say anything again. I had consumed enough coffee and weapons-grade headache pills to feel both a little better and a lot worse. I'd brushed my teeth and changed into a new shirt I'd bought on the way. As far as anyone could tell, I hoped, I looked almost like a normal person.

Eventually a guy in shirtsleeves and a tie appeared out of a door in back and said my name. I followed him down a corridor and into a room that had no windows. He introduced himself as Detective Blanchard and indicated for me to sit down at the other side of a table.

He spent a few minutes looking through the information I'd given earlier, and I found my hands tightening on the metal arms of the chair. The room was small and had gray walls and was not designed to provide diversion. I was stuck with watching the detective as he tried to memorize the stuff in front of him—or perhaps translated it to Chinook in his head. He was comfortably overweight, with soft-looking skin and pale, wispy hair that looked as if it was rapidly deserting his head to leave him looking even more like a large, confident baby. I tried to ignore everything else and concentrate on breathing deeply and evenly. I could feel it not working.

"My wife," I repeated fifteen minutes later, "is missing. Which word are you finding problematic?"

"Define 'missing' for me."

"She is not in the hotel where she's supposed to be."

"So she checked out."

"She never checked in. They have no reservation for her. As it says in those notes."

"Was it a Hilton? We got a few of those. Maybe you went to the wrong one."

"No," I said. "It was the Malo, as you also know if you were actually reading what's there in front of you."

"The Malo. Nice. What does she do, your wife?"

"Advertising."

He nodded, as if Amy's occupation explained something significant about her or me. "Travel on business often?"

"Seven, eight times a year."

"Seasoned. So she changed her mind. Or someone screwed up the booking and she had to find an alternative."

"I've been through this. She's still missing."

"You ever call her while she was here this week, get her on the Hotel Malo number?"

"No, because—and I'll keep repeating this until it gets through to you—*she was never there.* I always call her cell when she's away. It's easier."

"Right—except now she doesn't have it."

"It's been thirty hours since it was reported lost. She would have called to let me know what was going on."

"But you're not at home, right?"

"I have a cell phone, too."

"She tap in the number every time?"

"She had it on speed dial," I admitted. He had a point, annoyingly. If asked to quote Amy's cell number from memory, I wasn't sure how far I'd get. But Amy was different. Her brain was optimized for that kind of information. Although . . . I *had* changed networks when we moved, and I hadn't had the new number very long.

"So she wants to call to let you know the score, but she never learned your number by heart and her phone's missing. You see what I'm saying?"

"She'd remember it. The number."

"You're sure?"

"I know my wife."

He sat back and looked at me, judging that he didn't need to comment on this, given the current situation. Also that it might be unwise to. "Do you know how to pick up your home messages remotely?"

"No," I said. "Never had a need to."

"You do now. Got a neighbor with a set of keys?"

I knew this was bullshit, but it was clear I wasn't getting anywhere without jumping through this guy's hoops. Ben Zimmerman wouldn't mind going around and checking the machine, though I would mind asking him. I nodded.

Blanchard drove it home. "Excellent. See if your wife has been trying to get in touch. Maybe she's wondering where *you* are. Filing her own missing-persons report out in . . ." He consulted the form again. "Birch Crossing. Wherever that is."

"And if there's no message?"

"Come back and we'll talk again. Mr. Whalen, I appreciate that it maybe seems like I'm being obstructive. My wife went off radar for a couple nights, I'd freak out, too. But right now I can't do anything you haven't already done.

Meanwhile there's stuff going on in this city that needs people paying attention to it. I am one of those people. You were, too, from what I gather."

I stared at him.

"Yes," he said with a faint smile. "Guy comes in with an alleged missing wife, we run his name. You get no red flags, I'm happy to say. No reports about late-night shouting matches. No freaked-out calls to emergency services. But I got a Jack Whalen with ten years in LAPD Patrol Division, West. Resigned a little under a year ago. That you?"

"Yes," I admitted. "So?"

He did nothing but sit looking at me, remaining silent for long enough to become insulting.

I cocked my head. "You got a hearing problem?"

"Just intrigued," he said. "You present more like the kind of guy I'd expect to see on the other side of the desk. Wearing handcuffs, maybe."

"I had a bad night's sleep," I said. "I'm very concerned about my wife's safety, and I'm having more trouble than I anticipated in getting someone to take a missing-persons report seriously."

"Right now we don't *have* a missing person," Blanchard said firmly. His voice wasn't as flabby as his face. "We have a missing *phone.* Except it isn't missing anymore, because you've got it in your *jacket,* right?"

"Right," I said. I stood up, banging the table accidentally. This is precisely why I hadn't gone to the cops the day before. I felt dumb for doing so now.

"I'm curious," Blanchard said, folding my information in half. "Care to tell me why you left the force?"

"No. But I'm curious, too. You actually do any police work, ever?"

He smiled down at the table. "I'm going to tell you what I think your bottom line is, sir. Your wife didn't stay in the hotel she said she was going to, and in the last day and a half she's declined the opportunity to get in touch with you. Either there's a straightforward explanation or she's missing on purpose. That's not the law's problem, Mr. Whalen." He looked up at me. "It's just yours."

I walked fast and randomly for ten minutes and finally got out Amy's phone and scrolled through her contacts. I'd noticed yesterday that she had the Zimmermans in her list. Just as well, because I didn't.

My heart sank when Bobbi answered. She got straight to asking if their vehicle was okay and when it would be back, implying that she needed it *right now* to ferry carloads of sick children and wounded nuns to the hospital.

"The car is fine," I said. "I'm still in Seattle, that's all."

"You *said* you would be back yesterday afternoon."

"Something came up, and I'm sorry, but . . . look, is Ben around?"

"No," she snapped. "That's the whole point, Jack. He's flying down to the Bay Area this morning to visit an old friend of ours. Who is *dying*."

"I'm sorry to hear that," I said again, relieved at being able to apologize for something that wasn't actually my fault.

"Benjamin had to take the other car. I'm stuck here in the house because we *thought* you'd be back last night. Which is . . . Why do you want to talk to him?"

"I've got a problem."

"That much is abundantly clear," she said. "But—"

"Bobbi," I said, "would you just listen for one second? Amy's missing."

There was silence at the other end of the line for a long moment. "Missing?"

"Yes." I hadn't wanted to get into this but I didn't know how else to get through to her. "She lost her phone two nights ago, and I'm hoping it's just that she doesn't know my cell number to tell me where she is. She *might* have remembered the number at the house, and so I wanted to ask Ben if he'd go see if there were any messages."

"Jack—is this supposed to be funny?"

"Does it *sound* like it's meant to be funny?" I shouted, finally losing my temper. "Jesus, Bobbi."

"You want me to walk around to your house, let myself in, and check your machine, to see if Amy's called?"

"Yes," I said. "But I understand now that you have no car, and if it's too much trouble, that's fine."

"It's no trouble at all," she said. "In fact, I can do better than that." There was muffled silence, and then someone else came on the line.

"Jack," the voice said, "where are you?"

For a moment I believed I'd started hearing voices.

"*Amy?* Is that you?"

"Of course it is," the voice said calmly. It was like hearing my mother on the phone. My mother is dead. "Why are you in Seattle, Jack?"

"Where . . . where the hell have you been?"

"I've been here," Amy's voice said. "Wondering where *you* are."

"Didn't you get my messages? On the answering machine?"

"You know I can't work that thing. Plus, why would I think you'd leave me a message there?"

I opened my mouth to reply but couldn't come up with anything at all to say.

"Look, honey, just come home, okay? And drive carefully." Then she put the phone down, leaving me standing in the street with my mouth hanging wide open.

It began to rain then, with sudden firmness, as if it had meant to start earlier but forgot.

chapter FIFTEEN

I dropped the Zimmermans' car outside their house, leaving the keys in the ignition. If Ben had been there, it would have been different. I wasn't going to deal with Bobbi right now.

Or so I'd thought. She'd evidently been standing behind her door, possibly for the last two hours, and was out of the house before I had time to get away. I took a deep breath. My head hurt badly, and I wasn't going to give anyone a fight. Unless she asked for it.

"Thank you," Bobbi said, disconcerting me.

I reached inside the car and got out the keys. "Sorry for the delay, Bobbi, I was just—"

"I know," she said. "I'm sorry I was harsh earlier."

I nodded, not really knowing what to say. "I'm sorry to hear about your friend, too. I hope he's okay."

She smiled vaguely, and I headed up their driveway, back along the road, and into our own domain. I started slowly, but by the time I got to our house I was striding fast. Our car was standing outside the house. It looked big and black and reproachless.

Nothing strange happening in my life, boss.

I let myself in, closing the door quietly behind me. Took

off my coat and walked to the top of the stairs to look down into the living area below.

Amy was sitting in the middle of the sofa. She was wearing a red sweater and black slacks, cradling a cup of coffee in her hands and absorbed in a report. Other pieces of corporate paperwork were spread around her and strewn over the coffee table and the floor. This tableau was essence of Amy—stock photography of Woman Working at Home. The scene looked so normal I felt like a ghost.

She glanced up when I was halfway down the stairs, and smiled. "Hey," she said. "You made good time."

"When did you get back?"

"This morning." She looked confused but cheerful. "When I said I would. Jack, what's going on?"

"I got a phone call late on Thursday," I said. "From a guy who'd found your phone in the back of his cab."

"Aha!" she said triumphantly, shifting paperwork off her lap. She bounced up and came to give me a hug. "I *wondered* if that's what happened to it. I hailed the taxi off the street and couldn't remember what company it was. There's fresh coffee, by the way."

"What?"

She nodded toward the kitchen. "You look like you could use some."

"I'm fine," I said, keeping my voice steady and calm. "Had a couple beers last night, that's all."

"A couple, right. And then a couple more couples? Nice dent you've got on your cheek there, teetotaler."

"Amy, where the hell were you?"

"You know where I was, honey—Seattle. What I don't get is where *you've* been. I mean, it's cool, there's no rule says you have to sit around like a hausfrau while I'm gone. But you seem kind of . . . Are you okay?"

I didn't know where to begin. "Weren't you due back yesterday?"

She gently led me by the hand up the stairs to the kitchen. "Exhibit A," she said, pointing to the calendar stuck to the side of the fridge. An entry in her handwriting showed her leaving for Seattle on Tuesday and getting back Saturday morning. Today.

"I called your hotel on Thursday," I said. "They had no record of you."

"Which hotel?" she said, handing me a cup of coffee. It was too hot, and I didn't want it.

"The Malo."

"Honey, I *told* you I wasn't staying there."

I looked at her. "I don't remember that."

"I said I didn't think it was so terrific an idea to use what's basically the KC&H company hotel, when I was in town on scout. I could have run into anyone in the lobby, which would *not* have been cool."

"What do you mean, 'scout'?"

She smiled with affection—and a little exasperation. "Sweetie, we went through this, remember? We talked it through over dinner here—what, a week ago?"

I made a face that suggested I might be on the brink of recall, though in fact I wasn't. "There you go." She grinned. "The renowned Whalen brain clicks back in. I knew it would—I'm your biggest fan."

"So why didn't you tell me what hotel you were in?"

"I thought I did. Anyway, what's the difference? We always talk on the cell."

"But you had a note saying 'Hotel Malo' on your computer screen."

"Yes, that's right, Columbo—it's a note to *me*. I left my book there on the last trip. It's no huge deal, but it was a present and a signed copy, and I meant to call them before I left. I'm pretty sure I mentioned that, too. It was from Natalie last year?"

I rubbed my temples. "Why didn't you call when you realized you'd lost your phone?"

She laughed. "I couldn't remember the damn number. Isn't that ridiculous? Though actually it's kind of not funny. I think I'm getting old. Am I getting old?"

"No. The curse of speed dial," I muttered as Blanchard's smug face swam into my head. Simple lack of number recall, he'd said. She'll be at home wondering where you are, he'd said.

"And the modern age in general, right. But listen." She reeled off what I assume was my cell number. "I made a point of memorizing it this morning when I got back. Please feel free to test me on it at random intervals."

I took a sip of coffee, trying to work out what my next ten questions should be, and in what order.

"Look, I'm sorry," she said, suddenly more serious. "Were you worried?"

"Yes," I said. "Of course. Guy says he's found your phone. I call the hotel I believe you're at, you're not there. I go to Seattle and there's no sign of you. I even tried to file a missing-persons report."

"What?"

"Exactly. Plus . . . I talked to Todd Crane. Trying to find where you were."

She winced. "Really? That's not so good."

"Don't worry, you're fine. I said you were visiting a friend and I was just covering all bases."

"You certainly were. Long way to go to pick up my phone, babe. I mean, it's sweet, but I had it canceled ten minutes after I realized it was gone. A replacement will be here Monday."

"Canceled?" I got the phone out and handed it to her. "I used this to call Bobbi this morning."

She frowned. "Well, that's weird. I'll get onto it."

"It's okay. No sign anyone else tried to use it before I got a hold of it."

"Sure. But if I cancel it, I want it canceled. You could have been anyone. It's not good enough."

More vintage Amy. I waited for her to show some sign of being uncomfortable with the fact that I'd had her phone in my possession, even used it. There was nothing. Instead she stepped a little closer.

"I love that you went looking," she said. She touched my arm. "And I know that going to the cops couldn't have been easy, and I'm really sorry I didn't call. I just figured you'd know I was okay."

"I didn't," I said. "I don't live in a world where I assume people will be okay. I haven't for a long time."

"I know," she said, quietly. "It was dumb. It won't happen again."

"It's okay," I said. "I just got . . ."

"I know." She kissed me, her arms warm around me. "Really. I promise."

I stood under the shower for a long time, staring at the expensive limestone of the stall wall. I'd had very little sleep and was still suffering from a bad hangover, and so maybe that's why I felt like I did. I realized that I hadn't actually eaten anything the whole time I'd been away, which probably didn't help.

When I was clean and dressed, I went to the kitchen and fixed some eggs. I ate them methodically, hunched over the counter and without registering them as food. My body felt stiff and awkward. I thought maybe I should go for a run, try to iron the kinks out, but the idea made me want to go throw up.

Amy was back in position on the sofa, sitting Indian style and surrounded once more by paper. She was absorbed and didn't even sense me enter until I was a couple of yards away. I noticed that the paperwork seemed more text-dense than usual, bereft of bullet points and draft sketches, looking more like the product of a typewriter than a word processor. Also that the sheets didn't sport the relentless logo-branding characteristic of KC&H documentation.

"What are you working on?"

She looked up. "Deep background," she said, reaching out to gather some of the debris toward her. "And, frankly, bordering on the dull."

"Going to let me know how it went, later?"

"Yes, sorry. Got a headful right now. Need to get it straight. And sorry it's such a mess in here."

"No problem. Going to try to do a little work."

"How's it going, scrivener man?"

"Very slowly."

"Slowly as in . . . 'backward'?"

I smiled. "Maybe a little to the side."

"Well, the journey of a thousand miles . . ."

"Starts with me staring out the window. Right."

"I have faith. You'll get where you're going," she said. "You always do."

I went into my study, half closing the door behind me. I spent a while opening my research boxes and getting stuff out, making enough noise that it should be obvious what I was doing. Every book, magazine, or clipping made me want to grunt with boredom, but nonetheless I arranged them in piles on the counter. As I get older, I find I have a desire to have things in rows. Books, magazines, DVDs. I want them neat. I want them consecutive. I am coming to suspect that having the row may be more important than any specific issue or volume. It's the order I seek, rather than the contents.

When this task was completed, I moved my chair to the far side of the desk, so the screen wasn't facing the door. If need be, I could tell Amy I'd moved around to remove the distraction of the view, which was now behind my back, but she never entered the room when I was working. I was just being . . . what? Cautious? Sneaky? Weird, most probably. I opened the laptop, and the screen revealed itself once more, the same document with the same "Chapter 3" heading at the top. There were no chapters two or one. There was nothing written underneath "Chapter 3." But then I wasn't here to write.

I hesitated a moment. When I heard the distant shuffling of papers, confirming that Amy was still on the other side of the room, I got my cell phone out and put the laptop into "Bluetooth Receive" mode. When it was ready, I navigated through my phone to the relevant sections.

Then I sent to my laptop the things I had copied off Amy's phone before I left Seattle.

I didn't expect to be able to divine anything more from the text messages now that I was home, and I hadn't bothered to take them off my phone. All I'd transferred were the pieces of music, the sound file, and the three photographs. I plugged earphones into the side of the laptop and loaded up the first sound file. Hearing it louder and without background noise just confirmed what I'd heard in the bar. It was a man laughing. I turned up the volume until the sound stopped meaning anything, in the hope of spotting some kind of texture behind it, an indication of where the recording had been made. I couldn't hear anything. It was just a man laughing, somewhere neither unusually silent nor noisy. It had an unpleasant quality, but that could be because I didn't like hearing another man's laughter on my wife's phone. She could have been messing with it in an idle moment and recorded a sound from another table in a restaurant.

The pictures didn't do much for me either. They were bigger on my laptop screen than on the phone but remained dark and hazy, and I doubted I could recognize the guy if I saw him on the street. At first the other two pictures didn't seem to be of anything at all. Darkness with some lighter patches. Gradually I made out that one seemed to have been shot across a convenience-store parking lot and showed a man entering the store. I couldn't make out the second environment—a dark bar, perhaps?—but again there seemed to be a figure in it.

I put the files in a folder and lost it a couple of levels deep on my hard disk. Transferring them off Amy's phone had felt like stealing, and I was pissed off that nothing more had come of it. I still had Blanchard's words running around in my head, and I felt foolish. There was only one thing preventing me from feeling completely and utterly dumb, and I couldn't check it right now.

I heard a sound and looked up to see Amy standing a couple of feet into the room.

"Hi," I said, startled.

"Sorry," she said. "Didn't want to disturb you. You looked deep in thought."

"Yeah," I said. "What's up?"

"Bored, bored, *bored*," she said. "Heading up to the village for a couple things. I don't know what yet. You need anything while I'm finding out?"

For a moment I wondered why she hadn't asked if I wanted to go with her. Then I remembered I was supposed to be working in here and that she was being considerate by not leading me into temptation. This, even more than the tableau I'd discovered her in on my return, was the essence of my wife. Subtle by nature, blunt when required, the kind of woman who would breeze into the bathroom while I was shaving and say, "Yo, shithead—you going to fix that shelf like you said, or do I have to take you back to Husbands-R-Us?" I brought this up with a yard-yelling couple one time, suggested they try a more direct approach to managing their nebulous resentments. I got a Christmas card at the precinct from them every year after that, signed "The Shitheads—still together." I count it as one of my bigger successes on the force.

"I'm okay," I said, smiling, heart beating a little harder, feeling love toward her and thus all the more guilty for what I had to do, which she was about to make easier for me. "I got everything I need right here."

"Cheap date," she said, and left. She clanked around in the kitchen for a while and then called good-bye.

I gave it three minutes, then left the study and went quickly up the stairs. I made it to the window by the side of the front door in time to see our car pulling out of the driveway. I stood for a few more minutes, until I was sure it wasn't going to come back. Then I walked down to the lower level of the house and into Amy's study.

An hour later I was a couple of miles from the house, running a hiking trail in the forest. I have never liked running. It's grim in prospect, arduous in actuality, and it makes no basic sense. The human body isn't designed to run for long periods. My mind isn't designed for it either. But, though I hate to concede the fact, it does seem to meet the body's need to sometimes be taken seriously. The first stretch made my head ache badly, and I had to pause to cough up a lung a couple of times, but now I was moving smoothly and consistently through the trees. I was running in penitent mode, trying to overlay what had happened the night before. *I am the kind of man who runs, you will observe, not the type who wakes up in parks.*

I was running also in the hope of achieving some kind of clarity. Amy's computer screen had been blank when I'd gotten into her study. I'd considered switching it on, but with an unpredictable boot/shutdown time I didn't like the idea of her suddenly reappearing and finding me in there doing that. She'd consider it an intrusion, and she'd be right. I picked up the personal organizer instead. Looked at what it told me for a while, then turned it off, put it back on charge, and got changed to go running.

It was getting colder. I could feel the temperature dropping as I ran, and moisture was clouding more and more thickly up out of my mouth. When I could see the sky through the canopy of trees, it had a leaden quality, and muted light was turning the pines and firs a bluer shade of green. I decided to turn and head back toward the house. The light would be gone before too long anyhow.

What I'd seen on the PDA had been straightforward. An event bar marked "Seattle"—which is what I remembered. It was one of the reasons I'd been so confident she'd been there. But the bar ended on Saturday morning.

That was *not* how I remembered it.

When Amy had led me up to the kitchen and pointed at the pencil-and-paper diary on the side of the fridge, it had looked plain wrong. I knew I'd understood her to be there only until Friday. That had been what was in my head, what I believed I'd been told, and I knew I'd felt—when I saw it on her desktop machine—a simple confirmation of what I'd already known. So how come it now said Saturday on the PDA, and presumably also on her computer? There were only two possible explanations: She *had* been due back yesterday, as I'd believed. Something weird had happened—I had no idea what—but she'd gotten back this morning and decided to bull through with it. Made a quick entry on the fridge diary—she'd certainly been very confident of its being there, and quick to take me to see it. In the meantime she'd already changed the entry in the diary on her main computer, then done a sync to get it reflected on the PDA—just in case her husband required three forms of documentary evidence. A concerted campaign of tampering in order to throw me off, in other words. A risky one, too, because if I was sure of what I'd seen, then her making that kind of change would put up a huge red flag. But I hadn't been. And maybe . . .

Maybe I'd just gotten it wrong.

Maybe Saturday had been her return day all along. I'd been freaked out when I checked her machine on Thursday night. I'd already somehow gotten it into my head that she was coming back Friday, and that's what I'd seen confirmed on the screen. If I tried now to conjure an image of the diary with a bar stopping at Friday, I couldn't do it. It went to Saturday. Was that just because it was what I'd seen most recently, or wasn't it far more likely it had always been that way?

That's not the law's problem. . . . It's just yours.

Without the conflicting diary entry, I had nothing, and

that most likely meant there never *had* been anything. As I pounded along the trail back toward where the national land crossed over into our own lot, I became even more convinced. The feeling spread into my body as a softening across the shoulders. I felt embarrassed, too. The stuff on the phone remained odd, but other people's ephemera always are, and though it's hard to remember sometimes, your partner remains other people at heart. Amy's lack of concern at my access to her phone didn't jibe with its being an electronic den of iniquity. A running joke with a colleague was more likely, or snippets from an upcoming guerrilla marketing campaign. For a while my head had been full of darkness of an almost tangible kind, as if I'd been able to feel a weight suspended above it.

I recognized the feeling, knew that it had been born from things that had happened to me, and to us, in the last couple of years. I had come to find myself perpetually half braced for chaos and intrusion. For the sound of a window breaking at the back of the house, the scream of tires as a car flipped up the sidewalk and flew toward my back. A phone call to announce that one or the other of us had cancer, though neither of us had taken tests or had any plans or need to.

None of these things had happened. Other things had, but neither had been predictable. I hadn't received forewarning of the plans of the God of Bad Things. That's not the way he works, and it didn't mean something would happen again. I didn't have to be on my guard, expecting the worst, fabricating possibilities if necessary. Everything was okay.

I found myself repeating this under my breath, using it to keep my rhythm, as I hit the last, long hill hard and pounded up between the trees toward the house.

Everything is o-kay. Everything is o-kay.

It's a good rhythm to run to.

Amy was back when I reached the house, soaking in the tub and listening satirically to some public-radio conspiracy nut ranting about dark and hidden forces behind the previous year's bombings in Thornton, Virginia, as if normal terrorists weren't bad enough. I washed and changed and then did what I always did, somewhat perversely, after a run. I took a beer from the fridge and headed out to the deck to have a cigarette.

The deck lights came on automatically as I stepped out, and I went through my standard process of wishing they didn't, then remembering that to stop it from happening you had to flip a switch inside, which never occurred to me unless I had just stepped outside, in which case I couldn't. Amy preferred the lights on, but as she felt the cold more than I did and so didn't come out here at night, it was my call. I bookmarked the thought as usual, swearing this time I'd remember when I got indoors, and went to lean against the rail. A wind was picking up, moving the tops of the trees and making the tip of my cigarette glow brightly.

When I was done, I stubbed it on the underside of the rail and returned the butt to the pack. On the way back, I noticed a few flecks of ash on the deck, left from the last time I'd smoked out here. It struck me how chance and geometry could dictate that none of the last couple days' breezes had quite managed to move them on, how there are always particles of yesterday left lying around in the now. As I watched, a gust finally caught the ash and vanished it across the deck and over the edge.

chapter SIXTEEN

He drove fast but accurately, and he kept under the speed limit. He was careful to appear, as always, like just another man on the road. Though he'd enjoyed many privileges throughout his life, Shepherd understood the costs that came attached. You paid, somewhere down the line. The highest price, the one that could never be recouped, was that of time. You never get a minute back. If he got pulled over by the cops, he would lose half an hour, maybe more. He couldn't afford that. So he kept driving steadily up Interstate 5, hoping matters could be resolved tonight. It had been a simple plan. He had not suspected that things could go so wrong so quickly.

It was now over twenty-four hours since the girl had disappeared.

He hadn't expected his first stop to yield anything, but he had lived by doing things methodically, and checking the O'Donnell house first made sense. Before leaving Cannon Beach, he'd been up and down the highway and out onto the sands without expecting anything to come of it. The local cops were making a decent job of the search. If the girl had been there, they would have found her. She was not. So she'd gone somewhere else.

He needed to work out where—and fast.

He was Agent Shepherd again when he parked outside the house in the northwest district of downtown Portland, just a couple blocks from upscale shopping on Twenty-second and Twenty-third avenues. He knocked on the door, waited, and then let himself in. He was inside for six minutes. She wasn't there.

He went back out and sat in the car. He considered his next step. It was getting dark. There was one obvious location to head for. It had been the most likely destination from the get-go, but it meant committing himself geographically. If he went up there and she was still wandering dazed in Oregon somewhere, it was only a matter of time before she talked to someone, let something slip—bringing untold new variables into play.

Shepherd did not like variables. For over thirty years, his existence had been largely free of uncertainty, and he liked it that way. It was one of the advantages of the life he lived—the freedom to disregard the strictures that bound the lives of others. With freedom comes responsibility, however, the awareness that you have built your own fate and have little recourse to spreading the blame. He remembered sitting in a hotel bar a couple hours north from here, being given a proposition, and knowing that it spelled trouble, meant taking a risk with everything he'd spent his life moving toward. One look at the person on the other side of the table had been enough to let him know he would do it anyway. As marginalized as this person had become, Shepherd understood he wasn't someone whose wishes you denied. Shepherd had done things other people wouldn't like to think about, yet he knew who was in charge in that meeting, whose boundaries were the most absent, and whose will would prevail.

And then, of course, there was the money.

A very great deal of it.

So he had listened, and he'd left the meeting knowing he

would do as he'd agreed to do. In the last few months, he had started to develop his own, alternative plan, but until then Shepherd had played his agreed-upon part over the years. He'd kept an eye out, studiously, even after the target moved to a different state. He'd been on hand, invisible in the background, making an adjustment here and there to the course of personal histories, simply by being close enough to deflect the fates. He had, ten days previously, issued a warning to a man that had resulted in the abrupt cessation of a friendship Alison O'Donnell had been enjoying for the past five months. This friendship had threatened to become a variable. Shepherd cleaved to constants, always: The family needed to remain stable. This cessation had caused, in large measure, Alison's sudden decampment to Cannon Beach. Naturally, she had not told her husband what had been behind this new low in her intermittent depression, just as Mr. Golson had not revealed to her why he was no longer able to find time for coffee after work, that a man had sat down next to him in a Starbucks and quietly told him to drop it or face a very high personal cost.

It was likely that nothing would ever have happened between the girl's mother and her friend, but that was not a risk Shepherd had been prepared to take. Taking risks was not what Shepherd did.

Except once, in that hotel bar.

It had seemed an acceptable risk at the time, a farsighted plan to better his own future. Recently his position had changed. And so, a long time ahead of schedule, he'd done what he'd done, and immediately it had started going wrong. He'd claimed his due. That part had worked just fine. But when he returned to implement the short and violent second half of his personalized version of the plan, the girl was gone.

The phone call came half an hour later. He ignored it initially—assuming that it was the woman who'd been on his case for weeks and with whom he didn't feel like dealing right now—but grabbed the phone hurriedly when he realized it was not.

The call was short and came from a pay phone. He recognized the girl's voice immediately and asked her precise questions. She sounded confused and frightened, and he got little but for two words—"Creek" and "Rest"—before the call cut off. A look at the map gave him a destination within credible range. It would have been a needle in a haystack had it not lain in the direction he'd suspected right from the very start.

Given the distance, it might become one again.

So he drove fast out of Portland and up past Kelso and Castle Rock, along miles of near-empty night highway lined on both sides with gray trees, a vacant landscape that wore civilization like a thin overcoat recently acquired. It started to rain, but Shepherd kept his speed constant through Chehalis, Centralia, past other dots along what was effectively a tunnel north to Seattle, up the west side of Washington State.

An hour and a half after leaving Portland, he saw the turn. He pulled off the highway and onto a curving exit ramp, turning off his headlamps. Rain was hammering down now, and between the squeaking slashes of the wiper blades he saw a low, flat building sparsely surrounded with trees, a large parking area behind. Dim light shone from two small windows in the building, making it look even more abandoned.

A sign on the side said SCATTER CREEK SAFETY REST AREA.

The lot was empty but for a single car. He swung his vehicle in an arc to come to rest twenty yards away and killed the engine. The other vehicle was a Ford Taurus of the type favored by rental companies. It was dark inside. He gave it two minutes and then got out into the rain.

He walked slowly, his gun held low down by his side. The car *looked* empty, but methodical meant making sure. He checked through the rear window and found the backseats vacant but for a jacket, then came carefully around the side and bent down to look. There was no one inside. He straightened, reached down to open the driver's-side door. The interior of the car was cold. Either the driver hadn't used the heater or it had been sitting here for some time. The keys were missing from the ignition.

Broken down, abandoned, the driver safely spirited away by roadside rescue? Possibly. But then it would have been locked, and it was likely that the jacket would be gone, too. Maps lay in the space between the seats, flimsy and thin, again characteristic of rental vehicles.

A half-empty pack of cigarettes was wedged in the door on the driver's side, along with a disposable lighter. Lying on the floor in front of the passenger seat was a discarded Pop Rocks container, next to a wrapper for Chicken McNuggets.

Shepherd closed the door. He had never been a smoker, ironically, but he knew that people who need nicotine enough to ignore the DON'T FUCKING SMOKE signs in a rental car are not likely to leave the scene without their cancer sticks.

Somebody was here, somewhere.

He turned and walked toward the building. At the left end was a tiled privacy wall covering the entrance to the men's restroom. A foot-square window provided one of the two points of sallow light. Stone pillars supported the rest of the structure, enclosing a covered space. Racks of leaflets on local attractions. A hatch from which complimentary coffee would be available during the day, now closed behind a metal shutter. A bank of three pay phones. A couple of battered drinking fountains. Everything dark, cold.

But when he looked closer, he saw that one of the phones was hanging down off its cord.

He walked back out and into the restroom. It was tiled in cream and tan. Two basins, two urinals, two stalls. Surprisingly clean. The walls to the latter stopped two feet from the floor. Nobody inside either. The sound of rain was heavy on the metal roof above.

He came back out and headed through the covered area to the women's restroom. Three stalls, same deal. Except that a pipe was leaking, and the floor throughout was slick and wet. And except for the fact you could see feet at the bottom of the last stall.

Blue jeans, white sneakers. Wearer apparently in a kneeling position.

"Ma'am?"

Something else lay on the floor. Small, shiny plastic, purple.

He pushed the door open. A woman was curled into the corner of the stall. She could almost have looked like she was crouched, hiding in a game of hide-and-seek.

Shepherd bent down to pick the purple plastic off the floor. It was the battery compartment from a cell phone. He pulled on his gloves and took the woman's shoulders carefully in his hands. Pulled the torso back. She had died from an oblique head trauma, most likely her head striking the toilet bowl. The remainder of the phone lay underneath this, the screen cracked. Shepherd let the body slump forward and picked up its right hand.

Faint yellow discoloration along the inside of the index finger.

Smoker.

Probable renter of car in parking lot.

Possible provider of a ride to a Pop Rocks/Chicken McNuggets consumer, who had caught her during an attempt to make a telephone call in the restroom, her passenger having said something just a little out of place while they were on the road, something that didn't fit right.

Said passenger arrives at the stall door, woman is startled and slips on the wet floor, falls, is unlucky in the way some people are.

Probably.

Shepherd swore quietly and left the stall. As he walked

quickly through the rain to the trunk of his car, he was already making lists in his head.

Dispose of phone fragments. Wipe stall for prints, ditto restroom floor and interior walls of restroom. Wipe all public-phone handsets, remove one she's likely to have used. Search/wipe interior surfaces of victim's car. Wipe area around exterior handle of door. Remove body from stall and stow in trunk of car. Relocate vehicle.

This was not good, Shepherd knew. As he unloaded cleaning materials from the back of the car, he calmly appraised just how bad it was. *Assume victim didn't get as far as a connection to the police, since the place isn't crawling with cops. But someone, somewhere, might have seen the woman agree to give someone a ride. Seen them together at a gas station, the McDonald's. Just enough to point the people looking for her in the right direction.*

Shepherd pulled out an extra couple of tools and a folded bag made of thick gray plastic.

Messy work ahead.

Afterward he searched the perimeter of the parking area, in vain. Somehow the girl had found a way of leaving this place. It was hard to believe that some other traveler would have just taken her into his or her vehicle, been convinced of whatever explanation she might have concocted for her whereabouts. But Shepherd knew she could probably be convincing. Somehow she'd left here, just as somehow she'd gotten the dead woman to drive her this far, and she'd found a place or places to spend the day and the previous night, after somehow getting to Portland.

When he drove away, he left a car burning, flames flaring silently within it. There would be a few minutes before it exploded. This was not the rental car but the vehicle he himself had arrived in. The rental would have been too easy to trace, even if left in ruins, and that would have led investigators straight to the dead woman's identity. Her name had been Karen Reid. Her driver's license, credit cards, and purse had already been located and destroyed. The other potential sources of identification lay in the plastic bag in the back of his new vehicle, alongside a suitcase of the kind he'd lived out of for all his adult life. Fingerprints had been removed from the woman's hands, using her own cigarette lighter. Her head had been emptied of its distinguishing features. Her body, minus these telltale parts, lay in the trunk of the burning car. Somewhere between here and where he was going, all the remaining components would be dispersed. It wasn't perfect, but the only perfection is death. You can be perfectly dead, maybe. With everything else you just have to make do with what you can get.

It was after midnight now, and the interstate was almost empty. Shepherd got up to the speed limit and turned on cruise control. He barely noticed he was driving a different car. He had driven very many vehicles in his life and had not been attached to the old one. He was not attached to anything. It was easier to be in charge that way, and for the moment, he felt closer to being back in charge. It was clear what city he needed to be in, at least. It was also becoming apparent that the time was approaching to get some other eyes on the job. He was going to need to talk to some of the others, and soon, and that required coming up with a plausible history for this chain of events, just in case one of them got to her before he did.

But for now all he had to do was drive.

Five miles up the road, he opened the window and threw out the first of Karen Reid's teeth.

Part II

Unconsciously we envy the integrity of the dead: they are through with the preliminary stage, their characters are clearly drawn.

—Andrei Sinyavsky
Unguarded Thoughts

chapter SEVENTEEN

On Sunday we had breakfast in Birch Crossing. Afterward we went for coffee, sitting outside so I could have a cigarette. Amy was nice about this, withstanding the cold and denying herself even a pro forma reminder that I was supposed to be giving up. I flicked vaguely through the paper, remaining unchallenged by anything exciting in local news. Amy watched the mother and young daughters at the next table, but after a while her eyes drifted away.

We'd been there a half hour when someone said, "Hi," and I looked up to see Ben Zimmerman on his way into the coffee shop. He had newspapers under his arm and was wearing battered combat khakis, as usual, along with the kind of sweater you wear to go fishing after your wife has banned its use within civilized company. It struck me, however, that I'd be pretty happy to look the way he did at his age, and being greeted in passing made me feel like we actually lived there.

I nodded. "How's your friend?"

Ben shrugged, with a half smile. I wasn't sure whether this meant the friend was as well as could be expected or had died as expected, so I just nodded again, and he went inside.

Amy and I dawdled around the stores for a spell, surrounded by New Age and Mozart. I stood outside watching through a window as Amy fingered a blouse in a color I'd have to call pink. I was surprised. Men of my age and type remain barely aware of pink's existence, seeing it at close quarters only if they have a baby girl. Wives won't tolerate it in interior decor, wouldn't be seen dead wearing it either. It becomes like purple in the Middle Ages—exotic and unknown, and thus intriguing in its suggestion of otherness, among the earth tones and teals and ubiquitous blacks.

When Amy emerged, she raised an eyebrow at me. "What are you grinning at, monkeyface?"

"Never saw you as a pretty-in-pink kind of girl," I said. "But it's, like, totally rad. You want to make out at the movies later on? Or go hang at the mall?"

She flushed, slapped me on the arm, and embarked upon a series of unrealistic suggestions as to where I could stick a mall, complete with parking lot. We walked in companionable silence back to the house, wreathed in the smell of firs and pine. It was about as unlike living in L.A. as I could imagine, and in the best ways.

Back home, Amy hit the couch with work and I went into my own study. I didn't open the laptop right away but sat at the table looking out the big window. I had an idea, and I wanted to make sure it wasn't dumb. And also that it did not merely indicate how hard I was finding it to forget the life I'd left behind.

Being a cop is a strange existence, far more prosaic than the entertainment industry likes to make out. Basically you're a hall monitor with a gun, dealing with the venal, dishonest, and borderline crazy—and that's before you leave the precinct, ba-da-boom. You're the social janitor, patching and mending, trying to keep the place neat and in working order, once in a while joining the endless bar fight of the people who've been done wrong versus the people who've done it—or who might *look* like they did, except they were visiting their sister in the hospital at the time, they don't even *have* a car and certainly not that type, and why are you hassling me, pig motherfucker, ain't you got no real criminals to beat up?

The first thing you learn is that we never needed Esperanto. We already had a universal language: untruth. Everybody lies, about everything, all the time. You quickly stop believing what anyone tells you, and you come to realize that the victims will give you worse headaches than the perps will. Either they're the same people as the criminals but just happen to be on the receiving end this time (and are by Christ going to make the most of it), or they're middle-class assholes who regard the police as a private security force and who assume that their difficulties can be obviated through confidence and a hundred bucks, proffered discreetly or otherwise.

So you play a role. When you put on your uniform, you become another person. Someone able to block out the fact that this might be the day when the innocuous-looking guy you pull over is pissed at his wife or friend or because he *still* hasn't won the lottery and may boil over and reach under his seat for a gun that on any other day would have remained a secret. You try to forget how many weapons surround us: paring knives in kitchen drawers, bottles in bars where fights materialize like junk mail on the doormat, a rusty razor blade hidden deep in the filthy layers around the bum pushing his cart of mysterious trash along the highway—a known local wack job not doing anyone any harm but whom you have to spend an hour moving along because somebody complained and anyway *it's the law*—and who surfaces out of fizzy meditations on microwave beams and terrorists who've been stealing his pubic hair for long enough to perceive you as a threat compelling enough to defend himself to the death against.

A human being is rarely more than a yard from something he or she can use to damage someone else, and people I know got hurt in all those situations, one stabbed in the throat with a bottle opener by a woman whose mouth was pouring blood but who believed that her life would make no sense if her common-law husband got arrested. The cop got full honors; the woman got a long spell in jail; the guy who'd punched out her teeth in front of her kids is now living in some other woman's house. Sitting in her chair, fingers drumming on its shabby, ash-dusted arms, unable to understand why her kids are going out of their way to enrage him and why the stupid bitch won't do anything about it or bring him another beer, and what is it about her face sometimes that makes him want to smash her nose completely flat? Sooner or later one of his scumbag neighbors will run off with his television or his car battery or his shoes, and you'll turn up and have to treat this guy with the respect he now commands as a victim.

That's police work. It's hot sidewalks at twilight. It's banging on flimsy doors. It's telling big-eyed children everything's okay when it's clearly not. It's drunken girlfriends who swear that their guy never fucking did nothing—until they realize that their own position is precarious, at which point they'll volunteer yes, Officer, he might be a Nazi war criminal. And it's married couples shouting at each other in their yards, hoarse and inexplicable grievances grown so old that even the protagonists don't recall how they started, and thus it comes down this afternoon to someone forgetting to bring coffee back from the store and so you stand around talking about this for forty minutes, and then you leave, with handshakes all around, and a month later you or someone else will be back to stop them from killing each other over whose turn it was to take out the garbage.

I was on the job for ten years. I turned up and did what I was paid to do, entering people's lives only when they'd begun to go wrong, after the God of Bad Things had decided to pay a call. In the end my own life started to veer off course, as policemen's lives do. The problem with being a cop is, you wander into the field of play of the God of Bad Things so often that you wind up permanently on his radar—as a meddler, a spoiler, someone who has tried to mitigate his attempts to stir disappointment and pain into the lives of humankind. The God of Bad Things is a shitty little god, but he has a great memory and a long attention span. Once you've caught his eye, you're there for good. He becomes your own personal imp, perching on your shoulder and shitting down your back.

Or so I believed, every now and then. I know it's a heap of crap. But still it came to feel that way.

Being a writer actually made sense after this, and not just because I had long ago been an English major in college. Patrol Division is an intensely verbal profession. You spend every day judging what to say and how to say it; learning to get what you want via sentences even the drunk, drugged, or clinically stupid can understand; then interpreting and sifting the replies of people for whom the truth is a third language at best. If it comes to violence, they may have more experience at it than you do, and certainly fewer boundaries. Sure, you can have backup on site within minutes, but it takes only seconds to end your life, and if you had to call in the helicopters last time, then your next walk down that street will be long and hard. Your ability to choose the right words, to judge tone and stance—that's what the job boils down to 90 percent of the time, not least of all through the truly endless paperwork, in which you learn to express yourself in a clear, concise fashion, with just a touch of fiction here and there.

Certain terms take on an iconic role in your life. "Sir" or "ma'am" is how you reassure victims they're being taken seriously—but you employ these words with the perpetrators, too. "Sir, would you step out of the car?" "Ma'am, your husband says you have a knife." "Sir, I'm going to ask you *one more time* to put down the gun and get on the fucking floor." It signals theoretical deference, a withdrawable politeness, recalling the way mothers refer to their children by first and last name only when they're trying not to say "you little fuckhead." "Perpetrator" is a key term, one through which you reduce the infinity of difference all individuals represent to their being merely the punishable committers of an (alleged) crime, thus setting them in clear opposition to the victim/s, to yourself, to the universe at large. It's a big, weighty concept, often concentrated to "perp," and from it everything else follows.

A "weapon" is an object someone can carry that makes it likely he or she is or may become a perp. An "MO" is the characteristic way in which a perp perpetrates. A "victim" is a role created by the act/s of perpetrator/s. An "intruder" is a specialized form of perpetration, enshrining within its eight letters everything that needs to be said about the inviolability of private space (as defined through property law) and the wrongness of someone who puts himself inside the walls we erect against the chaos of other people. Even a murderer is just another kind of perpetrator, nothing more.

Not every cop is concerned with these matters, of course. But some are, just as there are neurosurgeons who scream at the ball game and priests who while away confession planning the evening pizza: *Okay, my son, so you harbor lustful thoughts about your neighbor—but the real question is, anchovies, or not?* Your job is to find the utterances that provide a structure for each situation, to show a path out of the present moment that does not involve jail or death. Armed with your words, you cleave the night with your judging hand and set the world to rights. In those written reports, at least. The judicial system has a way of blowing the fog right back in. Lawyers have different words and use them to different ends. Their structures are clean and theoretical and do not have to stand the test of working in stairwells, parking lots, and bars.

And when you leave this circus?

Leaving the police force is like getting out of jail, though not in a good way. It's like being fluent in the language, culture, and geography of a country—which overnight slides off the planet, taking all its inhabitants with it. Suddenly all this insight and autistic absorption means squat. You need instead to understand what's been happening in the *real* world, how to deal with people now that you're not wearing a badge, and what all these weird normal folks have been talking and caring about while you and your fellow inmates were blinker-focused on the bad, bad, bad.

As a readjustment it's pretty major. Probably only being dead is going to seem like more of a jolt.

The places I had photographed in L.A. were crime scenes, of a specific type. My book was called *The Intruders.* The cover showed the house where a woman named Leah Wilson had been found dead: just a standard murder by person or persons unknown, but one that really got under my skin. The pictures inside were also locations where a person or persons had unlawfully gained access to someone else's place of residence or work. Once there, they had committed a crime, from burglary to rape and murder. Houses, garages, the kitchen of a fast-food restaurant, hotel rooms both cheap and expensive, a coffee shop in Venice Beach. None of the photographs showed victims, nor did I try to capture the aftermath of the disturbance. In the text accompanying the pictures, I merely described what took place—as best I could, as a nonwitness—along with a flavor of the neighborhood. In the photos I was trying to take the places back to where they'd been in the world before something came from without and changed their texture forever. I have some idea why I was doing it. I had spent all my working life dealing with after-the-fact. In effect the photographs themselves were untruths, as they always are.

The idea I now had was simple. It'd occurred to me before but I'd dismissed it, because I'd seen *The Intruders* as a one-shot. Maybe Fisher's visit had given me a push, though I still believed that the cops were correct in assuming Bill

Anderson to be the best suspect in the murder of his wife and child, and so that crime did not revolve around an intruder.

I realized I could do the same thing again, for somewhere other than L.A. Seattle, say.

I wouldn't have access to information about crimes or long-term knowledge of the neighborhoods, but I could work around the former, and some research and talking to locals could cure the latter. A phone conversation with the crime desks of the major newspapers would be enough to put me on their radar. I could even try talking to Blanchard again, if I could face it. Missing-persons cases do sometimes start with an intruder, after all. The more I sat and stared out the window, the more the idea made sense. I guess I'd always seen myself as a one-shot kind of guy. But how had Gary put it? Something about nailing your colors to the mast. Enough time had passed.

Maybe I had to accept that an ex-cop was what I was.

When I surfaced from these thoughts, I realized I could hear music from the living room. Amy had something playing, which meant she couldn't be working too hard—and wouldn't mind my testing the idea out on her.

I was halfway to the door when I slowed, as the music registered as more than generic sound. I listened for a moment, assuming that what I was hearing would change. It did not, however, and so I walked into the living room. Amy was sitting on the couch. She had a sheaf of documents on her lap but wasn't looking at them. Instead she was staring into the distance, slightly hunched, as if she'd been in the same position for a while.

"Hey," I said. I felt tense. There had been a time, a year and half ago, when I'd seen her this way occasionally.

She blinked and turned to look at me. "Miles away."

"What are you listening to? Not your usual kind of thing."

"We all grow, babe," she said. "You want some tea?"

"You mean coffee?"

She frowned vaguely. "No. I'd like some tea."

I shrugged, not even having realized we possessed such a thing, and walked over to the glass doors as she went to the kitchen. While I waited for her to come back, I looked out at fir trees and dogwood and a sky that had lost the morning's blue clarity and was turning to cool gray. Many types of music go with such a view.

Old-time jazz is not one of them.

An hour later I was running through the trees and finding it hard going. I didn't usually go out two days straight, and my body didn't get what I was trying to prove. I wasn't sure I did either. I'd just felt like I wanted to be out of the house for a while.

I tried to return to what I'd been thinking about in the study, but my mind wasn't interested anymore. It wanted to worry on the idea of the music Amy had been playing instead. So I tried to empty my head, concentrated on the slap of my shoes on the ground, on the smell of the trees, the cold air as it sucked and pushed in and out of my lungs.

As I pulled back around toward the big pond at the bottom of our land, I realized I could hear my cell phone ringing. I slowed, trying to fumble it out of my sweatpants pocket, then stopped. I didn't recognize the number on the screen. I walked toward the pond as I put the phone to my ear, looking up at the house, wondering if it was Amy calling.

"Jack," said a voice. It was male.

Hearing his voice was no less surprising the second time. "Gary, hi. You caught me out running."

"Sorry," he said. "Look, we need to talk."

"I haven't changed my mind," I said. I was only half listening. Now that I could see the house, about a hundred and fifty yards up the hill, it looked as though someone was standing out on the deck.

"I'm not really calling about that," he said, and hesitated. "You were in Seattle a couple days ago."

"How do you know that?" I said. "And, in fact, how do you even know my cell-phone number?"

"I'd like you to come back here. As soon as you can."

"Gary, I'm kind of concerned by the idea that you might have been following me. Maybe you'd better come here, explain what's on your mind. Because—"

"I can't come to your house," he said quickly.

"This is starting to sound strange," I said, keeping my voice steady. I could see now that it was Amy standing out on the deck. Of course—who else? "Round about now you're going to need to give me a good reason not to end this call and block your number. And call the cops."

There was silence on the line. Amy was looking out over the forest, unaware that I could see her. Since she wasn't wearing a coat, she wouldn't be out there for long. She really doesn't like the cold, and it was sharp enough now to be sending a thick little cloud of condensation up around her face.

"It's about Amy," Gary said. "I'm sorry, Jack, but there's stuff you need to know."

chapter EIGHTEEN

You kept moving. You kept moving. You kept moving. That was what you did. If you were moving, then you were going somewhere. If you had somewhere to go, then you were a proper person and nobody bothered you—and so you kept moving even when your feet hurt and you could no longer tell the difference between where you were and where you'd been. If you stopped for a moment, they looked at you. They asked if you were lost. They asked if you were hungry or thirsty and where your mommy was. They didn't seem to realize that these questions hurt.

Madison was very glad she had her coat, and not just because Seattle's streets were cold. She was glad because it had been expensive, and other people seemed to know that. This meant that some did not bother her, people who she sensed would have been only too happy to bother her otherwise. It helped, too, that she was tall, like Mom.

She was also glad it was now day. The night had been very long. After she arrived in the city, dropped off near downtown by a man in a pickup who'd stopped to use the restroom at Scatter Creek and been glad to give a girl a lift when presented with one thousand dollars in cash, she had realized she still had no clue where to go. So she was in Seattle now—so what? The sense of purpose that had driven her since she left Cannon Beach was flagging. While it had been present, everything had seemed easier. It was like doing what a bigger girl said because you wanted to be her friend. It was like when you were in the kitchen and you'd had a couple of cookies and weren't supposed to have any more—but then suddenly you looked down to see that there was another one in your hand, half eaten. Whoops. As if there were another arm inside your arm, lifting it, doing things, but when Mom came in and found you there, caught cookie-handed, suddenly it was just you, alone.

Maddy had seen Daddy at dinner, too, saying this was the last glass of wine but then seemingly unaware of his hand lifting the bottle to pour just a little more. Mom had it, too, in stores, and maybe in other ways. At times over the last months, Maddy had seen her mother sad and quiet, as if she'd decided something. But that evening or the next day, she would be happy again—and how could that be, unless she had decided against an earlier decision? How could you mean something and then not mean it? And one time Madison had come into the house to find her on the phone, and maybe it was just her imagination, but she thought her mom looked like *she'd* been caught cookie-handed, too. Madison wondered if maybe everybody's life was like this. She hoped it wasn't just her. And she hoped it wasn't going to keep getting worse.

At least she wasn't hungry or thirsty now. The man in the pickup let her have some of his coffee and gave her half his sandwich when he dropped her off. She had known while offering him the money that many people would decide to bash her over the head and see what else she had, but this man hadn't been one of those. She'd known this before getting the money out. His eyes were pink, and he smiled a lot, and she knew he was a man who just wanted an easy life. Mom had often told her she was good at judging people. Her dad usually added "and getting them to do what you want," but he'd be smiling, and he meant it as a good thing.

She spent several hours walking the city streets, going

some other way when she heard footsteps or shouting. She tried calling home from a pay phone, using coins she knew she'd taken from her mother's purse before leaving Cannon Beach, which she now felt very bad about. She was not someone who stole. But the phone had rung and rung at the house in Portland, then gone to the answering machine. It was the middle of the night, okay, but there was a phone right there on their bedside table. Why wasn't Daddy at home? She tried calling Mommy's cell, too, but for some reason kept getting the number wrong. She knew it, she *knew* that she did—she'd gone to a lot of trouble to learn it by heart a couple of months before—but now it seemed to have dropped out of her head. She tried a few numbers that sounded right and woke up a few angry people, but none of them was her mom.

So she kept walking. She felt sometimes like she was looking for something, and at one point she found herself walking up a long and really steep hill and into an area where there were nice, big houses. She stood opposite one of these for a while, in the darkness, but it just made her feel angry and sad. When it got really cold, she found an alleyway back toward downtown that had a deep doorway some distance along it, and she sat huddled up in her coat. The doorway smelled of old pee. She meant to stay awake, but she couldn't. She was exhausted with all the walking. With pretending that she wasn't really, really scared.

She fell asleep, but it was not a good sleep. Things kept coming into her head and going around and around. Some made her happy, like a dream full of glimpses of little girls, pretty and smiling, and another of her sitting in a chair in a nice house with a view over the bay. Some were sad or frightening, like one where she was running along a concrete path down near the water itself, out of breath. She liked dreams, normally. They could be funny and interesting. These were not. They were like she was channel-surfing and found some new batch of channels that hadn't been there before. Some did seem a little familiar, from years back, from when she'd wake in the night to find that Mom or

Dad had run in to see why she was making that noise. Other were dark and noisy and grown-up . . . not nice. She never quite saw anything that she shouldn't see, but she believed that if she watched for long enough, she . . . would.

For most of the time Madison spent in the doorway, she wasn't even really sure if she was asleep or awake. But after a while it seemed to her that she was, and that it had started to become light, and she left the alleyway and started walking once more.

As soon as the stores opened, it got easier. She followed where all the people were going and found herself in an open area in downtown. Across the street was a Barnes & Noble. She went inside and knew she'd be okay for a while. You could spend as much time as you liked in a bookstore, as long as you had a nice coat. She looked at books and then at the magazines. When someone with a name badge came over to ask if she was okay, she said yes and then waved over the man's shoulder as if to someone on the other side of the store. The man smiled and left her alone after that. He was nice and reminded her of Uncle Brian.

There were some other girls about her age in the section, but they looked kind of weird to her now, after her dream. She felt that she was looking at them for a little too long. So she went up to the Starbucks and bought a water and a coffee and two things to eat. She did this without planning it, but when she got to the cash register, she realized that it had been clever. What a grown-up girl Maddy was, being allowed to go to the counter on her own, watched over by a mother sitting . . . just over there! She drank the coffee and ate the carrot cake and put the water and the granola bar in her pockets, which were now getting a bit overstuffed. Good to be prepared, though.

She had provisions. She was doing okay.

* * *

She went back up to the children's section and found a seat, then got out the battered notebook and leafed through it, hiding it inside a Richard Scarry.

The more Madison read from the notebook, the more different she felt. She couldn't understand why. The notebook was not laid out like a story. It wasn't as if it started out at the beginning and went from there, and you could follow what was going on, and then it ended—which was the case with all the books she'd encountered so far. Except for the really baby books, which had always driven her father nuts: Molly the Mouse gets out of bed, Molly stands on a hill near some flowers, Molly goes and looks at the sea with her friend Neville the Narwhal . . . The End. Her dad used to rant and rave about these books, saying there was no actual story and where the hell had Neville suddenly come from anyway? The notebook was like that. Just a bunch of stuff, with no shape, no beginning, no end. The big difference was that the baby books went all out to make things as clear and simple as possible. The hill would be big, the flower would be obvious and super-bright, Neville the from-nowhere Narwhal would fill most of one page. The whole point of them was to teach you how to read, to find out which words meant what.

The notebook wasn't like that. A lot of the time, it seemed that whoever had written it had put things in a way that you weren't *supposed* to understand, unless you knew what it was talking about in the first place:

I have always lived here.

For a long time trees were the only story.

But then the invaders came: breaking down the door as if it never occurred to them other people already lived here and called it home. I will be brief, the detail left as an exercise for the not-so-gentle reader.

In 1792, Vancouver and crew first enter Puget Sound. In 1851, claims are laid by the members of the Denny party. The local Duwamish and

Suquamish Indians provided food for the settlers at Alki Point during the hard winter of 1851/2. You might have thought they would have learned their lesson by then, but I guess they just weren't very smart. Chief Seattle at least had the wisdom of many lives, and encouraged "Doc" Maynard to join the settlement in 1852, knowing his friend was conversant with local lore, and might help preserve the integrity of this special place. Maynard staked the mudflats which are now Pioneer Sq and the International District, a curious choice, one might think. Denny/Bell/Boren took the ridges around Elliott Bay (now Downtown, Denny Triangle, Belltown), and in October 1852 one Henry Yesler arrived with a sawmill, looking for a site. After this the town started to grow. King County was created Dec 22, 1852, and in 1853 came a visit by the Territory's first governor, Colonel Isaac Stevens—his mission to remove the tribes from their lands. In 1854, Seattle gave the speech which comes as close to telling the truth as anyone ever has out loud. Paleface did not get the message, naturally. Paleface never fucking does.

In 1889 the town was razed, the blaze allegedly starting from a glue fire in a cabinetmaker's workshop. Though is it not more likely it was a last attempt to prevent a permanent settlement from covering the site? It was too late. Nobody thought to question why the Lushootseed name for this village had been Djijila'letc, "the crossing-over place"—because surely that referred only to the path across the inlet that could once be found there at low tide. It is still there, that place, the land around it charged now with the blood of the departed hosts.

I like to think I have done my part.

It was all like that, a list of things and facts. It looked as if it had been written in a hurry, too, and some words seemed to have lots more of some letters—*i*, and *j*, for example—than they should, and she didn't really understand about apostrophes, but she knew you didn't have them in the middle of long words.

She kept reading nonetheless, letting her eyes run over the red-brown ink, finding it obscurely comforting. There were pages with names, too, and addresses, but none of them meant anything to her either.

In the end she found herself on her feet again and back outside in the square. She noticed that there was a small mall on the other side of it, but she knew that it would feel strange going in there without her mom, and as soon as she realized this, she felt more like herself than she had in two days, and she started to cry.

It was as if something had been held down inside her and then set free, and suddenly her eyes were running with tears, her face cramped with a cry she could not get out, her chest hitching up and up as if it would never go down again, as if it would keep going until it burst.

Everything came at her at once. The realization that she was miles from home and her mom and dad and had no idea where she was. She could suddenly remember more about the last couple of days, but as if from a different perspective: Things that had seemed okay now seemed wrong and frightening. Sneaking past her sleeping mother and stealing her change, being on the bus to Portland and feeling excited but bad and confused, being in the car of the nice lady who had agreed to take her to Seattle because of a long story Madison had told her but then had started to look at her funny and gone off to the restrooms holding her cell phone and . . .

No, she couldn't remember that part. But everything else she could, momentarily. Including . . .

Her mom's cell-phone number.

Bang—suddenly there it was, right in the middle of her head, as if a cloud had moved out of the way.

Madison stopped crying, glanced around quickly, trying to spot a pay phone. She started running fast along the sidewalk, spinning around, looking for somewhere she could make a call. Finally she spotted one across the street and darted straight off the curb. Horns blared, and a yellow cab had to swing out to avoid plowing into her, but she kept running. At the other corner of the square was a bank of phones, and she knew she had to get there before she forgot the number again, before the cloud came back. The bottle of water fell out of her pocket, but she kept going, running directly toward the phone at the end, hands already reached out for it, going through the number again and again in her head. . . .

But by the time she'd punched two of the numbers, the rest of it had gone.

She shouted in frustration, smacking the phone viciously against the wall. Where had the number gone? *Why* had it gone?

"Hey," a passing man said. He was big around the stomach. "Careful, there. Or—"

Madison swung around to look at him, and he stopped talking, very abruptly.

"Get lost, fat boy," she snarled, and he stared at her, eyes wide, before hurrying on.

Madison was aghast. She'd never been that rude to an adult before—or to anyone, in fact. Ever. Not even in her head. That was worse than with the man at the airport. What was *wrong* with her?

She was motionless for a moment.

Then she blinked and put the phone carefully back on its cradle. She suddenly felt very clear in the head. She no longer wanted to call her mother. There was another number she *could* use, she remembered—one written on the white business card tucked in the front of the notebook. But she'd called him once before, and he'd been extremely bossy. For reasons she didn't understand, she also had a sense he was untrustworthy.

She turned from the phone and looked out across the square. It seemed odd to her that she'd been crying moments ago. Now everything seemed fine. She was away from home, away from Mom, from Dad, from everything that said she was a little girl and could be told what to do. For some months now, she'd been prey to a sense that it didn't have to be this way. That she had power. That people could be made to do what *she* wanted for a change. Sure, she'd get in touch with Alison and Simon. She wanted to ask them some things. But it didn't have to be right this minute. She was hungry again, and she knew what she wanted, and it was not a granola bar. She wanted a man-size breakfast, eggs easy up, home fries and hot sauce. She knew the place to get it, too.

She set off down the street toward the market. Her stride was long and her head held high, and now if people noticed her, they didn't wonder what such a young person was doing out by herself or where her parents were—but instead what was it about this little girl that made her look so self-possessed, so grown-up, so whole.

chapter NINETEEN

I was in Seattle over an hour before we were due to meet. I used some of the time in a book and record store on Fourth. I went into the jazz section, found the clerk who looked least like he'd rather be snowboarding, and got my cell phone out. I played him one of the MP3 files I'd transferred from Amy's phone. The clerk stooped with his ear cocked, listened for barely two seconds, and then vigorously nodded his head.

"Beiderbecke," he said. "'A Good Man Is Hard to Find.' A classic. And so true."

He led me into the section, ran his hands down the CDs as if down the spine of a man he loved, and plucked one out. The cover showed a black-and-white-era guy holding some kind of neo-trumpet device. I allowed the clerk to sell it to me.

"Such a shame," he said as we waited for my card to be authorized. "Bix, I mean. A prodigy. Could barely read music but played like an angel. Dead at twenty-eight. Drank himself to death." And then he sighed, as if it had been a personal loss.

I walked up Pike Street to the market and got a place at one of the tables outside the Seattle's Best across the street. I was still early. Fisher had refused to tell me anything more on the phone, probably judging—correctly—that he wouldn't get to see me in person if he told me what he knew. My head felt empty and bright. The atmosphere the previous evening had been stilted. I could not help feeling that Amy was being more normal than usual. She's one of those people who can grab random handfuls of ingredients, throw them up in the air, and have them land in bowls looking good and tasting great. Last night the food had been barely edible, and I don't think that was just a result of the churning in my stomach. Afterward she worked in her study for a while and emerged later seeming distracted. When I had a cigarette out on the deck toward the end of the evening, I watched through the window as she sat flicking through coffee-table books, as if looking for something she couldn't find. I'd seen her like this a few times over the last couple of years, but when I asked her if she was okay, she always said yes.

When I'd left her that morning, saying I was heading to the city to try to make some crime contacts, she looked up sharply, hesitated, and then shrugged.

"I just don't think it's so great an idea," she said, and went back to work. But after I'd been on the road barely twenty minutes, I got a text from her:

Good luck :-D

I didn't really know what to think, and I sat there in the cold early-morning sunshine not-thinking it. I heard a story once, about the early settlers of the region. It told that when Europeans finally landed on the northwestern shores of America, feeling like conquering heroes in a new world, they were disconcerted to find that the locals were not surprised to see them. This was not because unknown white men had forged a route overland from the East, however, but because over the last several generations the tribes had very occasionally seen trading ships far out to sea—once every ten, twenty, fifty years. They knew these could not be the work of local people and therefore surmised that some other group of men or beings were on their way, however slowly.

When I first heard this story, I shivered. I don't even

know whether it's true, but it has stayed with me: the idea of these hazy visitations, of inexplicable form, seen from afar, never coming closer—but, once seen, impossible to unsee. A first indication that the world held more than had been bargained for, a foreshadowing of events that would be impossible to change, impossible to hurry, impossible to stop. Portents of unknown type and provenance, far out in the mist of the seas, a future held in abeyance, for now, but irrevocably on its way.

The local people watched and saw, then turned their backs on the sea and got on with their lives.

I didn't think I was going to be able to do that.

When Fisher arrived, I was struck first by how tired he looked. He sat down in the chair on the other side of my table, took a deep swallow of the coffee he'd brought.

"Thanks for coming," he said.

I just stared at him.

"Okay." He reached into his coat pocket, hesitated. "I'm going to show you something. Then I'm going to tell you something before I explain what you're seeing. It's going to take a few minutes, and you're not going to want to listen, but you have to, or you're not going to understand my interest here. Okay?"

I nodded. He pulled out an envelope and handed it to me. I opened it and withdrew the contents. Two photographs, six-by-four. Both had the muddy, blown-out quality of digital pictures taken beyond the limits of the lens range.

The first showed a woman standing outside an unremarkable-looking doorway, in a street that could have been pretty much anywhere. The door was open. The woman's face was in profile. It was Amy.

When you looked a little closer, you could see there was someone else in the picture, a shadowed shape in the doorway. The quality of the light suggested that the photo was taken in the late afternoon.

"Big deal," I said. Fisher said nothing.

The second photograph was of another street, or the same street from a different angle. It showed a man and woman walking together, shot from behind. They were fairly close together, and the man had his arm around the woman's shoulders. From the angle at which the picture had been taken, it was impossible to tell whether this man was the one I'd seen in the photo on Amy's phone. He was a little over average in height, wearing a suit, could be either blue or black, dark hair. You couldn't see their faces, but the clothes the woman wore were the same as in the other photograph.

I glanced up. Fisher had his eyes elsewhere.

Photographs do lie, and one of the ways is by only capturing instants. Advertising people are tactile. Amy could have been walking along the street with a colleague or client, and he'd grabbed her shoulder to make some point or celebrate a corporate victory. Or she could have said she was cold and he'd momentarily looped his arm around her, awkward, feeling it was a man's job to do something and knowing that convention allowed this brief intrusion on personal space. Captured at the right instant, frozen beyond their true duration, any of these gestures could have looked like more than they were. Or so I wanted to believe. "Where are these from?"

"Taken in Seattle last Friday," Fisher said.

When I was also here in town. I took a long, slow breath. I've spent a lot of hours getting statements from witnesses. If you want them to talk, you have to let them. And you're not allowed to hit them first.

"So talk," I said.

He stood up. "Walk with me."

Fisher led me out of the antiderelict enclosure around the coffeehouse and up First. He took us north for a couple blocks, then steered several rights and lefts.

"I told you my interest in the Anderson murders came

from an estate," he said as we walked. "A client of the firm. Name was Joseph Cranfield. Heard of him?"

"No. Should I?"

"I guess not. Old patriarchal business type. Tough, six foot and still square-shouldered in his late seventies. Started work at thirteen—one of those kids who had a job when he was in diapers, crawls around delivering papers with his teeth. You ever wonder how some people are ready from the get-go, looking for the main chance and knowing what to do when they find it?"

I'd met people like that in my own life, the ones who hit the ground running. I'd never thought too much about it, and I wasn't in the mood to start now.

"I guess."

"By the 1950s Joe was into failing mills in New England, turning them around and then reselling them. Soon as that was killed by overseas markets, he sidestepped to retail, franchises, anything that kept money coming in. From there into real estate, became a partner in some of the earliest supermalls in Illinois. It wasn't like he never made a mistake. But he took the hits, moved on."

"An American hero," I said. "There should be statues everywhere."

Gary nodded. "Right. Could have been the smuggest asshole to ever draw breath. I met him when I was fresh out of law school. After a couple weeks, they sent me to Cranfield's office, to advise on some tiny thing. I was scared. I'm twenty-three, I've lucked into an all-star firm. If I fail this rite of passage, I'm history. So I show up in my new suit and shiny briefcase knowing that this is a meeting where my life can split two ways. My gastrointestinal tract was empty, I'll tell you that."

The thought of Gary Fisher being nervous was more compelling than what he was telling me, which appeared to have no bearing on any universe I cared about.

Despite myself, I said, "And?"

"He sat me down, got me coffee, explained what he

needed done. Thankfully, it was something I could handle easily, and once he saw that, he just told me to get on with it. A week later there's a note of thanks on my desk. From Cranfield, in his own hand. As the years go by, I wind up reporting to his office more and more. Finally one of the senior partners gets a little drunk and admits that Joe asks for me by name when he wants something done. This is a very big deal to me, and by now I know Joe well enough to understand he doesn't do anything by accident. He mentioned my name to someone and put a checkmark next to it. Six months later I was made junior partner."

"He have you running private work on the side, things he wanted kept out of sight?"

"You're a cynical man, Jack."

"I was a cop for ten years. And I've been a human all my life."

"No, he did not," Gary said as he steered us across an intersection. We seemed to be getting farther from the parts of Seattle that are featured in tourist brochures. "I'm sure Joe did things fast and loose back in the day—nobody gets rich playing by M.B.A. rules—but he never asked me to do anything your grandmother wouldn't smile upon. Life went on, except I scored a bigger office and got paid a bunch more."

"Until?"

"One morning the call comes in. Joe Cranfield died in his sleep. Bam—just like that."

We were walking more slowly now, and Gary was silent for a moment.

"I'm sorry."

"Yeah. It was a blow. Okay, he was eighty-one by then, but he looked like he'd make a hundred without breaking a sweat. Barely an hour after we find out he's passed, we get a call from some firm none of us have ever heard of. Turns out he'd used another crew to handle his personal affairs. Okay, it happens—but this is a tiny outfit based half the country away, and we're all like, *What?* The guy on the phone has instructions, however, and he wants us on it right away. And this is where it started to get weird."

"Weird how?"

"The will. Two million to his wife, one million to each child, two-fifty K to each of his grandchildren. A little over eight all told."

I didn't get what he was driving at. "How much was he worth when he died?"

"Nearly two hundred sixty million dollars."

I raised my eyebrows, and Fisher smiled tightly.

"Now you're listening. Strictly B-list in global terms, but hardly destitute. It had been more, but it turned out he'd been unloading briskly over the last five years, to institutions, charities, schools. A hospital ward here, drop-in center there, Old Master or two on permanent loan to some tiny gallery in Europe. We knew about a lot of it, of course, because of tax issues, but no one had really had a handle on exactly how much he'd moved out. It was close to seventy million."

I revised my opinion of the old man, and for the better. "So where was the rest of it destined for?"

"That's the thing. The afternoon of Cranfield's funeral, Lytton—one of the two named partners in this firm—turned up on our doorstep with a case of paperwork. Everyone with juice in the firm headed into the boardroom and went through it together. Cranfield left detailed instructions on how his empire was to be dismantled, and half of it was already started, triggered by Burnell & Lytton—who it turns out had overriding power of attorney. For the rest of it, Lytton basically deals with us like we're junior clerks: Do this, do that, do it now. Joe had thought of everything—down to the dispersal of a roadside food shack in Houma, Louisiana. That was a bequest to the old woman who'd been running it all these years, and there were other things like that, random citizens getting a chunk here and there, but everything else was to be liquidated. Even his houses were to be sold. And the resulting funds, minus ten percent, were to be split among nine main beneficiaries."

"Who were?"

"Battered women. Inner-city education and antidrug initiatives. Long-term medical supplies to godforsaken parts of Africa. Even a campaign to save the fucking sea otters, run by some hippie down in Monterey—who received six point five million dollars to keep up the good fight. I got to phone this guy with the news. He nearly heart-attacked right there on the line. He'd never met Cranfield in his life. Never even *heard* of him."

"Where did the last ten percent go?"

"A trust administered by Burnell & Lytton, which fed into an international charitable network."

"So how did the family take this?"

"How do you think? They went apeshit, Jack. I had men and women in their fifties, people who'd had *everything* on a plate since birth, coming into my office and screaming like crack addicts let down by the man. It went on for *weeks*. These people had lived their lives assuming they'd get a huge check someday, and now we're telling them it was all a dream? They contested the will, of course, but it was signed, filed in triplicate, and quadruple-witnessed by judges and priests demonstrably in their right minds. We had guys who'd built entire careers drilling holes in this kind of paperwork, real wolves, and they couldn't get their pencils sharpened. The only person who didn't go nuts was Cranfield's wife, and I'll come back to that. Bottom line is that he knew what he wanted to do and he did it. Everything else was after the fact. So . . . the children sued us instead."

We'd stopped at another intersection. Over the last minutes, my mind had found its way back to the photograph of Amy. I was trying to imagine what the man's hand had done in the moments after the picture had been taken. Gary had about another minute of me playing nice.

"How did that pan out?"

Fisher's face tensed, and I got the idea that the lines around his eyes had not been there long. "Ongoing. Everyone else in the firm has turned away from Cranfield's affairs, like a bad smell. But I couldn't do that. A month ago I came up against something that needed sorting out, figured what the hell, and flew here to Seattle. I went to the Burnell & Lytton office."

"And?" I asked.

"It wasn't there."

"What do you mean?"

"I'd been working with these guys for three months by then, okay? I know their address and phone numbers by heart. I landed at Sea-Tac, got a cab straight there. The neighborhood is more the kind of place I'd expect to find a bail bondsman, and when I walk up to the street address, I see it's a storefront that's been boarded up. And not recently. Before that, it looks like it was a coffee shop. There's a fucking *tree* growing out of the roof. No sign for Burnell & Lytton anywhere. There is an entry system, but it's really, really old. There's ten buzzers, and only the second to last looks like it's been used since I was born. So I press that one first. No response. I press all the others. Nada.

"By this stage I'm a little confused. I walk up to the corner, buy a coffee, call the office, double-check the address. So then I phone Burnell & Lytton. Lytton's secretary picks up. I ask to speak to him. She says he's out. I ask to check the address with her, say I have an important package. She reels off the same old zip code. So I ask her which buzzer you need to press.

"And she went quiet. Just completely silent. Then she said 'You're *here*?' And she sounded weird, really imperious, not like a secretary anymore."

"That's a little strange."

"Yes, it is. So I find myself saying no, I'm not in Seattle, but my assistant's sick and I want to fill out the waybill properly. She's all friendly again, tells me it doesn't matter, just the street address is fine. I thank her, leave a message for her bosses to call me, put down the phone. I sit there thinking for a minute, and then my cell rings. It's one of my colleagues, back in Seattle. Lytton has just called the office, asking for me. Luckily, my assistant only told him I was out, not saying I was in Seattle. It *could* just be a coincidence. But it's odd. So I walk back to the address. Ring the buzzer, still no response. Then I call their number again. There's no answer this time. But I realize I can hear something. A ringing sound, from above."

"Your call being received?"

"You got it. I disconnected and tried again, just to check. I took a few steps back from the door, and I could hear a phone ringing somewhere in the building. I let it ring, but . . . In the end I walked away. Flew back home."

He held his hands up, telling me he was finished and also asking a question. I wasn't sure what it was.

"You've been in contact with them since?"

"Many times. Once I got back to Chicago, it was business as usual. We've ground through the remaining work. It's almost done."

"Did you mention your trip to either of the lawyers?"

"No," he said. "I never could work out a way of phrasing the question: 'Hey, dude—how come your office is in an abandoned building?' I did mention it to one of the senior partners, but he did everything but stick his fingers in his ears and go la-la-la. No one's interested in hearing anything hinky about Cranfield's affairs."

I felt much the same way. "So these guys have a low-rent office. Big deal."

"Jack—when you die, are you going to hand your estate to a lawyer working out of a cardboard box? Assuming you've accumulated a couple hundred million by then and when you've already got one of the most prestigious law firms in Chicago on retainer?"

"Neither seems likely. And are you sure your interest amounts to more than an attempt to resist a drop in your personal stock once the old guy was dead?"

"Fuck you, Jack."

"Gary, just tell me what you got me here to say."

He pointed across the intersection, toward the other side of the street on the next block north.

I turned and saw a run of battered buildings. A tattered banner hanging from a lamppost said we were in the Belltown area. On the corner was a café, two people who looked like exhausted muggers sitting outside. Next to that was something purporting to be a secondhand bookstore, but which looked more like somewhere you'd head for porn and/or a tip on where to buy drugs.

And then a boarded-up window in a dilapidated dirty-brown building. It was wider than its neighbors, could once have held a small department store. Above the window on ground level was a peeling hand-painted sign, white on black, saying THE HUMAN BEAN. To the left of the long window was an anonymous door in gunmetal gray. I pulled out Fisher's envelope, took out the first photograph. I didn't need to hold it up to know that's where Amy had been standing when it was taken.

For a moment it was as if I could even see her standing there, head slightly turned as if she were gazing back at me, though she did not look like any person I knew.

chapter TWENTY

I walked across the street, barely noticing a truck that whistled past behind me. When I got to the far sidewalk, I turned, looked south toward downtown. I checked it against the second photograph and saw enough congruence to know that this was the view it showed.

"Yes," Fisher said as he stepped up the curb to stand next to me. "I was standing up at the next corner."

I walked up to the storefront. Tried to look through the window, but whoever nailed it over had done a good job. Went to the doorway and pushed my hand against it. No movement. It was a big, heavy door, decorated by rivets on all sides, and fitted tightly. Layer after layer of gray paint made it appear impregnable. I stooped to look at the handle and saw that the slot for the key showed flecks of bright metal. It had been unlocked recently.

I stepped back a few paces and looked up and down the street again. The entrance to the building was exposed, visible to anyone in a fifty-yard radius. It had the brutally monumental quality favored by turn-of-the-century boosters, a promise to stand profitably forever. It still stood, but it was not making anyone any money anymore. There were three big windows on each story. On the second and third floors, several panes of glass were broken, and the holes had been boarded up. On the next floor up, the glass looked complete, but the cloud reflections suggested that there was no light on behind. Clumps of grass and a very small tree were growing out of broken guttering right at the very top.

When I pulled my gaze back down, I noticed that the two guys hanging outside the corner café were taking an interest. I walked over to them, and Fisher followed.

Both men wore drab hoodies and stained blue jeans and Nikes that could barely have been five minutes out of the box. Apart from minor details of facial organization, they presented as functionally identical. There was nothing on the battered metal table between them. One smiled lazily at the other as I approached.

"I smell something," he said. "You smell something?"

The other nodded. "Makes me think of barbecue."

"That one's pretty old," I said. "I mean, like, fucking medieval. And you're probably just smelling each other. I can, from here. Next time it rains, you might want to stay outdoors."

The first one stopped smiling. "What you want?"

"That building I was standing at. You know anything about it? Seen anyone going in or out?"

They shook their heads slowly, as if being operated by the same lazy string.

"Right," I said. "You know shit about this corner. Probably new to the area. Just flew in from Paris on a student exchange program. Strolled down for a croissant and a café crème between classes. Am I getting warm?"

Both were staring sullenly at me now. I smiled in a flat, communicative way and broke eye contact first. I took a scrap of paper out of my pocket and wrote my cell-phone number on it.

"Call me. There's money on it."

I nodded at two pairs of pink, dull eyes and walked back up the street to the building. I wondered if there was any way in around the back.

"You find that works?" Fisher asked when he caught up

with me. He sounded relieved to have moved away from the café. "The openly confrontational approach?"

"Yes," I said, panning my eyes around the street level of the building. "And you're next, if you don't just go ahead and tell me what—"

I stopped talking and walked over to the doorway again. The entry system was a stained and rusted metal oblong with a grille at the top and a series of wide buttons. I pressed them one at a time and received no sense that anything was happening anywhere, that any connection remained to be made.

Then I looked at the remaining button but didn't press it. The rust wasn't as thick, and the patina was different. It appeared, as Fisher had said, as though it might have been used from time to time. It was the second from the top. I wondered if I'd discovered the meaning of the last of the text messages Amy had sent.

The one that said "Bell 9."

Around the rear of the building was a parking lot. The back of the structure was peeling and missing large patches of plaster. The street door was heavily locked. The windows on the floors above were boarded, and the fire escape was falling apart. I looked at this for a while, then walked away. A few streets back toward downtown, we walked past a bar. I stopped, turned, and went in.

The interior was dark, the counter running along one side. The lighting was dim. The walls were wood-paneled in a way that was not a recent design decision but an indication that the paneling had been in place since such decor was still in fashion. Many of the patrons probably remembered the way it was even before that.

The barman was skinny as a nail and looked like he knew how to get hold of things. He shot me just a brief glance and started to apologize for matters I had no knowledge of and cared about even less.

"Look, I'm not a fucking cop," I said. "We just want a beer. That going to be possible?"

I walked to the corner table and sat down. Fisher got a couple of drinks and brought them over. I sat in silence for a few minutes, smoking.

"Okay," I said. "So now tell me the rest. And really make it quick."

"After I got back to Chicago, this thing started eating at me," Fisher said. "I knew Joe pretty well by the end. It wasn't like he didn't get along with his kids. Clan Cranfield was tight—vacations together at the compounds, a photo of the bloodline on the Christmas cards. If you work in my field, you know a lot of families like that. Once in a while, it gets complicated when the old goat leaves the farm to a stripper no one knew about, but the patriarch never razes everything to the ground."

"But evidently this is what he wanted."

"It still doesn't make sense. I'm boring my wife senseless about it, barely spending any time with the kids. And so I went to visit Cranfield's widow. I'd met Norma often over the years, had dinner at the house a few times. This is not some trophy wife. They'd been together fifty years. So I went up to the house a few weeks ago and sat with her in a big room that's halfway through being packed up. I listened to how she was going to move into a small apartment in town, and every now and then I thought I could sense a confusion behind her eyes, as if she wondered when she was going to wake up. In the end I had to ask. Did *she* understand what was going on?"

"What did she say?"

"Nothing for a moment. Then she got up and went to a bureau in the corner. Opened a drawer, got something out. A card, old black-and-white photograph of an old pier stuck to the front, by hand. I asked her what the picture showed, and she said it was Monterey, the place she and Cranfield first met. Inside there's a message, in Joe's handwriting. It said, 'Don't hate me.' "

"That's it?"

"Those three words. I looked at her, and she shrugged and said, 'That's all I know.' She hadn't told anyone else about the note. Not even her kids. I drove straight back to the office, sat down with the documentation, and I went over it for the hundredth time. Not to break the thing, but to try to understand. I looked into the nine organizations that got the big money, but there's nothing strange there. Even the sea otters now made sense, up to a point. Norma told me they had a long weekend in Monterey ten years back, and Joe had been taken with the aquarium, loved watching the otters swim around. So I started looking at the minor beneficiaries. There's about thirty of them, people like the restaurant-shack woman, small figures from Joe's distant past. I can make sense of all of them, relate them to some old part of Cranfield's business, apart from one. A guy who seems to bear no relation to anything Joe's been into. And so I did a Google search, and *that's* when I find out this person lives in Seattle and also that his family has recently become dead."

"Bill Anderson."

"He was FedExed a two-hundred-and-fifty-thousand-dollar check—the same amount Joe's own *grandchildren* got, remember. It was signed for seven weeks ago, a whole month before he disappeared. But it still hasn't been cashed. Four, five years' salary, and he doesn't bother banking it? This being, incidentally, another reason I'm inclined to dismiss financial motive in killing his own wife."

"I can see that," I said. "And maybe you should have mentioned it when you first came to see me."

"Would it have made a difference?"

"Maybe."

"Bill is the closest thing I've got to a smoking gun with Cranfield's estate, something to unlock why he did something that no one—not his lawyers or children or his own wife—can understand. And I really did read your book when it came out, because I recognized your name, and I really *did* need a cop. I think Anderson's family was killed by an intruder. Your book was even called *The Intruders*. Tell me it doesn't make sense for me to come to you, get your advice."

"Start talking to me about Amy," I said.

"I'm going to. But you've got a bad look on your face, so bear in mind I'm just the messenger. I came over to Seattle again, to look into the Anderson murders. It's not hard for me to get the time. As you so nicely put it, my stock by then is falling fast."

I started to say something, but he held up his hand. "No, you were right, Jack. But what you *don't* know is what it's like in my world, once you start to drop rungs. The corporate world is based on confidence and very little else. Either you fix the slide fast or they simply take the ladder away. I'd accepted the glow of association while Joe was alive, so . . ."

"So what did you find out when you got here?"

"What I told you at your house. Bottom line, if I'm honest, I don't even really *care* if Anderson took out his family. I just want to know why he was sent the money and what it means. Meanwhile I'm sitting in a hotel room with a Web connection and time to kill. So I keep digging in any direction I can find. The first road that leads anywhere is the building you and I just visited."

"The Burnell and Lytton offices."

"Such as they are. I soon find out they don't own the property, they lease. The former coffeehouse is no help either. The company's long dead. Eventually I discovered that for a few years back in the mid-1990s the second floor was rented out as studio space for photography and video shoots—Belltown was a complete hole back then; you could pick up property for next to nothing. It's not used for that anymore, but the firm still owns the building. That company is called Kerry, Crane, and Hardy."

I nearly dropped my glass. Fisher rested his hands flat on

the table and leaned forward, with the air of a man who's glad that someone is finally listening to him.

"*Yes,*" he said. "Didn't mean anything to me at first. I check them on the Web, find they're some big ad agency, I can't see how that leads anywhere. I even called the company but couldn't get high enough to speak to anyone who knew what I was talking about. It's just another dead end for now. Which leaves me one final door to push on. Guess what that is?"

"The charity that got the ten percent out of Cranfield's estate."

Fisher smiled. "See," he said quietly. "This is why I believe you can help."

"What did you find out?"

"The charity is called the Psychomachy Trust, based in Boston. It has zero presence on the radar, never appears to solicit money from private individuals or the public at large. It's administered by Burnell and Lytton and a few other guys I can't dredge up anything about, probably not U.S. nationals. The interesting thing is that it's part of a network. Charity structures are easier to trace because they have to meet tax regulations. This trust, along with others in Paris, Berlin, Jerusalem, Tokyo, and other major cities around the world—they all feed back to a parent organization based in London. It's old. At least two, three hundred years, gets vaguer before that. Basically, I hit a dead end there, too, but just as that happens, I get hold of more information on the building we've just been to. I get a copy of the papers and find out whose names are on them."

He reached into his jacket pocket and pulled out a folded piece of paper. Flattened it and put it on the table in front of me. I didn't look down but lit a cigarette instead, and waited.

"There's three," he said. "One of them makes sense right away—Todd Crane, principal in the owning company. The second is a man called Marcus Fox, who I believe was once a business associate of Joe Cranfield's here in Seattle."

"It starts to come home."

"Exactly. Fox disappears from Cranfield's world in the mid-nineties, can't find anything more about him. The third name I can't get anywhere with at all until I have another scout around the Kerry, Crane, and Hardy Web site, where I spot someone with the same first name."

It wasn't hard to find, even in a page dense with the minutiae of property law.

The third name was Amy Dyer.

Seeing her name in print made me feel as if the car had finally smacked into me. It took me a while to notice that the document was dated 1992, six years before I'd met her.

"You knew about this when you came to see me."

"Yes, Jack. I found out that Amy Dyer was now Amy Whalen and that her husband is you. But at that stage she was still just a name on a piece of paper. I came to talk to you, and I heard your view, and I backed off. But I'm kind of camped out in Seattle for the time being and—"

"You're spending a lot of time away from home."

"While I sort this out, yes. And meantime I've developed a habit of walking past that building once in a while. Last Friday I spent a couple hours up at the next corner. There's another coffeehouse there. It's an okay place to sit. And toward the end of the afternoon, when I'm getting cold and beginning to feel ridiculous—and not for the first time, believe me—I see someone turn up at that door. And those pictures show what I saw."

"Do you have any more?"

He shook his head. "I didn't want to be too obvious. Surveillance is not my field. Plus, there were some ominous street people walking around, and I don't have your easy manner with them. I stayed the hell back and just snapped those two pictures. Never got a decent look at the guy. Honestly."

The door to the bar opened, and a group of parched-looking individuals entered in a brief glare of light. The start of the lunchtime crowd. Fisher sat in silence as I watched, though I was not really seeing them. In my mind's eye, I could see two people, a man and a woman, close together as they headed down a street.

I stubbed out my cigarette. "I want to see the originals of the photographs you took."

Fisher promptly pulled a small digital camera from his pocket, popped the memory card, and handed it to me. "Does this mean . . . ?"

"For now yes," I said. "Give me everything you have on Bill Anderson. Then go away and leave me alone."

chapter TWENTY-ONE

Todd Crane was sitting in his office. Most of his desk was lost under paper, which was in turn covered with bullet-pointed lists and slogans and sketches. He was supposed to have read, digested, and commented on it all. Creative teams were standing by. A pile of DVDs from commercial directors stood to one side. He was supposed to have watched all these, too, and passed down his views so that account handlers and production managers could get busy with checking availability and fees and booking talent and generally kicking KC&H toward further glorious triumphs in the pursuit of getting people to buy shit they didn't actually need.

He had done none of these things.

Instead he'd turned his chair to face the big window and was gazing blankly down across Elliott Bay. From up here you could see the piers, the roof of the market building hard to the right, and the sprawling docks over on the far left. Behind all this was the gray-blue expanse of the bay itself, and beyond that the cloud-shrouded Olympic Mountains. For many years Todd and a few college buddies had a habit of spending a long weekend every year in the forests of those mountains, hiking and drinking beer in moderation and openly one-upping each other on material success. He couldn't remember the last time this had happened. Six years, seven? Ten? Could be. In time, presumably, the memory would become a pleasurable thing, another example of the life-affirming activity he'd enjoyed as part of the richness of his existence, further evidence that you could—if you possessed character and money (and a tolerant wife)—live within one long advertisement for your own life.

But right now it felt like something that was slipping away, like the idea that he would ever become fluent in French or visit the carved-rock temples of Petra or play decent finger-style blues guitar. He didn't even really know why these things were important to him, or ever had been. He'd just assumed they'd happen sooner or later, that they'd be part of his life. For some reason he was no longer sure of that.

Sitting on the floor in one corner of the office was an old radio, which he'd come across in his den a few weeks before. It had been a present from his parents, back when Todd was in his early twenties. An upscale device, a significant gift from two people now both dead. It worked for a couple years, then stopped. It was likely that the problem was minor, and radios were easy and economical to fix, but somehow in thirty years he hadn't gotten around to it. It had sat on shelves, in drawers, drifting in and out of awareness, never formally sidelined or retired, forever on the verge of repair. It was absurd. He'd brought it into the office a week ago, in the hope that this would galvanize him to getting the job done. Yet there it sat. Maybe it was just never going to get fixed. Maybe life held a lot of things like that.

Todd turned irritably from the view. He was fifty-four years old, for God's sake. Barely middle-aged these days. So why did it feel like life was beginning to get away from him? Why was he becoming prone to notice the things he had *not* done instead of the multitude of things he *had* achieved? He wasn't sleeping well. He knew that this had nothing to do with the pincer movement of projects represented by the mess on his desk. He'd been busy all his life and slept like a baby ninety-nine nights out of a hundred. So what was the problem? Faced with no rational explanation, his famously creative mind had offered up several that made little sense. He'd become convinced for a few weeks earlier in the year, for example, that when he walked the streets of this city, something felt different about them. That they seemed unseasonably crowded. He'd even briefly taken to sitting outside coffeehouses in the midafternoon, ostensibly to work in peace, in fact to monitor the number of people on the streets. When he did this, he could see that they were not crowded at all. His analyst was no help. She never had been, with anything, even during the five months they slept together. The fact that they'd now successfully regained a straightforward therapeutic relationship suggested to Todd that neither the sex nor the therapy had ever made much impact on either of them.

Another thing that hadn't helped was the visit of the ex-cop. Amy's husband. There was something about the man that made you want to build a high wall around you. More unsettling still, Todd believed that the man had not been telling the truth. He didn't believe that Whalen had the faintest idea of what his wife was doing in Seattle, and he didn't buy the lost-phone story either. But it *was* likely that Amy had actually been in town; her husband didn't seem the kind of guy who'd be wrong about something like that. So what had she been doing here? A side deal? Possibly, in which case he didn't care. But maybe it wasn't that simple. Maybe it had to do with other matters. Something told him this was more likely, especially considering the fact that Bianca had on that afternoon deflected another man, who had come to ask questions about a certain building. Something told him that it was this that was creating the hard, dark lesion in his stomach, that people were knocking on the door of a part of his life he'd never really understood.

He had never been a man prey to self-doubt or prone to concern about the passage of time. But now he was. And why would that be, unless it was something about this past that was bothering him?

He'd finally begun dealing with the paperwork when he was startled by the buzzing of the intercom. He stabbed the button.

"Christ, yes?"

"It's Jenni, at reception?"

Todd considered reminding her that everyone except Bianca had been advised not to bother him with anything short of world-shaking news. Unfortunately, he believed he had a reputation as a good boss, which meant only chewing out the staff once in a very great while. He'd realized long ago that being a good boss sucked, but it was too late to break the habit. "What is it, Jenni?"

"There's somebody here from Meadow's school," she said. "They'd like to talk to you."

He frowned. Someone from his youngest daughter's school? "What do they want?"

"She wishes to speak with you privately."

Todd told her to bring the person up. He grabbed the phone to call Livvie, to see if she knew what was going on, but then remembered that his wife had Pilates or yoga or some other body magic this afternoon. It didn't matter. He hadn't gotten to be CEO of the Pacific Northwest's most profitable advertising agency without being able to deal with people unbriefed. And there was a limit to how much trouble a twelve-year-old could have gotten into, surely.

Hopefully.

He took a minute to check his reflection in the hand mirror he kept in his bottom drawer. He looked tired but otherwise fine. The door opened, and his assistant entered, accompanied by someone who was clearly not a teacher at his daughter's or anyone else's school. Todd froze, halfway to his feet.

"Who's this?"

Bianca indicated via a raised eyebrow that she had absolutely no idea. Meanwhile the person in question looked at him steadily and answered for herself.

"My name's Madison," she said.

Bianca hovered. Part of her job was to second-guess and covertly undermine every call made by whichever girl was currently working reception. Thus were the subtle hierarchies of the corporate world maintained where they really mattered—at the bottom.

"Are you—"

"I'm fine," Todd said. She nodded once and left.

"So," he said warmly, coming around to sit on the edge of the desk and indicating the nearest chair, "you're at school with Meadow, right?"

"No," the girl said as she sat neatly in the exact center of the chair. "I've never met her."

"But you told—"

"How else was I going to get up here?"

Todd didn't have an answer for that. The girl pointed at the photograph on the corner of his desk. "She's what? Thirteen?"

Todd nodded, wondering at what point he should get Bianca back in. Soon, he was thinking. Maybe even . . . very soon. "Yes. Nearly."

The girl smiled cheerfully. "And I'm nine. But I told the woman downstairs we were in the same class. And she believed me. So I guess she's not very bright, huh?"

"She's . . . never met Meadow. I'm sure she was just being polite." This came easily into Todd's mouth, though privately he was wondering what had gotten into Jenni, letting a random child into the building.

The girl nodded. "Maybe. Are you sleeping with her?"

Now she had his full attention. *"What?"*

"You look a bit ancient, it's true. But I'm sure you can still hear reasonably well. And still do the old dirty bop."

The . . . *what*? "Look, kid, whatever your name—"

"Madison. I just told you."

Todd moved back around to the chair side of his desk. It was time to get Bianca the hell in here.

But then a thought occurred to him. He hesitated, hand over the phone. "If you're not at school with her, how do you know my daughter's name?"

The girl made a face. "Actually, I don't know. I just do. Like I know that your other daughters are a lot older. And your wife used to drink, too—"

She stopped talking, and her head slowly dropped. "I'm so sorry," she said. "That's really rude."

For a moment she appeared blank. Then she looked up again suddenly, and her face seemed different. She was blinking rapidly and seemed extremely agitated.

"Please," she said, "can I have a piece of paper? And a pen?"

Todd's hand was still over the button on the phone system that would summon his assistant. He moved it to point at a Post-it pad. The girl grabbed a pen from his desk and wrote something on the top note. It looked like a series of numbers.

She got four or five down and then faltered. "No," she said, angrily. "No . . ."

She quickly added two numbers to the beginning. Tore off the note and stuffed it deep in the pocket of her coat, looking for an instant like some juvenile street person, hiding her favorite piece of string from aliens or the CIA or naughty ghosts. Then she threw herself back into the chair and covered her face with her hands.

Todd watched all this wide-eyed. Soon he could hear her crying behind them. It was a low, measured sound, more exhaustion than sobs. He stood again, disconcerted. Why on earth had he let Bianca even leave the room?

"Look," he said, trying to sound more friendly than nonplussed. "Can I get you something? A drink?"

The girl said nothing, and Todd began to think she couldn't

have heard. Then, in a voice muffled by the hands in front of her face, he heard her say, "Coffee."

"Coffee? Really? Not . . . a soda? Or water?"

She shook her head. "Coffee. Black."

He went to the machine in the corner, poured a cup. Brought it back over. He slipped into the role of subservient waiter easily, having done it often enough with his own daughters. Sometimes an apparent reversal of power was the only thing that would placate a kid enough to get them to do what you wanted. Children seemed to arrive with keenly political natures, to understand how things worked right from the start.

"Here," he said, realizing she couldn't see him.

Slowly she pulled her hands down. Looked at the cup and reached for it with both hands. She brought it to her face and took a long, deep sip, though Todd knew that it came off the plate hot enough to sear. Cradled the cup in her hands afterward, looking down into the remaining liquid.

"That's what I'm talking about," she said. Then she turned her face up toward him and slowly smiled.

"So, Todd," she said. "How have you been?"

He blinked at her. Everything about her—her voice, her smile—seemed different. The distraught child had been replaced by . . . he wasn't sure what. But he did know that he didn't want her in his office anymore.

"You're going to have to leave now," he said. "I can get someone to call you a cab if you need a ride home."

"Yes," she said, looking past him out the window. "Always generous with the small things."

"Look—who *are* you?"

"Guess," she said.

"I really have no idea," Todd said firmly. "You got in here claiming to be a friend of my daughter's. We both know that's not true."

"Please," she said. "Tell me. Tell me who I am."

"You're a little girl."

She laughed, apparently genuinely, an uproarious guffaw that took him entirely by surprise.

"I know," she said. "Isn't it priceless?"

"It's a riot," he said, leaning over to press the button to summon Bianca.

"Don't do that," the girl said. "Don't you dare."

"Listen," Todd said briskly, "I'm done with this. I don't know what you're doing here, and you seem to me to be an odd little person. That's your parents' problem, thankfully, not mine. I've got work to do."

"Oh, hush," she said. "I've got no desire to spend a moment longer in your company than necessary, believe me. You recall the saying about the organ grinder and the monkey? You're a flea on the monkey's ass, and you always have been. But beggars can't be choosers, and so you're going to do a few things for me. Lucky boy."

"I'm not doing—"

She ignored him. "First, somewhere for me to stay. I need a shower, and I'm tired of dealing with street trash from a position of weakness. Not to mention that I could use a good night's sleep. As could you, by the look of it."

Her voice was firm and confident now, and Todd could see how she might have been able to convince Jenni to let her up here. He was also horribly reminded of his cousin, when she'd been in the hospital recovering from a bad car accident, back in '98. During most of the critical period, she'd floated on a river of morphine, but occasionally she fought her way free of chemicals and pain to deliver remarks whose normality came to seem extraordinary and bizarre. The contrast made the hairs rise on the back of your neck. This girl had the same effect, even though you knew she could only be mimicking some adult she knew.

She seemed to take his silence as acquiescence. "When I arise, bright like a phoenix from Lethe's snoozy flames, there's someone I *very* much want to meet again. A mutual friend. You're going to make it happen."

"I can't imagine who you're talking about," Todd said, finally pressing the button, glad to be on solid ground. "We don't feature anyone from boy bands or TV shows. It's a policy."

"A 'boy band'? What on *earth* are you talking about?"

He heard his assistant's door opening along the corridor, then her hurried footsteps. Bianca was paid 20 percent more than anyone else at the same job level in the company. She was worth it.

The little girl heard it, too. Her face darkened. "Toddy, this is one of those times where you can make a bad choice or a good one. Don't fuck it up."

The door opened, and Bianca came striding in. "This person's going to leave now," Crane told her.

The girl sighed histrionically. He ignored her. "If she makes a fuss, call the police. She's here under false pretenses, wants to meet a celebrity."

Bianca stood by the chair, looking balefully down at the girl. "On your feet," she said. "Now, princess."

"Oh, you tedious people," the girl muttered wearily. She stood, ignoring the hand Bianca held out, her eyes still on Crane. "I don't want to cause a fuss. You're forcing my hand, don't you see?"

Todd retreated stiffly behind his desk. Bianca would handle this, had indeed already taken the girl's upper arm in her hand and gotten her as far as the open door.

He looked down at his papers, suddenly anxious to immerse himself in work. There was something about the way the girl had spoken in the closing stages that was tugging at him. Tugging hard.

"Good-bye," he muttered.

The girl winked. "Watch your back," she said, and then she was gone.

Todd Crane's head jerked up, and he stared after her as she disappeared down the corridor.

* * *

Five minutes later he saw her emerge into Post Alley, two stories below. She drifted to a halt. Slowly she started to turn, to raise her head—and though Todd darted back from the window as quickly as he could, she caught him.

When he leaned cautiously back, she was still there, looking right up at him. She shifted her face into something that was like a smile and raised one hand, the index finger extended. Using her whole arm, she moved it to describe a symbol in the air. A short spiral, like the number 9.

Then she turned away as if he were of no account and walked rapidly up the alley and out of sight.

Todd watched the alley a little longer, in case she came back. He wasn't really sure why the prospect worried him. Something about that last phrase. It had seemed so ridiculous, coming from a little girl, that it . . . it had reminded him of something. Someone.

A meaningless coincidence, nothing more, the mind joining unrelated dots from across the years. Time was weighing on him, that's all—he'd worked that out before. What he needed was a rejuvenator. He tried to remember exactly what Jenni in reception looked like and was a little worried to find that he could not. He could redress that later. Perhaps over a drink.

As his mind clicked back onto old paths and the work in front of him started to get done, Todd began to feel more like himself once again.

chapter TWENTY-TWO

The Anderson house was on Federal, near Broadway Avenue, up on the ridge overlooking downtown and Elliott Bay. The avenue itself is a major thoroughfare, a long, wide street sparsely lined with generic businesses, redbrick banks, and more places to buy coffee. As a nation in general, we like our coffee, but the Northwest is insane on the subject. I'm surprised you can't get it out of ATMs. Federal was a couple of streets back and overhung with big trees now shedding copper and yellow leaves. The speed limit was twenty, because people actually walked around here, and many houses had low hedges that someone remembered to cut or picket fences that had been painted sometime in living memory. Most were small. The cars on the street also said you did not have to be rich to live here, but it was easy to see why you might want to be.

The house itself was one back from a crossroads. Evidence of fire damage was minor from the outside, though the street-level windows had been covered with plywood sheets. I walked straight up the stairs onto the shallow porch, which is what you do when you have a right to be there. The door was sealed with tape, but I had a tool ready for that and another to pop the lock. A lot of cops have rudimentary breaking-and-entering skills. Mine are a little better than most.

I stepped into a dark space that smelled of old smoke and shut the door behind me.

I stood still for a few minutes, letting my eyes adjust. There was little ambient light making its way around the window boards, however, and it didn't get any better than very dark. I reached out to the side of the doorway and found a switch. The lights came on, the bill presumably still being automatically paid from the account of a man whose whereabouts were unknown.

I went upstairs first. Other than the smell and some shadowing on the walls, the fire had made few inroads here. Two bedrooms, a bathroom, another room used for storage and a home office. A hatch in the hall ceiling opened into a roof space thick with dust that had not been recently disturbed. I looked quickly through the bedrooms, doing little more than opening drawers and glancing into closets, then checked the obvious hiding places in the bathroom. Found evidence for nothing more than a middle-aged couple living with a teenage son. No sign of anywhere a gun would likely have been stowed, either: no lockbox, no wrap cloth, no carton of old shells.

Then I went back downstairs and halted a couple of steps short of the bottom to look down over the living room. The air was dead and quiet. This was obviously where Joshua Anderson had died, given the oblique blood splatter across one smoke-stained wall and the charred patch in the carpet. I descended the last couple of steps and walked around the room, not trying to make anything of it. There was no telling the degree to which things had been moved after the crime-scene people had logged and recorded the environment. But I was already beginning to think I could tell what had happened here. I'd seen it many times before.

I went through into the kitchen, then back across the hall to a den containing a smaller TV with a PlayStation attached and walls lined with shelves of DVDs and books. The latter broke down into paperback novels of a King/Koontz/Rice bent and a large array of hardcovers and papers relating to the physical sciences. Bill Anderson's, presumably. I ran my eyes around these for a while, seeing a few titles that surprised me—Cremo, Corliss, Hancock, alternative-archaeology theorists—but it was not enough to stop me from leaving the room.

To one side of the doorway into the kitchen was another, narrower door. Beyond it lay a flight of makeshift steps down to the basement. When I reached the bottom, I found a pull cord that shed light over the most damaged part of the house. The floor was ankle deep with charred shreds of paper that had been burned and then soaked. The remains of a wooden workbench lay along one wall. Tools and electrical components of various sizes were mixed in with the other mess, and a couple of buckled filing cabinets lay on their sides down at the end. It didn't look like someone had merely trashed the basement. It looked like a bomb had gone off.

Sometimes you have to be in the place. You have to stand there to tell. People do strange things in their own environments, behave in ways you or I might find impossible to understand. But the chaotic intrusion of otherness leaves a distinctive quality, creates a fracture at some very deep level. The place is changed.

I pulled out my phone. I took a picture. I left.

As I was walking down the path, I saw a man standing in the doorway of a house on the other side of the street. I changed course and walked over to him.

"Are you supposed to be in that house?" he said.

"Yes. You live here?"

He nodded. He was early sixties. Gray hair thinning over the top, the mild eyes of a man who watches, and thinks, and is content to live that way. "Terrible, what happened."

"Which was?"

"Well, you know—the murders."

"You think Bill did it?"

He opened his mouth, hesitated. I knew what he needed to hear from me.

"I don't," I said. "I think Gina and Josh had another caller that night."

"I didn't see anyone," the man said firmly. "And I don't know anything, really. I . . . well, they've lived here over ten years. I saw them every day, near enough, one or the other, sometimes all. Wave, say hi, you know. Not a week before it happened—three, four days—I saw the two of them go out one night. They were arguing about something, bickering, kind of. Not loud, but right there in the street, as they walked to the corner. Happened once in a while. You understand what I mean?"

I did. "Thank you. That's very helpful."

The man nodded again, folded his arms, and slowly returned indoors, still looking back at the house.

I headed a further block south down Federal and knocked on the front door of something that might have once been a Craftsman bungalow worth preserving. After a very, very long time, a light went on behind it. I was mildly surprised by this—it was only early afternoon and, by Seattle's standards, barely overcast—until the door was opened and I saw it was very dark inside, almost as dark as the Anderson house had been.

She stood in front of me now. Perhaps eighty, bent over to half my height, her face like an apple that had been left in the sun for a summer. When she looked up, her eyes reminded me of the windows in the building I'd stood outside in Belltown that morning, reflecting nothing but the clouds behind my head.

"Mrs. McKenna?"

"Yep."

"You mind if I ask you a few questions?"

"Nope."

"You told the police that on the night of the fire up at the

Andersons you saw someone coming down the street, see what had happened, then run away. That right?"

"Nope."

I hesitated. "Did you say 'No'?"

"Yep."

"My understanding was that—"

"Didn't see 'someone.' Saw Bill Anderson. You understand me now?"

"Yes I do."

"Good. What's your point?"

I looked across at the front of your house. "You always have your drapes drawn like this? Day and night?"

"Keeps out the light."

"I can see how that would work. So, if you don't mind me asking, how were you able to notice Mr. Anderson as he passed by on that evening?"

The old woman looked up at me suddenly, and her eyes were no longer reflective. You could see something inside now and tell that it was still very much alive.

"You one of them?"

"One of who?"

She stared hard at me a moment longer, shook her head. "I can see you're not. Okay, so. I keep a watch. Especially at night. I hear someone walking up or down the street, I take a look. Someone's got to. Keep a watch. Always. 'Round these parts it's me."

"Keep a watch for whom, ma'am?"

"You know. Those fellas no one can see. So I hear footsteps. Sound familiar, but I think I'll check anyhow. Move aside the corner of the curtain, just a little. See it's Bill. He's okay. I don't mind Bill. He walks a few yards past, and he stops. Stands there staring. I cain't see what he's looking at. But he starts to back away, and he turns and runs. I haven't never seen Bill run before. Twenty minutes later you got sirens and what-all else."

She coughed, violently and without warning, making no effort to cover her mouth but letting the dislodged materials rocket out and hit the ground. When she was done, she shook her head wearily.

"Don't catch cancer, son. It's a pain in the ass. Need anything else? I got a show to watch."

I walked back to the crossroads, stood on the sidewalk there watching falling leaves while I smoked a cigarette. I wouldn't want to count on Mrs. McKenna in court, but she didn't come across as completely unreliable either. Even without the experience of being in the house, the conversation with the guy living across the street might already have started to change my mind. Couples living in long-term abusive relationships, the real heavy hitters, rarely exchange harsh words in public. Out in the world, everything's fake peachy or icy polite, an occasional flash of angry eyes but no more. Their real business is private, an indoor sport. Add this to what Fisher had told me and maybe Bill Anderson hadn't whacked his wife and child. So the question became who did.

That, and where Anderson was now.

I wasn't kept waiting long at the station, which surprised me. Either they were having a quiet day or perhaps he was just intrigued.

Blanchard took me into a different room from the one where I'd sat with a hangover three days before. This room looked like it might be his office. It was certainly messy enough.

"I wanted to apologize," I said.

"That sounds nice."

"You were right. About my wife. She *had* just forgotten my number, and she *was* right there at home."

He nodded. "So everything's cool?"

"Right as rain."

"That's good. Well, you didn't need to come here, but I appreciate it."

"Actually, I wanted to pick your brains on something else while I was here."

"That figures. Shoot."

"What do you know about the Anderson murders? Up near Broadway, three weeks ago?"

He looked surprised. "Nothing. Well, two people died hard, word is the husband did it. No more than that."

"Anderson is listed as a missing person?"

"No. As the suspect in a double homicide. Which is a different department, as you know."

"You buy that? Him killing them?"

"It's not a case I know anything about. The-husband-did-it is normally how it breaks down, as you'll also know. Why—you got a different perspective?"

"I've just been up there," I said. "Talked to a couple people."

Blanchard frowned. "Are congratulations in order? You join SPD and make detective the same day? I'm a little surprised I didn't hear about that."

"Just a private citizen," I said. "Talking with other private citizens."

"Uh-huh. So what's your interest, citizen?"

"Personal."

"And what do you think you've discovered, in this new hobby of yours?"

"I don't think Anderson killed them."

"Uh-huh." Blanchard started doodling on the pad in front of him, small looping spirals.

"The only eyewitness says she saw Anderson approaching the house after the fact. Okay, she's not a great advocate, but she can't be ignored. I talked to someone else who confirms the Andersons as a functional couple, which I gather is the general picture. If you take away the notion of some long-overdue boil-over, then I can't find a reason for this happening. Can you?"

"You realize there was an eighty-thousand-dollar policy on Gina Anderson?"

"Didn't know the figure. But that's a bullshit motive. He didn't even own a gun."

"Far as we know."

"There's no prior, no flags, no indicators."

"Come on, Jack, you were on the job. You know how it is. These people are like sleepers. They get up and go to work, day in, day out, have cookouts in the yard, fishing trips with the neighbors. Just like regular human beings. Then one night it turns out they're a pod person after all, the thing inside comes out, and bang—it's a whole different world and there's blood on the walls. Eighty thousand is more than enough, especially if there was something else going on in his life."

"That's just it," I said. "There *was* other stuff going on, but not the way you think. Things the investigators don't know about."

Blanchard stopped drawing on his pad. "Like what?"

"Couple months ago Anderson was a beneficiary in the will of a rich dead guy from Chicago. He received a check for a quarter of a million dollars."

Now I had his attention. "How do you know this?"

"A lawyer involved in the case. He's all bent out of shape over this and convinced Anderson didn't do it."

"Just because of the money? Proves nothing."

"I know," I said. "And that's something my guy hasn't considered, because he's never been a cop. You're thinking Anderson comes into this money, decides he wants to reinvent his life, and though he was okay with the wife and kid before, he doesn't want them hanging around his neck now, taking up space on his new beach towel."

"Why *did* you quit the job?" Blanchard asked. "Seems to me you might not have been the world's worst cop."

"But here's the thing," I said. "That check was never cashed. He had it for a month before he disappeared. Even if you've decided you're going to move to Mexico and grow fat on fish tacos and Dos Equis with a series of loud women, you're going to open an account and put that money in the bank. Not take the risk of this new life getting lost or stolen—or found out by your wife."

Blanchard's eyes were on the wall behind my head now, or at a point somewhere in between it and me. He ran his tongue around his mouth for a moment, then nodded once.

"Okay. Maybe. What's this guy's name? The lawyer?"

"Gary Fisher. I don't know the name of his firm."

"But he's on the level?"

"I've known him a long time."

"You got a number for him?"

"I left it back at the hotel."

He looked at me. "Right. Have it your own way, concerned citizen. I'll talk to some people, throw this into the pot. See if I can get anyone to care."

"Thank you," I said, standing up.

"We're here to serve. In the meantime go home and stay out of trouble."

"What?"

He stared me straight in the eye. "You just got that look about you. You did the first time I ever saw you."

I'd told myself I wasn't going to do it, but I'd known that I was lying. I did what I could to avoid it. I called Fisher, arranged to hook up later at the bar at the foot of Madison where I'd met Georj. I then took a long walk in the wrong direction, as the afternoon got grayer and darker and colder. As I walked, I noticed more than ever the shape of the land, the way it tilted sharply down toward Elliott Bay. Walking to the natural contours, seeing buildings only as things in my way, it was as if the work of man became insubstantial. I knew from my tourist visit with Amy that there had been extensive regrading work throughout the city in the last century. Given how hilly it remained, it would have been hard to imagine what attracted people in the first place, if you didn't know that the ridge had once been thickly covered in profitable trees. I cut diagonally down to hit First and kept going south. Followed the odd forty-degree swerve that First makes around the bottom of James, and continued toward

Yesler Way, where the streets suddenly run east-west instead of parallel to the water. I hadn't headed for this area in particular, but it seemed that whenever I went walking in Seattle it was where I wound up, as if the city tipped me down in this direction.

I stopped at the corner of First and Yesler, looking across at the totem pole on the corner of Pioneer Square. On the other side was the terra-cotta bulk of the Yesler Building, to its right a monstrosity of a parking lot, built in the sixties to replace the fine old Occidental Hotel and so ugly it helped spark the campaign that saved the old town from being leveled into yet more parking lots. A few homeless people walked this way and that in the drizzle, single men, shoulders hunched. The irrelevance of the surrounding buildings seemed even more acute here, as if they could have no bearing on these passing humans and their lives. These were street dwellers, not the building kind. If they had a home in this city it existed at ground level only, and the appearance of sidewalks and road surfacing had not changed it much.

I went and stood in Pioneer Square, under blood-leaved trees in front of the drinking fountain with the Indian's head on it, and read that it showed Seattle himself, chief of the local Suquamish tribe, one of the peoples who'd been living here before the white man came. This fountain, the city's name, and the totem pole appeared to be the sole memorials to the tribe's passing. There are middle-class dogs that have done better than that. I wondered if Seattle or his forebears had ever stood on the shores of the bay and seen tall ships in the distance and what their response had been. Whether they could have done things differently and, if so, whether anything would have changed.

There was something calming about the square, and I stayed awhile, sitting on a bench. Then I walked through the old town, stopping in the Elliott Bay Book Company, killing time any way I could. I stood in front of the bookstore's True Crime section, wondering if I had it in me to produce something that could be filed next to the single copy of *The*

Intruders they stocked. I doubted it, and wasn't sure I wanted to. The big local seller of the moment appeared to be a garish hack job on the darker corners of Seattle's last few decades. Arson and scandal. Famous suicides and murders. A long series of unexplained disappearances in the seventies, eighties, and early nineties, kidnappings of young girls, only a couple of badly mangled bodies ever being found, both having suffered abuse even this author balked at specifying, along with cuts into their faces so deep they'd gouged the bone.

I put the book back on the pile. I didn't want to write that kind of thing, and even if I had, someone had beaten me to it. In the end I bought a thin précis of the city's early history and wound up walking the streets again, until they ran out and deposited me unceremoniously in a tangle of busy new roads that showed so many twisting ways to go that ultimately there was no way to decide.

So I turned back around and tried to go some other place. Anywhere except where I'd been heading all along. But a little before five o'clock, I still found myself walking up Post Alley, in the direction of the Kerry, Crane & Hardy offices.

I went straight past their offices and checked out a couple of things. Then I returned to the corner deli with the window seats. I got a coffee and sat facing back up the alley. I had no way of telling if Crane was in there, and I told myself this was a good thing. I'd just sit awhile. Watch people go in, come out. Then people only coming out, and finally the lights dimming, and someone shutting and locking the door behind him at the end of the business day. Crane was a big wheel. Chances were that he'd be out of the office, sitting in some other people's boardroom, making them feel good about whatever he wanted them to do. That was his job, and when we met, I'd been able to tell that he would be good at it. He'd go straight from the meeting to dinner with a client, or home to his picture-book family, and that was for the best. Sooner or later I'd get tired and bored and thirsty and hoist myself up off the stool and go into the night.

I sat there forty minutes, becoming more and more convinced of this scenario. Then Todd Crane came out.

He was alone, and he looked preoccupied. I was paid up and ready to go, in position at the door within seconds. He didn't do what I expected, however. My scouting around had been to establish the closest entrance to the multistory parking lot. It was back up the alley, and I'd assumed that Crane would be the kind of man to arrive at work in something expensive. But he was walking toward me instead.

I faded back into the aisles of imported produce, but he walked straight past, eyes cast down and hands pushed deep into his coat pockets.

I slipped out of the deli and followed.

He walked quickly, heading for where the alley opened out into the underpass beneath the off-ramp. I would prefer privacy in which to ask this man if he'd been the person in the photographs Gary had taken, the man with his arm around my wife. I picked up my pace.

My phone rang. It was loud enough that I couldn't just let it go on. I pulled it out of my pocket, still walking, suddenly convinced it would be Amy. The screen did not say AMY, however. It said ROSE.

I don't know anyone named Rose. I put the phone up to my ear. "Who the hell—"

"Don't do this," said a woman's voice, talking very fast and loud, and then the connection was cut.

I thumbed the green key twice to call the number back, but it rang and rang and was not answered. I stared around as it continued to ring, looking back along the alley and up at the windows of the buildings, but could not see anyone.

By the time I gave up and ran down to the end of the alley, Todd Crane had disappeared.

chapter TWENTY-THREE

I was at the bar a while before the time I'd arranged to meet Fisher. I needed somewhere to think. And I needed to call home. I had to let Amy know I wouldn't be home tonight. The thought of her made me defensive and angry, though I didn't really know what about. The building in Belltown was Fisher's obsession, not mine: Amy's name on the papers didn't necessarily have any bearing on my life. We hadn't even known each other when she was involved. A business formality, a company name on a company deal. I hated having these questions to consider, however, just as I hated my inability to stop wondering who the man in the photographs was. In the end I gave up trying to prepare myself and just pressed her number.

"Hey," she said. She picked up quickly, as if she had already been holding her phone. Had she? Did it mean anything if she had? "What's the news in the bright lights? Thought you'd be home by now."

Her voice sounded as it always did. The telephone, though a remarkable device, is not designed for real communication, for the heavy lifting of personal interaction. For the big stuff, you have to be in the same physical space. Questions are asked and answered on a chemical level: Our species lived and loved and dealt with each other for millions of years before we developed language. It's still only ever background music.

"Been talking to a few people, took longer than I thought. Chance I may be able to grab a beer with a couple of crime reporters later on."

"That could work. You thinking of staying overnight?"

"Maybe. Okay with mission control?"

"Of course. I'll inform the kitchen. So it's looking like it might pan out, huh? The book idea?"

"Could be." I felt bad about lying to her. I realized I had a handful of text messages, mainly blank, a couple of photographs that didn't show much—and not a lot else.

"Well, that's good. And honey, sorry if I was down on the idea last night. I was in kind of a funny mood."

"Yeah, I got that." I took a deep breath and stepped closer to the precipice. "Is everything okay?"

"Oh, sure," she said. I couldn't tell whether she said it too quickly, too slowly, or in an entirely normal way. I was listening too hard. "Just work, you know, the usual work crap. Blah-blah-blah in the head."

"I thought moving out of L.A. was going to stop all that."

"It will. Give it time."

She said something else then, but I didn't hear it, as there was a surge of noise in the background.

"I didn't catch that."

"Sorry," she said quickly. "It's the TV—got a *Sex and the City* marathon about to start, and the microwave's set to ping any second now."

"So you're in a happy place."

"I am. You'll be home tomorrow, though, right?"

"Around lunchtime."

"Good. I miss you, trooper."

When she said those words, she sounded so like Amy, so like the person I'd known, and married, and stood beside on many days both short and sweet and long and hard, that I couldn't believe that anything was wrong, or that it ever could be.

It still took me a beat too long to say.

"I miss you, too."

Fisher had claimed Anderson as his smoking gun. I wasn't confident he merited this status, but I wasn't sure I had one either. Maybe I should just have *asked* Amy about the building up in Belltown—which presumably had to be the place the cabdriver had dropped her on the evening she went missing. But how could I bring it up? I'd actually be asking something else, and I wasn't sure I was ready to open that box. Even if it turned out to be empty, it would never be properly reclosed. Utterance is a one-way street. Questions can never be unasked.

My phone buzzed. I had a text message. It was from Amy, and it said:

Hav fun. Dn't drnk 2 much! :-D x

And it was a nice message, and it made me smile, but the smile didn't stick for long. Two instances—this and the message that morning—were enough to make me notice that a woman who had always written a smiley as :-) had recently begun using :-D instead and started employing shorthand. Previously she'd always pecked out every letter of every word. Why change, unless she was picking it up from someone else? Or was this just another piece of dust that meant nothing unless you piled it up with others, almost as if you were *trying* to make a heap big enough to cast a shadow?

I rubbed my face in my hands, hard, and shook my head, dismissing this for the moment. It was time to go back to what I'd been doing since losing Crane.

Trying to work out who the hell Rose was and what she was doing on my phone.

I'd already realized that the name coming up on the screen meant there must be an entry for it in my contacts. I'd checked and found that yes, I had such an entry. A phone number, and a name. ROSE. But I hadn't put it there. I'd owned the phone only about a month, having changed networks when we moved to Birch Crossing and discovered that my old provider's coverage sucked. I had fewer than twenty numbers stored, could place every one except this. I didn't even *know* anyone named Rose. Never had.

I selected the number and dialed it, as I had four previous times since whoever called herself by that name had derailed me—deliberately, I assumed—from having a private conversation with Todd Crane. As before, the number rang and rang, without being diverted to an answering service. I could have gotten access to a reverse directory, tried to find some information about it that way. But something told me it would be a dead end in any case.

So I kept returning to how the number could have made its way onto the phone. I could think of only one time it could have taken place. After the fight with the guys Georj had denied knowledge of, I'd found myself in the bar near Pioneer Place. There had been a long blank spot between my sitting on a stool there and waking up in the park. I'd evidently been very drunk. Could I have stored the number on the phone then, the number of some person I'd been talking to? I would have called this a possibility were it not for one thing. The name was all in caps. ROSE. I use upper and lower, always, and when I text, I spell out every word—just as Amy used to. You might think if I was drunk enough to enter a woman's name without remembering, then I'd have forgone typographical niceties, too, but that shows how little you know me. Being that drunk meant I would have been even *more* tight-assed about getting it right.

To prove to myself that I wasn't drunk, see?

So I was back to someone else putting it there. And that left me in the middle of my own question, a question I appeared unable to solve and had no one to ask about.

* * *

Just after seven, Fisher walked into the bar. He was with someone. They came to where I was sitting in the corner.

"Who's this?"

"Peter Chen," Fisher said. "A friend of Bill Anderson's. They were out together on the night that . . . you know."

Chen was one of those slender, round-shouldered guys whose body knows that its sole function is to chauffeur the brain around. I put out my hand, and he shook it. It was like briefly holding the hand of a child.

He looked at Fisher with mild accusation. "You said he wasn't a cop."

"Jesus," I said. " Listen, Peter, just sit down."

He did, diffidently. Looked dubiously at a small bowl of nuts the waitress had brought against my will.

"Why did you want reassurance you weren't being brought to talk to a policeman?" I asked. "You don't present like someone with problems with the law."

"Of course not," Chen said. "It's just that they're so wrong about Bill, and I'm tired of listening to them bad-mouth him."

"We're aware that Bill didn't kill Gina or Josh."

"You are?"

"I've heard enough to believe he wasn't that kind of man. And I've seen what happened to Bill's basement. He didn't do that himself."

Fisher interrupted me. "You've been in the *house*?"

I ignored him, kept Chen's attention. "So what do you think happened?"

"I don't know." He seemed a little more comfortable now. "Like I told the cops, Bill was on edge for a few weeks, maybe a couple months. I told them that, and they ran away with the idea that it was something in his personal life. But Bill didn't have one. A personal life. I mean, he had Gina, and Josh. He didn't want anything else."

"So what was bugging him? Any idea?"

"Not really. But I think maybe it was a work thing."

"Something to do with his job? At the college?"

Chen shrugged. "Don't know. Probably not, he would have said. We got hassles there, we all talk about it."

"Chew on it around the coffee machine."

"Exactly. Right."

Fisher spoke up. "But you think his work was involved?"

"Maybe. We've all got personal projects, you know—hobbies. We talk about them all the time. But for a while, I don't know . . . seemed like Bill was holding back."

I nodded. "And I'm assuming you haven't heard from him, right? No contact that you're keeping secret?"

"I wish." Chen looked down. "I keep my phone with me all the time. I sent him e-mails every day for the first two weeks. I still check all the time. First couple days, I even left the back door of my house unlocked. Gerry did, too." He looked up. "I think Bill's dead."

"Which e-mail address are you sending to? One associated with the college?"

"Yes."

"He's not going to be using that. Not going to be phoning you either. He knows that those will nail him. If he's innocent, he's terrified out of his mind and going through grief and survivor guilt simultaneously, and doing it on his own. That would be enough to put most people in a psych ward within two days. Right now he's probably one of the most paranoid individuals in the state. You've got no other e-mail address for him, something he can access anonymously on the Web?"

"No. I thought of that, but I don't know one. And he could have set one up anytime, used it to e-mail me."

"Except that as far as he knows, you buy the prevailing story and would try to trick him into giving himself up."

"No. He'd know I wouldn't do that."

"With respect, Peter, you have no idea what paranoia is like. What about online science forums, Usenet groups, anything like that? Virtual places you'd expect him to hang out."

Chen cocked his head. "Hadn't thought of that."

"He's hardly going to be swapping equations back and forth," Fisher said. "Given the position he's in."

"Of course not. But remember: For us, what happened to Bill is just a part of life. For him, it's everything that exists. If he's still alive, he's been in hiding for three weeks. He needs to talk to someone, very soon, and he's going to be trying to work out how. But he's going to be very scared of physical contact or anything he fears might lead a bad guy to him. We have to find a way of making that easier for him."

"But we have no idea where he is."

"He's in the city," I said. "He's not Rambo. I don't see him taking to the mountains with a hunting knife between his teeth. He has no money, because he'll know that an ATM will tag him. But he's a bright guy, and I'm sure he could panhandle enough cash for half an hour online. That's the best way I can think of trying to get to him."

I grabbed a napkin off the table and wrote my cell-phone number on it. I gave this to Chen.

"Go home," I told him. "Get online. Go to the places you and Bill and Gerry used to hang out. Leave messages. Don't make it obvious they're for Bill, but put something in them that will catch his eye and at the same time confirm it's from a friend. And put this phone number in it. Not in plain sight, obviously. Find a way of hiding it, but in a way Bill will get. Can you think of a method of doing that?"

He nodded quickly. I knew he would. He looked like a puzzle kind of guy. "Good. And try to communicate that there are people who believe he's innocent and that the person on the end of that phone line is one of them."

"Okay. But why your number? Why not mine?"

"Because if we're right, then someone who *wasn't* Bill broke his wife's neck and shot his son in the face before setting him on fire. Whoever Anderson makes contact with stands a chance of running into this person." I stubbed out my cigarette and looked at Chen. "Want that to be you?"

"Uh, no," he said.

chapter TWENTY-FOUR

When he'd gone, Fisher turned to me.

"You didn't say you were going to get into the house. I would've liked to have been there."

"Which is one of several reasons I didn't tell you," I said. "And there was nothing there for you to find."

"Jack . . ."

"Jack nothing. You pulled me into this by throwing my wife's name in my face. She's my interest here, and I'll do what I have to in order to find out what's going on. Just liked you turned up here with that friend of Anderson's without letting me know first."

"Bad idea? Talking to him?"

"Not unless he's involved with whoever killed Anderson's family."

"Christ—you think he is?"

"No, I don't. But you didn't even consider the question. What if Chen had let someone know that Anderson would be out of the house that evening? Or if he'd even agreed to make *sure* he was? If either of those were true, we've just put ourselves squarely on someone's radar."

Fisher looked down. "Jesus. I didn't think. Sorry. I'm . . . This isn't really my kind of thing."

"Remember that. Something else—when you called, you knew I'd been to Seattle. I want to know how you knew."

"Just happened to see you," he said, shrugging. "I didn't even mean to tell you about it."

"Where?"

"Road at the foot of Post Alley, near where the Kerry, Crane, and Hardy offices are."

"We just *happened* to be in the same place at the same time?"

"I have no idea why *you* were there," he said irritably. "I was on my way to try to talk to Crane. About the building in Belltown. I told reception I was interested in buying it. He wasn't in."

"Actually," I said, "he was. I'd just come from there."

"Oh." Fisher frowned. "Why?"

"I got a call the night before. From a cabdriver. He'd found Amy's phone in the back of his car." I hesitated before continuing. It felt disloyal to speak of Amy to Fisher, as if by doing so I was joining some campaign against her. But that was absurd. "There appeared to be discrepancies in her whereabouts. I went to see Crane to find out where her meetings were that day, to work out when I could return her phone."

"And?"

"He didn't know she was in town. Or so he said."

"But now you're wondering if he was the guy in the pictures I took."

I didn't answer. I didn't have to.

"I'm sorry, Jack," he said.

"I'm not convinced there's anything to be sorry about."

"I hope you're right. But the downside of what you've just told me is that we both visited Crane's offices within a half hour and mentioned your wife's name. We've probably put ourselves on *his* radar, don't you think?"

"Fine by me," I said. "I talked with the guy. I don't see him for murder."

Fisher said nothing. For just a moment, I began to feel

that my hands were not my own. "You're going to have to stop looking at me that way," I said quietly.

"What way?"

"Like we're back in school and I've said something naïve."

"That's just in your head, Jack."

"It'd better be," I said.

"You think Anderson will call?"

"I have no idea. Chen may be right. Anderson may be dead. Whoever took out his family could've caught up with him. He could've gotten randomly mugged. He could've thrown himself into the bay. I'll give him until midday tomorrow. Then I'm done."

"But what if he calls after that?"

"I'll redirect him to you. I don't care about Anderson. Neither do you, though I can see that it's interesting that Bill's odd mood maybe dates from around the time he received the check from Cranfield's will. I'm giving you twenty-four hours as a favor, and because you showed me something it's possible I need to know. After that, I'm going home. If I've got real problems, then it's there that they're going to be solved."

"Thank you for coming," he said. "I do appreciate it."

"Good. So buy me another beer."

Our waitress seemed to have been abducted, and so Fisher went up to the bar to deal direct. I watched him as he handled the girl there, saw the flash of his artless smile, and realized that in the end I'd wound up joining his game after all. He came back soon enough, and we set about doing what two men in a bar in a strange town usually do.

We got drunk.

Sometime later we were in Fisher's hotel. It was sort of in downtown but had little else to recommend it. Amy wouldn't have set foot in there, put it that way.

The guy behind the bar was an asshole, by which I mean

he wouldn't serve us. So we went upstairs. Fisher's room was large and frank in its rectangularity and had a window over yet another of the city's ubiquitous ground-cover parking lots. I looked out over this as Fisher turned on a couple of lights. People came and went with greater regularity than the need to park usually requires. Most of them didn't even have cars. Had I been in need of an easy drug collar, instinct told me the lot would be a good place to start. After a few moments, I spotted the seller, recognizing him instantly. Not because I'd seen him before but because I knew his type. The subspecies. Thin, pale, pinch-faced, with short, dark hair like a pelt, the kind of man you'll see emerging nonchalantly in the early hours from a car he's just broken into. Without morals, guilt, or empathy, culturally imbecilic. Ratlike, perhaps, though rats are actually far more noble, a species whose reputation we've sullied to provide a cheap symbol for members of our own, the ones prepared to gnaw their way into anyone else's life in the hope of an easy score.

The minibar was well stocked and proved willing to accommodate us. Fisher and I sat on opposite sides of the room, in its two armchairs. The walk had been cold and long. It was after eleven, and it had occurred to me to send a text message to Amy. I wasn't sure what. Something short. Preferably something nice. I knew I should probably not do this, at least not without a clearer intention in mind, and I'd already made the decision not to. Twice. But the idea evidently didn't feel it had been dealt with as it wished, and it refused to get out of my head. If things got much later, she'd be in bed.

I sat there, arms hanging over the side of the chair, head tilted back, not knowing what to do, feeling tired but as if I would never sleep.

"How come you don't have kids?" Fisher asked after a while.

"Amy works hard," I said, feeling bad.

There was another silence. Then Fisher spoke again. "I dream of her," he said.

I was confused. "Who?"

"Donna."

I struggled for a moment, then realized who he was talking about. I tilted my head down to look at him. "From school? The girl who killed herself?"

"Yeah."

I didn't know what to say. "I guess it's going to crop up. From what I could tell, it changed your life."

"It did," he said. "But you don't get it. I never used to think about her at all. What happened was bad, sure. I was screwed up over it for a while."

"It wasn't your fault."

"I know that," he said, with a very brief smile. "You told me back then, and I was grateful. To be frank, if we hadn't had the conversation at the track that afternoon, I probably wouldn't have remembered you at all. My point is, after a while I came to terms with what Donna did, realized I couldn't be held responsible for her choices. I was a kid, I was probably kind of dumb and definitely too full of myself—but neither of those is actually a crime, right? I didn't do anything to lead her on and certainly nothing to make her kill herself. I saw a therapist for a couple years while I was at college, and I gradually stopped feeling bad about it. I got on with my life. It was a pretty good life."

"Was?"

He ignored me. "She didn't cross my mind for years at a time after that—and when she did, it was like some story I'd been told, one that had a moral I'd already absorbed and didn't need to hear again. Then one night about a year ago, I dreamed about her."

He stared down at his hands. The light in the room was low, but it looked to me as if they were trembling.

"I dreamed I came home from work early, and the house was empty. I wasn't worried—I knew that my kids would still be in kindergarten and my wife would be at the store or having coffee with the neighbor. I had papers to go through, and so I went into the den. But after a while I thought I could hear water running. I couldn't figure out where the sound was coming from. Finally I realized it was upstairs. That's very odd, because I'm alone in the house, so I go to the bottom of the staircase. I look up." His face twitched. "And a shadow crosses the hallway at the top of the stairs."

"Did you go up?"

"Of course. It's a dream, right? It's all about me going up those stairs. I *ran* up them, in fact, because the shadow . . . it was pretty low on the wall. I have two little kids, and I'm worried. Scared. I run up the stairs convinced one of them is in trouble, and when I get to the top, the sound of the water is much louder. I run to the end of the hallway, and the door to the bathroom is closed. I pull at the handle, but I can't open it. I know there's no lock on the door—we had it taken off when the kids got old enough to shut themselves in. I kick it. I can hear someone inside, someone making a sound, no words, just a noise like they're frightened, and I know it's one of my kids. And I'm so desperate that I take a step back and throw my shoulder at the door, and suddenly it has no resistance and I go tumbling into the bathroom.

"There's no one in there. No water in the tub. The room's exactly as it should be. All my wife's shampoos in ten neat rows. Line of books above the john. A green plastic whale full of little kiddy toys for bathtime. Everything's fine. But then I hear this tiny *click*.

"I walk back out into the hallway, and one of the doors ahead falls open, just a bit. I reach for the handle, but suddenly I don't want to open it. The door's ajar enough that I can see through into my daughter's bedroom, a patch of carpet and a slice of wall. And I see a shadow fall across it, but this time it's too big for a child, and I hear the crib rustle as if someone has pulled aside the bedspread and climbed in, curled up into the space, and I don't understand how I know this, but I know that person is naked and she's waiting for me—but it's only when I start to push the door open that I realize it's going to be Donna lying in the bed."

He stopped abruptly. "And by then it's too late."

"Too late for what?"

He shook his head, as if either I should know already or he just couldn't say. "And since then I can't get her out of my head. I have that dream every couple weeks, sometimes more. Each time the door gets a little wider before I wake up. And I know that if it's ever wide enough for me to see her face, then I *won't* wake up. That I'll step in and she'll be lying there smiling and the door will close and I'll never get out again."

I wasn't sure what I could say. "We're getting older," I tried eventually. "Today's too muddy and confusing, and so you retreat to when it all seemed simpler, even if it actually wasn't."

He let out a short, harsh laugh. "What she did wasn't simple."

"I know, but . . ."

"There's something else. The dream kept coming back. I was exhausted, couldn't focus at work."

"Did you talk to anyone about it?"

"Not really. I never told my wife about it. I was so over the whole thing by the time we met. And . . . you know, when something's really in your head, if you *tell* someone else about it and they don't get it, don't understand its weight, you feel even worse for opening your mouth and blabbing your dark secret. So . . ."

He stopped again. Outside the window a police car went by, siren blaring. I imagined the dealer and his clients scattering like frightened mice, to return within minutes.

"But, so . . . anyway," Gary said. "How well do you remember Donna?"

"A little. I knew her some. She wasn't unattractive. Plus, you know, she died."

He nodded. "All the time I was in therapy at college, I was barely able to recall what she looked like at all. But after I started having the dreams, I could remember her in every detail."

"That's because—"

"Just shut up, Jack, and let me speak. So one Saturday afternoon I'm in the park with Bethany. My daughter. Just turned two. I'm pushing her around on one of those trike things, you know, a handle up out the back so they don't have to pedal. And I'm very tired because of work and not sleeping, and it's gotten real cloudy and is clearly going to rain, and I've basically had enough. I tell her it's time to go home. She turns and looks up at me, and that's when I see it."

"Saw what?"

"I don't know how to describe it. She was mighty pissed, because she wanted to keep going around the park, but that wasn't it. Not just that. There was something else coming out of them at me. Out of her eyes."

"I don't get what you mean."

He shrugged. "Over the next few days . . . Well, kids change week to week, even day by day. You know that. She's at that age. But . . ."

"But *what,* Gary?"

"A few weeks later, we're all having breakfast, the standard chaos, and my wife leans forward and peers at Bethany's face. 'How did she get that?' she says. I have no clue what she's talking about. She points to the side of Bethany's eye. And there's this little ding there. Like a little curve, a scar. I say I have no idea, didn't happen on my watch. Megan says it certainly didn't happen on hers. It escalates. And all the time while we're 'discussing' this, Bethany is watching me. I see this . . . *look* in her eyes again, and suddenly I know I've seen that mark somewhere before. I had to just leave the table. Immediately. I got up and left the house with Megan still glaring at me, pissed as hell. And as I'm driving to work, I finally get it."

His voice was dry now. "I think about these dreams I've been having for months, and how I know there must be some point to them. How they've got to be trying to tell me something. And bang—this thought hits me. It hit me so hard I have to stop the car. Where I'd seen that scar before. On whose face, in my dreams. Donna."

I was staring at him now. "Please tell me you're not serious."

"Of course I'm not. But you must have had times like this when you were a cop, when you thought, *Yes, that's what happened,* or *Yes, he's the guy,* and you're only saying what some part of you has already known for days or weeks. Then, when you finally get it, it's like everything drops into place, and you know you're right."

"Yeah, I know that feeling. But sometimes it just means you've got it so wrong that you've stopped making sense to anyone other than yourself."

Fisher wasn't listening to me, though. "For a second I actually wondered if she'd come back," he said quietly. "Donna. To get a lot closer to me this time."

I just sat there staring at him.

"I *know* how stupid it sounds," he said. "Worse than stupid. But why the dreams, Jack?"

"Because . . . Look. Did you ever sleep with Donna?"

"Jack, I really didn't notice that she existed. That was the *point.* That was what I felt so bad about, that there was someone who had thought so much about me and I barely registered she took up space on Planet Earth."

"Here's what I think," I said. "Donna is dead and gone everywhere except in your head. You still think what happened is your fault. But the truth is, you can't do anything about other people. Everybody's a pod person in the end. There's the person you know and the person you don't—the one who was around before you met them, who does stuff when you're not there, who will persist and do further things after you're gone. The person you *do* know becomes almost an extension of your own mind, your own self. So it's the one you *don't* know that's truly them."

"Yes," he said. "Yes. I guess that's right."

I nodded, pursing my lips like a sage eighteen-year-old, and for a moment it was as if the walls had shaded away and the two of us sat in chairs by the side of a deserted running track, as if all our friends had gone on to other things and left us far behind, and we would be left sitting there for all time.

I think we talked some more, but not much, and at some stage I fell asleep. I woke to the sound of ringing. I jerked my head up to see Fisher crashed out in the other chair, the red lights of the bedside clock saying 3:18.

The ringing sound was my phone. I fumbled it out.

“Yeah,” I mumbled.

“Is this Jack Whalen?”

“Who is this?”

There was a pause. “My name is Bill Anderson.”

chapter TWENTY-FIVE

Finally Shepherd called Rose back. He had more freedom than most, but there was such a thing as pushing it too far. He hoped she'd get it over with on the phone, but she insisted on meeting him face-to-face. She had wanted to do it in the old town, near the Square, but he said no. He'd never liked it there. The air was too rich. It felt crowded even when no one was around.

He arrived early. Victor Steinbrueck Park, past the northern end of the fish market, on the edge of what had once been a high bluff overlooking the bay. The grassed section was dotted with sprawled or sleeping homeless people, and a couple of the picnic tables also held small groups of the alcoholic and/or stoned. He could tell that these were not the only people present. The feeling was nowhere near as acute as it would have been at the Square, but it was stronger at night wherever you were. He felt it more and more now, everywhere. He took a table at the paved area near the front of the park, where he could look down across Alaskan Way and the traffic viaduct below to the wide open coldness of Elliott Bay. On a clear day, you could see right from the mouth of Puget Sound down to Mount Rainier in the south. Now it was all dark, and cloudy, and dead.

It was the first time he'd been motionless since reaching

the city, having spent the whole day on foot. He had been to a residential street up in the Queen Anne District. He had been to a plush hotel bar in downtown. He had worked the streets, up and down, walking the central area, the international district, and also Broadway, in a grid pattern.

He had not found her.

Rose arrived an hour late. She came by herself, but Shepherd noted that none of the derelicts did more than glance at a woman, not so tall, walking alone across a park at night. Far more than those at the center of society, people on the edge have a fine sense of whom to avoid. There is evolution among the dispossessed, too, natural selection at work through violence and bad drugs: They sense things that others do not.

She sat the other side of the concrete table and did not smile or say hello.

"Evidently I misunderstood," she said. "I believed that the idea was you returned calls right away. Not ignore them for three fucking weeks."

"I've been busy," he said. "Doing things you told me to do."

"And?"

Shepherd realized that lone figures, male and female, now sat at some of the other tables in the park, in nondescript clothing, could-be-anybody style. Another stood thirty yards away, a guy with short red hair. None was looking at him, and none looked familiar. He knew who they were, however. Others like him, people who carried their lives in a suitcase. He was intrigued that Rose had felt the desire to have protection tonight.

Assuming that was what it was.

He refolded his arms, allowing his right hand to slip inside his coat toward the gun there.

"The last one is done," he said. "Which was a waste of time. No one was going to listen to Oz Turner. But whatever. Anyone who ever communicated with Anderson over his thing is now dead. His notes were destroyed. It's finished."

"Are you kidding me?"

He shrugged. "He's vanished. Probably dead. So . . ."

"One of your colleagues got a sighting of him," she said. "Yesterday. He's still here in the city."

"If you've got someone who knows where he is, why don't *they* deal with him?"

"Because it's your responsibility. And your job."

"The situation is not my fault," he said calmly. "I said that whacking Anderson was unnecessary from the start."

"Strange. Word's always had it you're the go-to guy for black-and-white solutions. You were when we met."

"I still am. But once in a while that means choosing white. Getting Anderson fired would have been enough. They shouldn't have let one of the Nine try to handle it his own way."

"The others had no warning of it. Once Joe Cranfield had done what he did, it was always going to have to be tidied up. I was given the task of coordinating it. Yours not to reason why, Shepherd."

"Don't patronize me," he said. "I've been doing this since you were still shitting your pants."

"Congratulations. And your point?"

"After a while you start to reason why."

"But then you do what you were told in the first place, right? That's the deal."

The deal, yes. A cold wind came up across the bay. Shepherd's gaze was on the cars that came and went along the Alaskan Viaduct, donkeys following the carrots of their own headlights. When he'd been young, the big science-fiction ideas had included cars that needed no human intervention, that followed predetermined tracks. He wondered how many people realized that it had already happened, and you didn't even need a car.

"I'm worried about you," she said. "Are you okay?"

"I'm fine," he said.

"Really. You don't look so well."

He glanced away from the view to see that her sharp, gray eyes were on him. "I'm fine, Rose."

"I'm assuming you must be. Because of how dumb it would be for you not to say."

"Give me what you have," he said.

She handed him a piece of paper upon which something had been written. "No collateral damage this time. Don't fuck it up, in other words."

He looked up at her slowly and was glad to see her move back a little from the table. He was also aware, in the background, of the men and women at the other tables getting up, as if to protect her. He wondered just how far Rose's star had now risen.

"I won't," he said.

The others melted away, leaving Shepherd and Rose alone. They walked up the slope of the park past the tall, thin shapes of totem poles placed there by civic-minded individuals of the past who either had not known or did not care that such things had never been made by the local tribes, nor by any Native Americans at all, before the white men had arrived with their metal tools, and who had felt it reasonable to steal the city's poles, including the celebrated one in Pioneer Square, from Indian villages that lay hundreds of miles away.

Just before they got to Western Avenue, the boundary of the park, he stopped. Now was the time to get this under way.

"There's another problem," he said offhand. "Maybe. A girl's gone missing in Oregon."

"So?"

"I think she's one of you."

"What makes you believe that?"

"I tracked her down, had a conversation with her. She's extremely confused. It could be dangerous if she talks to anyone. She got away from me."

"That's clumsy."

"It was a public place."

She raised an eyebrow. "Some random kid runs away from home and you leap straight to a major crisis?"

"I've been doing this a long time, Rose. It's the way it works sometimes. They start to remember, things get ahead of themselves. A child, a good family, normal life, no history of problems—one morning they just disappear. Adults, too. Vanish off the face of the earth. Everyone assumes they got killed by accident or design or wound up two states away on crack. Not always so. They crop up elsewhere sometimes, yes. But alive. And feeling different about themselves."

She considered this. "And?"

"I think she's in Seattle. Or at least headed this way."

Rose swore. Shepherd knew that the very last thing this woman wanted was trouble in the city. Especially right now.

"When you say 'ahead of time'—how old is she?"

"Nine."

"Nine?" She stared at him. "Shepherd, do you know something about this that you're not telling me?"

"Me?" he said, holding her gaze. It was not easy. "I'm just here to serve."

"Kill her," she said, and walked away.

Shepherd watched her go and smiled.

chapter TWENTY-SIX

"He's not going to come."

"So he doesn't come," I said.

Fisher shook his head, went back to staring out the window. It was a little after eight. We were in Byron's, on the street level of Pike Place. You entered through the market, walked past bulky men bellowing about fish, and found yourself in a dusty, low-ceilinged and hazily sunlit diner that couldn't decide whether greasy breakfasts or strong cocktails were its main business. Some of the patrons couldn't either. In the center was a battered and grimy cook's station, around which battered and grimy men perched on stools sucking down one type of fare or the other, occasionally both. Some wore the stained white coats of men who'd already been up for hours shifting raw seafood and ice, others were dressed white-collar, on the way to work, and trying to look like they'd wandered in by accident and found a beer in their hand the same way. One wall was mainly glass and looked out over Elliott Bay. The tables along the side were occupied by tourist families in defensive huddles, patriarchs staring into guidebooks with a look of worried betrayal.

I had a bucket of strong coffee. Fisher tried breakfast. He had admitted he didn't drink much these days, and his leaden movements this morning confirmed he was out of practice. I didn't feel so hot either. When the waitress stopped by to offer more coffee I said yes and left Fisher to toy biliously with his congealing food, while I went to have a cigarette outside.

My phone conversation with Anderson had been short. He wouldn't say where he was. Wouldn't come to Fisher's hotel. Wouldn't let us come to him. Chose Byron's presumably on the grounds that it was a very public place. I said yes because I knew it, having nursed my head there the morning I woke in Occidental Park, before going to report Amy missing.

I stomped out the cigarette on the cobbled street and looked blearily at the people milling around. Tourists, market traders, adults, children. Selling, buying, browsing. Talking, shouting, silent. Everyone doing normal things, yet looking so strange. Bodies moving apparently with purpose, but controlled by intelligences whose existence I could determine only through their actions. Of course, it could have been the hangover.

To kill a few minutes, I walked across the way and got some money from an ATM. As I waited for the bills, I rubbed my eyes, hard. I needed to get my head together. I was feeling wide open, broken down, and far too tired.

Twenty minutes and half another coffee later, I spotted something.

"Okay," I said to Fisher. "I think we're on."

He looked up. The diner's door was jammed open, and through it you could see and hear the passing throng. There were intermittent gaps in the press of bodies outside, and through one I'd seen a man about thirty yards away, not far from where I'd stood to have a smoke. He was gone for a moment, then came back, a little closer. He was average height, gaunt. The skin around his cheekbones was gray and hung a little too loose, but in general he didn't look very different from many of the other people around, except in his eyes. He was either about to attempt to overthrow the American government by force or a man standing on the edge of a steep drop only he could see.

"That's him," Fisher said. "At least, I think. He's lost weight from the picture I saw."

I looked the man in the eyes and gave a small upward nod of the head. Sat back in my chair and indicated for Fisher to do the same, giving Anderson a chance to confirm that we were only two, that our hands were empty and on the table, and that we had another chair. Then I went back to my coffee.

A couple of minutes later, he sat down.

When seen close up, the bright, turgid fear in his eyes was terrible. I pushed my coffee toward him. He picked it up, took a gulp.

"You okay?"

He did something with his face. I don't know if it was supposed to be a smile. In his position I'm not sure how I would have answered either. It was a dumb question. Sometimes they have to be asked.

"I'm Jack," I said. "This is Gary. And I want you to know right away, Bill, that neither of us thinks you did what you're supposed to have done. I've been in your house, and I know it was the work of an intruder."

"I can't think about that at the moment."

His voice was husky, like he was fighting off the flu.

"Sure," I said. Not thinking about what had happened to his wife and child seemed to me a sound policy. I'm sure trauma counselors would advise differently, but they have homes and families to go to at the end of the day. "Where are you living?"

"Around," he said. "I keep moving."

"Do you have any money?"

"I had nearly fifty," he said. "I bought a toothbrush, soap. Cheap change of clothes. Some food."

I put my hand on the table close to his, moved it slightly

to partially reveal the money I had folded over small. When he saw it, his face threatened to crumple.

"No," he said, and shook his head.

"It's only a loan. I want it back."

After a moment's hesitation, his hand moved to where mine had been and then down into his pocket, and there was nothing on the table anymore.

"You want something to eat?"

He shook his head. "Coffee."

I waved to the waitress, and nothing was said until that was done. I knew that Anderson would need time to settle.

Fisher took the lead. "What happened, Bill?"

He shook his head again. "How am I supposed to know?"

"Why did you run?"

"Because I was afraid."

"You didn't want to get to the house, check if they were okay?"

"I would have run, too," I said. "You'd know that the neighbors would do whatever you could do. That the cops were on their way. And you also knew that whatever happened was no accident, too, right?"

Anderson was crying now. There had been no change in his facial expression or posture, no indication he knew it was happening. His cheeks had been dry, and now they were wet. He put his coffee cup unsteadily back on the table.

"I should have gone in there anyway," he said.

The truth was yes, he should have—assuming he could've held back from contact with his wife or child, thus muddying what might otherwise have been a strong forensic defense. But he didn't need to hear that.

"You're going to feel that way, of course, but it's the past and there's no changing it. They were dead before you entered the street. There was nothing you could have achieved except getting caught or killed, too. You understand that, right? It's important that you do."

He didn't say anything. Up at the cook's station, the grill

flared suddenly, as a couple more burgers got flipped. Two children down at the far end of the diner were bickering about something, noisily, going at it so hard you almost believed they'd remember what it was tomorrow.

"Bill," Fisher said, "I know it's tough, but—"

"Oh, you know?" Anderson said. He turned away from us, the action resolute and possibly permanent. "You have absolutely no . . ."

His head dropped. He wasn't going to say any more.

Fisher made a face. I let a silence settle, allowed Anderson to follow whatever thought was in his head and be left empty when it had gone.

"My father was murdered," I said.

It felt strange to say it, to unearth this fact that lay as a semipermanent coloration in the back of my mind and had for so long that it was hard to believe that everyone didn't already know. Strange, and also calculating. But if anyone was entitled to use this information, surely it was me.

Fisher stared at me. "I never knew that."

"You wouldn't. It happened a couple years after we left school. While I was at college."

"Who killed him?"

"I don't know," I said, and by now Anderson was looking at me. "We never found out. I was away. My mother was visiting her sister overnight. Somebody broke in to the house. My father came downstairs, found them. He was not a man who was going to back down in that circumstance. They killed him—deliberately, accidentally, I don't know—and then they took the stuff anyway. An old television and VCR, a handful of jewelry, and around eighty dollars in cash."

Fisher looked as if he didn't know what to say.

"I'm not equating this with your loss," I told Anderson. "Point is, I can't bring him back. You can't bring your family back either. Somebody came into a place that was not theirs and took these people. They had no right. The question is, what do you do about it?"

Anderson sat completely still for maybe a minute. Then he turned back to face the table squarely.

"What *can* I do? The cops think I did it."

"So tell us something that will help them see it differently. Like what this has to do with a check you received for a quarter of a million dollars."

His eyes went wide. "How the hell do you know about that?"

I nodded to Fisher. I wanted a cigarette. Talking to Anderson was making me sad beyond belief, and I didn't want to do it for much longer.

"I'm working on Joseph Cranfield's estate," Fisher said. "I'm a lawyer. You were one of a very limited number of individual beneficiaries. I couldn't help noticing that the check was never deposited. Why?"

"I never met the guy," Anderson said. "I never even heard of him. Then one morning there's this ridiculous check. I have no idea what to do with it, why it's there, nothing. But there's a letter with it."

"I know," Fisher said. "I wrote it."

"Then where the hell do you think you get off?"

"What?"

"Sending someone that much money, with conditions like that?"

"What do you mean? What conditions?"

"You wrote it, you know."

"The letter I wrote just said, 'Here's the money, have a ball.' And where it had come from. Nothing else. There were no conditions stipulated in the will."

Anderson kept looking at Fisher, evidently not inclined to believe him. For a moment I wasn't sure either, but Fisher's face was just too confused.

"What was in the letter you received?" I asked.

There were two small spots of color on Anderson's cheeks now, livid against the gray. "It said this Cranfield person had bequeathed me the money on the condition that I stop my work. That if I did so, the money was mine. That if I took the money and kept working, there would be consequences. And, between the lines, that I'd better take the money."

"What work? Teaching at the university?"

"No," Anderson said, and for a flicker of a moment he looked cagey. "A private project."

"Private?" Fisher said. "Private from whom?"

"Everybody."

I remembered the way the basement workshop in his house had looked. "So how did Cranfield even know about it?"

"I have no idea. I was in contact with a couple of people on the Internet. Had a few covert discussions. All I could think is, the information got to him that way."

"And you made the decision not to take the money?"

"Yes."

"Did you tell anyone that's what you were doing?"

"No. I just didn't take the check to the bank."

"Do you still have it now?"

"It was in the house."

Fisher was looking into the middle distance. I imagined I knew why. He'd thought he was running the Cranfield estate, or at least in charge of his end. But someone had replaced his letter to Anderson, and somebody had been monitoring the account from which the bequest had been drawn. How else would they have known that Anderson had refused to be paid off, setting in motion the visit to his house three weeks earlier?

"How could they have done that?" I asked. "Replaced the letter?"

"It was part of a batch of stuff that went via Burnell and Lytton's office," Fisher said quietly. "One of them must have done it."

"Did you lose everything?" I asked Anderson. "In the fire? Relating to the work, I mean?"

Anderson nodded. "Everything. I forgot to take my backup with me that night. Only place any of it's left is in my head."

"What was it?" Fisher asked. "What were you working on?"

"I can't tell you."

"Yes," Fisher said firmly. "You can. I have to know more."

Maybe it was only the harsh morning glare coming at him through the glass, but right then Fisher looked a little strange. The lines at the corner of his eyes were pronounced, his mouth thin.

"More?" I said. "I didn't realize that you knew anything at all about this."

Fisher looked away, and I knew he'd been lying to me.

"What Gary means," I said, turning to Anderson, "is that it would assist us if you could give an indication of what led to the events that occurred in your house. To help the cops look at this differently, we need to build a credible case toward an alternative perpetrator."

"How do I know you're not one of them? Or that *he* isn't?"

"You don't," I said. "Neither of us has a badge saying 'Certified Good Guy.' If that's what you need, you're going to have to wait until you get to heaven."

"I'll tell you," he said, looking at me.

The implication was clear. I turned breezily to Fisher. "Gary. Wonder if you might want to get some more coffee for Bill? I could use a refill, while you're at it."

Fisher kept his face composed. "Whatever you say."

He got up stiffly, walked toward the counter. Anderson looked around the restaurant for the hundredth time, eyes darting in every direction.

"Going to give you a tip," I said. "Don't be looking around the place like that the whole time. If you want to be invisible, then you have to look like you're heading from A to B and you have the right to pass through all points in between. If a cop with time on his hands catches you doing the shadows-in-every-corner thing, he'll check you out just on the off chance."

"How do you know?"

"Because I used to be one."

"You're a *cop*?"

"Listen to all the words, Bill: *used* to be. Not anymore. Not on their side necessarily. Though I know they're not all assholes either. You would be the main suspect for this case in any town in the U.S.A., trust me. Cops learn to break situations down according to the way they usually shake out. It saves time. It can save their lives. You've fallen on the wrong side of that process, but it doesn't mean that the police are the axis of evil. Your best-case scenario right now is to get yourself to the point where you can go to them instead of hiding."

Anderson shook his head. "How can I—"

"Tell me what this is about," I said. "I get that it's private. Something even Peter Chen doesn't know about. It's not my business, and I don't even really care. But right now you're running out of options, and this secret has already gotten people killed."

"You're not going to believe what I tell you."

"Somebody evidently does," I said. "So try me."

He hesitated for a long time. I glanced toward the counter to signal to Fisher that I might be getting somewhere, but he wasn't there. In the restroom, I guessed, or maybe he'd stomped outside. He was in a very spiky place this morning, especially for someone who'd found what he was supposed to be looking for.

When Anderson finally spoke, I knew it was not just in the hope that I might be able to help him but also because it was something he'd kept to himself for a long time. It's not true that everyone wants to confess a crime, but most people do want to tell something of their story, to stop hiding for just a while.

"My field is wave dynamics," he said. "Specifically those relating to sound. At college I just cover the physics of it, basically. But a couple years ago, I started to get interested in broader issues. How sound affects us in other ways."

"Like how?" I said. After only a few sentences, I was

finding it hard to believe that this was going to relate to anything of importance in my world.

Anderson's response showed he'd read something of this in my face. "Sound is underestimated," he said earnestly. "We all go on about *seeing* things, but sound is a *lot* more important than people realize. It gets taken for granted. Everybody knows we played heavy rock at Noriega to flush him out. Some people know that music was used when the FBI stormed Waco. But there's a lot more to it than bombarding people with tunes they don't like. You go to a restaurant where there's loud music, and see how much less you enjoy eating. You can't concentrate on the food—you almost can't even *taste* it. Part of the brain switches off. Or you hear a piece of music, some song, for the first time in years, and it takes you right back to the time you associate with it. You'll feel the same, even remember smells, tastes, relive other sensory data from this other time. You know this, right?"

"I guess. Yes, I do."

Talking through something he cared about seemed to have momentarily helped Anderson forget the rest of his world. "Or you're alone at night, in a place you don't know—and all at once you hear a noise. It doesn't matter that you can't *see* anything wrong—suddenly sight doesn't rule the roost anymore. You don't need to see anything to be scared out of your wits. Your brain and body understand that sound matters a whole lot."

"Okay," I said. I knew I had to let him talk, but for some reason I felt unsettled, uncomfortable. I still couldn't see Fisher, and this was beginning to stretch the length of a viable trip to the john. "I'll take your word for this, Bill. You're the science guy. But what's your point? What were you working on specifically?"

"Infrasound," he said. "Very-low-frequency sounds. Most people have been looking at eighteen hertz, but I went to nineteen hertz. It has . . . effects. Your eyes may water or blur when you're exposed to it. You can get odd sensations in your ears, hyperventilation, muscle tension—a physicist called Vladimir Gavreau actually claimed that infrasound is a key component in urban anxiety. More simply, it just makes you feel like you're afraid. And if you hit the resonant frequency of the human eye, which is right around this point, you can start thinking you're *seeing* odd things, too. Everyone's been assuming this is physiological, just a side effect of the physics of the eye, but it's . . . not. It's more complicated. Infrasound does strange things to us. Very strange things. It enables us to glimpse things we can't normally see."

I found myself looking around the restaurant, just as I'd told Anderson not to do. I saw nothing to explain what I was feeling, a sensation I didn't even know how to describe. I looked out through the open door into the crowds. Just people, moving back and forth.

"What kinds of things, Bill? What are you actually talking about here? What was it that you did?"

I pulled my eyes back to him. He was looking down at his hands. When he spoke, his voice was very quiet.

"I made a ghost machine," he said.

But that's when I saw a tall figure heading toward the diner through the crowds, walking quickly. He was dressed in a dark coat and looking not left or right but straight at Anderson.

"Get down," I said quickly.

Anderson blinked at me, confused. I tried to stand, pushing him to one side as I rose, but I got caught under the table. I saw Fisher coming around the side of the center station, coffee cups in hand, just as the man in the coat pushed his way into the restaurant and removed one hand from an inside pocket.

I finally got clear of the table and shoved Anderson harder, shouting, "Bill, *get out of the—*"

It was too late. The man fired three times, measured, unhurried shots from a silenced handgun.

He'd disappeared back into the crowd before I even realized that none of the bullets had hit me. The shots had been quiet, but the sight of Anderson's blood as it sprayed across the window was not—and everybody started running and shouting at once. When I bent over Anderson's body and tried to find where he'd been shot, I couldn't hear what he tried to say to me through the noise and the blood welling up out of his mouth, but I saw it open and close and knew it would be for the last time.

chapter TWENTY-SEVEN

"He's dead."

I looked up to see Blanchard standing over me. It was two hours since Anderson had been shot, and I was sitting in a plastic chair in a corridor of a hospital I didn't know the name of. A crowd of cops were standing down the far end. I'd been interviewed by two of them.

"So where does that leave us?"

"No idea," he said. "And there is no 'us.' Be clear on that. I'm only here because I used to partner one of the lead detectives. You're here as a courtesy and because witnesses are very firm on how you reacted when the gunman came in. Where's your buddy? Fisher?"

"Getting some air."

Blanchard sat down heavily in the chair beside me. "What the fuck happened? Really?"

"What I told you. We got a message to Anderson through one of his colleagues. He came to talk to us."

"Why? That's what I don't get. Why you?"

"Maybe because our pitch was that we knew he didn't kill his family. We arranged to meet at the diner, at Anderson's suggestion. How the guy with the gun found him, I have absolutely no idea."

"What did you get out of Anderson?"

"He'd barely started to open up before it happened. He received the check I told you about but didn't do anything with it because it came with conditions he wasn't prepared to meet."

"Which were?"

"That he stop work on some private project."

"Which was?"

"We were getting into that when the ceiling fell in."

Blanchard turned to look at me but didn't say anything.

I shrugged. "Believe what you like. I was helping Gary out. Now that Anderson's been found, it's over. It's up to your guys to sort out the mess."

"Mess?"

"This makes Anderson a strikingly less credible suspect for the double homicide, don't you think?"

"Doesn't have to be any link between the two events."

"Yeah, right. I'll just bet everyone in SPD is telling themselves that. Better than admitting they spent a month looking for an innocent man and not finding him before someone came from nowhere and blew him away."

"Anderson fucked himself. He should have turned himself in. Gotten in contact, at least."

"That what you would have done under the circumstances?"

"Yes."

I nodded slowly. Truth was that I still didn't really get why Anderson had done as he had. I'd only intercepted when Fisher had pushed him on it because I knew that increasing Anderson's feelings of guilt was not the way to get him to talk. Coupled with the caginess of his response when talking about his work, however, plus Chen and others' view that he'd been on edge before the murders took place, I believed that Anderson had felt himself to be in a dangerous position even before the events of that night. The covering letter with the bequest had carried ominous weight. Was that enough to explain his running from the scene? Or was it something inherent to the work he'd been doing? Was he already spooked?

"Yeah," I said. "Me, too."

I got up. There was nothing more for me to do here. "I appreciate the way you've dealt with this."

"You're welcome. Just don't make me regret it."

"What do you mean by that?"

He looked down at his cupped hands. "I know a little more about the circumstances under which you left the LAPD," he said. "We wouldn't want anything like that happening here."

"Whatever you think you know isn't what really happened."

"I know there were some dead guys involved. And you."

"Am I in jail right now?"

"No. But what I just said still holds."

"Gotcha." I started walking away.

"Jack," he said when I'd gotten about ten feet. "How deeply are you tied in to Fisher's universe?"

I stopped, turned back. "Not at all. Why?"

"Keep it that way. I also talked to someone in Fisher's firm. Why do you think he's here?"

"He's tying up loose ends for them."

"Wrong. He's on enforced leave. 'Personal reasons.' The colleague I spoke with was very discreet. But I got the sense they were distancing themselves. If I were you, I'd do the same. I think there's stuff going on in that guy's head you don't know anything about."

I left, walking more quickly now. Fisher was not standing in front of the hospital. That could have been because of the media presence beginning to build there—the killing had been pretty public—but he wasn't answering his phone either.

And when I got back to his hotel, the man behind the desk told me he'd checked out a half hour before.

* * *

I retrieved my car and drove out of town. On the way down to the freeway, I pulled over opposite Pioneer Square. I got out on impulse and walked over to it. My hands were shaking. I don't know why. Because of Anderson. Because of what Blanchard had brought up about things that had happened in L.A. I sat on the bench for twenty minutes, taking deep breaths, until I felt okay again.

Then I left the city, headed east toward the mountains. The morning was clear and bright at first, a few fluffy clouds only for decoration. Traffic was light, and I seemed to slip along almost too easily, as if the world was colluding in letting me run from a place where I'd been instrumental in a man's death.

As I pulled toward the top of the Cascades, it began to get colder, the scene more muted, rusty dogwood the only color among the trees and bushes, their stems looking a little too much like sprays of dried blood. The sky frosted over, and clouds crept down out of it to touch the land, roosting in trees like the ghosts of long-ago campfires, a damp and silent echo of the lives of the people who had once lived peacefully here with the wood and the earth and the water.

Would something of this kind persist now in Byron's, the impression of a man sitting hunched at a table in slanting morning sunlight, or would people sometimes see or sense a shape at the door or the window of the house up on Broadway, the remains of a man trapped on the other side of a curtain, trying to find his way home?

A shadow of my father had remained in our house in Barstow after his death, I knew that much. My mother had lasted only five months before selling the place and moving to be closer to her sister, of whom she was not overly fond. I went home for the weekend perhaps three, four times during that period, and each time the house felt as if it had been dismantled while I was away and put together again exactly the same. I always felt like I was trying to catch up with what had happened in it, partly because of the way I'd received the news.

At college I had a notably progressive professor who, among other fine qualities, was open to having favored students hanging out at his house on Friday evenings and—while engaged in suitably brainy talk—helping themselves to the alcohol-based contents of his fridge. It had been on a morning following one of these freewheeling tutorials that I'd woken to the knock of two cops on my dorm-room door. I was hungover, majorly freaked out—there was a small stash of marijuana in my drawer—and their presence made me feel caught out, late, permanently off balance.

My father was found on the kitchen floor, wearing pajama bottoms and nothing else. He'd heard something in the night, come down to investigate—as men must. He had suffered extensive stab wounds from a large, serrated hunting knife but died of blows to the head from a claw hammer. The hammer lay next to him on the floor. It was his. I'd been with him when he bought it, on a Saturday-morning walk, and had watched him use it to mend chairs and fences and put up pictures. As I'd told Anderson, the intruders had stolen little. The household's money had always gone toward making sure that there was good food on the table, that I had clothes and the books I needed for school. The stuff that matters can't be taken—except, I suppose, for fathers: stolen by strangers looking to finance the evening's drinking or a new set of tires or a bet on a horse that was already set to lose.

It was clear that whoever had shattered Bill Anderson's life had not been on so mundane a quest. In a few days, it would rotate off the television and radio coverage, but not out of my life. I had lied to Blanchard. Up until 8:51 that morning, Anderson's existence had been of tangential relevance to my own. But no longer. There is an intimacy to carrying someone else's blood on your hands, in seeing their eyes as they realize the sharp and finite limit to how much more of the world they themselves will see. Anderson's soul had now been nailed to my own, which meant that Joe Cranfield's estate and the building in Belltown were problems I had to solve, together with the question of how this related to my wife.

By the time I turned off onto 97 and started into the woods toward Birch Crossing, I knew that this was something I could not now let go of, and that this would not be a good thing for me, or for others. The God of Bad Things still knew where I lived. He always would. If I did nothing, he would come and find me anyway.

Maybe it was time to take the fight to him.

chapter TWENTY-EIGHT

Madison's second night on the streets had felt even longer than the first. After going to see the silly man in his office—an episode that was a little cloudy to her now—she had walked for quite a while. She bought some food at a small market and ate it in a park, and cried for a bit, then went walking again, going on and on, long after all the stores and restaurants were shut, keeping to alleys and moving within shadows. She stood for a while in front of a building that was boarded up, even went and pressed on one of the buzzers. She took out the keys she'd found in the back of the notebook, tried them in the door. They did not fit. This annoyed her a great deal. Something had been stolen from her, she now believed. This was where it was.

She turned away from the building and stalked back into downtown and along near the Barnes & Noble, past the public library with its weird glass and metal. She let herself be led down the right side of the slope, diagonally toward the bay. She walked for so long that after a while it seemed to her that she was asleep and only *dreaming* that she was a little girl, always on the move, trying to find something she knew was important. The only problem was, no one had ever told her what that something was. She finally wound up in an area from which she had no inclination to move. It was a tiny park in front of an old building, but there was nothing obviously special about it—except, she noticed, that the building had the name "Yesler" on it, one she recognized from reading the notebook. The park had no grass, just trees and a covered place to sit and a totem pole. There was also a small statue of an Indian chief's head, where you could get a drink of water.

She had to move away often, because there were others around, homeless people who appeared on the corners of streets opposite and wandered over to stand in the park for a time, not doing anything, before shuffling on. Sometimes they took a drink of water. They seemed to want to be there for a while, but not to stay. She wanted to stay, but she could not. When you're a little girl you're not allowed to do a *lot* of things. Being a little girl sucked. She had never realized just how much before now, how bad it could make you feel.

Eventually she just got too tired to keep moving. She climbed over a low wall and found a door where the bottom half was broken, and via a short passage made her way into a parking lot that was shaped like a sinking ship. On the very top level was a single car, left alone and by itself overnight.

The car was like her, she decided. The back door was unlocked.

She climbed in and made herself comfortable.

And woke, very suddenly, an hour later. For a moment she had absolutely no idea where she was. But there was something else that she *could* remember now. Very clearly.

She pulled out the Post-it note and pen from her pocket and quickly wrote down the four numbers in her head, as fast as she could, convinced that they would be snatched away from her as they had been before.

But no, this time she made it. She counted the numbers, feeling her heart start to race. It looked like enough. It finally looked like the whole number.

Moving quickly now, she got out of the car and ran down through the parking lot and back out through the passageway. She emerged in the side street and spun around, looking for a phone. Couldn't see one and started running again, knowing that this would draw attention but also that she had very limited time.

She ran and ran until she finally found a phone that worked. She grabbed the handset and stabbed in the numbers from the piece of paper. She let out a short, fierce shout of triumph as she got the last one done.

Hopping from foot to foot, she waited until she heard it picked up at the other end and a voice—and then she started to babble, talking as fast as she could.

But a blackness poured down across the inside of her eyes, and she stopped being able to hear what she was saying. She fought it, as she had fought in that man's office the previous afternoon and seemed to be always fighting now, struggling against this dark cloud that got thicker and thicker around her, a cloud that sparked and was lit from within with thoughts and memories that made no sense, that made her want to do bad things. She screamed in her head and pushed harder and harder, trying to keep them away from her.

But the next thing she knew, she was walking away from a phone that was now broken, and the piece of paper that had been in her hands was shredded to pieces and floating away on the wind, and her knuckles hurt, and when she realized that there was blood on her hands, her first thought was surprise that for once it was her own.

She was woken again sometime later by the sound of a car door opening.

"Jesus Christ," said a voice.

Madison sat up quickly. She was back in the car, and it was bright now. She felt like she'd slept for quite a while. She felt a little better, too. Less . . . confused.

A man was standing outside the car, staring wide-eyed at her. He had pale skin and sandy hair. He was looking not at her face but lower down. She looked, too, and saw that both her hands were speckled with patches of dried blood. There was a little on her coat, too.

"It's okay," she said, though actually she now realized that her hands hurt quite a lot. "I'm fine. I broke a phone, that's all."

"What are you *doing* here?"

"I needed somewhere to sleep. You left the door unlocked. Don't worry. I haven't stolen anything."

"That's . . . look . . ."

The man evidently didn't know what to do. He was wearing a suit and a tie and had the glaze in his eyes that Madison's dad did when he was *really* busy and was having trouble seeing past the front of his own head. But he obviously also believed he had to do something nice.

"It's okay," she said soothingly. "I'm fine. Honestly."

"I need to . . . I'll take you to the nearest police station. Come on."

"That really won't be necessary," Madison said, slipping out of the car and smiling up at him.

"I think it kind of is. Necessary. I can't just . . ."

She shook her head. "What time is it, friend?"

"What? It's nearly midday. But . . ."

"Perfect," she said. "Thanks for everything. I shall recommend your facilities *very* highly."

She reached her right hand up toward him. Disconcerted into an automatic response, the man shook it limply. Madison shook his hard and then walked away. As she started down the stairs, she turned and glanced back. He was still standing there, looking down at his hand. She knew he wouldn't be coming after her. She'd never understood how easy it was to deal with grown-ups, after you realized most of them were basically frightened of you. Sure, moms and dads were okay with their own children, but they always watched other children out of the corner of their eyes, as if all other kids were wild and ungoverned. And children could be, Madison knew. Little girls had a power and light all their own. It was something most grown-ups couldn't see—but something that, once glimpsed, you wanted to share. You wanted to spend time with them, to get to know them thoroughly, get to know them very well. This was what the man in the yellow car in Portland had been about, she now realized, though he'd been an amateur. He didn't know you could find the spark and keep it, too. If she had her time again, she would have talked to the man properly, told him what she knew.

She emerged from the parking lot and walked down toward the square with the totem pole and the drinking fountain. A lot of things were clearer to her now, even parts of the notebook that had originally been inexplicable:

The seven ages of man?

Of course not. As with everything, there are nine.

By 9—we must be rooted, living securely above or below. 18—we may start pulling strings. By 27—there should be sufficient control to be consistent in aim. At 36—adulthood, true Dominance begins. 45—without integration, the crisis point. 54—the age of Power. 63—Wisdom. At 72—the search starts again. 81—time to leave: we do not die as others do, and so the parting of this place must be under our control. Add the numbers which make up these nine ages—3 + 6 or 7 + 2—all in turn resolve to a digital root of 9. So it has been enshrined, hidden in plain sight. A triangle = 180° (1 + 8 + 0 = 9); the square and circle are 360° (3 + 6 + 0 = 9)—all regular geometrical shapes have a digital root of 9. Even 666—do I need to tell you by now to add those three numbers, and then add them again?

This is not an accident. Our mathematics was created to honor the power of 9. To the power of the Nines. But the Nines themselves have become weak in the meantime, spiritualized, have even come to believe in their own cramped version of the lies. To believe that our power must be constrained, that we must enter life as a newborn—must hide in plain sight, just another tree in the forest.

But the forests have all been cut down.

I will not fall with them. Did Aristotle not say "The weak are anxious for justice and equality: the strong pay no heed to either"? What happens to those who do not believe as the Nines do? Those who dare contradict them? Ah—over those souls, the truly free, then they would make themselves gods, sitting in judgment upon us.

St. Thomas Aquinas said: You must know a soul by its acts.

You are free to know me by mine.

And Lichtenberg said: We imagine we are free in our actions, just as in dreaming we deem a place familiar which we then see doubtless for the first time.

I am what you dream
I watch your back, always.
I am what guides your hand.

As she entered the square, she caught sight of her reflection in a plate-glass window and was surprised at how short she was. She looked at herself for a long time, remembering the day when she and Mom bought the coat in Nordstrom's, at the head of Courthouse Square in Portland. Remembered the two of them seeing it for the first time and knowing they were circling it together, that it was *really* expensive but they both wanted it in their lives. Madison had said nothing, knowing that this was a decision her mother had to come to under her own steam, that an extravagant spur-of-the-moment gift would appeal to her sense of hip motherhood, where acceding to a demand—however muted or subtle—would not: Madison not understanding how she knew this, but knowing it all the same.

They left the store and walked around others, looking but not really looking, and Maddy had known that if she just kept quiet and was sweet, they would find themselves back in Nordstrom.

They had.

And she realized now how she'd known how to get what she wanted that day, and on other days. She realized that something within her had always known how to dominate, how to quietly get people to do what she wanted. Someone had been at her back then, too.

He had always been inside.

It was nice in the square, but it did not feel as it had at night. Though there were more people around, it somehow felt less crowded. Maybe that was because the people here now were not the same. They were not like the homeless men, but rather were tourists, passing through. People who took pictures of things instead of seeing them, who thought they owned a place because they stood in it, instead of understanding it worked the other way around.

One of them was different, though. When she'd been there about half an hour, sipping her way through an Americano from the Starbucks on the corner, Madison saw an SUV pull up on the other side of the street. A man got out. He walked straight through the traffic and into the square. He didn't seem to be there for any reason, but sat on a bench for a while. He was quite tall and had broad shoulders and for a moment Madison had an urge to run over to him and tell him her name and ask him to help. She could see that he was different from the man whose car she'd slept in, that if *this* man knew that there was something he should do, then he would not stop until it was done.

But instead she found herself slipping off the bench and walking quickly out of the square—not looking back until she was sure the man wouldn't be able to see her. Madison might want the man's assistance, but the man in the cloud did not. She dimly recalled the attempted phone call in the night—largely through the aftereffects on her hands—but not what it might have been about. Instead she realized that she now wanted to make another call, to the man she'd previously been avoiding. She felt stronger now. She could deal with him.

When she located a phone—this time in the lobby of a hotel a few streets away, a fancy one with an awning with red and gold stripes—she got out the notebook and removed from it the white card with the number on the back.

He answered immediately.

"It's me," she said. "I need some information."

"Where are you?"

"Did you hear what I said, Shepherd?"

"Look," the man said. His voice was patient and annoying. "I want to help. But I need to know where you are. You're nine years old. You're . . . not safe."

"Are you done talking?"

"No," he said. "Madison, nothing's going to happen until you tell me a place to come and meet you. Do that and we'll talk. I'll find out whatever it is you need to know. But you're making it hard for me to do my job."

"You've *done* your job," she said. "And have been paid. Despite the fact that you didn't do as you were told, did you? Which means I have no reason to trust you."

"What did I do wrong? I came to you—"

"*Too early.* You were supposed to wait until I was eighteen, like always, but you wanted your fee *now* and didn't care that I wasn't ready. But I *am* ready, in fact. I've *always* been ready to take control. Though I guess you remember that. You had better anyway."

"Look," the man said. "You had an accident, that's all. You fell over on the beach. You saw me there and thought I meant you harm. You started to run, you banged your head. Your hurt yourself. That's why you keep blacking out. That's why you're having these strange—"

"Oh, *do* shut up, Shepherd. I'm going to ask you to find

out something. Then I'm putting the phone down. I'm going to call again in fifteen minutes from a different location. If you don't give me the information—and make me believe in it—I'm going to start doing things that really *will* make your life difficult. Doing things and telling things. Understand?"

"Madison, you've got to trust me."

A wheedling note had entered the man's voice, but Madison knew that this was fake—him trying to appear weak, caught off guard, in the hope she'd fail to take him as seriously as he deserved. This man didn't wheedle. "I've done everything you want. . . ."

"No," she said coldly. "You *haven't.* But you're going to. You really are. You and everyone else."

She told him what she needed and put the phone down without waiting for a reply. Checked the time and headed toward the elevators. This was a pretty big hotel. She could lose herself in the corridors for fifteen minutes without people bugging her, she thought, and it would be a change from pounding the streets.

As she got into the elevator, she passed a slim young woman in a smart suit and blouse, eyes bright and hair sleek. She caught the faint scents of coffee and breath mints and knew that the woman had been sitting alone in her hotel room until moments before, muttering self-confidence mantras, reapplying her corporate mask before some drab meeting, trying to convince herself she was a grown-up now, no longer a little girl.

"Nice tits," Madison said.

The doors closed on the woman's astonished face.

As the elevator climbed, a car was rapidly approaching the outskirts of the city. Simon O'Donnell was driving. Alison was in the passenger seat with two maps and her cell phone. She had just gotten off a call which had succeeded in getting her put through to someone in the Missing Persons

Bureau of the Seattle Police Department, a man named Blanchard, who had appeared to take her seriously. He said he would meet them, at least.

"This exit?" Simon asked.

"Next one," she said. "I think. I should remember, but . . ."

"I know," he said. "It's been a while."

It had been a little over ten years, in fact, a figure that was easy to remember because they'd moved out of the city soon after Alison learned she was pregnant, soon after they had decided to name their baby after the street in the city where they had first met. Simon started to pull through the lanes of traffic, doing so with his usual judicious care. There'd been times when this had irritated Alison. Right now it did not.

They'd spent the last twenty-four hours waiting with a desperation that would prevent the passage of time from ever seeming the same again. The police said there had been a possible sighting of a girl trying to get on a plane in Portland, but that she'd been prevented from doing so, and so they should just stay put and wait. And so they had. But they had also talked. The absence at the center of their life was so vast it seemed pointless not to open all the drawers and pull everything out, to make the void universal. Alison admitted the friendship she'd maintained with a man her husband had never met, swearing—truthfully—that it had never been more than that. As she did this, a bubble burst in her head, revealing that nothing had ever been inside.

Inconsequential, too, had become many of the things she'd thought were wrong with Simon, with their relationship. It wasn't that they didn't exist or had just blown away. But if everything in the world seemed wrong and broken, maybe that actually proved the opposite. Not everything could be wrong about the universe. Simon (for once) had the tact not to say this out loud. He didn't need to. She got there by herself, somewhere during those hours of talk, or perhaps during the few hours of sleep that followed. It didn't solve anything, didn't make everything all right—but it turned things around, tilted them so they reflected the light differently, and for the moment that was enough.

Simon meanwhile had admitted that he sometimes behaved as if Alison's moods swings were deliberate, and this wasn't fair. Also—and this was only to himself—that his accidental one-night stand with a colleague three years ago actually *did* count, and the price he might have to pay for this event's having remained secret could be cutting his wife some slack, not least because his own drunken error had caused him more confusion and discomfort than anything Alison had ever done. The behavior of others can be withstood. Less so the occasions when we stab *ourselves* in the back. A brief hatred of someone else can be refreshing to the soul. Not so a hatred of one's other self, which is never brief.

Both of them knew, but did not admit, that they said or thought these things as offerings, to whichever power held their daughter in his hands. No matter how long they talked, however, the absence stretched with every additional minute the phone failed to ring.

In the end it became too wide to speak across, and they were left in silence, staring out windows into the dark.

Finally they'd lain down on the bed together, closer than for some time. At 3:02, Alison had woken to the sound of her cell phone. She scrambled across the bed, fell off the other side, and sent the phone clattering to the floor. Got it open and to her ear just in time to hear someone talking loud and fast. It was barely two sentences, but the voice cut through Alison's head like a knife. Then the line went dead.

Alison turned, eyes wide, to see Simon levering himself up onto one elbow.

"Who's that?" he slurred. "Police?"

"No," she'd said, trying not to start running in all directions at once. "It was Madison. I think she just told us where she is."

chapter TWENTY-NINE

When the door to the house didn't open, I was confused, until I realized that Amy must have gone out. I unlocked the bolt and let myself into a space that was supremely quiet, suffused with the distinctive emptiness caused by the absence of the person with whom you share your life.

I headed down into the living area, sneakily glad of time to myself, a period to decide how to broach the subject of the photographs I'd seen and the fact of her name being on the paperwork Fisher had shown me. The living room was tidy. The current work frenzy was over, or in abeyance, and presumably she'd walked up into the village. In which case maybe I should call her, go meet up. Grab lunch. Talk to her long enough to overlay the dark aftermath of the morning and decide what to do about everything else. We'd always been able to talk the world away. I hoped this was still the case.

I'd traveled a couple more steps before I stopped, however, looking through the door into Amy's study.

What I saw would not have struck anyone else the way it did me. You'd have to know Amy, to have been married to her, and to understand how important her work spaces were. Her office was where she lived and who she was. And what I saw was not the way it should be.

The computer was on, the screen a mass of open windows. Amy closed computer windows the way old men keep a single bulb burning in their house, turning lights on and off as they move from room to room. The surface of her real desktop was covered in papers, notepads. Box files had been removed from the shelves and left open. Whoever had been here had hardly trashed the place—many people's studies probably never looked this neat—but they had been thorough. Her laptop was gone. So was her personal organizer.

I pulled out my phone to raise Amy right away but stopped as two more things struck me. First that she would have called me if she'd known that someone had broken in. She had not. So this must have happened very recently.

And secondly that the front door had been locked.

Thumb hovering over Amy's speed-dial number, I went out into the living room. Stood and listened, letting my mouth drop open. The house was as quiet as when I'd first arrived. I walked quickly and silently to glance into the other rooms on the main level, then up the stairs. My study looked as it had, laptop lonely in the middle of the table.

I searched the rest of the house. Within five minutes I was confident there was no one there.

And by no one, I now meant Gary Fisher. I couldn't imagine who else might have come here. He not only knew where I lived but had tied Amy in to the story he was building around Cranfield's estate. If he'd walked straight out of the hospital to his car and gotten on the road, he could have beaten me here.

Though not by much—and there was still the issue of the front door. Only way he could have managed that was with a set of keys. I still had mine, and there'd been no opportunity for him to copy them. Unless when he'd come to visit, he swiped the spare set from the bowl in the kitchen . . .

The keys were still there. Across from the breakfast island was access to the garage, but a quick twist of the doorknob confirmed that this door was locked, too. That left one remaining option. I headed back down the stairs and over to the windows. Grabbed the handle of the sliding door and yanked it to the right, hard, expecting it to slide open. But it did not.

I unlocked it and stepped out onto the deck, finally pressing the speed-dial number on my phone. It took Amy a while to pick up, and when she did, she sounded distracted.

"Yes?" she said.

"It's me. Look . . ."

"Who?"

"Who does it say on the screen, honey?"

There was beat. "Answered without looking. Sorry, miles away."

Again, I added silently. "Look, where are you?"

"Home," she said. "Where are *you*?"

I turned back to the window, prey to the bizarre idea that I'd somehow missed her, that she was inside the house doing something mundane, working, making coffee, or tea, that she'd just happened to move from room to room in such a way that I'd not seen her since I got back.

"At *home*?"

"What time are you getting back?"

"Amy, you're not at home. I'm in the house now. You're not here."

There was a pause. "Not in the *house*."

"In Birch Crossing?"

"No. I'm in L.A."

"You're in *Los Angeles*?"

"Yes. The city where I was born? Grew up? Did that back-in-the-day stuff?"

"What are you *talking* about? Why are you in L.A.?"

"I left a message on your phone," she said. She sounded confident now, as if she'd worked out the precise way in which I was being obtuse. "Like, about an hour after we spoke last night? I flew into LAX last night."

"Why?"

"KC and H called a big powwow. God and his angels are flying in, business class."

I held the phone away from my ear, looked at the screen. There was an icon there to show I had voice mail.

"I didn't notice it come in," I said. "Amy . . ." I didn't know what to say and instead got mired in the trivial. "And you couldn't conference-call instead?"

"My point entirely, honey. I fought tooth and nail. But apparently not. This is face-to-face action."

"So how long are you down for?"

"Meeting's tomorrow A.M., stupid early. Been at the office all morning. I'm on my way to Natalie's for the afternoon now—thought I'd catch up with the brat, be big-sisterly at her. She's probably feeling undernagged."

"Right." I was distracted by a tiny spot of unexpected color, pale and sandy, deep in the undergrowth twenty feet below the deck.

"You still there?"

"Yes," I said. I was leaning over the rail now. "Was everything okay at the house when you left?"

"Well, sure," she said. "Why—is there a problem?"

"No. Just feels . . . kind of cold, that's all."

"So check the furnace, caveman. That where big fire spirit lives. Want you nice and toasty while you work."

She said she would keep me updated and was gone.

I'd barely heard the last few sentences. I went to the end of the deck and ran down the flight of stairs to the path. It wasn't designed to enable access to the area directly underneath the balcony, which was heavily sloped, but to deliver you to the more landscaped area below. I had to come off it and push my way through bushes to get to where I'd been looking.

It took me a couple of minutes to find the first one. Soon afterward I'd found three more.

I made my way back out to the path and stood with them in the palm of my hand. Four cigarette butts. Each had been stubbed out on something firm, then dropped over the side. The color and condition of the filters said they hadn't been there long. Yesterday at most, this morning more likely; overnight mist would have made them soggy and dull.

I walked back up to the deck. Found the point above where I'd found the butts and discovered a discolored patch on the upper surface of the rail. I always stubbed mine underneath, precisely to avoid causing this. I didn't just drop the remains into the bushes either but carried them indoors to put in the trash.

Somebody had been standing right here, smoking.

There were two things I didn't understand about this. The first was, whoever was out there should have been visible from the house if anyone was inside.

The second was, I knew that Gary Fisher didn't smoke.

Another question occurred to me. The SUV had been with me in Seattle. So how had Amy gotten to the airport? Birch Crossing didn't exactly rate a cab service. The only solution I could think of was one I'd taken advantage of myself, a few days before. The Zimmermans. This made me remember something else.

The Zimmermans had keys to our house.

They were, in fact, the only people in the world who did. I couldn't for a moment see either of them letting themselves in. But they were helpful folks. If someone came to them with a convincing story, I was far from sure they wouldn't have tried to help. Ben, at least—Bobbi would have been a harder sell. But wouldn't even Ben have come into the house with them, hovered in the background?

Five minutes' search failed to turn up their phone number in the house. I decided to walk over there instead. The first question was settled as I walked up their drive. Both Zimmerman vehicles were present.

I went to the front door and rang the bell. The door

opened immediately. Bobbi stood there holding a glass of wine. The broad smile on her face faltered but then reattached in a slightly different shape.

"Jack," she said. "How *are* you?"

The Zimmermans' house was arranged all on one level, ranch style. Over Bobbi's shoulder I could see that some kind of get-together was taking place in their living room, a wide, open space with a view of the creek. There were people standing there, at least fifteen, perhaps twenty. Ben didn't appear to be among them.

I stepped inside, trying not to be overly aware of the people in the living room or the way some of them seemed to be looking at me.

"Wanted to check something with you," I said quietly. "You've got a set of our keys. Has anyone asked for them? Or asked you to let them into our house?"

Bobbi stared at me. "Of course not," she said. "And I wouldn't have let them in if they did."

"Right," I said quickly. "I didn't think so. It just looked a little like someone might have been hanging around the property. Is Ben home?"

She shook her head, started explaining that their friend had taken a turn for the worse again and that Ben had gone back down to be with him. I tried to listen but found myself distracted. I realized that I recognized some of the people in the other room. Sam, the fat and bearded man who owned the grocery store. A gaunt, gray-haired woman whose name I didn't know, but whom I believed to be the proprietor of the bookstore. The smooth-looking gent who owned the Cascades Gallery and others also who appeared familiar. I was aware that I should probably feel embarrassed for Bobbi that I'd arrived to witness a gathering we hadn't been invited to. But that wasn't what I felt. The people who glanced my way didn't look like they were preparing to greet another guest. It felt more like being a kid who had wandered into the wrong classroom by mistake, to be confronted with a group of older children, their faces familiar but their gazes flat and closed.

"I'm sure it's just my imagination," I said, smiling. "Sorry to have disturbed you. What's the occasion?"

Bobbi took me by the elbow and led me gently to the door.

"Just a little reading group," she said. "Give my regards to Amy, won't you?"

And then I was back outside, the door closed behind me. I stared at it, then turned to go. As I walked down the drive, I saw someone else I recognized.

The sheriff nodded to me as he passed and continued on his way up to the Zimmermans' house.

He'd never struck me as a man who read a lot.

I stood out on our deck and smoked as I drank a succession of cups of coffee. I tried to find something to eat. I tried to do most things I could think of, but in the end I did what had been brewing all along.

First I called Natalie in Santa Monica. She said Amy had just left, which meant she couldn't have spent barely an hour there. So then I called the other number, the main switchboard for Kerry, Crane & Hardy in Los Angeles. My heart was thumping hard. Someone perky answered.

"Hey," I said. "Seattle mailroom here. Got a package needs to get to, uh . . . Ms. Whalen, I think, for the meeting tomorrow. You know where she's staying, or can I just ship it direct to your office?"

"Well, sure. Which meeting is that, by the way?"

"No idea," I said. "It just says 'the meeting, Thursday A.M.' Some big thing, I guess."

There was silence for a moment, and then she came back on. "Actually, I don't see anything in the diary," the girl said. "It looks kind of quiet tomorrow, in fact. Can you be more specific?"

"I'll check and get back to you," I said.

I sat in the chair that looked out over the forest. I tried to be dispassionate. The absence of Amy's laptop and PDA now made sense. So did the state of her desk, if she'd had to leave in a hurry. Direct evidence for an intruder had faded. I was left with what I'd found outside—that, and a very strong feeling.

I sat with my elbows on my knees, hands held in a triangle up to my face. Instead of trying to think about things in straight lines, asking them questions in an attempt to force-fit them into a scheme of rationality I didn't yet possess, I let them float around in my head, following their own shapes and paths and gravities, in the hope that there was some order I didn't understand because I was looking at them the wrong way.

If there was, I didn't find it. All I managed to do was find another fact and add it to the pile. When I'd gone out onto the deck after my run on the day Amy came back from Seattle, I'd noticed ash on the wooden floor. I'd made an assumption about its being left there from my own last cigarette. But was that likely, given what I'd just found? Or had someone perhaps been standing in the shadows of our lives back then, too?

In the shadows, but very close?

I went through to the bedroom and put a change of clothes into an overnight bag. Then I walked up the stairs and unlocked the door that led to the garage.

Boxes of possessions, ours and those belonging to the owners of the property, stood in dusty, monolithic piles. Some contained objects that belonged to me, like my family's photo albums, just about all that remained of my childhood now. It seemed hard to believe that I would ever feel the need to open them again.

I walked past all the crates and leftover pieces of furniture to the far corner, where I moved aside a heavy workbench. Behind it there was a cupboard built into the wall. I used two keys from the house key chain to unlock it.

Inside, wrapped in a cloth, was my gun.

It had been there since the day we moved in, like a memory pushed far back into the shadows of my head. It was something I'd carried every day for years, at work. It was something I'd carried one night. It was something I should have gotten rid of.

I picked it up.

Part III

At night when the streets of your cities and villages shall be silent, and you think them deserted, they will throng with the returning hosts that once filled and still love this beautiful land. The white man will never be alone. Let him be just and deal kindly with my people, for the dead are not altogether powerless.

—Chief Seattle,
excerpt of the 1854 speech,
from the original translation by Dr. Henry Smith

chapter THIRTY

At LAX, I took a cab to Santa Monica. I got the driver to stop fifty yards short of the house, and I walked the rest. When I arrived, I found a boy in the yard outside, playing in an orderly fashion.

"Hey," I said.

He looked up, checked me out. Didn't say anything.

"Uncle Jack," I added.

He nodded, head to one side, as if conceding the truth of my observation but failing to find that it rocked his world.

I walked past him up the path and knocked on the door. It opened immediately, as I'd expected. This kid's mother wasn't going to be letting him mess around in the yard in the early evening without keeping an eye out.

"Well, how *about* that?" she said, hands theatrically on hips. "You don't see a Whalen for months, then bang—a full house. Must be some kind of astrological thing, right? Or biorhythmic? Is a comet due?"

I felt tense. Amy's sister was hard work at the best of times. "How are you, Natalie?"

"*Still* not a movie star and a bewildering ten pounds heavier than I'd like, but otherwise in an acceptable place for my culture and type. I told you on the phone you missed Amy, right? Like, hours ago?"

"We're meeting later. Just thought I'd stop by and say hi, since I'm in town."

She looked at me dubiously. "I'll alert the media. You want coffee while you're doing this hi saying?"

I followed her inside. There was a big pot ready and waiting in the kitchen, as always when I'd visited Natalie's house. It was one of the few points of congruence between the sisters.

She handed me a large cup, filled it. "So. Amy didn't say you were gracing the area."

"She doesn't know. It's a surprise."

"Uh-huh. Tangled web you guys weave. Speaking of which, is it just me or has big sis been acting a little wacked recently?"

"In what way?" I said, careful to keep my voice flat.

"She drops by here today with no notice, then asks me if I have tea. Well, *of course* I have tea. I am the homemaker from hell, but I do *try,* and Don likes it first thing. Tea, I mean. But Amy? Tea? That's a new one."

"She's been drinking it some recently," I said. "Maybe she's doing a campaign on it."

"Okay. So I'll tell Mulder and Scully to stand down. But here's item two: Any idea what the date is?"

"Of course," I said, reaching for it. "It's . . ."

"Right," she said. "Given a couple seconds, you could name the month and maybe even the day. That's not what I meant. That's Man Time. I'm talking Woman Time. In my people's calendar, it's Annabel's Birthday Plus Six Days."

"Annabel," I said. "Your Annabel?"

"She was twelve last week."

"Your point being?"

"Whalen card and gift conspicuous by their absence."

"Christ," I said. "I'm sorry. I—"

She held up her hand. "Jack, you couldn't name my daughter's birthday if your life depended on it. Mine either, or Don's. You probably have your own written on the palm of your hand. So how come we always get cards?"

"Because Amy knows."

Natalie drew a checkmark in the air. "Not just birthdays. When Don and I got married. When Mom and Dad died, *their* wedding anniversary. She lives the family chronology. Year in, year out, she gets the job done."

"Did she mention this when she—"

"That's the thing. She stops by without warning, drinks her tea, goes upstairs, comes back down, kiss-kiss, good-bye. She's exactly the way she always is, which is mainly a sweetie, also slightly killable—but she neglects to mention forgetting her niece's birthday, which by now she *must* have realized she's done."

"She went upstairs?"

"To her old room. It's Annabel's now."

"Did she say why?"

Natalie shrugged. "Amy's what—thirty-six this year? Maybe it's a memory-lane deal. Gather up the past before the Alzheimer's really kicks in."

"You mind if I go take a look?"

"I already did. She didn't touch anything, far as I can tell. Why would she?"

"Still . . ."

Natalie cocked her head to one side, and you could tell immediately how the boy in the front yard had acquired the habit. "What's this about, Jack?"

"Nothing. Just intrigued."

"Go nuts, Detective. Annabel's at band practice. Second on the right."

I left her in the kitchen and went upstairs. The second door along the hallway was slightly ajar, and for a moment I remembered Gary Fisher's dream so clearly that I hesitated. But then I pushed the door open.

It would have been different in detail when Amy lived here, naturally. Posters of different bands. Merchandising goods associated with different movies that had now probably been remade twice. Otherwise it was archetypal.

It's strange being in the childhood space of someone you love. Knowing her now is not the same as having known her before, and that pre-you person will remain a stranger even if you go on to die hand in hand. It's odd to imagine someone so much smaller and younger, to see the shapes and angles through which she learned about the world. You hear echoes. You cannot help but wonder whether she now always feels most comfortable in spaces of similar size or height, or if the bedroom you share with her adult incarnation feels wrong to her for not having a window in that same position. You picture her sitting on the edge of this bed, feet neatly together, staring into the future with the acquisitive and slightly alien gaze of the child.

It didn't take long for me to notice something Natalie couldn't have been expected to spot. The room was in flux—it had been neat recently, and it would be again—and objects and clothes and bits of furniture were strewn around. But the rug that covered the center of the floor was at precise right angles to the bed, with no wrinkles at any point. I doubted that Annabel had left it this way.

I moved the wooden chair off it, flipped it up. Nothing to see except floorboards that had been painted shabby-chic white at some point in the last ten years. I went to the other end, did the same. Thought I'd drawn a blank but then looked closer at the end just under the bed. I went down on my knees and felt beneath the frame, close to where it butted against the wall.

It was tight, but a small section of board could be levered out. Underneath was a dusty gap, an ideal child's hiding place. It was empty now, but I didn't think it had been that way when Amy arrived.

Natalie was standing by the kitchen window, cradling her coffee in both hands and watching her son in the yard.

"So?"

I shrugged. "Like you said. Memory lane." I caught something in the way she was observing the boy. "Everything okay?"

"Sure. Just a . . . Matthew seems to have gotten himself a little imaginary pal. No biggie. You just wonder what gets into their heads."

"You asked him about it?"

"Sure. It's just a friend, he says. They play together sometimes, you hear him talking quietly to himself once in a while. It's not like we have to set an extra place at dinner. And it's better than nightmares, for sure. Amy had those super bad."

"Really?"

"God, yes. One of the earliest things I can remember—I don't know how old I was, three maybe, four?—was these horrible noises in the night. Like a scream but deeper. Loud, then quiet, then loud again. Freaky. Then I'd hear Dad trudging down the hall. He'd get her back to sleep, but then it would start again an hour later. Went on for a couple of years."

"Amy never mentioned that."

"Probably doesn't even remember. Sleep's a war zone with kids. Babies especially. Friend of mine's kid used to push his fingers into his eyes to stop himself from falling asleep. Seriously. Matthew was hell on wheels, too—you couldn't get him to nap without pushing him from here to San Diego. And he'd wake up in the night four, five times. Like an on-off switch—straight to Defcon Five. You'd be lying there in the dark, house peaceful, baby asleep and all's well with the world. Then, bang—he'd be wailing like his room was full of wolves."

"Makes sense. Suddenly you're awake and alone in the dark with no mom or dad to be seen or smelled or found."

"Sure—that explains bad waking. But why fight sleep so hard in the first place?"

"Because it wouldn't have been that way when we lived in caves. The whole family would be sleeping in a pile together, instead of exiling Junior into a room with scary murals he doesn't understand and inexplicable things dangling from the ceiling. The baby thinks, *Fuck this, are you* insane*? It's not* safe *to leave me alone.* So they do the one thing that reliably affects their environment—scream their heads off."

"You surprise me, Jack. I never realized you were so much in touch with your inner child."

"Always. It's the inner adult I keep losing track of."

She smiled. "Yeah, well, maybe you're right. But I don't know. Kids are weird. They pick up TV remotes and hold them to their ears like phones and talk to people who aren't there. You give them a toy saxophone and they put it straight in their mouths—and blow instead of suck, which is what they've done with everything else. They put empty cups to their mouths and go 'Mmmm,' and you think, *Where did* that *come from? Have I* ever *gone 'Mmmm'?* Then one day they stop doing it. It's how they break your heart. Some unbelievably endearing habit they develop, from nowhere—then bang, it's gone again. Makes you miss them even when they're still there in front of you, and that's part of what loving is about, right?"

Suddenly she stopped, and her cheeks went bright red. I'd never seen Natalie embarrassed before. Wouldn't have believed it possible, in fact.

"What?"

"I'm so sorry," she said. "I have been a numb fucking bitch."

I shook my head. "No you haven't."

"But—"

"Seriously. It's not a problem."

"But with Amy? How—"

"Everything's fine."

"Okay," Natalie said. "I'm sure it is. She's pretty tough." For just a moment, she looked fiercely proud of her sister, and I wished I had a sibling to feel that way about me. "She has been . . . I don't know, a little different since, though. Don't you think?"

I shrugged. "I guess."

Natalie persisted. "Maybe even before that?"

I looked up at her, surprised, and was disconcerted to find her looking at me, hard, with eyes very similar to her sister's.

"People change," I said, dismissively. "They get older. Grow up. May even happen to you someday."

She stuck her tongue out. "There's one thing I never understood, though," she said, leaning on the sink and looking out the window again. Her son still playing sensibly in the yard, staying a statutory six feet from the road, as if a force field operated to keep him within a safe distance of the house. Perhaps it did. Amy wasn't the only Dyer girl who ran a tight ship.

"What's that?"

"How Amy wound up in advertising."

"Things happen. I ended up a cop."

"I never knew you when you weren't, so that's not strange to me. Plus, your being a cop made sense. What happened to your dad, and . . . You just made sense that way. More than you do as a writer, that's for sure."

"Ouch."

"Say it ain't so. But Amy, I mean . . . When she was a teenager, she was always the complete geek."

I frowned. "Really?"

"You don't know this? Totally. Forever making something out of weird bits of crap. Poring over books with titles that would make you lapse into a coma."

"That doesn't sound like the woman I know."

"For sure. For years she's the science-fair queen and poised to do something appallingly nerdy, and then suddenly one day she's all 'I want to be in advertising,' as if it's 'I want to be a movie star.' I didn't even know what advertising *was*. She'd just turned eighteen, and she comes out with it at dinner one night. I remember it because the old folks had spent years backing her up on all the tech stuff, giving her rides to clubs, being proud—more than they ever were with anything I did—and then bang, that's all history. I remember watching Papa across the table as she's saying all this, seeing his shoulders slump." She smiled, gaze still on her kid outside. "I was fourteen. First time I ever realized that being a parent maybe *wasn't* a complete walk in the park."

"She ever give a reason? Why she switched?"

"She didn't have to. She was golden."

"Natalie . . ."

She smiled. "I'm just kidding. No, she didn't. Though I did ask her about it this one time. She said she'd met a guy."

My heart thumped, once. "Someone at school?"

"No. Somebody older, already in the business maybe, though that's totally a guess. I figured she was attracted to this guy, didn't work out . . . but she stuck with it. You know what she's like. Dogged. Doesn't matter how long something takes, how long she's got to wait. Always been a girl with an eye to the long-term view."

I'd turned to look out the window, though I had no interest in what was outside. I didn't want Natalie to be able to see my face as I asked the next question.

"Don't suppose she mentioned the guy's name?"

"Actually, she did, and the strange thing is, I remember it. Pure coincidence. We'd had this one dog for years, and he'd died like two, three months before. He'd been around almost all my life, and I still missed him *really* bad. So I guess it stuck in my head."

"This guy had the same name as your dog?"

"No, sweetie. The dog was called Whooper. Calling a person 'Whooper' would constitute cruel and unusual punishment, even in L.A. It was the breed. A German shepherd."

I had been so prepared for hearing the name "Crane" that I had to check if I'd heard her right.

"The guy's name was Shepherd?"

"Yep." She looked blank for a moment. "Funny. Nearly twenty years go by, and you can still miss a damned dog."

* * *

Ten minutes later her husband returned home with a clarinet-toting child. My relationship with Don had always revolved around his getting me to tell cop stories. We hadn't arrived at a new MO since. His daughter greeted me with grave politeness, as if part of a self-imposed practice regime for interacting with the nearly elderly. I had no idea how to broach the subject of her birthday, and so I didn't.

Natalie walked me to the door soon afterward. "Been nice to see you, Jack," she said unexpectedly.

"You, too."

"Sure everything's okay with you guys?"

"Far as I know."

"Well, okay then. So—where are you going tonight? Amy was dressed up mighty nice."

"It's a secret," I said.

"I hear you. Keeping that magic alive. You're an inspiration to us all. Well, come see us again soon—or we'll come to you, and you don't want that. Oh, that was the other thing today." She laughed. "I thought you guys moved to Washington. Not *Florida*."

"What do you mean?"

She held up her hand, fingers splayed. I shook my head, no clue what she was talking about.

"Amy in bright pink nail polish?" she said. "What's up with *that*?"

I left not knowing where I was headed, walked down residential streets in soft, midevening air. People parked their cars, drove away, got home or went out. Others stood in kitchen windows, glanced down out of bedrooms, stood watering plants in their yards. I wanted to head up those paths, stand in those kitchens, sit in a big easy chair in one of those living rooms, and say, *So—what's up? Tell me how you live. Tell me all.* Other people's lives always seem more interesting, coherent, simply more *real* than my own. Television, books, celebrity culture, even plain watching the world go by: all a desire for an existence that has a directness and simplicity we never feel, that seems real and true in a way our own smudged and fractured days never do. We all want to be someone else for a while. Seem to believe, almost, that we already are, that something stands in the way of the lives we were supposed to have.

My phone rang. I didn't recognize the number. "Yes?"

"Whozis? Who?"

The voice was thick and hard to understand. "It's Jack Whalen," I said. "Who the hell are you?"

"This L.T. here. It's the building, you said."

"What building?"

"Shit. You told me money."

I realized who I was talking to. "You're the guy who was sitting at the café in Belltown."

"It is. You want what I got?"

"No," I said. "I'm not involved with that anymore."

My interlocutor became loudly disquieted. "You a lying mother*fucker*! You said you had money. I made the call, cop motherfucker."

"Okay, sir," I said. "Tell me what you have."

"Fuck you! How I know you going to pay me?"

"You got me. But I'm not in Seattle right now. So either you give me what you have, and I pay you later, or I put the phone down and block your number."

He didn't hesitate long. "It's a girl, bro."

"What?"

"She a kid. Come up the street, last night, late, she stand a front the building. Look like she try a key. Don't work. She go away up the street. She gone."

I laughed. "You saw a little girl come look at the building, then go away? And you want money for that?"

"You said—"

"Right. Well thank you. The check's in the mail."

I ended the call and made a note to block the number

when I sat down. In the old days I'd be doing something like that once a week. Giving out my number to people who might have information they would feel more comfortable giving out later, when no one was around—then blocking it when they got to thinking they had a friend on the force who would fix their parking tickets or get their aunt out of jail. I did not miss those people. Black or white, young or old, these baffled, violent men with their unhappy, shouting wives, hermetically sealed off from their dreams by drugs, poverty, and fate—and laziness, too, often, along with short fuses and shorter attention spans and a bitter yearning for the easy life that guaranteed that theirs would be anything but.

I kept walking, and after a time I found myself on Main, passing places like Rick's Tavern and the Coffee Bean, iBod and Schatzi, Say Sushi and Surf Liquor, environments that had been a casual part of my existence for years. I'd even met Amy in a bar not far from here. I'd been killing an evening with a colleague when a couple of drunks started working a table of women. The deal with a bar's being cop-friendly is the understanding that—should anyone not realize that the place often contains off-duty policemen and that good behavior is therefore mandatory (for non-cops, at least)—it will be made clear to them. So I got up, walked by the other side of the women's table on the way to the men's room, and communicated via a pointed finger that the guys' attention would be better deployed elsewhere. One looked like he wanted to make something of it, but his friend got the message, and they left without a fight. There was a fresh beer waiting for me on the counter when I got back. So it goes.

Several months later I dealt with a minor collision a few miles away. One car was inhabited by a pleasant man in his early seventies who was profoundly stoned and admitted his culpability even before he fell down on the sidewalk. The other contained a woman I recognized as having been at the table in the bar. She was sober, calm, and cute. She'd never even noticed me in the bar, but she had by the time this incident was sorted out. I was brisk and efficient with the public. She liked that, I guess. As I came to understand, Amy Ellen Dyer valued the brisk and efficient above most else.

A couple weeks later, I was back in the bar, and so was she. Facial recognition occurred in both parties, and I briskly and efficiently stopped by to say hello. Though hitting on the victims of crime was viewed by many as a key perk of the job, it lay outside my own personal experience and I expected nothing to come of it. The women left while I was out back sharing a joint with the cook, but when I returned to the bar, I found she had left her number with the bartender.

"Call me," the note said. "Without delay."

We met up a few days later and had one of those dates where you start one place and then find yourself in another, and then another, not remembering how or why you moved—because the talk just seems to keep coming and this sense of freedom, of not having to stay put to protect your position and mood, seems to be at the heart of the evening. In the end it became kind of a game, each of us suggesting somewhere more obscure or offbeat to go next, until finally we found ourselves sitting side by side on a bench in a very touristy location and realizing that it felt okay because we didn't feel much like locals either that night, but as if our lives and selves were in the midst of being freshly minted before our eyes. They were.

When you meet someone you love, then you change for good. That's why the other person will never know or understand the earlier you, and why you can never change back. And why, when that person starts to go, you'll feel the tear deep in your heart long before your head has the slightest clue what's going on.

It was hard not to think of that evening now that I was here, and of others that had come after it, good and bad. I dropped down Ashland to Ocean Front, headed up past

Shutters Hotel, under the long ramp road from the pier up to Ocean Avenue, then onto the concrete path on the beach itself. There's a run of buildings just up from there, right down on the sand, some of the earliest houses built in the area. They've always looked strange to me, incongruous, faux-English mansions behind fences on the beach, squatting in the shadow of the high bluffs like imps on the chest of someone who sleeps.

The lights on the pier were all on now. I got out my phone and called Amy's number.

"Hey," she said. "Sorry I haven't checked in. Got hung up at Nat's. Only just left. You know what she's like." I didn't say anything. "How are things back at the homestead? Got the place warmed up?"

"I'm not in Birch Crossing," I said.

"Oh?"

"I'm in Santa Monica. I flew down this afternoon."

There was a pause. "And why would you have done that?"

"Why do you think?"

"No idea, hon. Sounds kind of wacky to me."

"Hardly seen you this last week. I thought it might be nice for us to meet up. Check out the old haunts."

"Babe, that's a really sweet idea, but I've got like a *ton* of work to do. Need to get my ducks in a row for the meeting tomorrow."

"I don't really care," I said. "I'm your husband. I'm in town. Come meet me, for coffee at least."

There was silence for maybe five seconds. "Where?"

"You know where."

She laughed. "Well, actually, I don't. Not being a mind reader."

"So pick a place," I said. "And be there soon."

"You're really not going to tell me where?"

"You choose. And just go there."

"Jack, this is a dumb game."

"No," I said. "It's not."

chapter THIRTY-ONE

On the pier, groups of tourists strolled in the softening light, coming in and out of souvenir stores or suspiciously eyeing restaurant menus. I leaned against the rail and waited, the knot in my stomach getting tight and tighter. Twenty-five minutes later, I saw a woman walking down the ramp from the Palisades. I watched her come onto the pier and move purposefully through the crowd. She was in her mid-thirties but looked younger and was very smartly dressed. She glanced neither left nor right but headed straight to where she was going. She held something in her right hand, something that looked so wrong as to be trick photography, and I realized there had been things I'd misunderstood.

I let her go by, then got up and followed.

By the time I got to the end, she was leaning on the railing, looking across the water back toward Venice, a yellow glow surrounding her from the lamp at the corner of this section of the promenade. There were other people nearby, but not many—we had passed the restaurant sections and stores, were almost as far as possible from land. Most people got to this point, nodded at the sea, and turned to head back to where they could buy stuff.

Amy turned around. "Hey, you found me," she said. "You're good."

She looked strange. Taller, yet more compact. As if she had edited or improved her form, become Amy 1.1, without consulting me on the development process.

"Not really," I said. "This was the only place that made sense."

"Exactly. So what's with the cloak-and-dagger?"

"I just wanted to see if you could remember."

She rolled her eyes. "Come on, Jack. We came here on our first date. You proposed to me on this actual spot. We . . . well, you know. I'm hardly going to forget."

"Good," I said, feeling tired and sad, unable to completely remember what I'd thought the point of the exercise had been. I leaned on the rail next to her.

"So what's up?" she said. "It's lovely to see you, obviously, but I've got miles to go and promises to keep and a stack of work to do before I sleep."

I shook my head.

"What's that mean?"

"No you haven't. Got work to do."

"What are you talking about?"

"I called your office before I left home."

She pushed back from the rail. "Honey, you've really got to stop bugging people where I work. It just doesn't look very—"

"There's no meeting here tomorrow."

She cocked her head, Dyer style. I could see her judging how to proceed. In the end she nodded.

"That's correct."

There it was. *Yes—I lied to you.* It felt like a cold wind was blowing across the back of my neck, though the night was warm, and there was no breeze.

"So what *are* you doing here?"

"I wanted to see Natalie."

"Not according to her. She says it was a drive-by and she wasn't even sure why it happened." There was a cliff in front of me, the edge of which I could clearly see, yet toward which I was persisting in taking steps.

"You've been to *interview* her? Wow. Shame you were never this go-getting when you were a policeman, Jack."

"I never wanted to be a detective. You knew that."

"But now you do? When it's too late?"

"I care about this more, I guess."

"How come?"

"Because it's you. Because something's happening that I don't understand. And you're not answering my question."

"There's nothing going on, babe."

I got out my cigarettes. Took one, then offered the pack to her—something I'd never done before in all the time we'd known each other. She just looked at me.

"Saw you walk by with one in your hand," I said. "Found your ash on the deck the night you came back from Seattle, though I didn't realize it. Saw you smoking out there last Sunday afternoon, too, when I was running. I thought it was just condensation. But it wasn't."

"Jack, you're being ridiculous. I don't—"

There wasn't enough force behind the lie. I didn't even have to raise my voice to interrupt.

"Plus, I found a collection of butts in the bushes. Couldn't figure how someone could have been out there without you seeing them from inside. But that's because it was you doing the smoking. Correct?"

She looked away. Being right brought me no pleasure. "So what starts you up again after . . . what—ten years? Twelve?"

She didn't answer. Her eyes remained elsewhere, and her mouth was pursed. She looked like a teenage girl stoically enduring being chewed out for breaking a curfew she believed was dumb and unfair.

"Is it the same thing that's started you using abbreviations in text messages?"

"What are you talking about now?"

"You're a bright woman. You're capable of understanding the question," I said.

"I understand the words, but not what you're getting at. You're out on some weird kind of limb here, honey."

"I don't think so. You're the one who needs to get your head straight. Whatever or whoever's clouding your mind has you falling down all across the board."

"I'm really fine," she said. "Seems to be you who's running red lights."

She looked so chillingly smug then that I wanted to turn and walk away from her. Or even, for a fraction of a second, to shove her over the railing. To punish this impostor for stealing the identity of someone I loved.

"Annabel's birthday," I said instead.

She frowned. Even when she spoke, it was with the air of someone treading water. "What about it?"

"When is it?"

The penny dropped. She rubbed her forehead. "Oh, crap."

"No big deal in the grand scheme of things. But—"

"Of *course* it's a big deal. *Shit.* Why didn't Natalie say anything?"

"Probably didn't want to embarrass you."

"Natalie? Does that seem *likely*?"

"Actually, no. But before you leave town, you should see about getting something to the kid, don't you think?"

"Yes. Christ. What did we get her last year?"

"I have no idea," I said. "Call Natalie tonight, make your excuses, and get a gift suggestion at the same time."

"Good thinking."

Neither of us said anything for a while. We seemed to have taken a turn down some baffling side street, and I didn't know how to get back to where we'd been. So I simply picked up the car and put it back on the other road.

"Amy, if you're just going to stonewall, then—"

"There's nothing that needs to be talked about."

"So how come you're suddenly listening to Bix Beiderbecke?" I asked, feeling absurd.

"Christ—you're really pushing on this, aren't you? I

caught a couple tracks on the radio, thought it sounded okay, didn't bother to change the station. And anyway—how do you know that's who—"

"Your phone is full of it."

"You looked through my *phone*? For God's sake. When?"

"The day in Seattle. As far as I could tell, you'd vanished off the face of the earth."

"What's on my phone is private."

"From me? Since when did we have secrets?"

"People *always* have secrets, Jack—don't be a moron. It's how you know you're a different person from somebody else."

"I don't have any."

"Oh, yeah, right. Is that why you tell people you left the police because you'd finally had enough? Why you don't volunteer the information that one night you just got up and fucking—"

"Secrets from *you,* I meant. And what would you prefer me to say? That I nearly wound up on a—"

"Of course not. But . . ."

She breathed out heavily. The air was beginning to turn, to lose its warmth. We looked at each other, and for a moment it was only the two of us, as if a bubble had burst and any disagreement between us was absurd.

"You want some coffee?"

She nodded.

"Or is it tea these days?"

She smiled a little, against her will. "Coffee will be fine."

We got drinks from a stall thirty yards back up the pier. Started walking together toward the shore but wound up back at the end without discussing it. Whenever we'd come onto the pier together, that's where we always went, where our feet took us when they were together.

I found myself saying something from nowhere, something that sounded odd and clumsy in my mouth. "Do you think there's any of him still here?"

"Any of who?"

She knew who I meant. "Don't you remember the wind? How some of . . . some got blown back at us, back onto the pier?"

She looked away. "There's nothing left. Nothing here, nothing anywhere. It was two years ago. It's dealt with."

"No," I said. "We *haven't* dealt with it."

"*I* have," she said. "It's history. Leave it there."

It was only for an instant, but I saw her chin tremble, two tiny little twitches. I realized that it had been a long time since I'd seen her cry. Too long, for what had happened.

"We don't talk about it," I said. "Ever."

"There's nothing to say."

"There must be."

She shook her head, and now her face was firm. "I was pregnant. It died at five months, and I had a dead thing inside me for a while. It came out. It was cremated. We spread the ashes over the sea. My womb is broken, and I'm never going to have a child. There's nothing else to say, Jack. It happened, and I'm done with it now."

"So how come you changed the picture background on your phone?"

"You know why. Because I was pregnant in the photograph. I'm moving on. You should be, too. *Not* thinking about it. Not letting that or things that happened fifteen years ago rule my life. Sometimes people die. Children, fathers. You have to move on. Your dumb God of Bad Things is only in your head, Jack. There's no one to catch, no perp. Nothing to be done."

"You can't pretend things never happened."

"I'm *not.* I'm just not wallowing in it. I don't want that crap anymore. I want to be someone else."

"Congratulations, it's already happened."

"That's an asshole thing to say."

"Well, you're *being* an asshole."

And then we were at each other like vicious children, two people shouting at the end of a pier, and passersby watched us curiously and either changed their course to avoid the embarrassing couple or slowed a little to catch a sentence or two, neither knowing nor caring that they were witnessing a universe as it split in half.

For this to be happening, and happening here, made me so sad that my words started to catch in my throat. I could barely hear what Amy was saying.

"Amy, just look me in the eyes and tell me this isn't about some other guy."

Asking the question out loud made me furious, and sad, and exposed: There's little difference between it and saying, "Mommy, why don't you love me anymore?" It made me feel fourteen years old. This only worsened when she didn't answer me.

"Jack, this is stupid."

"Is it Todd Crane?"

"Jesus."

"Don't laugh at me, Amy. I'm asking you an adult question. Are you having an affair with Crane?"

"I . . . Look, a long, long time ago, years before you and I even met, Crane and I were an item. Briefly. Not since. There's nothing inside that guy's head, Jack."

"So who is it? This guy Shepherd?"

She stared at me. I hadn't scored a hit—at least, not of the right kind—but I'd clearly unbalanced her in some way I didn't understand.

"What . . . how do you know about him?"

"Yes or no, Amy?"

She looked away, eyes clouded. "Of course not."

"This relationship with Crane—would that have been around the time the company bought the building in Belltown?" Amy had started to look very unsettled now, and I realized that Gary Fisher had been right about at least one thing: The building was important after all.

"Jack, you really . . . you shouldn't be getting into this. It's got nothing to do with you, and it's not something you're going to understand. Believe me."

I was unable to stop pushing now that I'd started, and I tried the remaining name I'd heard in the last few days, the name that appeared on the building's papers, along with Amy's and Crane's.

"What about Marcus Fox?"

Amy's face dropped. She actually looked pale. I nodded, suddenly disbelieving anything she had to say. Disbelieving Amy, period. All that had happened to us in the last few years no longer seemed like events we'd weathered together. Instead, the time had coalesced between us, like ice: transparent at first, stealthily growing harder and more opaque with every day that passed.

"Last chance to do this right," I said. "Tell me what's going on."

She pulled a pack of cigarettes out of her purse, her hands shaking a little. She took the last one, lit it, and threw the empty pack over the rail. A woman who, when I first met her, took part in volunteer walks to pick litter off the beach.

"I don't respond well to threats," she said.

Her gaze was level and flat and cool. The fingers curled around the cigarette ended in splashes of pink. I realized I did not know this woman. Someone, some person who for now existed only in the shadows, had pushed his way into my life. He'd found his way in and was destroying the things that mattered most to me, either stealing or changing them so they were no longer mine. I'd thought I kept my house empty, protecting myself from the outside. But I had not. Amy had been inside all along, and it was she that he had come in to find.

And somehow he was taking her away from me.

I felt something very bad and dark rising in my head, a shaking I knew I might not be able to control.

"You're not you anymore," I said, thickly.

"Yes, Jack, I am. I'm sorry. But this is me."

"I really hope not. Because I don't even know this person. And she's very hard to like."

I walked away.

I left her standing there and stormed to the bottom section of the pier, walking stiff-legged around the final bend to where I could not see her. I was blinking fast and mechanically, my hands in fists by my sides, my arms and shoulders feeling as if they were under someone else's control.

When I reached the very end, I forced myself to stop, to take a series of long, deep breaths. The pier felt as if it were rocking under my feet, but I knew it was not. It was the whole world, and I understood now that this was what had been in my head when I'd stood out on the deck of the house in Birch Crossing and been unable to remember where I was.

An intuition that for many years I'd been living inside a dream, and that I was now about to wake up.

When I got back, she'd gone.

I headed quickly along the pier toward land, no longer angry. I had to dodge in and out to get through the packs and couples of contented, random people, and it felt like being a ghost. I started to run.

When I got to the beginning of the pier and gazed up the ramp, I could see someone who looked like Amy, sixty yards away, almost at Ocean Avenue. I shouted her name.

If she heard me, she didn't turn around. She walked straight to a car that was waiting on the corner, opened the back door, and got inside. The car pulled out quickly. There was no way I could catch it.

I grabbed my phone and dialed. It went to voice mail. She wasn't taking calls from me now.

"Amy," I said. "Call me. Please."

Then I dialed another number and asked someone if he would find something out. While I waited for him to call me back, I hiked up the slope to the avenue and sat heavily down on one of the benches in the park. My phone rang five minutes later.

"What do you know about this guy?" Blanchard asked.

"Just the name. Why?"

"Fox was a businessman. A pretty big deal in the city for a while, apparently."

"Was?"

"He disappeared nine, ten years ago."

"Owing money?"

"No. But it sounds like Homicide was beginning to pay him a little attention. A witness maybe put him in the area when a young girl disappeared, up in the Queen Anne District, four, five blocks from his house. There'd been other missing girls in the city over the previous few years. More than a few. Detectives got access to Fox's property and found a very clean basement."

"Suspiciously clean?"

"Maybe. But he was gone. I talked to one of the guys who was in the house, and he said it was like the *Mary Celeste*. Uncorked bottle of wine on the table, a cigar cut and ready to smoke, the whole deal. The file is still open, but it's full of dust, and I should stress that nothing ever got tied to him. So what's he to you, Jack?"

"I don't know," I said.

"I'm not sure I believe that," Blanchard said, sounding tired. "The guy I spoke to said someone else was asking about Fox, a few weeks back. This other person said he was a lawyer. Do I need to spell it out?"

"No," I said.

I called a final number.

"You've been lying to me," I said, before Fisher had a chance to speak. "I'm coming to Seattle. You're going to meet with me or I'm going to come and find you. If I wind up doing that, you'll regret it the rest of your life."

I cut the connection and walked across the road to hail a cab to the airport or a motel or bar, somewhere I could camp out for the night before flying north.

chapter THIRTY-TWO

Rachel stood at the corner, mouth open. She looked up the street, then down again. Turned in a melodramatic circle, as if it might help. It didn't. Son of a *bitch.*

She'd really gone.

Oh, beautiful.

Thanks, Lori. A perfect end to another stellar night.

Naturally, it was agreed that if either woman met someone five-star, then she was authorized to take off with him without having to track down the other to explain. The arrangement was more pertinent to Rachel, though, because Lori always insisted on driving and so was never the one who got abandoned outside Seattle's hottest bar (this week only), facing a walk home that would get longer and longer as the last glass of wine wore off. A walk in a skirt not designed for locomotion. And without a sensible coat.

"Fuck," Rachel said, wearily. But no use crying over spilt milk. Or split girlfriends. Ha. Was that funny, or just clever? Was it even clever?

Given that the exchange was happening inside her own head, did it even fucking matter?

She glanced indecisively back at Wanna:Be. She guessed she could go into the bar again and see if they knew any special cab-summoning spells, but there was no telling how long she'd have to wait. Nor did she relish trying to talk her way back past the doorman, a tall, smooth black dude flushed with self-importance and clearly unaware that a month from now he'd be on the streets again, handing out passes to drunks just to keep the background hubbub up to marketable levels.

"Fuck," she muttered, again. She arranged her wispy coat around her neck like a scarf and sent up a prayer that Lori's new best friend would turn out to have major issues and a dick the size of a cashew nut. Said "fuck" a final time, quietly.

And started walking home.

"Twenty-seven," Rachel said under her breath.

She was keeping careful count. She didn't want to be ballpark about it. She wanted the *exact number* to insert between the phrases "I had to walk . . ." and ". . . fucking *blocks*" in the e-mail she was sending Lori first thing in the morning.

She took the opportunity to rest for a minute. Another couple blocks would get her to the correct cross street, and *then* it would be fifteen minutes before she got to her house, a dinky place in a semimarginal neighborhood. Her house, where she kept her things, and slept, and ate in front of the television. Home, she guessed, and she knew she was lucky to have it and that without help from her dad she'd be sharing some dope-reeking dive with three other people drifting through their early twenties.

Eventually she started walking again, more slowly now. The streets were deserted but for an occasional car rocketing up or down or across, other people doing whatever it was they did. Rows of decent houses were set behind small and well-tended yards, every window dark. Nobody stayed up late around here. They'd already gotten what they needed and didn't need to pretend that it could be found in cool-for-this-night-only bars full of light and chatter, which still felt like the insides of empty closets. Who needs that crap when you've got a two-car garage? Everybody here was tucked in happy and warm. Everyone except for . . .

. . . whoever was making that noise.

Rachel stopped, turned. The noise was footsteps. It pissed her off that the sound affected her this way—so there were footsteps, what*ever*—but it was dark and late, and she couldn't help it.

There was no one behind her. The steps sounded like they must be a little distance away, they were so quiet and light. Rachel flipped open her purse, got out her phone.

"Right," she mumbled into it. "But penguins are *always* like that, you know? Most of them can't even drive a car. Except those ones with the big crests. The CIA bred them for cross-country rally competition."

She paused a moment—faking conversation in the hope of putting off a stalker made her feel dumb, but a friend of Lori's claimed it had saved her butt more than once—then listened again.

Silence now. Whoever walked alone had gone some other way. Cool. She kept the phone in place, however, as she turned the corner that put her just six blocks from home. Then her hand slowly drifted down from her ear.

Someone was standing twenty yards up the street.

It wasn't a very tall someone, but Rachel couldn't determine much more than that because there was a streetlamp behind them.

She walked a little farther, slowing down, squinting.

The silhouette resolved into the shape of a little girl, standing neatly in the middle of the sidewalk.

"I'm lost," the girl said.

"Where are you supposed to be?" Rachel asked.

"Somewhere else."

"Okay, then. How . . . um, how come you're out this late anyway?"

The girl ignored the question. Rachel didn't blame her. She knew she was crap at relating to kids, with the exception of her baby sis. No children worked in her office or went to her gym. Or hung out in bars, much. So the only other shorties she encountered belonged to her older sister, who never left them alone with her but always hovered in the background, as if she suspected that Rachel might try to borrow money off her brood or try teaching them to smoke.

Nonetheless, she tried bending down, to seem more friendly. "Does your mom know where you are?"

"No."

"Where do you live, honey?"

"I just want to be indoors. I don't want to go home."

Uh-oh, Rachel thought. Suddenly this was looking more complicated. A lost kid was one thing. Chance to be a good neighbor. A runaway was different. Problems at home. Weird Uncle Bob. The whole nine yards.

"Why not?" she asked. "It's late. And cold. Be nicer to be home, don't you think?"

The girl waited patiently for her to stop talking. "Where is *your* home?"

Rachel raised her eyebrows. "Excuse me?"

"Where is it?"

"It's not far," Rachel said. "But—"

"Take me to your home."

"Look," Rachel said firmly, "I'll help you find your own house. Your folks must be flipping out. But—"

Suddenly the child flew at her.

Rachel wasn't ready. She threw a hand out to break her fall but crashed awkwardly anyway, the momentum from the child's attack causing her head to crack resoundingly against the concrete. The whole thing took about a second. Whiteness filled her head, as if light were splitting across the night sky.

Then she saw the bulbous shadow of the little girl's face above hers. "Take me to your home."

Rachel pushed herself back along the sidewalk, her wrist yelping in a bony way. "What's *wrong* with you?"

The girl's face had swum into focus. Her mouth was a thin line. "Take me to your home."

"I'm not taking you anywhere, you fucking freak."

The girl hesitated, kicked her in the stomach, and then ran off. Rachel caught a final glimpse of the child as she clambered quickly over a low fence into someone's front yard, and then she disappeared.

Rachel was moving fast as soon as she was on her feet. Within a couple of blocks, she'd started shaking, as shock kicked in. She thought about calling the cops to tell them they should get the hell out here and to bring a big net, but decided she'd wait until she got home.

It started getting odd once more when she was only a couple of blocks away. At first she thought she could hear the footsteps again. This time they stopped her dead in her tracks. She heard only silence. She turned in a slow circle, expecting to see a small figure standing shadowed under a streetlamp, some distance away but not far enough.

Nobody.

She was just spooked. That was all.

She started walking even more quickly. Her ears felt like they were sticking six inches out from her head. Her shoulders felt strange, too, as if she'd banged them up a little bit. But she kept her feet moving regularly, in a marching rhythm. *Click-click-click,* as the heels came down again and again. She tried to keep her eyes looking straight forward. To just keep moving . . .

Then she snapped her head to the left.

She saw a pair of houses, almost identical, standard-issue ranch style with a little fence in between. Silent and motionless under thin moonlight. But hadn't she seen someone slipping over the fence, way in back? Her brain wasn't sure, but her heart was beating hard enough to sound confident. And very unhappy about it.

She hesitated. She'd turned quickly. There were five, six yards between the fence and the side of the next house. Could a little girl really have made the distance in that time? Probably it was just a cat, prowling its territory. Jumped the fence, catching her eye, melted back into darkness in time-honored feline fashion.

But . . . if it *had* been the kid, it meant she was now ahead of Rachel. She could be waiting a few houses along the street, hidden behind one of the fences.

No. It was just a cat.

And if not . . . what was Rachel going to do? Run Christ knows how many blocks back to the bar, ask the cool black guy to come help? Or call the cops? *Right, ma'am, and how much did you have to drink tonight? Really*—that *much?*

And besides, it was only a kid. She'd had the element of surprise. This time Rachel would just deck the little nutcase.

Nonetheless, she covered the last block and a half at a trot, keeping a close eye on each fence as she approached. Her neighborhood signaled a small drop in the size and value of the houses, and her yard was neither deep nor wide. It was obviously empty, thank God.

She ran up the path and unlocked the front door with the key already in her hand. Closed it fast behind her.

And started laughing. Jesus. What a *shitty* night.

She poured herself a big glass of wine right away, swallowing half of it in one gulp. So she'd lost count of the number of blocks. She had *more* than enough juice to make Lori's mouth drop open. And maybe even, for once, apologize. She walked into the living room, stood aimlessly for a moment. The shock and spent adrenaline were losing their fizz and going flat. What was she thinking of doing now?

Sitting in silence? Turning on the television? Lori wouldn't be doing either of those things right now.

Rachel took another swig of wine. It refreshed the alcohol still in her system, and she felt a bit drunk. Drunk and bad-tempered. And *freaked out.* What was going on in the world that little girls were out in the middle of the night attacking innocent single women?

And what was going on in Rachel's world that those last two words applied to her? She shouldn't be walking late at night alone. She shouldn't be standing here alone now either. It sucked.

She raised the wineglass defiantly, thinking she might just throw it back and have another—there was nobody here to judge, right?—but then she heard something.

The quiet shattering of glass.

She turned so fast that the mid range Merlot slopped out and splattered on the carpet.

The sound had come from upstairs.

She set the wineglass down quietly on the table and went quickly out to the hallway, heart beating hard. Stood with her hand on the banister, looking up. Thought again about calling the police but knew it would be too long before they got here. Thought about running out onto the street but then thought, *No. This is my fucking house.*

She climbed the stairs slowly, feet to either side of the treads to avoid the creaks, and got to the top without a sound. She waited a moment. No more noise. She took the two steps required to cross the hallway and pushed open the door to her bedroom.

She could immediately see that the lower pane of her bedroom window was broken, a jagged, glinting hole. Glass lay on the floor just underneath it. She looked carefully all around the room. She knew only too well that there was no space for another blouse in her closet, never mind a human being. Her bed went right down to the floor, so there couldn't be anyone under that either.

Then she noticed something out of place. A small rock lying up against the bottom of her closet.

Somebody must have thrown it at her window from below. It had broken, and the rock came flying in. Somebody? How many candidates were there?

Rachel went to the window. Carefully got up against the wall and angled herself so that she couldn't be seen. Then very slowly moved her head so she could glimpse the yard below—ready to jump back out of sight fast.

There was no one down there, but Rachel decided that this had gone far enough. She was finally going to call the cops. She walked quickly back out of the bedroom and clattered down the stairs.

The girl was standing at the other end of the corridor, silhouetted against the light in the kitchen.

Rachel could see immediately what she'd done. Sent her upstairs with the noise, then quietly broken a pane in the back door, put her hand in, and unlocked it. But was that something a little girl would be able to plan? What kind of child was she dealing with here?

"Get out," Rachel said.

Her voice was dry and not loud enough.

The girl was holding something. Rachel recognized it. A professional-standard ten-inch chef's knife, from when she'd decided she ought to learn how to cook French. She'd bought an armful of books and a food processor and gotten as far as badly fucking up a confit of duck before abandoning the idea. The knife hadn't gotten much use since it left the store, bottom line. It was still very sharp, and out of scale with the person currently holding it. A child that age should look silly with such a thing in her hand. Unfortunately, she did not.

Rachel turned and ran to the front door. Grabbed the catch and pulled it. It didn't move.

She'd locked it when she got back in.

The girl was now in the living room. "You're going to help me," she said.

"Listen, honey," Rachel said shakily, hands on hips, "we are *so* done here. I don't know what your problem is, but I'm calling the cops. I mean it."

The girl moved the knife until the point of it was right against her own throat. "No you won't," she said.

"You're wrong. Get out of my house."

"Don't make me do this," the girl said, and now the point of the knife was making an indentation in the skin of her neck.

"What are you—"

"Do you want the police to find things this way?"

"Look . . ."

Suddenly the girl's eyes were wet. Rachel watched as she pushed her hand upward a little more, and a dark drop welled up around the point of the knife jabbing into her throat. Saw the girl's hand tighten as she prepared to shove the blade up. Knew that she wasn't going to stop.

"Please," the girl said, her voice quiet and very afraid and not the way it had sounded moments before. "Help me. I'm not doing this."

"Jesus," Rachel said quickly, holding her hands out. "Okay. You win. Just don't . . . do that."

The girl took a step forward. This brought her into the light, and for a second she looked less crazy, as if the blade had gotten into her hand by accident, Mommy not paying attention while they cooked together, and it would be put down with ostentatious care at any second.

"Promise?"

"You bet," Rachel said. "I promise."

The girl slowly moved the knife away. She smiled tentatively. It was a nice smile, and Rachel allowed herself to relax just a little bit. A child who had that inside her could not be all bad. Hopefully.

"Okay," she said, in the same calm and friendly voice. "So we're cool. Why don't you tell me your name?"

The girl's face changed. "Why do you want to know?"

"Well, how else am I going to know what to call you, honey? I'm Rachel. See? No big deal."

The girl was holding the knife loosely now, as if she'd forgotten about it.

"My name is Madison," she said. "Mainly."

"Great." Rachel smiled. "That's a real pretty name. Madison and Rachel. Friends, right?"

The girl was silent for a moment, motionless. Then she blinked. "I already knew your name," she said.

She smiled again, but something had changed. It was as if everything about the girl—her face, body, clothing—were irrelevant. Only her eyes told the truth. Rachel's stomach turned. She tried to look away but could not.

"Time," the girl said, looking Rachel over, "is not kind. You were *perfect,* so much my kind of thing. I even found myself prey to a little crush, would you believe it? Oh, well. That was then, and this is now. Understand something, not-so-little Rachel. You're too old, and we're not friends, and even if we were, it wouldn't stop me from cutting you up. So it would be a very good idea for you to do what you're told."

Rachel nodded. She didn't know what else to do.

"Good," the girl said. "We're going to make a phone call now. You should find it interesting. Instructive, at least."

The girl was holding the knife more tightly again now. This realization distracted Rachel, and she did not notice the girl's other hand swinging toward her head until it was too late.

"Excellent," Madison said brightly, when Rachel lay unconscious on the floor. "Now let's find out just how much the great Todd Crane loves his daughter."

chapter THIRTY-THREE

I have been here before. Many times has this scene replayed in my head, but never has it been so much like it was when it was real.

I am in Los Angeles. I am sitting in a cramped armchair, in the dark, surrounded by the smell of other people's debris. I am waiting for two men whose identities I have determined through the closest thing I will ever do to detective work. Men who have been places that were not theirs to enter, and in which they stole, committed at least two rapes and a murder. I have come to believe that being human is most of all to be a social animal and that if you do not understand that you are not allowed into other people's places without their permission, then while you may be a *Homo sapiens,* you are not a human being.

I am aware I am committing the same crime as they, and as the men who killed my father, many years ago and hundreds of miles away. I am not allowed to be in this house. Even if I had a warrant, I should not be here. I should be at home with Amy, who is close to broken and needs me with her. Instead I am here. I cannot help Amy's grief, or my own, and have run out of ways to try. So I sit in the rambling ruin of a house at the back end of a canyon, where all the windows are shut and there is no air. What do I really think

I'm doing here? Am I waiting to arrest two people whose identities I have established or instead for two unknown men from long ago, whose names I can never know and whom I can never catch?

I am not thinking about this. I am not thinking about anything. Thinking means remembering the face of the prenatal technician as she stared at the images on the ultrasound for a beat too long, before quietly summoning a supervisor. It involves the sight of my wife moving slowly around our house, waiting in vain for the thing inside her to go away. It culminates in a spray of fine dust, thrown back in my face by the wind at the end of Santa Monica Pier, just two days before this night, as if all creation wanted to make sure I understood that this event was something that would never, ever go away. The material that came out and was cremated and dispersed was not him. Our son never made it to the outside world. He got stuck inside, still wanders those interior halls, affecting the world only through his shadowy presence in our minds. Those who share their lives with someone dead know that there is nothing as loud as the recounting of all the things that now can never be said, or the memories of events that will never take place.

Cut off from the generations in both directions now, I have nowhere else to go. And so I sit here, and wait. Someone can be held responsible for something. Somebody, somewhere, has to pay. Finally I hear the door of the house open. I hear loud voices and the heavy thud of footsteps, and I sense that more than two people have entered. The sound of their voices is harsh, alien, and jagged with a frustration as toxic as my own.

Within three minutes of this moment, I will have shot four men to death.

I do not want to experience this again. When I finally fight my way up from the dream, I scare the life out of the person stuck next to me on the morning flight up to Seattle; and as I cry out, I realize that it is not the sound of footsteps

I have heard but the plane's wheels being lowered, ready to land.

We touched down just before midday, and I turned my phone on immediately. It buzzed thirty seconds later. The message was not from Amy, as I'd hoped. It was from Gary. An address.

His hotel was on the west side of downtown, close to the canyon of Interstate 5 as it cuts through the center. It looked to be around the same price point as the last one. After the conversation with Blanchard the previous morning, this made sense. Fisher was paying his own way, not charging it off to some deep-pocketed client. I parked the car under the hotel and went around to the trunk. Then headed inside.

Gary had said he'd come down to the lobby to meet me. Instead I got his room number from reception and went up. I knocked on his door. A muffled voice answered.

"Honor bar," I said, facing the other way.

"I don't need anything."

"I have to check stock, sir."

As soon as the door opened, I kicked it straight at him, catching him in the face. I slammed the door shut again behind me as I strode in.

"Jack, what the—"

I shoved him hard in the chest, sending him stumbling. He fell onto his back, and I put my knee in the middle of his ribs, pulling out the gun and pushing it hard into the middle of his forehead.

"Shut up," I said. "Do not say anything at all."

He still started to open his mouth.

"I mean it, Gary," I said, pushing down harder. "I really do. I am done being fucked around by you and everyone else. Do you understand?"

This time he just blinked.

"Did you get Anderson killed?"

He stared at me. "What?"

"Only three people knew where we were going to meet. You, me, him. I didn't tell anyone else. I'm assuming he didn't. Which leaves one person. You."

He looked alarmed. He started to push himself up, saw my face, stopped. "Jack, you've got to believe me."

"No. I don't have to believe anything from a guy who leaves a hospital when we've just seen a guy gunned down in front of our eyes. Who checks out of his hotel and disappears."

"I had to, Jack. There's . . . People have been following me. Someone had been in my hotel room."

"For God's sake, Gary. Go back to your therapist and take it seriously this time."

"There's nothing wrong with—"

"Really? So how come you told me you were still working for your company, when it turns out you're on enforced leave?"

"How do you know that?"

"What exactly *are* these 'personal' reasons, Gary? What the fuck is *up* with you? Actually, you know what? I don't care. I've got bigger things to worry about."

"No you haven't," he said. "There's nothing bigger than this."

I looked down at the man lying on a hotel carpet and wondered how on earth my life had come to this. How we'd somehow gotten from a high-school running track to here.

"Whatever," I said. "I don't care about Anderson, Cranfield, or any of this crap. I want you to tell me anything else you know that pertains to Amy, and then fuck off out of my life."

"Jack," he said, "I've kept things from you. I admit that. But I had to. Please, just let me explain."

I should've started walking toward the door. The gun felt too good in my hand. But I didn't know where else I could go except to see Todd Crane, and I knew that would be a bad idea. I was being drawn toward easy solutions. I wanted someone to hurt.

"Please," he said. "Give me five minutes."

"For what? More bullshit?"

"Look in the briefcase."

I glanced at the briefcase lying open on the chair. "Why?"

"Just look. I'll stay right here. On the floor."

I went and looked. Photocopies of contracts, reference books. A Bible, dog-eared, marked with Post-it notes. "What, Gary?"

"In the side pocket."

I pulled out a small, hard rectangle. A Mini DV videotape. "Is Amy on here?"

"No," he said. "It's nothing like that."

"Then I don't care."

"Please, Jack. Literally, five minutes. And then I'll tell you everything I know."

"Does what you know affect anything I care about?"

"Yes."

I tossed the tape down onto his chest.

I sat in the chair, still holding my gun, and watched Fisher get off the floor. He took the camcorder out of the briefcase, along with a thin black cable. Went around the back of the room's television to plug one end in and stuck the other in the side of a camcorder. Put the mini-tape into it.

"I'm going to have to find the right place."

"Fine," I said. "The time that takes is included in the five minutes."

He stood hunched in front of the set, doing something to the camcorder. I couldn't see the screen from where I sat. "Okay," he said after a moment. "We're set." He stepped out of the way. The television screen was still black. He went to the window and pulled the drapes.

"Why are you doing that?"

"Because what's on the tape is pretty dark."

He sat on the edge of the sofa. The room was now murky enough so you could tell that the television was on, from the slight warmth on the screen. Fisher pressed a button on a tiny remote.

The screen was suddenly bright with picture. A park, on a cold afternoon. Grass, trees still with leaves, a couple of joggers in the distance, the sound of someone walking on gravel nearby.

The camera swerved and zoomed in to show a child, a baby girl, tottering along a path, holding a stick and waving it insistently at nothing in particular.

"Beth?" said a voice. Gary's voice. *"Bethany?"*

The child turned, after a pause, evidently still having to remember that the sound her father had just made related to her in some specific way. She grinned up at the camera and made a babbling noise, flapping the hand not holding the stick.

"Look," Gary's voice said. *"What's that?"*

The camera panned left to show a large dog ambling up the path toward the girl, whose face lit up.

"Ooof-ooof!" she said. *"Ooof-ooof."*

"That's right, *honey. It's a dog. Woof-woof."*

The child moved confidently toward the animal, hand held out conspicuously flat, as she'd evidently been taught. The dog had brought with it an elderly couple.

"It's okay," the woman said. *"He's quite safe."*

The little girl glanced up at her for moment, then at her husband. She raised her hand and pointed.

"Granna," she said firmly. *"Granna."*

Gary laughed as the camera dropped to her level. *"Granddad? Well, no, honey."* He then added, not to his daughter, *"She thinks everyone, who . . . well, you know."*

The man smiled down affably. *"Has gray hair. I know. And hell, I* am *a granddad. Five times over."* He bent carefully toward Bethany as she patted the dog's back. *"What's your name, honey?"*

She didn't say anything. Gary spoke. *"Bethany, what's your name?"*

"Batne?" the girl said.

Then she patted the dog one more time, a little too hard, and went running away up the path.

The video froze abruptly, then went to black.

"Very fucking sweet," I said. "But—"

"Wait a second," Gary interrupted. "You had to see that. But this is the thing."

The image on the television's screen changed again, flipping from pure black to a kind of mottled purple. Some kind of view in very low lighting conditions.

As my eyes got used to the dim light, I figured out that the glow came from a bedside night-light and that a collection of paler dots in the middle of the frame was a mobile, dangling animal shapes twisting slowly. I was looking into a child's bedroom, in the dark.

"What the—"

"Please just watch," Gary said.

The camera remained motionless for a while, evidently positioned in a hallway outside the room. I realized I could hear the sound of its operator breathing, trying to do so as quietly as possible.

Then the camera moved in a series of slow steps, as the person holding it stepped into the bedroom and then back and to the side. There was a quiet swishing sound and then a click. The image got even darker.

The camera panned slowly and unsteadily around the room. A faint, cold light through drapes showed shadowy, grainy images of a jungle mural on the wall, a baby-size chair and table, an orderly collection of toys stowed in a shelving unit. The view turned in a complete circle to pass the door, now closed, and ended back on the area made lighter by the clock. Looking down into a child's bed.

The bed had bars on all sides, a crib designed for someone not yet old enough to be allowed to traverse the world under his or her own steam. You could make out the shape of the sleeping child within. Hear it, too, the slow rise and fall of its breathing.

Nothing happened for a couple of minutes. You could tell that the camera was still capturing the scene in real time, however, because of the quiet sounds of two people breathing and the noise of the image as the camera tried to cope with the near darkness.

This wasn't anywhere enough to hold my attention. I was just about to get up when I heard something very quiet out of the television speakers.

"What was that?" I said.

Gary held his hand up, gesturing me to keep silent.

On-screen, the camera changed position. It moved quickly back from the bed, around to the side, and dropped a couple of feet. From here it had a view between a couple of the bars, of the side of a baby girl's head.

I leaned forward, peering at the murky screen.

Nothing for a moment. Then the noise came again. It was a long, drawn-out sigh. From its quality it was obvious it hadn't come from the person operating the camera—Gary, I assumed. Nothing for maybe another minute. Then, out of the speakers, very quietly:

"I don't know."

I blinked. I knew what I thought I'd just heard. There was silence again for fifteen, twenty seconds.

"Can anybody *hear?"*

This time there was no doubt. The words sounded strained, unevenly inflected. The child's eyes were shut. Her body was motionless.

And she was two years old.

"Go 'way," she said then, and this time her voice did sound right, the words vague and unformed.

"No," the other voice said, still coming out of Bethany's mouth. *"I'm going nowhere."*

The child suddenly turned on her side, toward the camera. The motion was angry.

The operator caught his breath, evidently afraid she was going to wake, see him, and wail the place down.

But her eyes did not open. There was the very faint sound of crying, the child's chest rising and falling more rapidly.

"I can wait," the voice said.

Then the girl turned quickly onto her back again. There was another long sigh, and she went quiet. A moment later the screen flicked to black.

I turned to Fisher.

"Play it again."

He rewound the tape. At no point was there a perfect view of the child's mouth at the same time as the voice was audible. It was too dark in the room, and her face was generally at least partially obscured by the bars of the crib. But it was hard to believe that the voice had been dubbed in afterward—it shared too much of the same quality as the background sounds of breathing. Even harder to ignore was the way the child turned over at the end. There was something adult about it, fast, bad-tempered. Did children move like that?

I didn't know. I hit PAUSE and froze the tape on the image of Bethany lying in her crib.

"How does this relate to Amy?"

He stared at me. "You're kidding, right? I even got the name for them from you. From your book."

"Name for what?"

"You've just *heard* one, Jack. Heard its voice, coming out of my baby's mouth."

I stared at him. "You think someone's *inside* your child?"

"Not just her. Don't you get it?" He leaned forward, his eyes sparking with inner light. "They're the intruders, Jack. They're the people inside."

chapter THIRTY-FOUR

There's a feeling you get to be very familiar with as a policeman. The realization that the person you've been talking to has, all this time, been lying. It might be something big, could just be some small detail. But suddenly you understand that the world he's been describing, with plenty of eye contact and the apparent desire to be helpful, is simply not real.

I didn't think Gary was lying. But otherwise it felt the same. You want neurosis to be heroic, to confer a shamanic majesty upon the tangled and pathless inner landscape some people are unable to escape. It isn't. There is no upside. It's just bitterly sad.

He saw the way I was looking at him. "No, Jack. You just *saw* it, right there on the screen."

"I saw a child sleeping. I heard some words."

"Some of which she is *not capable of saying.*"

"Some part of your kid's brain has gotten ahead of itself, Gary. That's all. It's practicing in downtime. Talking in your sleep is no big deal. Amy did it for a while. Back when she was a kid, and recently."

Gary smiled in a strange, overconfident way. "Really."

"What's that supposed to mean?"

"Explain Mozart to me, Jack."

"Excuse me?"

"The guy was composing at four, yes, and we all know this, but instead of pointing out how fucking freaky it is, we just say, 'Cool, how super smart he must have been.' But how could that *possibly* work—unless he came into the world with a flying start?"

"Are you talking about reincarnation, Gary?"

"No. This is not an individual coming back into a new body. This is when you have two people *inside the same mind.*"

"You think Bethany has an additional person in her head."

"I know it. And who it is."

"For God's sake—you told me you didn't *believe* that crap about Donna. I thought you were just drunk."

"You didn't watch me carefully enough that evening," he said. "I didn't finish half my beers. I don't drink much anymore. I'm too smart for that."

"Right. Sure. Whatever. And what exactly does this have to do with my wife?"

"Joe Cranfield had an intruder, too, Jack. He *was* the intruder, in fact, the older personality roosting in the body of the person I met. This is why Cranfield was able to hit the ground running. A *financial* prodigy, yes? A Mozart of music. He's what clued me in to the whole thing in the first place. That's why he cleared his estate at the end, without warning his wife—who wasn't an intruder and so didn't know the score. That's got to be part of the system. The way these people work."

"*Which* people, Gary? Your two-year-old and a dead businessman from Illinois? They had some conspiracy going between the two of them? That's what you're saying?"

"Jack—of *course* not. There's more of them, all over the world. A group who've organized things so they can come back, who've done it time and time again—figured out how to do this hundreds, thousands, maybe *tens* of thousands of years ago. You said it yourself, back at school. You said that thing about Donna, remember? That she came into the world knowing things."

"Gary, that was just a figure of speech. I was eighteen, for Christ's sake. I was just trying to sound smart."

"But you were *right.* That's the thing—some people *do* come into life knowing things they shouldn't, or at least the second soul that lives *inside* them does. A group of people figured out that they could come back, get into other people's heads. Hitch along for another ride. They found ways of reminding themselves who they'd been before. They started to plan ahead, coming up with ways to be truly themselves next time, instead of just thoughts in the back of someone else's head. This is why some people are born bad, Jack. This is—"

"Gary, listen to someone with experience. People are not born bad—"

"Really? You think all cops would say the same? All social workers? All defense lawyers? All the parents out there dealing with a kid who just cannot seem to behave, who is determined to go through all the wrong doors and kick them hard? Some of the intruders are good people, decent people. Joe Cranfield was. But some of them are not. They only come back because they didn't fuck the world hard enough last time. The intruders wait until they've seen that a baby's not going to die of some infant-mortality thing, then bed down inside it. This is why tantrums start around age two or three—as two souls start to struggle together for prominence. And why some kids have nightmares for the next five, six years, as they try to fend these things off in their sleep—confused, frightened, not understanding what's moving into their heads in the night, when they're vulnerable and weak. Note how prodigies always either die young or go nuts, Jack. It's okay if you *know* what's going on, if the intruder takes center stage and is in conscious charge of its destiny—if it's part of the gang. But if you *don't* know that this is what's happening to you, then it's too confusing and

too much of the endless inner voices, and people drink or drug themselves to death or go insane."

I didn't know what to say to him. "I keep failing to hear how my wife fits into any of this bullshit, Gary."

"The firm that handled Joe's estate works out of the building that has her name on the papers, Jack. Burnell and Lytton are tied in to the organization that keeps the system going. The intruders must have to fiscally reboot each time; otherwise you'd have people with huge amounts of cash they'd accumulated, without any inheritance route, which would blow things out into the open. So my guess is that when you're coming to the end of your present lifetime, you have to get rid of everything. Start next time afresh. Which is what—"

"Gary, you can't use a *lack* of something to prove—"

"I know that, Jack—I'm a fucking lawyer. But face it: Amy and Cranfield are connected. In the end it comes back to the ten percent kept aside from Cranfield's estate. I didn't tell you one thing because I didn't think you'd believe any of this back then."

"I don't believe any of it now."

"The charity Burnell and Lytton helps administer? The Psychomachy Trust. You won't find the word in a modern dictionary. So at first I assumed it was made up. But it was in use a couple hundred years ago. It means 'a conflict between the body and the soul'—or between a person and *the thing that's inside*. The trust's a front. When an intruder dies, it pays a tithe—in Cranfield's case nearly twenty-six million dollars. This money is used to keep the system going, or staff, or . . . Look, I don't know exactly how it all works," he admitted irritably. "But—"

"Okay," I said, standing up. "I'm going to leave now. And seriously, Gary—go home. I mean it. Spend some time with your family and talk to someone good before this gets any worse."

"I don't blame you for thinking I'm . . . I know this

sounds very strange," Fisher said. "I have evidence, Jack, *lots* of it. I've done my research. But you already *know* what some people are like. The dissatisfaction, the yearning to be or to have someone or something else, people who can't stop themselves from doing things they *know* are wrong, other people who seem to be able to tap into some kind of higher power right from the get-go."

I was putting my gun in my jacket by now—I wasn't going to need it here, I could see that, and being in this room with Fisher was making me feel worse even than talking to Anderson had. I wanted out.

But I hesitated. I guess I was thinking of a woman who'd had nightmares as a child, started talking in her sleep a year ago. Who was not behaving like the woman I knew. Who almost smelled different. Since Natalie had asked me the question, I'd been forced to realize that, when I thought back, Amy had been changing subtly over the last couple of years, from even before what had happened with our son. Was all of this explicable through the hidden presence of another man? Some tea-drinking, pink-liking enabler, promoting the emergence of a different Amy? Was it simply time in her journey for a change, a chaotic swerve into midlife, with old baggage being abruptly thrown over the side?

Or was there something else going on?

I shook my head. No. I was leaping at anything that would explain Amy's behavior in a way less injurious to me, less to do with lack of love and irreversible change. Almost anything felt better than the obvious.

However ludicrous.

"So why did they kill Anderson?" I asked, losing momentum. "What does he have to do with this?"

"You tell me. You were the guy he talked to."

"He barely said anything before he got shot."

"Right. And what was *that* about? What could a man like Anderson do that would provoke someone to tear down his life and shoot him to death in a public place? You think that killer was working alone? Of course not. So what merits all this? What's *big* enough? Tell me."

"I don't know. I don't care. I—"

My phone rang. I yanked it out. "Hello?"

"Mother*fucker,*" a voice said.

I swore. I'd forgotten just how much some guys won't give up on the prospect of an easy buck. "L.T.," I said. "I meant to block your number. I'll do it now."

"You owe me. Last chance."

"Or *what*? I owe you shit. I already told you, I'm not interested."

"You sure? They here now."

"Who is?"

"At the place. Three people just go in."

I reevaluated. "Into the building? What did they look like?"

"You interested now, huh?"

"Just tell me what they look like."

"Like any other white motherfuckers. One a businessman. He wearing a suit. Other two, I don't know."

"Stay where you are. Call me if they leave."

I closed the phone. Fisher was sitting on the bed, staring at the frozen image of his daughter on the screen. He looked older. Older and smaller and alone. There were wet tracks down both of his cheeks.

"What?" I asked, feeling cold. "Gary?"

"I miss her," he said quietly. "I miss them all."

"So go home. Forget about all this."

"It's too late for that." He looked at me. "You don't believe me, do you? You don't believe in this."

"No," I said. "I'm sorry. But some people just went into the building in Belltown. You want to find out who they are?"

He rubbed his face with his hands, as if having to haul himself back into the here and now.

But when he looked at me again, his eyes were clear. He

stood and reached for his jacket. "Why would they even let us in the door?"

I got a clip out and clicked it into my gun, so that—for the first time that day—it was loaded.

"I'm not planning on giving them a choice."

chapter THIRTY-FIVE

The call came in the dead of night. Todd had fought waking. Fought it hard. He'd lain wide-eyed for hours when he went to bed. When he finally found sleep, he wanted to stay there. The sound of the phone ringing had been faint, from downstairs. Livvie had banned a telephone by the bedside a decade before, after a spate of strange calls, some wacko calling up in the night to speak to their middle child, then only eleven years old.

The ringing stopped as the machine clicked in. But barely thirty seconds later, it started again.

Todd opened his eyes. That was weird. People hitting a wrong number usually understood their error as soon as they heard someone else's message. They didn't call back. Anyone with a legitimate message left a message.

He rolled over. The clock said 3:21. Jesus.

No call at that hour of the night can be ignored.

He grabbed his robe and hurried downstairs. By the time he got to the hallway, the ringing had stopped again.

He heard the answering machine click in. Nobody said anything. It clicked off. Then the ringing started once more. He grabbed the handset. "Look—"

"Be quiet," said a voice. A young girl's voice. It made the hairs on the back of Todd's neck rise.

"Who is this?"

"Listen."

There was silence for a moment.

"Dad?" A different voice. Older. Scared.

Crane gripped the phone.

"Dad, it's me."

"Rachel? What's going on?"

He heard the catch of her breath. As if she were crying, trying not to let him hear. He felt frozen in place, heavy, blurred sleep turning to anger and fear.

"I'm sorry." Then she was gone.

"Okay," said the other voice, and he knew now where he'd heard it before. In his office the previous afternoon. "You're going to listen now, Toddy. I found myself somewhere to stay. Guess where?"

"Put my daughter back—"

"That's right. Rachel's going to describe her situation to you now. Listen carefully."

A pause as the phone was handed over, and then his daughter spoke slowly into it. "I am tied to my table. She is standing behind me. She has a knife."

The other voice returned. "A little Hemingwayish for some tastes, perhaps, but I hope it gives a clear picture? I need you to be fully focused, Todd."

"Please," Crane said. "Please don't hurt her."

"I may not," the voice said, as if considering the idea. "You never know. But that's going to depend. I said I wanted to meet with someone. You were a bore about it. I need you to find another way of looking at the situation. A more workable solution, as a someone close to me might put it. I need you to set up that meeting."

"Who—"

"Rose."

Todd opened his mouth, shut it again. "But—"

"No. There can be no buts here, Todd. Don't be thinking in a 'but' frame of mind, or I'm going to fuck Rachel up. Arrange it, and do it fast. If you don't, I'll just kill Rachel. If you talk to the cops, tell anyone else what's going on, I'll know. And then I'll just work on her instead. So she'll be around for you to see afterward. For you to know you made her this way, as you take out all the mirrors in her sweet little house and refit it for wheelchair access."

Todd opened his mouth, but it was dry.

"Just do it," the voice said, and then was gone.

Todd was on the road in minutes. It didn't occur to him to go wake his wife. This wasn't something she could help with, and nothing he could do or say would stop her from getting on the phone to the police.

He raced across the sleeping city in a daze, running red lights without even realizing. Drove past his daughter's house, careful not to slow down. It was dark inside. He pulled the car around the next corner and came to a halt, trying to work out what to do.

Would this person really know if he called the police? How *could* she? He was pretty sure that part had been a bluff, but the threat she'd made was not. More than anything, he'd been convinced by his daughter's voice. What had he heard—twenty, thirty words? It was enough. Rachel was independent, tough, more like her father than either of her sisters was. Couldn't seem to get her private life together, but it took a lot to knock her confidence. She'd sounded about four years old on the phone. And very, very scared. She was convinced by the person with her, and that was enough to convince Todd. If he called the police—even assuming they'd take seriously a report of a grown woman being held hostage by a child—and they knocked on the door politely, instead of just busting their way straight in . . .

Todd couldn't take that risk. Rachel could be dead and her killer away over a back fence before they got into the house.

What if he went up to the door himself? That wouldn't

constitute calling anyone, would it? But he didn't know if it was just the girl inside or if she had someone else helping her.

He sat in the thrumming car, horribly irresolute. This was what fathers were supposed to be able to do, wasn't it? To make this kind of call. To protect their young. To go charging in, confident of their ability to handle the situation, to prevent harm.

But now he knew that this had to do with that other thing, the oddness that had circled in the back of his world for half his life, the people for whom he had once in a while done small things and from whom he had received career-making favors in return.

And so he was not confident of his ability to control the situation. He was not confident of anything at all when it came to Rose.

"You've got to listen to me," he said twelve hours later. "I really have to meet with you. Today."

"Tell me over the phone," she said. "I'm very busy."

Todd put his head in his hands. His palms were slick with sweat. He felt sick. It was now a little after three in the afternoon. It had taken all this time to get the woman on the phone. He had this shot, and that was it. He could not blow it.

He raised his head. Stared out over the bay, at the mountains, tried to lock himself into the way he usually felt while at his desk, the habitual confidence.

"I can't do that," he said, in a voice that sounded very reasonable and professional. The voice of a good boss. The voice of someone in control.

"Why?"

"I think my phone's being tapped."

There was a pause. "Why would you think that?"

"I hear strange noises."

"Are you quite all right, Mr. Crane? You haven't been

drinking? Had too long and convivial a lunch, in the pursuit of a client? Or a young lady, perhaps? Have you possibly reverted to the excessive use of cocaine that we once had to assist you in relinquishing?"

"No," he said, and he knew he could not keep this up for much longer. "I just have to talk to you in person."

"That's not going to happen, Mr.—"

"Oh, for God's sake! Come on—it's *Todd.* You know I'm not going to screw you around. I've just got to see you. I—" He stopped just in time.

"You . . . what?"

Todd hesitated. He knew what he was not supposed to say. But he also knew that without giving Rose something, she wasn't going to do what he needed her to.

"Someone came into the office yesterday," he said carefully.

"What do you mean, 'someone'?"

"A girl. But there was something weird about her."

There was a beat of silence.

"I'll call you back in half an hour," the woman said.

The phone went dead. Crane sat there with it in his hands, shaking.

As he sat waiting, he stared at the radio still lying on the floor. Tried not to see it as a symbol for all the other things he should have taken more care of while he had the chance. But once the mind thinks it's found a sign or portent, it will not let go even if it discovers too late and only to punish you. When he reached KC&H that morning, he'd tried phoning Rachel's work number. She had called in sick. Halfway through the morning, Livvie phoned, complaining she'd tried to get hold of Rachel on her cell to arrange lunch later in the week and gotten no reply. Todd told her he'd received an e-mail ten minutes earlier saying she'd lost her phone at some club the night before, was getting a replacement sent, sorry—he meant to tell her right away.

He was doing all the right things. He was behaving well. He was going rapidly out of his mind.

Rose called back twenty minutes later.

"I can see you," she said without preamble. "Around seven. I'll confirm a venue closer to the time."

"I need to—" Todd stopped. He knew he couldn't demand to know where they were going to meet. He couldn't ask for a specific place either. Not yet.

"Need what, Todd?"

"To see you, that's all."

"And it's going to happen. I just hope I find it worthwhile." Then she was gone.

Todd pulled on his coat and hurried out of the office. Bianca tried to wave him down as he passed her office, but she could wait. Everything could wait.

He emerged into Post Alley with his phone already in his hand but didn't call his daughter's house until he was halfway down the street, shoulders hunched against the rest of the world.

As he pleaded with the person who answered, getting her to accept the fact that he hadn't yet been able to confirm the venue she'd specified, he didn't notice a stocky, red-haired man coming out of the deli on the corner: a man who heard every detail of Todd's phone conversation and quickly relayed it on.

In a hotel ten minutes' walk away, a man sat on the end of a bed. He had been there most of the afternoon. It was not a nice bed. It was not a nice room. It was, all in all, not a great hotel. Shepherd didn't care. He'd stayed in good hotels often enough. Unless you are in urgent need of spa treatment and don't mind spending thirty bucks on breakfast, the difference isn't very noticeable when the lights go out. You're still just a man in a room in a building in a city, surrounded by strangers, hoping that tonight you will sleep.

His phone rang. He checked the number and did not answer it. It was Alison O'Donnell's cell phone. Again. She'd left a number of messages during the day. Her husband, too. They were in an excitable state, having hooked up with some policeman in Seattle, one who'd had the sense to realize that the reason Shepherd had specified Alison should call him on her cell was that the alleged FBI agent who'd left his card with her would accept calls only from that particular number. Give a cigar to Detective Whatever-His-Name-Was: Evidently the SPD Missing Persons Bureau recruited from a higher IQ bracket than the sheriff's department in Cannon Beach. Shepherd had no interest in talking to Mrs. O'Donnell now. Things were closing in. Not just the situation he'd brought about, but everything. He could feel it getting closer by the hour.

Behind him on the bed lay his suitcase. It had lasted four years so far. Before that there'd been one exactly the same, and another before that. How many had he gone through in his time? He had no idea.

The suitcase was full of money. This was what had made him accept the bargain and stick to it, a bargain that had seen him lending material assistance to someone who'd been declared far beyond the pale. The first thing the girl remembered on the beach was the money's whereabouts. It had been arranged that way—with the 9-by-9 symbol as a trigger—and Shepherd had gone straight back to Portland to pick it up from the old Chinese woman to whom it had been entrusted. He'd broken the terms of the initial bargain because he couldn't wait any longer. He needed the money *now*. It was to be his stake, his first birthday present, his head start next time. It was utterly forbidden to do this, but he wasn't one of them, and he would not be even when he took advantage of the older deal, the one struck when he was twenty.

Work for us, that deal went, do our dirty work, and we'll arrange that you, too, will be reminded, when you come back. Shepherd had not merely been present at deaths, after all; he'd been instrumental, as all who took the title were, in rebirths. He had arrived in people's lives, sometime after their eighteenth birthday, and supplied the trigger they'd registered with the trust. A phrase, a piece of music, a picture or symbol, on a couple of occasions a specific flavor: memory joggers, carefully selected so as not to be something the person would run into by accident, before he or she was ready. Before someone like Shepherd was on hand to guide the subjects through the process of realizing that their current feet were not the first with which they had walked the earth.

Shepherd knew that if a count were made in his life, however, the deaths far, far outweighed the rebirths. He had become a specialist. People who found out something, however small. People who guessed next to nothing at all. And once in a while even one of their own. Someone who had become a threat to the system or had returned damaged in transit—either of whom was *not* then supposed to be helped to come back again.

Murders and motel rooms—in the end they all flattened into one. Now Shepherd could feel his legacy gathering around. With Anderson's machine he might even be able to see them, if it had really worked. The people Shepherd had sent away grew thicker around him. Like invisible cats, but larger and far colder, rubbing insidiously against the back of his legs and neck. Waiting. How far away were they? Not far enough.

Shepherd needed this situation to be over with. Then he had to admit his condition to Rose and start putting things in place. He needed certainty, more than ever. Now that the time was approaching, he'd found himself prey to occasional doubt, to the idea that maybe there *was* no deal, that all those like him had been tricked. Perhaps this notion had come to him in a dream or a waking thought in one of the long night watches when he looked back over the things he'd done. Or perhaps one of the shadows that surrounded him had whispered it in his ear, not as a warning but as a taunt. Either way it occurred to him one night that he'd never met someone like him who had come back. Never heard of one from the others either, and he'd known more than a few like him who *had* died, after years of long service. The man who'd recruited Shepherd, for example, who found a gangling youth in a small town in Wisconsin and made him a promise compelling enough to make that boy leave everything behind, even a sweetheart whom he loved. That man had died twenty-five years ago. Since then there'd been no sign of him, even though it had been agreed that he could get in touch with Shepherd once he'd been reminded.

But he must be out there somewhere.

The deal must be real. It had to be. These doubts were nothing more than a variation on those that every human felt when faced with the end of the road.

Shepherd could smell the bathroom from where he sat. His stomach was in near-constant revolt now, and yet still he tried to eat. It was a habit the body found hard to break. Like a wounded dog, viciously rejected, kicked for years, but still returning with cowed back to its hateful master or mistress, in the hope of love this time. He could remember his mother, in her last days, when he was thirteen. In the months of her slow death, she'd made little notes in a book, jotted down memories of her early life, as if gathering fallen leaves to her chest, to stop them from being scattered and lost by the coming winds. In the final few weeks, she stopped doing it. She merely sat in her chair out on the porch, reeking of cancer, and done nothing but wait, with increasing impatience, for the end. Ready to go home alone, to leave, waiting for her wounded dog of a body to finally lie down and *die,* so she could be free of its relentless needs and loves and demands.

At the time Shepherd had accused his mother of giving up. Now he understood.

After a while his phone rang once again. He looked at the screen, answered it.

"We've found who you're looking for," Rose said. "Arrangements for a meeting are being finalized."

"Okay," he said. "I'll be there."

"When I call, be there *fast,*" she said. "This situation has to be resolved immediately, I've got a bad feeling about who this might be."

"Who?" he asked, to see whether she'd gotten it right, making it sound like it didn't matter to him.

"Someone we all used to know," she muttered, and cut the connection.

Shepherd stood. She knew. That didn't matter. It merely made it all the more important that Madison O'Donnell wound up dead, and that it happened fast.

He got his gun out of the suitcase and closed it up.

chapter THIRTY-SIX

"I don't see how we're going to do this," Gary said.

We'd spent five minutes inspecting the back of the building in Belltown, confirming that the windows were boarded from the second story up. Their condition was academic: The fire escape stopped ten feet from the ground, and I wouldn't have trusted a cat's weight on the rest. The ground-level door had a pair of Dorling bolts, which could be opened only from the inside. It would have taken time and a sledgehammer to get through the door from here, an endeavor that would arouse comment in the parking lot that ran right up to the back wall and in which we sat, peering up through the windshield. Patrons came and went, and an officious-looking man was sitting in a booth. He'd already given us a long and suspicious glare. Nobody was going to be dealing drugs on this guy's watch. Or smashing down doors.

We got out of the car and walked around the side to the road that ran along the front of the building. Crossed the street and stood looking at it from the other side. It was coming up to five o'clock. Passing road traffic was light and moving fairly fast. Nobody in a car was going to notice much. The problem was pedestrians. There was enough cause for people to be on their feet in this part of Belltown—a few battered bars, hopeful new ones, restaurants dotted here and there. Most people would mind their own business. Some would not.

"Go over and ring the buzzer," I said.

Fisher went across the street. I watched the windows of the upper story as he leaned on each of the buttons in turn. The sky was overcast and dark enough that the reflections were muted, but there was no discernible change behind any of them. Gary looked back at me. I held my right hand up to my ear, nodded upward. He got out his phone, dialed. He shrugged. Nothing changed.

He walked back. "So now what?"

I went into a convenience store, and then we met L.T. outside the coffeehouse on the next corner up from the building, the one Gary had been sitting outside when he took his photos of Amy. L.T. was on the sidewalk with a friend, a tall guy who looked so disreputable you could have arrested him just for being alive and probably made it stick. He regarded Fisher and me with something between hunger and open hostility, but he probably looked at his own reflection that way, too.

"I said to meet inside," I reminded him.

"Threw us out," L.T. answered.

I offered him a cigarette, a folded fifty lying on top of the pack. He took the note, along with two cigarettes, winked at his friend.

"So?"

"Nobody come out," he said. "They still inside."

"You want to earn another fifty? Each?"

"Shit," L.T. said, which I took as assent.

"Either of you holding?" They shook their heads. "No, really." After a beat, both nodded. "You don't want to be," I said. "Stash it somewhere. Now."

They touched hands with the lightness of magicians, and then the tall one trotted around the corner to hide their drugs.

"Okay," I said when he got back. "Here's what we're going to do." I pointed down the street. "I want one of you on each of those corners."

"And do what?"

"Just stand in the middle of the sidewalk. Eyefuck anyone who looks like they're heading your way, but don't do or say anything. To anyone. Okay? I just want five minutes without too many people passing that building."

"What this shit about?" L.T. asked.

"None of your business." I gave him the money. "When you can't see us anymore, you can go."

L.T. took the cash, nodded at Fisher. "This dude ever say anything?"

"He's choosy. Only talks to other narcotics cops. And he's seen where you hide your shit. Understand?"

L.T. made the money disappear. "Don't you want to know about the girl?"

"What girl?"

"Little girl I told you about, man."

"Not really," I said. "Why?"

"See her again, last night. She come back later, go right up to the door. Keep pressing a buzzer. But there ain't nobody answer. And then I see her later watching outside some new bar, a couple blocks downtown. *Way* after little-girl bedtime, you know?"

"Great," I said. "Now go stand where I told you to."

Gary and I waited as the two guys crossed the street. L.T. took the corner nearest us. His friend loped down to the other end of the block. Within a couple of minutes, most pedestrians were electing to cross to the other side rather than walk close to either of them.

"Let's go," I said.

I went across the street and straight up to the door of the building, Gary following right behind. "Get out your phone," I said. "Make it look like you're placing a call. Glance up at the building once in a while."

I got out my key ring. I took it slow, trying to feel confident that the combination of a largely empty sidewalk behind me and a colleague who looked like he was trying to get hold of someone in the building to achieve legitimate entry, would make me invisible for long enough.

"Christ," Fisher said after a couple of minutes. "There's a police car."

"Where?"

"Down at the intersection."

"Keep an eye on it."

I kept moving the tool. Trying just to feel the metal inside the lock, the balance of tensions, the ways the hidden components did and did not want to move. It wasn't happening. I switched to a more flexible tool.

"Fuck—he's gone," Fisher said, looking up the street the other way.

"The police?"

"No—your friend. L.T. Just vanished, didn't even see him go."

"What are the cops doing now?"

"They've pulled over. Where that other guy is."

"He'll be fine."

"He's running this way."

"Oh, crap," I said. I glanced around and saw L.T.'s friend pounding up the sidewalk. One cop was running after him, the other stood at the car, on the radio.

"Stupid fucker kept L.T.'s drugs," I said. "You can't trust *any*one."

"Jack, he's heading toward us."

"I know that. Put your back to the street."

I turned to the door again, closed my eyes. I heard the sound of the foot pursuit, the cop shouting at the running suspect, but tried to concentrate only on the feel of the thin piece of metal in my hands.

"Jack—"

"Shut up, Gary. I'm nearly there."

The sound of chaos got closer. "He!" someone was bellowing breathlessly. "He, there! He the man!"

L.T.'s friend had stopped running. He was twenty feet away, pointing straight at me. The pursuing cop was slowing, hand on his gun, figuring this new twist. His partner was heading our way, too, now. I could hear sirens in the distance.

"He," the tall guy said again, jabbing his finger in my direction. The closest cop was approaching him warily, but casting looks in my direction. "He pay me, he tell me be there. I ain't sell no shit to no one."

The second cop had made the sidewalk now. While his partner grabbed the tall guy's arm, he walked toward Gary and me.

"Excuse me, sir," he said loudly. "You got any idea what this guy is talking about?"

"Sorry, no," I said, looking at him with an honest citizen's unthinking deference. There was a faint click at my hands as the tumblers finally fell. I pushed the door open behind me as if it were a twice-daily occurrence. "Is there a problem?"

The cop looked at me a beat longer, then lost interest and went to help his colleague subdue the tall guy, who was kicking and shouting and raising hell.

I stepped into the building, Fisher right behind.

chapter THIRTY-SEVEN

After the door closed, we were in pitch darkness. I hadn't wanted to fumble for a switch with the cops right there.

"Christ," Fisher said. "That was . . ."

". . . fine," I said. "Keep your voice down."

I pulled out the cheap flashlight I'd bought in the convenience store. I pointed it back toward the door, ran the beam along the wall at shoulder height. Saw a bank of switches. Flicked them one by one. Nothing happened. Pointed the light down at the floor instead. There was nothing lying there.

"No power," Fisher said.

"But no mail or junk either. Someone picks up."

We were standing in a wide, high-ceilinged corridor, peeling paper on the walls and an uneven floor. Once it had been tiled in a simple, businesslike way. Now many of the tiles were broken or missing. I made my way along it, treading carefully. The building smelled damp and fusty and old. Ten feet away a door hung ajar slightly, on the right. It opened into a long, narrow kitchen, the service area of the coffee shop that had been the last occupant of the front part of the building. In the glow thrown by the lamp, it looked like the proprietors had left work one evening and decided never to come back. Broken cups, rusty machinery, the scent of rats' passing, and beneath all that the smell of Seattle itself, old coffee and fog. This building was dead. It was like being in the hold of a shipwreck, hundreds of feet under the sea.

The two doors farther along the corridor were both open onto a wide, dark area cluttered with large pieces of display furniture, dating back to when the place had been a department store, moved out from the walls and left stranded in the space like more tall, abandoned ships.

I came back out and found a door in the back wall, too. I gave this a shake. It didn't move at all. This must be the one we'd seen in the parking lot. There was another door around the back of the staircase. I opened it, looked down. Pitch-black and cold, with narrow wooden stairs leading to a basement.

I went back and headed up the stairs, climbed quietly to the next floor, shifting my weight along the banister until I was sure the treads of the staircase were sound. Fisher followed. When I got up to the second level, I gestured to keep him still and listened.

No sound of conversation or movement, no creaking floorboards.

All the doors on this level were shut and locked. The same on the next. Someone had gone to some trouble to make sure fire precautions had been followed, closing the doors to stop a blaze flooding from room to room. On the third level, I chose the door at the front of the building and quietly jacked the lock.

The other side was a wide, empty space, the full width of the building's street frontage, faint lines of light around boarded-in windows. A flick around with the lamp revealed a few pieces of furniture, extension cords running the perimeter and up and down the walls, and a collection of rolls of mildewed backdrop tilted into one corner. Presumably this was the area that had been used as a studio. I tried to imagine a much younger Amy perched in one of those chairs, cradling a coffee, watching a shoot. I couldn't.

Fisher had stayed in the doorway, his face a paler patch in the gloom. I pointed at the ceiling.

"Try them again."

He called. We could hear a phone ring on the floor above, the kind that sounds like someone hammering frenetically on a tiny bell, a dusty, echoing sound. It wasn't answered, and no machine clicked in.

The tension in my stomach and shoulders was starting to fade back, and I felt a sense of focus that had been lost to me for over a year.

"Are you okay?" Fisher whispered. His face was pinched and nervous, and he was looking at me strangely.

Not at my face, but down at my right hand. I realized that the tension had not faded at all, merely spread so it was throughout my entire body.

And also that, without any recollection of doing so, I had taken out my gun.

"I'm fine," I said.

I walked past him to the end of the corridor, crooked my head to look up the next flight of stairs, directing the little light obliquely off the side wall. Held my hand up again to keep Fisher back.

I went halfway up, stepping carefully. Stopped and listened. I could hear nothing except the faint sounds of traffic outside the building, a drip of water somewhere. I gestured for Fisher to follow and made it up the rest of the way. I waited where I was until he stood next to me on the top level, at the mouth of the staircase.

This landing was arranged in the same way as the lower floors with a long return, doors to spaces at the front and side areas of the building. I switched the flashlight off. Darkness. The long arm on our left was as featureless as the void of space.

But beneath the door to the room at the front of the building, there was a faint glow. Fisher saw it, too.

I stepped quietly over to the door, cupped the end of the light in my hand, and turned it back on. Close up, you could see that this door was different from the ones on the lower levels. Thicker, newer, reinforced. A padlock the size of my fist hung off the handle.

I turned the light back off, slipped it into my pocket. I felt my right thumb flicking the safety off my gun and decided not to interfere. Reached for the door handle and pushed the door inward a breath, to give the mechanism a chance to turn soundlessly.

It was heavy, but the doorknob turned all the way.

Holding it steady, I moved to the right and gestured with my head for Fisher to come behind me. Then I pulled the door open. It moved slowly and silently.

I stopped when the gap was less than two inches wide.

The space on the other side was dimly lit by a lamp on the corner of what looked like a desk, one of the old low lamps with a folded green shade. I could make out a narrow strip of wall beyond, a bookcase lined floor to ceiling with leather spines. Now that the door was cracked open I could hear a faint skittering sound.

At first I thought it might be a rat, or rats, pattering across a wooden floor within. Then I recognized it. It was a sound I had made myself from time to time, though not lately.

You don't take a breath before entering a room. You just do it.

I stepped right into a space that was, except for the desk and shelves, completely empty. The dividing walls on the floor had been removed, creating one very large, L-shaped area. Bare floorboards. No chairs. The windows boarded over. Just that single lamp.

A man was sitting behind the desk, his face bathed in the pale light of a laptop screen. He looked up mildly. I stared at him.

"Ben?" I said.

Fisher stopped in his tracks. Ben Zimmerman looked at him, then at me.

"Oh, dear," he said. "You were right."

"Who?" I said. "Was right? About what?"

"I did warn you," said another voice. I turned to see Bobbi Zimmerman standing by the other wall.

"First time she met you," Ben said, to me this time. "Bobbi said you were trouble. I should listen more often."

"Yes, you should," his wife said.

Ben went back to typing. I realized I was still pointing my gun at him. I lowered my arm. It hadn't seemed to unsettle him much. He looked different from any way I'd seen him in Birch Crossing. Instead of the usual battered khakis and sweater, he was wearing a dark suit with a shirt and tie, and his entire posture was altered. Gone was the stooped air of benign neglect. He didn't look like a history professor anymore, and I knew immediately where I'd seen his likeness.

"Jack," Fisher said. "How do you know this guy?"

"He's my neighbor," I said. There were blotches of color on Fisher's cheeks, and the lines around his eyes were more pronounced than ever. "His name is Ben Zimmerman."

"No," Fisher said. He sounded like a petulant child. "It's Ben *Lytton*. He's one of the Cranfield lawyers. He's the one who came to our office in Chicago."

I pulled out the photos that had been there since Fisher gave them to me, only a couple days before and five minutes' walk away. "So how come you couldn't tell he was the man you photographed with Amy?"

Fisher looked at the photo, back at Ben. He seemed baffled. "I was a block away. I didn't see his face."

Ben ignored the whole exchange.

"Which is it?" I asked him. "Your name?"

"Zimmerman," Ben said, without looking up.

"So why did you say it was Lytton?" Fisher said.

Ben's fingers kept on going *tap-tap-tap*. "It's traditional," Bobbi said. "Lytton has been dead for *quite* some time. As has Burnell. This is rather an old firm."

Fisher stared at her. "And who the hell are you?"

Ben looked up at me. "Mr. Fisher was never judged to be

worth troubling about, what with . . . his situation. But you I foresee problems with, Jack. Something might have to be done."

"Is that a threat? If so, be careful."

"I'm well aware of your record."

Fisher looked at me. "What's he talking about?"

"Jack has shown a certain facility with violence," Bobbi said. "Didn't you know?"

My face felt hot. I was finding it hard to understand how come these people knew a lot more than they had any right to about my life. Had Amy told them?

Fisher was still staring at me. "What does she mean?"

"There was an incident," I said as I remembered that Amy had been at the Zimmermans' the morning I'd called after waking up in Seattle—when Bobbi handed the phone to her. "I saw suspicious activity one night. Found that the back door of a house had been forced. I went inside."

"And?"

"People got hurt."

Suddenly the phone rang, the jangling we'd heard from downstairs. The sound was coming from Zimmerman's laptop. Ben reached forward, hit a key.

"Coming to collect," said a woman's voice from the laptop's speakers. It sounded like the voice that had called my phone to derail me from confronting Todd Crane a couple days before.

Ben stood and started gathering papers from around the desk. Bobbi came over and picked up a handful of manila folders. They seemed to be in a hurry.

"What's going on?" I said.

"Is Shepherd here yet?" Ben asked, looking up and smiling briefly. I realized he wasn't looking at me.

"On his way," said a voice.

I turned to see two men standing in the doorway. One was blond. The other had short red hair. Both were armed this time. I realized that Georj had been right after all. These guys hadn't come into the alley for him.

That didn't seem important right then, however, because between them stood a third person. A woman.

My wife.

My head felt cold and my body as if it had turned to air. I couldn't move. *"Amy?"*

She didn't even look at me. It was as if my voice had made no sound. The Zimmermans walked past me.

"Out the back," Amy said.

The red-haired man raised his gun to point it at me. "Your weapon, please," the other man said.

"Yeah, right."

Finally Amy glanced at me. "Do as he says, Mr. Whalen."

"Amy . . . what . . ."

She just reached out, took the gun from my hand, and gave it to the red-haired man. Then she turned and left.

The two men backed out of the room after her and pulled the door shut.

As Fisher and I stared at it, we heard it lock.

chapter THIRTY-EIGHT

When the phone rang, Todd yanked it out of his pocket so fast it slipped and went skittering across the sidewalk. He crawled after it on hands and knees, people snorting and laughing and not moving out of the way. He was beyond noticing. He'd spent three hours walking the streets. He couldn't have gone back to his office, dealt with Bianca or the rest of them. He couldn't possibly go home. He had to do something, and so he'd walked, attempting to lose himself in the press of normal people, trying not to feel once again that the streets were even more crowded than they looked, growing more so as the evening came on, that this feeling was worse than ever before.

"Yes?" he said into the phone.

It was Rose. She gave him the address. It was where it was supposed to be. Todd knew it well. A long time ago, he'd spent many hours in the building, supervising shoots, sitting in a chair with his name stenciled on it, selecting which PA would receive the offer of a quick and expensive dinner somewhere discreet. Since then, more than once, he'd raised the question of selling it. He had not been allowed to. Even though it was never used anymore and had small trees growing out of the roof, apparently it had to be kept. Maybe now he knew why.

As soon as Rose had gone, he called his daughter's number. He gripped the phone till it nearly broke. Finally the other end picked up.

"Todd." The little girl's voice.

"It's happening," he said. "Now."

"Excellent."

"It's in—"

"Belltown?"

"How did you know she'd choose where you wanted?"

"Because I'm a clever little girl. They changed the locks. They have something there that belongs to me."

"Let me talk to my daughter."

"She's fine. How else do you think I'm going to get there? You remember what her car looks like, I assume?"

"Of course I—"

"Keep an eye out for it."

Todd shouted in the street, a hopeless sound. He reeled off the main sidewalk and into an alley between buildings, away from normal people. He knew that the police couldn't help him now, that this was about that building, and those people, and the things he'd never tried to understand.

He started to run.

When he got to the address, he was appalled to see police cars parked in the street. A tall black guy was hollering as he was manhandled into the back of one of them, barely twenty feet away from the door to the building.

Todd's head was pounding from the journey, and his lungs were on fire. He looked at his watch—he'd made it here in fifteen minutes. Would the police be moving on in the next twenty? If not . . . Todd suddenly came to believe he was about to have a heart attack.

He stopped, made himself breathe evenly. Walked across the street and positioned himself under the awning of a gallery that had closed for the night. He watched as the black guy fought the law, and he called upon whichever sleek god looked after admen of a certain age to send the junkie motherfucker a heart attack of his own. Now. Right *now.*

That god was not listening, however, unless he operated with kindness and through the offices of a cop from the second car, who eventually came over and helped his colleague shove the guy sharply into the backseat. Then the policemen stood around for a while, talking, pointing this way and that. Todd watched them, aware of nothing but these men, knowing dismally that they would take an hour or so to wrap this up and he would never see his daughter alive again.

But then, unbelievably, the cops all got in their cars and drove away. It was over. With five minutes to spare.

Todd's phone rang. He didn't know what to do when he saw who it was, but he knew she wouldn't just go away.

"Hey," he said. "Look, honey, I'm really busy."

"For God's *sake,*" Livvie said, entering the conversation at full tilt, a skill of hers. "You're supposed to *be* here."

Todd had no idea what she was talking about. Then he remembered. New clients. Japanese. Due at his house for dinner in . . . about an hour.

"Christ, I—"

"No, Todd. No. There is no *conceivable* end to that sentence that is going to work for me. So don't even finish it. Just come home."

"I will. I'm . . . look . . ."

For a split second, he remembered the Livvie of twenty-five years ago, when life had been brighter and so much more straightforward. He wanted everything that had happened since to have not happened. He wanted to wipe all the slates clean, to do whatever it would take to make Livvie not angry at him all the time, to find inside her the raucous college girl he'd not been able to stop thinking about, who had for a while made the rest of her sex obsolete. Most of all he wanted to tell her what was going on now and ask her to help, for her to make everything all right. In the end that's what men want most of women, and the thing they can never ask for out loud.

Then he saw it. A pale green VW Beetle, his twenty-first-birthday present to his daughter. It was coming quickly up the street.

"I've got to go," he said.

He closed the phone on whatever his wife was now saying and ran across the road.

The car pulled over just past the building. Todd ran up to it, heart thumping. Rachel was hollow-eyed in the driver's seat, staring straight ahead through the windshield. The passenger-side window was already rolled down. The girl was sitting there.

"Observe my hand," she said.

Todd had already seen that the girl's arm was up against his daughter's stomach and that something hidden in her sleeve protruded a little past the tips of her fingers. Also that there was a splash of dried blood under Rachel's nose and a livid bruise on the side of her head.

"Baby, are you okay?"

"I'm fine," Rachel said. Her voice was dry, quiet.

"Open the front door," the girl said. "Go inside, leave it ajar."

"No. You—"

"Do what she says, Dad," Rachel said. "Please."

Todd turned, walked stiffly over to the building. Found a key on his ring that he hadn't used in six or seven years. Opened the door and went inside, leaving it open behind him. He turned back to watch what happened in the car, wondering if he could make it there in time.

He saw the girl talking to Rachel. Saw his daughter nod her head, slowly. He saw in her face the tiny being he'd held in his arms, the ghost of that long-ago child. And he wondered what, if anything, was left inside Todd Crane, what dead thing unable to comprehend or affect the cramped prison it had built around itself.

The little girl got out of the car, came across the sidewalk and toward the building. Past her shoulder Todd saw his daughter slump forward until her head rested on the steering wheel. His stomach rolled over.

But then he saw Rachel's head lift again and turn toward him. Her eyes locked with his.

The girl walked straight past him and into the hallway of the building, pulling the door shut behind her.

The sudden darkness made Todd's eyeballs twitch. He moved back involuntarily, as if he were here not with a child but with someone larger and older and incomparably more dangerous. Which he was, of course. He knew that now. It made no sense, but there was no other way it could be. He realized he should have listened harder to the voice within him that had said it recognized the parting shot of the child who'd been led out of his office by Bianca the previous afternoon. An expression he'd heard a certain man use a long time ago, a man he'd had few dealings with but had instinctively disliked a very great deal.

There was a click. A strong white beam of light from a flashlight illuminated the little girl's face as she stood there between Todd and the door.

She cocked her head. "Let's make sure we're on the same page here, Todd," she said.

The girl let the long knife slip smoothly out of the sleeve of her nice, expensive coat. "You hearing me?"

Crane felt sick. "Yes, Marcus, I hear you loud and clear."

She smiled. "Glad you got there in the end."

chapter THIRTY-NINE

Five seconds too late, I was all about movement. I threw myself at the door, calling Amy's name.

"Can't you open it? Pick the lock?" Fisher had gone straight to the bookcase and started pulling books off the shelves.

"It's padlocked on the other side."

Gary leafed through another book, dropped it to the floor. "They're all just law manuals."

"It's a lawyer's office."

"Lytton works out of here. Zimmerman. Whatever his name really is."

I kicked the door, uselessly. "So either they've got the sense not to keep anything in an obvious place or maybe there's just nothing to be found."

"Jesus, Jack. What does it take?"

The truth was, I wasn't sure anymore.

"Two armed guards plus your wife," Fisher said. "Heavy backup for just some lawyer, don't you think?"

For either a lawyer or an ex–history professor, and I couldn't begin to understand what Amy had been doing here. My only chance of finding out lay in catching up with her. I headed into the portion of the room that led to the back of the building. The doors in this section were as thick and heavy and locked as the first one.

"Why replace the doors up here?" Gary insisted. "Why make them so tough? What are they protecting?"

"I don't give a shit, Gary. I have to get to Amy. Anything else is your problem."

The window at the back had been secured with a sheet of plywood. I wedged my fingers under the bottom and tugged. It didn't feel like it was going to move easily. I took a step back and slammed my heel into it. After a couple more kicks, it began to splinter.

Fisher continued to pull books down at random, flicking through them, throwing them away. He was getting more and more frustrated.

Finally a crack split across the bottom third of the wood. I gave it one more kick and then took it in my hands and gave a hard yank inward. The bottom pulled away. Fresh, cold air flooded in, along with the sound of traffic from far below. I hooked my fingers under the higher portion. With a couple tugs, it started to come away, revealing a few square feet of open space.

I stuck my head out the gap. It was totally dark now. We were four stories above the parking lot. A handful of overnighted cars, a chain across the entrance. No light in the attendant's hut. But right in front of me was the fire escape. I hadn't liked the look of it before. I did now. "We're out of here," I said.

Fisher came over to see. "The hell we are."

"We can get down to the next level."

"Yeah—or straight to the parking lot, fast."

I stuck my head out and shouted. There were a couple of people walking along the street at the end of the lot. Neither of them even glanced up. We were too high up, the lot too deep, couldn't compete against traffic sounds.

I vaulted onto the sill. Reached out and grabbed the sloping ironwork of the escape. Gave it a push. It moved ponderously. Hanging on to the window frame with my left hand, I lowered my right foot onto the level patch of the metalwork. Gradually moved my weight onto the foot on the platform.

It made an unreassuring sound. I lifted my other foot off the sill, then slowly lowered that, too.

"We may not have a lot of time on this," I said. "Be ready to move fast."

I went down the stairs, watching the wall brackets. All were rusty. A couple were missing. I disturbed a large bird as I reached the platform below. It took off, and I felt the whole structure move. The window on the next level down was boarded up from the inside.

The floor below was boarded, too, however, and the supports looked even worse down there. So I stayed where I was. The panes in this window were mainly broken, jagged remains of glass studded into the wood frames. I smacked my elbow against the point where the cross-joins met, then again.

The join in the window splintered. I tore off the pieces of frame around it until there was a big enough hole. Went back a couple of steps up the ladder, then swung my foot and kicked. The first impact told me the board was damp and wouldn't hold for long. A grinding sound said the escape brackets wouldn't either.

"Get ready!" I shouted. The area of board directly in front of my boot split, breaking inward. I moved down a step, started kicking again. The fire escape above me gave out a loud, grinding sound, and for an instant I felt weightless.

Fisher's head jerked out of the window above. His face was white. I was now very aware of how far I was above the ground. "Jack . . ."

"Wait until I get in," I said. "This isn't going to take both of us at once."

I shoved the broken board with my hand, holding the frame to minimize the stress on the brackets. The board started to push away from the wall, and a chunk bent inward, wide enough for me to get my head and an arm in. I knocked away the bigger pieces of glass left around the sill and levered the upper half of my body through.

Couldn't see anything. Couldn't get to the flashlight, stuck in my pocket. So I kept shoving against the plywood, pulling myself over the sill until I toppled forward to the floor inside, making ringing contact with an iron radiator under the sill.

I got up quickly and stuck my head back out the hole, yanking more of the board away. "Come on. Now."

Fisher's feet emerged from the window above. The escape made a grinding noise again, and this time it was longer, like an old door opening. There was a thunk, too, and a small fragment of metal dropped past my face.

"Shit," Fisher said. "One of the supports just—"

He took the last three steps in one. I grabbed his hands and started pulling, but he'd given himself a good push with both legs and came through fast enough to knock me over onto my back.

"If we can't get out of this room, I'm going to kill you," Fisher said, wiping the blood off his palms.

The flashlight showed a room cluttered with upturned furniture, boxes, and inky shadows, filled up almost to the door. We made our way across quickly, shuffling our feet against obstructions on the floor.

We got to the door and threw our shoulders against it together. Banged them hard and fast and with something approaching panic. In the end I pushed Fisher to one side and forced myself to go at it the right way, ducking low and hitting it where it would make the lock casement splinter fastest. When it started to go, I switched to kicking.

Fisher joined me again, and finally the door blew open and we crashed out onto the landing. We ran down to the second floor, around the landing there.

I was heading straight for the stairs to get down to the next but Fisher grabbed my arm.

"What's that?" he whispered.

I heard something, too. A sound from below.

I went to the top of the stairs. From there I could make out hard breathing, someone moaning softly.

We had no other way to go. I kept my back to the wall. Fisher followed two steps behind. When I hit the half landing, I shone the light directly below.

There was a man lying on the floor. A dark pool around him said he was bleeding to death. He slowly wrenched his head up as we came down to reach him.

It was Todd Crane.

chapter FORTY

It was too dark to see, but the stifling air and heavy smells of brick and earth were all too familiar. Madison knew she'd been here before, in dreams and nightmares. Though the man inside kept her plunging forward into the dark, if felt like he was pulling her backward. The darkness didn't bother Marcus. He knew he had nothing to fear from it. Madison did not want to have him in her head anymore, but it didn't feel as if she had any choice; if anything, it felt like it was she who was being shoved out. He was increasingly out of control now, too—or she was less able to stop him from doing the kind of thing he'd always wanted. She hadn't known he was going to stab Rachel's father—she'd just found herself doing it, before she could do anything to try to stop it. He'd been angry that the woman he wanted to see wasn't here after all, that this was supposed to be a trap, though Madison believed he'd known this was a possibility all along, that his anger was partly a pose, and this was all just part of the endless game he played with whoever was available.

There were huge amounts of blood all over Madison's hands and coat, and now she could remember shoving the nice woman in the Scatter Creek restroom, tripping her so she fell and smashed her head against the side of the toilet bowl. Tears were running down her face. She was unaware of them. She was pulled ever forward, as if someone had tied ropes to her arms and legs and was tugging her deeper into the cloud.

Marcus wasn't interested in the upper part of the building, it seemed. He'd brought her straight down into the basement, opening the door with the second key on the ring from the envelope Madison had carried since Portland. He was muttering things to himself, things she hated to hear in her own voice . . . horrible, sick things, tasting his own memories on his tongue. Rarely did he use the lighter he'd taken from Rachel, holding it up to get his bearings, before plunging onward into the blackness.

After a couple of minutes, the echoes were different, and Madison realized they'd come into a bigger space. Marcus dragged her onward, not caring if she crashed into things or fell or cut herself.

She stepped on something crackly on the floor, and he paused, her face splitting with his grin, but there was something far more important in this place, something he was desperate to see again and for which this man felt the closest he was ever going to feel to love.

He scrabbled on over piles of chairs and boxes. He flicked the lighter once again, and Madison saw they were in a long, low room now, like a bunker. At the far end was another doorway, blackness beyond. There was a shape to one side of it. It was slumped in a chair.

When Marcus saw this, he caught his/her breath, holding the lighter up above her head until it got so hot that Madison cried out. Then he let it go out and started toward the corner again, like someone going home.

"You have to warn her," Crane said. His voice was weak.

"Warn who? About what?"

I was squatted next to him, trying to establish where and

how he'd been hurt. So far all I could see was blood, and all I could tell was that it was bad.

"Marcus is back."

"What?" I said.

"Marcus Fox," Fisher said, misunderstanding me. "The other man on the documents for this building. The one I couldn't find anything about for the last ten years."

"You wouldn't," Crane said. "He was dead. You've got to warn her. Warn Rose."

My hands froze, and I stared at him. "Rose? How do you know about Rose? Who is she?"

His eyes were unfocused. "Oh, you know Rose," he said, with affection and bitterness. "*Everybody* knows . . ."

His face contorted, and the words became a sharp intake of breath.

"Where did he go? Marcus?"

His face slack, Crane jerked his head to the left.

"In one of those rooms?"

He shook his head. I flicked the flashlight down along the corridor toward the back of the building.

"Into the basement," Fisher said.

I thought for a second. Amy and the Zimmermans would be long gone by now. There was no point in my running after them. "Gary, go out on the street and get help. Quickly. Get an ambulance."

"What are you going to do?"

"Find the person who did this."

"I'm coming with you."

"No. This guy's badly fucked up. He needs an ambulance, and he needs it now."

Fisher pushed past me and headed along the corridor. "I don't care. I have to know what's down there."

"For God's *sake*."

I started to move back past Todd toward the street door, but his hand reached out and grabbed my leg. "Don't let him go down there alone," he said. "He'll die."

"Todd, you *need a doctor.*"

"Go after him," he insisted. "Please." His eyes were strong again, for the moment. "Or he will die."

I hesitated. "Hold your hands over the wound," I said. "I'll be right back."

I ran back toward the staircase down into the basement. Fisher was already heading down the steps.

"You're an asshole," I said, shining the light so he could see his way into the darkness. He just started descending more quickly. The stairs hit a return halfway down and kept going. There was a full story belowground, which didn't make much sense. I knew that there were areas like this in the old town, but here?

We came off the bottom into an open space. There was a door on the left side. Beyond it lay service areas, full of pipes and dampness. There was another door on the right, hanging open. It was three inches thick, with the same reinforcing we'd seen on the top floor. I pointed the flashlight through the gap. A narrow corridor led away into total darkness.

Fisher went through. I followed. The walls on the other side were of old brickwork, the mortar rotted out in parts. I passed a bank of switches and flicked them, but nothing happened.

"Gary, slow *down.*"

Fisher wasn't listening. When I caught up with him, I found he'd hit an intersection. The flashlight revealed only about eight feet in any direction. Darkness led three ways. The place smelled of rock and old dust.

"I don't get it. We must be out under the street by now."

We heard a sound then, from down one of the corridors. A moan, which abruptly climbed in pitch.

We turned together. The sound came back, splitting into something that could have been fractured laughter or someone choking, then broke into silence. It came from the left corridor.

"Down there," I said.

* * *

He made her go right over to the corner. The thing in the chair was sealed into a plastic bag. When Marcus forced her hands to open the bag, a smell came out that was the worst thing *ever,* so bad that in the darkness it seemed to fill the universe. Her eyes watered, her stomach dropped out like seasickness, but instead of moving back he yanked the sides of the bag wider. He pushed her hands inside, needing to touch the last place he'd called home. From the smell you thought it would be warm, but it was cold. It was like stringy, fatty mucus with things in it, and there were bones. He made her come farther toward it, bringing her face to the gap, opening her mouth, as if he meant to taste the . . .

No way.

She'd thrown herself backward, flapping her hands spastically, and stumbled howling back into the darkness, frantically rubbing her hands on her poor coat, the coat now covered in dirt and blood and this appalling, horrendous crap. She'd gone running back across the room then, smashing into things and not caring, until she found another corridor and ran down it—and then into another, bigger space, not caring where she went because she knew now that all corridors were the same.

It didn't matter how far you went. There was no escape from what was inside.

Gary ran down the left corridor. I began to smell something else, an earthier note underneath the dust.

We came to a doorway and stepped through it into a more open space. Forty feet square, a low ceiling, upturned furniture and wooden crates and debris all over the place. One whole wall was bookshelves, very old-looking volumes, leather-bound, most of them little thicker than notebooks. The room had thick concrete walls and was bone dry, but the odor was stronger here, far worse than the damp and mold we'd been enveloped in before.

As we started across the room, I stepped on something. It made a flat, crackling sound and gave way, dropping my foot onto something uneven.

I pointed the light down. There was a stretch of dark gray plastic beneath my foot, less than five feet in length, an uneven two feet wide.

"What's that?" Fisher's voice was dry.

I knew. I'd seen one before. It was a body bag. A good deal of packing tape had been fixed over the central zipper and reinforced the join at the top. The tape had curled a little at the edges, as if it had been in place for some time. I reached down toward it.

"Don't open it," Fisher said.

I peeled the tape back, found the zipper. Ran it down six inches. The smell that emerged was like nothing on earth. Fisher turned away jerkily. I shone the light into the hole. A face, or the remains of one. This person had been there awhile, sealed into a tough, nearly airtight bag. She had once had long red hair. She had not been very tall, or very old. Her face had been deeply sliced, in a series of wounds that together looked a little like the number 9.

I pulled the zipper back up, pushed the tape back down around the join. The smell did not go away. That smell is not just a smell. The brain keeps sending out alarms even after the source is taken away. It knows that this odor is a gateway to places you cannot go and stay alive.

Assuming I *had* removed the source . . .

I straightened up, remembering I'd been able to smell something of this as soon as we'd entered the room.

"Jack," Fisher said. "There."

I pointed the flashlight. Another bag, the same size, on the floor, partially underneath a table. I moved the light again. Found another bag, then another, and for a moment it was as if they hadn't been there before we came but were appearing now in front of our eyes, multiplying to fill the space, coming closer, surrounding us.

And then one final bag. This was not on the floor but

propped upright in a rotten armchair in the far corner, near another entrance. For a moment when the light bounced off the top, it looked like a face, though that must have been the folds, the remaining structure of what was sealed inside. This bag was a good deal longer than the rest. It had been opened, the sides pulled apart.

Fisher grabbed the light from me and pointed it to the side, fast. In the wall there was another door. I saw something in the corridor beyond.

Something running, like a shadow that had peeled itself up from the floor.

Fisher was in motion immediately, shoving a pile of chairs out of the way and starting toward the door. Over his shoulder I saw the shadow again, at the limits of where the light reached, vanishing around a corner.

It had looked like a little girl.

Then it/she was out of sight, just the sound of footsteps running away into the void. Fisher started running, too, calling out something that made no sense.

Calling out his daughter's name. Her name at first, but then Donna's, and then just sounds. I began to realize that Gary was not even clear on where he was anymore, or who he was with.

All I could see was the shape of his back as we hurtled onward down the corridor. The walls were stained and wet here, and water dripped from above. The floor seemed to be sloping down. The corridor, this whole subterranean section, had to have been laid when the area was regraded, before the building was even built, a route preserved along the original ground level.

Why?

Fisher shouted again. The sound was flat. The corridor was getting wider now. The echoes of our footsteps were changing, too, and there was another noise up ahead, a sound of fear and dread. We seemed to be running straight toward a dead end now, but right at the bottom it banked sharply right.

And then the walls on either side disappeared.

"Gary, *wait.*"

My voice sounded different now as well. Fisher slowed, as he became aware that something had changed. It wasn't just the sound. The air was cooler here. The other sound became clearer, ragged and hitching sobs.

We kept moving forward, more cautiously now. Twenty feet, thirty. Fisher held the light out, spinning it slowly. White jags of light cut through the air without hitting anything.

There was a scream, something that had words hidden in it. Gary pulled the flashlight around, fast.

Someone staggered into view. A young girl, standing in the flashlight's beam like something transfixed in the night on a backcountry road. Her hair was whipped in all directions, as if she'd been trying to pull it out. She was wearing a coat that was covered in blood and something dark and viscous. Her face was wet with tears, smeared with dirt, the tendons in her neck pulled taut to the snapping point.

"Go away!" she screamed.

As Fisher moved toward her, the girl started hammering at her head and face with her fists. "You're not *allowed* in here!"

Fisher held out his hands to her. "Shh," he said. "It's okay. It's—"

The girl's head jerked up. She stared at Fisher as if he'd appeared out of thin air. She blinked. Her voice changed, rasping deeper.

"Who . . ." she snarled, ". . . the *fuck* are you?"

"It's okay," Gary said, taking another step closer. "Everything's okay. We're—"

But then there was a clunking sound, and lights started to come on from the far end of the space, flicking toward us out of the darkness, coming on in groups.

I began to see that we were in a big, big space—about fifty yards long and forty yards wide. It was difficult to be exact, because the low ceiling was supported by brick columns that obscured the view. There was a central area of floor. In this was a circular wooden table. There were nine chairs around it, heavy, oak. A glass pitcher in front of each of them, opaque with dust. It looked like something mothballed since the Victorian era, or transported from a medieval hall, or discovered in a bunker on another planet.

Rows of wooden seats ran down both sides of the room, behind a flat front, like pews, each banked higher than the one in front. The light was coming from small, dusty electric lamps set along the rows, making it look like a Catholic church on a long-ago winter afternoon when no one had done much remembrance.

Fisher was openmouthed, taking it in. The girl was staring past him, back the way we'd come.

I turned to see that someone had entered the room. A tall figure, dressed in a coat. I knew immediately where I'd seen him before. In Byron's. It was the man who had killed Bill Anderson.

He walked slowly down the center of the room, not giving the table and chairs or any of the rest of it a second glance. He wasn't looking at Gary or me either.

He was here for only one thing.

"Hello, Marcus," he said as he slapped a clip into the gun he held in his right hand. "At least this time you'll know it's me, right?"

The girl turned and ran, heading straight for a door at the other end of the room.

"Time to die!" the man shouted after her. "Again!"

Gary ran after the girl.

I turned back to the man in the coat. "Who the hell are you?"

He raised the gun and shot me, in passing, and then kept on walking as if I were already dead.

chapter FORTY-ONE

Madison sprinted through the door, back into the dark, and went careering along a series of twists and bends into black corridors. She was the fox now, cunning and at home. She hardly even *knew* who she was anymore, in fact was barely sensible to her body's crashes into walls, the stumbles and falls. As her body ran, she ran, too, inside, through a head that was no longer hers and no longer a haven, no longer even safe.

There were running footsteps behind her for a few minutes, and a flicking light, but for the moment she had lost her pursuers, dodging down a maze of corridors that Marcus knew but Shepherd and the other man did not: Shepherd, the man who'd come to her on the beach and smashed a hole in her mind wide enough for Marcus to start coming through. Shepherd evidently wanted to kill her now, and it sounded like maybe he'd done so before.

She'd been right not to trust him, huh.

She tripped over something, hard, and fell sprawling.

As she picked herself up, she suddenly realized she was in a place she'd been in already. She recognized it from the smell.

Which meant that the door, a way out back up into the building, was on the other side of this room.

She was exhausted from days of walking. She was exhausted just from being alive. She kept moving because she was terrified, but the man inside was not. He was not afraid of darkness or dead girls or anything else, had never understood the emotion properly. Never in all his lives. He'd seen too much. He'd known this place before it was even here, after all, known it when it was trees and rock and water. It was his. Everything was his to do with as he wished. Or so he believed.

Not everything, Madison decided.

As she stumbled through the chaos of the room, she tearfully pulled off her coat. She didn't want it anymore. Not with so much blood in it. She didn't want it because it hadn't been she who'd known how to make her mother buy it for her. She wanted her mother now, and her father, but she did not want this coat. If she was ever going to see them again, it could only be as herself.

She threw the coat on the floor, but her legs stopped moving immediately, knees locking.

Of course. He wanted his notebook, which was still in the coat pocket. He didn't want it left here. He needed it. Madison was glad to make him angry, and suddenly she had an even better idea.

She pulled the cigarette lighter out of her pocket. She knelt and held it to the coat, right where the dumb notebook was, with all its stupid words and sums and things she did not want to remember or understand. She flicked the wheel more awkwardly than when he did it, because he had smoked and she did not.

But she kept at it. He tried to pull her arm away, but she held firm, straining every muscle against his will, until she got a flame and the coat was on fire. Everything around it was dry. She moved the flame to a pile of dry and musty books.

The fire spread quickly. She started to laugh and scream, feeling her head split open, and then she was completely in the cloud.

* * *

It feels like someone hitting you with a sledgehammer, to which they've stuck a thumbtack, point out.

The bullet hit me high in the left shoulder, spinning me to crash into the first bank of seating. For a moment my vision went black, the impact to the back of my head hurting more for a moment than the shell wound.

I hit the ground hard and rolled, tried to push up with my left hand, felt something like cracking glass shoot along my arm. I reached up and grabbed the top of the wooden frontage with my right hand, hauled myself up.

Blood was running out of my jacket. My whole arm felt hot. The pain in my head already felt like nothing at all, and I knew that my shoulder was going start feeling worse real fast.

I ran into the corridor at the end of the room. A sharp, right-angle turn took me into darkness. I could hear the echoes of Gary shouting from somewhere up ahead, however, and I chased the sound.

When I made another right, I heard the sound of my footsteps change, flat and quiet, and knew I must be in a chamber of similar size to the one I'd just left. I pulled out my cell phone and flipped it open, the screen shedding a weak light as I stumbled forward.

This room had no seats, was more like a storage vault or an antechamber for the other room. I ran straight through it toward the other end.

On the other side was a door to another short corridor, with two possible exits on either side. I realized I must now be close to the series of tunnels that had delivered us to the large chamber in the first place.

A high-pitched laugh/scream echoed down one of the corridors toward me. The girl. Then a shout that didn't sound like Gary. It had to be the man who'd shot me. I wanted to see him again, and soon.

I held the phone up toward both of the openings in turn

and saw a smear of something dark that could've been blood on one wall. I took the corridor next to it. It felt like this was angling upward again. As I ran up it I could smell something new. Not the body smell from before, though that was present. Something acrid and dry.

I started to hear different noises ahead, too, and thought I must be gaining on either Gary or the other man, even though they didn't sound like voices or footsteps.

It was getting warmer.

Then I knew what the smell was. It was smoke. Something was on fire. The noise I'd heard was crackling and the sound of burning wood. I stopped running. I didn't want to head into a dead end full of fire. I wasn't sure I could find my way back the other way, however, and I didn't want to get stuck on the wrong side. Whatever I wanted to do, the longer I took, the harder it would get. So I started onward again.

Soon the light from the phone was reflecting back at me, bounced against billowing smoke, showing me nothing, so I stuffed it into my pocket. I pulled my coat off, crying out as it snagged the wound, then held it up over my mouth. I could breathe less painfully, but it didn't help my eyes, and as I kept pushing forward, I was half blinded, keeping my back to the wall and sliding sideways along it, knowing I had to keep going however much my body wanted to run in the other direction.

Then it was suddenly hotter and louder, and I lurched into a room I'd seen before, the one with the body bags. This time I'd come into it from the far end, near the body in the chair. It was still there, the plastic flicker-lit by flames that filled the center of the room.

I headed away from it toward the right-hand wall, now a blaze of burning books, pulling myself over furniture, shoving crates aside in an attempt to put something solid between me and the flames.

I stepped on at least one of the bags on the floor, breaking something inside. At the other end of the room, I saw a shape silhouetted in the doorway.

I shouted Gary's name. He didn't hear me, or if he did, he just kept on running anyway.

In her head, Madison was now sprinting along a tide line, as if she and her mother and father had gone for a walk on Cannon Beach at the end of a long afternoon, and her parents were chatting happily, and the weather was fine, and so she'd gone running ahead, feet pounding over the sand, running along the edge of the world. She would run to the end and then turn around, come back to her parents with open arms, and her father would bend down to catch her, the way he always had, even though she was too big for that now and they both knew it, though they pretended they did not.

But somehow she was also running beside a different body of water, and in a different time. She was running along Elliott Bay, here in Seattle, ten years ago and in the dead of night, fleeing in the knowledge that someone was coming after him/her and that whoever it was wanted her/him very dead. That they discovered what lay buried beneath the basement of his house in the Queen Anne District, and the others hidden under the building here in Belltown, and decided that his behavior could not be tolerated anymore. They had come for him just ahead of the police, and he'd managed to get out of the house, but he knew they were serious, and his advantage would not last long. Marcus had always suspected that Rose had been behind the decision, Joe Cranfield's little protégée stretching her wings. Now he knew that it had been Shepherd who'd been there to do the Nine's killing work, barely a month after he'd agreed to the bargain struck in a hotel bar here in Seattle—a bargain Marcus had designed, because he'd known, with the experience of many lifetimes, that the shadows at the end of this life were drawing in.

They had chased, and he had run, toward a trap with Shepherd standing at the end.

In a way Marcus respected this. Shepherd was the obvious choice, and who could blame him for working both sides? But had they known that Marcus was still alive when they'd sealed him in the bag and left him to scream himself to death in the pitch-black of that cellar room?

Yes, he believed they had.

That was not nice. That was not the way they were supposed to leave. It doesn't matter how many times you've died. It's never something you look forward to. And as Marcus watched the child try to deal with the situation she was in, he began to feel darkness gathering once more. Shadows he was not prepared to confront again so soon.

Though her head was full of movement, in reality Madison was going nowhere. She was crawling on hands and knees along a corridor, dragging herself through dust and ash, unable to see anything. Her lungs were so full of smoke it felt like someone had shoveled earth into them. She'd burned her hand and arm in the room where she'd set the fire, caught by surprise at how quickly it had taken, and the pain was intense. She did not know in which direction to go, and she'd had enough. Of everything.

She was not going to survive this. She knew that. So she was trying now to find the way to another place, one deep inside, pushing the man away, knowing how much he wanted to be back but feeling his grip falter as he realized she'd rather be dead than live like this, that this girl was not prepared to be his home.

Then she banged into something. She raised her head, sensing that it was a fraction lighter here. There was cooler air coming from somewhere, too.

In a flash of clarity she was aware that she was no longer in a corridor, but in more open space—and that what she'd run into was the foot of a staircase.

She hauled herself onto the bottom step and started pulling herself up the wooden stairs. All she had to do was get up them and then run, *really* run this time. There was a door to the street up there, and past it was the outside world. She could get out through it and then keep running.

Straight into the busy road, without looking left or right. It would be a sad solution, but it was workable. And it would teach Marcus a lesson. Be careful which little girl's body you try to steal.

Not all of them will stand for it.

The right side of the room was a wall of fire now. I kept heading down the middle, plowing through the debris, smelling my hair and coat as they began to burn. A stretch of the bookcase fell away from the wall, toppling in slow motion and showering me with burning paper and wood and sparks. I ducked my head and just kept going through it, shouldering forward until I got to the doorway, flapping at the parts of me that were on fire.

The corridor was choked with smoke, but I could hear retching sounds ahead. I stumbled straight through the thick, gray clouds, covering my whole face with my jacket now. The muscles in my shoulder had begun spasming, and I could feel how wet it was, and my arm had started going numb. I hit it with my fist to keep the blood flowing and to send a jag of pain up into my head.

As I made it into the room at the bottom of the staircase, I nearly fell over someone crouched on the ground, rolled into a ball, coughing his guts up.

It was Gary. I grabbed his jacket collar and pulled him along with me, hauling him to the foot of the stairs, screaming down at his face. He finally started moving under his own steam, and we fell up them together. I could barely see his back through my stinging, watering eyes. At the bend in the stairs, I slipped and crashed to my knees. Fisher turned and wrenched his arm under mine, pulling me around and back to my feet.

We stumbled up the last stretch side by side.

This hallway, too, was clogged with smoke. Gary ran straight down it toward the door to the street, which was hanging wide. I stepped over Todd Crane's body but knew I couldn't just leave it there and bent to grab his wrist. He made a sound as I pulled him down the hall toward the door, and I realized he was still alive. I felt a muscle in my back tear but kept dragging him until I fell over the doorstep and out into the cold night air.

It was like being reborn.

Cars, night sounds, glints of light. People were backing and running away from the building, shouting, pointing. Smoke was billowing out onto the street. I heard a siren in the distance, heading in this direction.

I staggered a short distance from the doorway, leaving Crane slumped over the step. Gary was shouting somewhere in the melee, though at first I couldn't see where he was. Everyone seemed to have a much clearer idea of what was going on than I did, to be moving faster and with greater intent, and what took place next happened so quickly that it's only in recollection that I was even really there.

The man with the gun was advancing toward the little girl, who was caught in the middle of the sidewalk. A gap opened up around her as people ran to get out of the way.

Gary was not running, however.

He had the girl's arm gripped in his hand. He was trying to drag her behind a big SUV, to get her out of the other man's line of fire. He was trying to save her.

The girl was fighting him. She was struggling hard, screaming at him, frantic. Gary was shouting, too.

"Bethany!" he said. "Wait!"

The man aimed his weapon straight at the girl.

Gary saw it happening and yanked her back again, rolling his own body to get between them, and the man's first shot went wide.

People started screaming louder. The sound of sirens was closer now.

The girl suddenly got away from Gary. I can't imagine where she thought she was going to go. She was trapped, and she wasn't even running. It was as if she were making it *easier* for the man who was coming for her. Gary must have known he couldn't get to her in time, couldn't get her to safety. But he threw himself toward her nonetheless, knocking her off her feet and shielding her with his body as they stumbled forward.

The man fired four times.

All four shots hit Gary, knocking him back and down.

Gary kept his grip on the girl and crashed down on top of her. They hit the ground together, the girl's forehead smacking onto the pavement with a sound I heard from twenty feet away.

I was running at the gunman by then, throwing myself at him to smash into his chest—as his gun went off once more, then twice. We fell together into a car door.

The man bounced off, but I was twisted and dropped straight into the gutter. I wrenched my head up to see that police cars were now hurtling into the street.

The man with the gun was back on his feet. He glanced over to the girl and saw a swelling pool of blood across the sidewalk. He hesitated. Then he turned and slipped away, dodging into the crowds.

I pulled myself up onto the sidewalk, pushed myself up to hands and knees. Crawled over to where Gary lay.

The girl was not moving. Her eyes were closed.

Gary's shirt was red, all over, and the pool beneath him was spreading fast.

My arm gave out, and I collapsed to the ground next to him, my face landing no more than two feet from his.

Much of the back of his head was missing. His eyes were open and flat and dry.

chapter FORTY-TWO

"We didn't get him," a voice said.

I was sitting in a chair in a hospital room, after the most recent of a series of conversations with members of Seattle's law-enforcement agencies. I'd given a selective account of events during the altercation inside the building in Belltown. It was not the first time I'd given this account. I doubted that it would be the last. I had burns on my face and arms, had lost a chunk of hair. The pain of the wound in my shoulder and its associated stitching was bitterly emphatic, even through a pile of painkillers. My lower back felt like I'd been hit by a truck, and my head hurt in a way that felt as if it would never go away. I was not feeling receptive to news of any kind. I glanced up. Blanchard stood in the doorway.

"I hope you feel better than you look," he said.

He came in and leaned against the side of the bed, folded his arms and stared down at me. I waited for him to say whatever it was he'd come to say.

"You could be worse," he said eventually. "You *were* a lot worse, until half an hour ago. You're a lucky guy."

"In what way?"

"Forensic report came in. The bullets that killed Mr. Fisher and the one they dug out of you share a profile with those they found in Bill Anderson."

"I said it was the same guy."

"You did. But you know what? Ballistics reports carry a little more weight than the word of an ex-cop, especially one who's happened to be on hand at every gun fatality Seattle has seen in the last week."

"And there's no sign of this guy? He just melted away on the open street?"

"Like he walked away from killing Anderson, and Anderson's family. The guy is evidently a professional. A professional *what,* I have no idea. All we do know is that it seems like his name might be Richard Shepherd."

I don't think I did more than blink, but Blanchard was watching me closely. "Mean something to you?"

I shook my head. "How do you know his name?"

"I'll tell you in a minute. I want to be sure on something first. You really have no idea of how the fire in the basement started? In these 'storage areas'?"

"No." This at least was true. "How bad was it?"

"Bad. The fire department is only really getting down there now. Anything that wasn't rock is gone. Assuming there was anything there to be found?"

I made a face indicating I had nothing to say on the matter.

Blanchard smiled tightly to himself.

"Come on," he said. "I'll walk you out."

"I can go?"

"For now. That's what I'm telling you," he said, standing. "You're a lucky man."

I followed the detective down the corridor. Walking hurt more than sitting had. Nurses made a big deal out of not watching us. There'd been a couple of armed cops sitting outside my room since I arrived. They were gone now.

"They can't specifically put the gunman at the scene of the Anderson-family murders," Blanchard said. "But since he killed both Bill and Gary Fisher—who was the only person making noise about that case—nobody has any problem assigning those to him, too. And you have no idea why he might have done all this?"

I shook my head. It was barely a lie. "What about the other guy? Todd Crane?"

"Private hospital across town. Lost a bucket of blood and took a lot of sewing up, but he's going to be okay. He'll live to hike again."

"What?"

"He was babbling about it to his wife when he came out of surgery. Going hiking in the Olympic Mountains. So apparently Shepherd stabbed him, right?"

"If that's what Crane says."

"Busy guy."

Though the environment was clean and bright, it felt oppressive. I was glad to be alive, more or less. Other than that, I wasn't sure what to feel. I'd spent the night awake, my eyes open, watching and rewatching the memory of Gary Fisher being killed. I'd told myself that the man in the long coat, Shepherd, had planted killing shots in Gary before I could have made a difference. It was true. It hadn't helped a great deal. You always feel you should have been able to do something about events in the past, more even than those that may lie in the future. I don't know why that is.

Blanchard paused near the nurses' station. Across from it was a room where a young girl was lying. A man and a woman were holding hands across the bed. I realized that this was the girl I'd last seen lying under Gary Fisher, covered in his blood.

"She's okay," Blanchard said. "Serious concussion, some burns and scrapes. Seems to have lost a lot of the last week, though, big chunks gone like they never happened. Could just be she's blanking stuff, abuse or something, but the psychologist thinks it's permanent."

"What was she doing in the building?"

"That's the other thing I mentioned. Madison O'Donnell was abducted from a beach house down in Oregon five days ago. What happened since isn't clear, or how she got up here, but a man was evidently involved. The girl says it was the man with the gun last night, who *you* say was trying to kill her. Her parents gave a good description of him, and the guy even left his card with them, which is how we know his name. Or the name he uses, at least."

I stared at him. "He kidnaps a child and then leaves a *business* card? How does that make sense?"

"I don't know," Blanchard admitted. "But we're never going to be able to join all the dots on this one until we find the guy. And on that, I'm not holding my breath."

I watched the family in the room for a moment. The girl's face was badly bruised, but she was smiling. Her mother and father looked happy, too. Very happy.

How nice to have a family, I thought. *What a simple thing, and yet how lucky it is.*

When I turned back, I realized that Blanchard was looking awkward. "What?"

"I don't know how much of this you know," he said. "So I'll just tell you. Fisher's wife and child were here very early this morning. Mrs. Fisher flew over to identify the body. She did it and went straight home again."

"Child? He had two."

He nodded slowly. "Okay, so you don't know. The daughter died. Three months ago."

I stared at him. "Bethany's dead?"

"Yes, that was her name."

"How? What happened?"

Blanchard's face was composed. "She drowned. In the bath. Mr. Fisher . . . well, her father was the supervising adult at the time. According to his account, he went out to get her pajamas from her room, and in the meantime she slipped, banged her head. He tried to resuscitate her. He failed, even though she could not have been under the water for very long."

"You're not saying . . ."

"Nobody's saying anything. But there had been some

crisis at Mr. Fisher's office. He was named in a massive negligence suit over some guy's will. Subsequently Mr. Fisher had become unfocused in his professional and personal lives. Started refusing to sleep. This thing in the bath happened, and then a few weeks later he went out one day and just didn't come home. His wife didn't even know he was in Seattle. He's been missing for over a month."

I suddenly had to get out. I didn't want to be in the hospital anymore, didn't want to hear anything else.

"Wait here," I said.

I walked over to the bedroom where the O'Donnell family was. They looked up, all at once, as I entered. The parents frowned, doubtful and concerned. I probably didn't look like the kind of person you wanted walking into your life.

"I remember you," the girl said, though. "I think."

"Right," I said. "I was there. In the building. You don't remember much, from what I hear."

She shook her head. She seemed groggy. "Not really."

"Do you remember a guy? Not me, not the . . . not the man with the gun? Another man?"

"Is this important?" her father asked. He wanted to protect her, and I didn't blame him. His wife was ready to back him up hard. I wasn't going to stop, however.

"Yes," I said. "Madison—do you remember him?"

The girl thought a moment, then nodded.

"Yes," she said. "There was a man who was trying to pull me out of the way."

"His name was Gary Fisher," I said. "He saved your life."

Blanchard went down in the elevator with me and walked me to the door. Stood looking up the street as I lit a cigarette.

"There's no call for you to be leaving the country, right? Or the state?"

"No," I said.

"I guess we'd like it if you kept it that way. Being lucky doesn't equate to a free pass just yet."

"Whatever you say."

He nodded, seemed to hesitate. "Don't feel bad about what happened," he said. "It seems to me that everyone put themselves in their own place. Fisher most of all."

"Okay." I didn't want to talk about it.

"Right," he said. "Well . . . oh. Here."

He handed me a slip of paper.

"What's this?"

"Left at the nurses' station for you this morning. Now. Tell me you're not going to try driving anywhere today."

"I'm not going to try driving anywhere."

"Good man. See you around, Jack."

I waited until he'd walked back into the hospital before I unfolded the piece of paper. It took me a moment to recognize the handwriting. Something about it had changed. The note said:

Meet me somewhere.

chapter FORTY-THREE

First I cabbed over to Belltown to retrieve my car. The area around the building was heavily cordoned. Police and firemen were going about their business. Passersby stopped to watch for a while, no idea what they were looking at. Just another thing in the background of their lives. The visible fabric of the building didn't appear badly damaged, but if fire had been through the foundations, I guessed it was most likely coming down.

To become another parking lot, and then apartments, and get knocked down again, and then be something else in some future world. Things go up and then come down, and the years go by.

I got into the car and drove down to Pioneer Square.

I bought a coffee in the Starbucks and took it outside. The metal tables were all empty. I chose the one with the best view of the square and lowered myself gently into one of the chairs. The process hurt. I told myself I'd give it an hour and then go.

While I waited, I looked across at the trees. There was something about the quality of the light filtering down through them that lent the square an elusive quality. For a place that gave birth to so much, a whole city, it is actually rather small. Just those few trees, the sheltered seat, a drinking fountain, and that totem pole, all dwarfed and in shadow from the stolid stone buildings that stand around, like a defensive barricade.

And yet it doesn't seem small.

It felt okay to be sitting there, and after a time I shambled inside again and got another coffee. I returned to the table and went back to watching people walking up and down, tourists and locals on their way somewhere, the homeless passing through, stopping in the square for a few moments, then moving on.

I was halfway through the second cup when I heard a chair being pulled out from the other side of the table. I looked around to see that someone had joined me.

"You're good," she said.

I didn't know what to say. She levered the top off her cup of tea to help it cool. Lit a cigarette and leaned back in her chair. Looked at me.

"Are you okay? Physically?"

"I'll live," I said.

"Well, that's good."

"Glad you think so."

"You were locked in the top office for a reason. You were intended to stay there for your own safety."

"Shame you didn't explain that at the time. Gary Fisher might still be alive."

She shrugged. Something had changed, more so than when I'd seen her on the pier in Santa Monica and even since last night—though I hadn't had much chance to observe her closely then. Her hair was brushed differently, or maybe it was the same, but her suit was new in some way, its fabric or the cut, something that hinted at an older fashion. Perhaps it was something less tangible. Body language, the light in her eyes, or lack of it, whatever it is that makes someone altered from the person she was before, that says she stands at a different angle to you now. Whichever, I knew that this person was no more my wife than the girl who used to go to sleep in the bedroom of what was now Natalie's house.

I started with that. "What did you take?" I asked. "From Natalie's?"

"Nothing important. A keepsake."

"Of what?"

"Being a child. I used to stash my little treasures under the floorboard there."

"Why go back for it now?"

She hesitated, as if deciding how much she wanted to confide in me. Or what I could be trusted with.

"When I was about eight," she said eventually, "going on nine, one weekend we went to a swap meet over in Venice. Me, my mom, Natalie. We wandered around, looking at the usual crap, you know, and then I saw this one stall and knew I had to go look at it. The woman had all this really old, dusty stuff."

She reached into her purse, pulled something out. Put it on the table. A small, square glass pot, with a tall Bakelite lid. Whatever was inside had once been brightly colored, a hot pink of a kind now out of fashion, but it had dried and cracked and gone mainly murky and black. There was a faded label, in the kind of lettering you see on old cinemas. It said JAZZBERRY.

"Nail polish," I said.

"Original 1920s. I didn't know that then. Just knew I had to have it. My mom thought I'd gone nuts. I used to take it out and look at it once in a while. Didn't understand why. Until I was eighteen."

"What happened then?"

"Things changed."

"You started to believe that you'd been here before."

"So you think you know some things, huh?"

"I don't really know what to think."

"Your friend Gary built quite a castle in the air, by the sound of it. In which he'd have lived alone. Probably just as well things turned out as they did last night. No offense."

"Was he right? About any of it?"

"I don't know what he told you. But . . . people guess things. Sometimes they guess right. The mental institutions of the world are riddled with sane people who just never had the sense to shut up."

"What's the Psychomachy Trust?"

"What do you think? What's *your* guess?"

"Something to do with the intruders."

She raised an eyebrow. "The who?"

"That's what Gary called people who got it into their head that they keep coming back."

"A name he got from your book, I suppose. I'm sure that, if any such people exist, they'd prefer the term 'revisitors.' "

"The place under the building in Belltown," I said. "What was that for?"

She glanced at her watch. "A gathering. One that happens very rarely, and quite soon. It's why I've been spending so much time here."

"But now it's burned down."

"Oh, we wouldn't have been using that place anyway. It was prepared long in advance. A hundred years ago, that's how it was done. The world is far less formal now. You have to move with the times."

"Wasn't there a risk someone would find it?"

She laughed. "Find what? Some chairs, a table? Big deal. Hiding things is for amateurs."

"What about the bodies?"

"That was different."

"Who *was* Marcus Fox?"

"Someone who used to be important," she said, as if the subject were distasteful. "He has always been . . . difficult. He developed worse problems during his most recent time away."

"Away where?"

"The place where you go. In between. It's not far. Marcus became very cruel. He hurt people. Little people."

"I saw. Why keep the bodies?"

"They were as safe from discovery there as if buried in a forest or thrown into the bay. Until you and your friend started digging around."

"And Fox?"

"He became a security risk. He was dealt with."

"Killed, you mean. By the man who shot Gary."

"So you say."

"Why did Todd Crane say Marcus was in the building yesterday?"

"You do have good ears. And a busy little mind. That could be a problem. But, of course, we know where you live."

I stared at her. "It's where you live, too."

"No. I never lived there, Mr. Whalen." She stubbed out her cigarette, looked at me with blank indifference. "I assumed you understood. You're not talking with Amy. You're talking to Rose."

Maybe I'd already guessed. I'd certainly realized during the night that Amy could have put a number for ROSE into my phone, at any time in the last few weeks or months, and I wouldn't have noticed until she called me from that number. Called why? To warn me, maybe. Or to stop me from screwing with something I didn't understand. Presumably the same reason I'd been approached by the two men in the alleyway with Georj. Men in the pay of the intruders, whoever the hell they were.

"So who is Rose, exactly?"

"Just a label for a state of mind."

"I don't believe that. I don't think you do either. Why was Shepherd trying to kill that girl? Was Fox supposed to be inside her?"

"He was. But Mr. Fox appears to have left the building."

"That happens?"

"Very rarely. She was strong. She was also far too young. There's some concern over how Marcus got through in the first place. One of our helpers may have been involved." She shrugged. "Sometimes revisitors jump ship. Once in a blue moon, they get kicked out. Someone will keep an eye on the girl. We'll see."

She saw how I was looking at her and shook her head. "Not going to happen here. I told you on the pier. This is who I am. How I've always been, underneath."

I noticed a gray limousine parking fifty yards away up Yesler. A man got out, old, African-American, distinguished-looking. The car drove off, and the man walked down toward the square. He sat on a bench by himself. This struck me as odd in some way.

I was distracted by Amy lighting another cigarette. It's the simple things that seem the most wrong. Even though it was clear to me that I was not there with someone I understood, I didn't want her to leave. Once this person left, whatever she was now calling herself, I could be left with no one at all. So I started asking questions again.

"What was Anderson's ghost machine?"

She sighed. "You shouldn't know about that either."

"Tough. I do. What was so important that a guy like Bill had to be killed? And his wife and child?"

"He chanced upon something that allowed the eye to glimpse certain things."

"Christ, Amy—just be straight with me. What things?"

"The clue's in the title, Mr. Whalen."

"The machine meant you could see *ghosts*?"

"Souls. While they're waiting to come back again. They're all around us, they live in a . . . Trust me, it was a bad machine. No good would have come of it. People are better off not knowing certain things."

"So Cranfield paid Bill to drop his research."

"Joseph was a kind man, and he had become rich and powerful and gotten used to handling things his own way.

Even people with his experience forget the broader picture once in a while. It was a mistake. It should have been discussed among the Nine."

"Who are they?"

"The people who look after things. Make strategic decisions. First among equals. You know the kind of thing."

I realized that another man was sitting on the bench in the Square now. He was not communicating with the first man, just sitting at the other end, watching the world go by. And a woman in her late fifties was standing by herself on the other side, near the totem pole.

"Unfortunately, the money made Anderson aware he was onto something," Rose said. "He started hinting about his work to people on the Internet."

"That was his big crime? Hinting?"

"There will come a time when the Internet will be our best ally. Sooner or later someone there will have said everything that can be said, proved every cross-eyed piece of lunacy, and then there'll be no distinction between what's true and what's not. We're not there yet."

"So your people had Anderson murdered."

"Nothing should have happened to his family."

"But now *I* know some things. So—"

"You *think* you know, that's all. And I'm sure you realize how it sounds. How seriously did you take Gary when he told you what he thought he knew?"

"So what happens to me?"

"That's up for discussion—though not with you." She hesitated. "I find myself unable to mandate the usual course of action. Amy's still strong. But that will pass."

"I wouldn't bet on it," I said. My voice felt shaky. "She's pretty tough."

"We do, however, know about the night when you allegedly chanced upon suspicious activity in Los Angeles. We know that your colleagues and Internal Affairs elected to accept your version of events on the basis of exemplary previous service and on the fact that the four men you shot dead would not be missed by their own mothers. But I also know, because Amy knows, that's not the way it was. You went out that night looking for two of those men, and you took your gun but not your radio or your badge. What happened was premeditated. Amy could testify to that."

"She wouldn't," I said.

"Maybe. But I would."

"In which case I'd start talking."

"And all that gets you is a cell with thicker padding on the walls. Your record is not your friend here. Nor your personality in general."

There was coldness in her voice now that made me realize I'd spoken with this woman at least once before. The day I'd seen Amy, on the pier, for some of the time I'd been dealing with Rose. And before that? Presumably. Maybe from the day we met, those moments when my wife had seemed just a little different, unaccountable, not quite like herself. As we all do, from time to time.

When had Rose started to take fuller control? When we lost the child that would have kept us together? Could an event like that have made Amy start to withdraw deeper inside herself, leaving the stage empty? Or was it just something that was destined to follow its course, an assumption of power that happened according to schedule?

"So who's the guy in the pictures on your phone?"

She smiled. It was a warm, private smile, the kind to make a husband sad. "His name's Peter, since you ask."

"I didn't ask his fucking name. I asked who he was."

"Oh, sorry. He's a computer programmer, Jack. He lives in San Francisco. He's twenty-four. He plays guitar in a band. He's very good. Is that more what you meant?"

I didn't know what I'd meant. "How long have you been seeing him?"

"We've only met once. Night before last, in L.A."

"That's why you were down there?"

"Yes."

"I don't understand," I said. "How come you had pictures of him, if you never met before?"

"One of our other helpers tracked him down. She took some pictures, sent them to me. She had the preliminary conversation with him, which is one of the tasks the shepherds perform. We exchanged text messages after that."

"I still don't get it. What do you mean, 'tracked him down'?"

The smile still hadn't left her face, and it made me aware how long it had been since I'd seen a glow like this on her. I wondered how much of that was my fault and how much of it had been outside our control.

"A long time ago," she said, "there lived a young woman who was very, very much in love. With a jazz musician. An incredibly talented man, someone who could create music like nobody else, who could . . . Well, I guess you had to be there. But this man was also someone who couldn't come to terms with the nature of who he was, of the way things worked in his head. He fought himself. He drank too much. He died very young. But I've found him again now, and it will be different this time."

"So is he here? In Seattle?"

"No. He needs time to adjust. But the first meeting went very well. I think he'll come here soon. I hope so."

"Do you love him?"

"I always have."

For a moment I hated her very badly, of course, yet still I didn't want her to go. I'd spent the last seven years of my life with someone who at least looked like this woman. I knew that when I stood up, the first step I took would be into a world I'd never been to before.

She was glancing across at the square more often now. There were now five or six people standing there, unconnected but in the same space.

I looked at her face, remembering all the ways I'd seen it, all the places.

"Did you do anything about Annabel's birthday?"

She grinned, and for a moment it was different, and in her eyes I saw something of a woman I used to know. More than something. A lot.

"Check," she said. "Girl's going crazy in Banana Republic 'round about now."

Then she was gone. "Don't worry," Rose said briskly. "Amy will continue to do her jobs, perform her roles in other people's lives. No one but you will ever know."

"And what about me?"

"What *about* you?" she said, and the conversation was over. Her cup was empty. I'd run out of time.

"What is it about this place?" I asked nonetheless. "This square? Why does it feel like it does?"

"There are places where the wall is thinner," she said. "This is one of them. That's all."

I counted the people now standing beneath the trees, as if they were eight strangers, looking in different directions. One of them over the far side, I now noticed, was Ben Zimmerman.

"I only see eight."

"Joe was the ninth," she said. "A replacement has been selected."

I nodded. I understood. The move to Birch Crossing had started soon after Cranfield had died, I now realized, though presumably the grooming process had started long before: when Amy had been chosen to be part of the transfer of ownership of the building in Belltown.

Perhaps even back when she was eighteen, and had met someone named Shepherd, and her life had started to change track.

"So what happens now?"

"I say good-bye."

She got up, started to walk across the foot of Yesler Way, toward the square.

"Amy," I said loudly. The woman hesitated. "I'll be seeing you again."

Then she resumed walking. When she reached the other side, she stepped into the square beneath the trees, stood among the others there. None of them spoke, but for a moment all bowed their heads. They could still have been random passersby, pausing in a place that had been here long before this modern city, that had been the real reason, perhaps, that it came into being.

This city, in what had been far wilderness, a place that certain people could call their own: somewhere that had been special and revered even before they found their way here. On the flight to L.A., I had read some of the book on local history that I'd bought only a couple of blocks away. I knew that there'd once been a village called Djijila'letc on this spot. The translation usually given for the name was "the little crossing-over place."

Or, I suppose, the place where you can cross over. From here to somewhere else. And perhaps back.

I let my gaze drift up to the few remaining leaves in the trees, as a soft wind seemed to move the branches. I could not feel it where I sat, but I was close to the building behind me, and the afternoon was cold anyhow.

I watched these leaves for some time, listening to their dry, whispering sound. It seemed then as if it were raining, too, yet not raining, as if it could be both at once, as if many things and conditions could exist in the same place, together, hidden only by the splendor of light.

When I looked back down, the square was empty.

chapter FORTY-FOUR

As soon as I let myself into the house, I knew that everything had changed. Houses are pragmatic and unforgiving. If something alters in your relationship to them, they shift, turn away. I saw that Amy's computer had gone, some of her books, a few clothes. In a way it was distressing to see how little had been removed, how small a part of the life that had been lived here was now judged to be worth moving on.

I limped back to the living room and stood in the center. Took out my cigarettes and lit one. Defiantly, thinking, *That's the end of all that.* But I couldn't go through with it. I unlocked the door onto the deck and went out there instead.

People never really leave. That's the worst crime committed by those who go and those who die. They leave echoes of themselves behind, for the people who loved them to deal with for the rest of their lives.

I hardly slept at all that night, or the next. Even if my mind had been able to find any quietness, the pain in my shoulder wouldn't have allowed it to settle. Lying on my back hurt. So did lying on my front and my side. So did sitting. Existence in general, in any posture, hurt.

I spent the days in the living room or out on the deck.

Eventually I dragged one of the chairs out there and stopped going back inside, except when I was trying to sleep. It was far too cold for that.

Two days later the snows finally came.

They came all at once, in the night. I missed their arrival, having at last managed to get some rest. When I hauled myself out onto the deck the next morning, I gasped aloud.

Everything was white. Everything I could see. I knew that it was all still there underneath, of course, but for the moment the world looked as if it had been made afresh, as it always does.

I love snow. I always have. And in loving it at that moment, I was wishing Amy were in the house to go wake up, to bundle into a robe and drag out onto the deck to see it with me. To stand there shivering with her, not caring about the cold, looking at all that white and feeling as if we'd been reborn together, reborn into a new world we could make our own.

And finally, and savagely, I cried.

In the afternoon I forced myself to consider going into town. I was running out of the only things I had appetite for, coffee and cigarettes. As I was checking my wallet for cash, I realized there was something wedged among the bills. A small blue plastic rectangle, barely thicker than a credit card and a sixth the size.

It was the memory stick Gary had given me, from the camera on which he'd taken the photographs of Amy in Belltown. I'd forgotten about it.

I went into the study and put it into a card reader attached to my laptop. There were only four files on the disk. The first two were the pictures I'd already seen. Even at greater magnification, and with the benefit of hindsight, Ben's identity wasn't obvious. I couldn't blame myself for not working it out earlier, though I tried. The next file was a Word document. When I double-clicked it, nothing seemed to happen for a moment, and I thought the document had been corrupted and crashed the machine. When it finally came up on-screen, I realized that the delay had been caused by the fact that it was huge. Tens of thousands of words, littered with diagrams.

I scrolled through it, trying to figure out how the document was organized, but soon decided that it simply wasn't. It started with a list of people Gary believed had been intruders (Frank Lloyd Wright, J. S. Bach, the Wandering Jew, Nikola Tesla, Osiris, vampires, the builders of Stonehenge, Thomas Jefferson, all of the Dalai Lamas, to name but a few). The prophets of the Old Testament, too, with their extraordinary ages—four, five, eight hundred years. Naturally, they didn't live that long as the same person, Gary wrote; it was the same soul returning time and again to different bodies. From here he moved to another quasi-historical figure: one who on the morning of his birth received three visitors bearing "gifts"—symbolizing this child's experiences from previous lives. Gary claimed that the boy's mother was told not that the Holy Ghost would come upon *her,* as the Bible had it, but that one would come upon her *son.*

The promise of life everlasting. The Lord, who is our shepherd. Father, Son, Holy Ghost.

"Oh, Gary," I said.

But I continued to read, and it soon dawned on me that he'd been hiding the truth even on the day he died. He'd spoken then as if he thought the intruders were an isolated phenomenon, a few individuals who'd worked out a way to persist down the generations, a cabal who were different from the rest of us. But he hadn't believed that at all.

He wrote that the word "nightmare" was derived from the Scandinavian legend of *nachtmara*—demons who squatted on the chests of sleepers, bad dreams long having been believed to be caused by evil spirits trying to force their way inside. He claimed that the original role of midwives had been to scout for healthy pregnant women, whose babies would probably live past infancy, who would make good sites for aging intruders to move into next time around. He noted that nobody knows how antidepressants work and claimed they masked a badly integrated intruder—which was why initial benefits often turned to worse depression or self-harm: suicide an unconscious attempt to kill an intruder, the thing roosting inside, conflicting our lives. He believed that this also explained our species' affection for drugs and alcohol, as they dampen the main personality, allowing the intruder some time in the sun, a chance to direct our behavior once in a while. The intruder was less inhibited, more experienced, and simply a different person, and prone to make us behave uncharacteristically. This, presumably, was why Gary had given up drinking, and why it's said God looks after drunks and small children. It's not God, of course. It's the hidden person inside.

The person, Gary believed, inside all of us.

Only a small group of these were aware of coming back. To keep the rest of us sane, secure in our identities, we were happy to have the second soul fenced off, gagged and occluded from our conscious minds. When something leaked through the wall in our head—a piece of déjà vu, a dream about somewhere we'd never been, a confused body image, a facility for a foreign language or a musical instrument, the simple feeling that we should be somewhere else and having some other life—we shrugged it away as being merely the human condition: fucked up, fractured, never masters of our own minds.

Gary even had a scientific rationale. It was an adaptation, he said—and the real reason humans ruled the world. At some point on the flat, grassy plains of Africa or in the cold mountains of Europe, our species derived evolutionary advantage from being able to support two souls within a single body. The modern soul didn't realize but was able to make intuitive decisions—lifesaving and thus naturally selecting calls—on the basis of experience gained in the intruding soul's previous lives. But there was a cost. When the souls cooperated, the person worked. When they didn't, the person was damaged. Broken, dysfunctional, violent, alcoholic. This was why some of us are mentally ill, or bipolar, or just can't get our shit together, and seem to enter the world like that.

The soul goes somewhere for a while, but then it comes back, forcing its way into children, into our babies. Then it waits, consolidating, growing in power, until the time is right. Why do we hear nothing about Jesus until he was in his mid-thirties, Gary asked? Because that was when the intruder was mature, ready to assume control. Any internal threat to the security of the system was dealt with swiftly, as he claimed Salieri had done with Mozart, when the latter grew disenchanted and worn out and started dropping hints in his work, disguising them as hidden references to Freemasonry. And why had Jesus himself never returned, as he promised? He got lost on the other side, was just another shadow among those who Bill Anderson's machine would have enabled us to glimpse, had it not been destroyed.

And so on.

There was more of it. Too much to read or believe, far too much evidence for it to be true. I didn't know what to think about the person who'd been my wife, about what had caused her to change. But I couldn't help wondering if I'd helped cause Gary's obsession, through something I'd said by the side of a running track long ago, if my dumb comment had lain festering at the back of his mind all these years, as Donna's death had, gradually taking over his mind. I closed the document.

The final file on the disk was another picture. When it came up onto the screen, I caught my breath. It was a photograph of Gary, with Bethany. A badge on her dress said she was two years old that day, which meant that the picture must have been taken only a few weeks before she died. She had a big old slab of cake in one hand and whipped cream all over her face and in her hair—and was grinning up at her father, her eyes bright with the shine of someone gazing upon one of the two glowing souls who make up her entire world.

The picture had been taken indoors, with flash, and was very sharp. I magnified it and scrolled to the area at the side of Bethany's right eye, then sat there looking at it for a long time.

She did have a scar there. Small, crescent-shaped.

When I closed my eyes, I knew, as Gary had, where I'd seen that scar before.

I walked into town. It took a long time. Pushing through six inches of snow caused a sharp pull in my shoulder and neck with every step. By then I had accepted the pain. There was no escape from it.

Birch Crossing was almost empty of cars, but Sam's Market was open. I walked alone along the aisles, staring without comprehension at all the things you could buy. My hand hovered over a can of sauerkraut for some time, but then I realized I didn't know why I liked it and left it where it was.

When I got to the checkout, Sam himself was standing there. He bagged my few purchases without saying a word, but as I shuffled toward the exit, he spoke.

"Could get the boy to bring things up to you at the house," he said. "If you wanted."

I stopped, turned. I remembered the last time I'd seen him, at the gathering at Bobbi Zimmerman's house. I thought it was unlikely I would be buying anything in Birch Crossing again, but I nodded.

"Thank you."

"Need to look after that shoulder," he said.

I hadn't managed to make much sense of this by the time I struggled back to the road that led to the house. And by then I'd noticed that the gate had been pushed wide open and there were tire tracks leading up our drive.

A car I'd never seen before was sitting next to the SUV. I let myself into the house and went to the top of the stairs to look down.

A man was sitting on my sofa.

I went back to the kitchen. Poured a cup of coffee from the pot. I had gotten badly chilled on the walk back. I took the coffee down the stairs and sat in the chair opposite the sofa. The man had a cup on the table in front of him.

"Make yourself at home," I said.

"The keys," Shepherd said, nodding toward the table. "Rose doesn't need them anymore."

"Why are you here?"

He reached into his coat, pulled out my gun and my cell phone. Put these on the coffee table, too. Then finally the clip from the gun. "How's the shoulder?"

"How do you think?"

"It was nothing personal. You just looked like the kind of man who would get in the way."

"You killed a friend of mine."

"Like I said. Nothing personal."

"You're the second person who's shown concern for my shoulder this afternoon."

"I assume you've figured out that this town is one of their places? A headquarters?"

"I was getting there. I chanced upon a pre-meeting celebration, I think, at my neighbors'. Are there a lot of towns like this?"

"Only two in this country. There aren't many of these people, all told."

"And who are they, exactly?"

"I assume Rose gave you the wacky version. She likes to kid around sometimes. They're just a club, Mr. Whalen. Like the Masons. The Rotarians. The Bohemian Grove. Successful people who scratch one anothers' backs. Some of them have this mythology thing going. Doesn't mean anything. It's like having Santa Claus as an excuse to give presents at Christmas. Nothing more."

I looked at the stuff on the table. "How come I'm getting these back?"

"They're yours, and the big meeting is over. Evidently you were discussed."

He reached into his coat once more, brought out a small box, which he put on the table next to the other objects. "If you decide to accept, walk up the hill and talk to Mr. Zimmerman. He'll explain the deal."

"Whatever it is, I'm not doing it."

He rose. "That's up to you."

I watched as he ascended the stairs. At the front door, he stopped, turned.

"Let me just make one thing clear," he said. "These people only take yes-or-no answers. If it's no, someone will come to call on you. That won't be personal either."

He left.

I picked up the cell phone first. Amy's number had been removed, along with Rose's, and the call log had been erased. I could look up Amy's number easily, of course, but I knew that there would be no point. If I hoped ever to see her again, it would not come about through a phone call. At the moment I had no idea what an alternative course of action might be.

I put the phone back and moved the small box toward me. Inside were business cards, printed on pure white stock. There was nothing on them but a name, or perhaps it was a job title.

Jack Shepherd

I left the cards on the table and went outside to the deck, closing the sliding door behind me. The world sounded dead and flat.

And very quiet.

I walked to the end of the deck and down the stairs. Instead of heading onto our land, I turned and went around the side of the house, up the slope, pushing the snow-covered bushes aside. When I neared the front, I got in close to the wall and moved my head out carefully.

The car was still parked in our drive.

I pushed the clip into my gun and flicked off the safety. Kept low as I moved across to the back of the car. Straightened quickly as I slipped out around the driver's side. There was no one in the car. Just a black suitcase on the backseat.

I walked over to the door to the house. Stood to the side and pushed it. It opened slowly. I swung out, gun in front. My shoulder didn't hurt anymore. I nudged the door with my foot and stepped inside.

The house was still and silent. I took four steps, five, until I was within six feet of the top of the stairs. I waited there.

Moments later Shepherd came out of Amy's study and into the center of the living room, moving quietly, swiftly, at ease in someone else's place. There was a gun in his hand.

I fired three times.

When I got down to the living room, he was still alive, lying twisted on his back. He seemed to be gazing at something behind me, something or someone, staring past me like a man facing down a crowd. He was trying to raise his gun. I didn't think he was going to make it, but you want to be sure.

I shot him again, and it was done.

I stood over him for five minutes, perhaps ten, as his blood pooled out over the wooden floor. It was spattered over the coffee table, too, and across the sofa where I'd last seen Amy when she was in this place, sitting working, as she so often had. I remembered the way she would look up at me and smile when I came down the stairs, making me feel I was home. I remembered also something that she/Rose had said:

There's some concern over how Marcus got through in the first place. One of our helpers may have been involved.

It occurred to me to wonder whether Rose had sent Shepherd here to tie me up as a loose end or if the hope had been for it to pan out the other way around. If I had already started working for them.

"You killed a friend of mine," I said again, to the man at

my feet. But I knew in my heart that was not why I had done what I'd done.

He'd come to murder me. I had no choice.

I am not a killer. Not Jack Whalen. Not my father's son. But something inside me is, and with every year that passes, I feel it struggling harder to get out.

I am on the road now. I am in Shepherd's car. I brought nothing from the house except a photograph of myself with a woman I once loved and may once more, if I ever see her again. I have looked in the suitcase that lies on the backseat. There is a change of clothes that will probably fit me, and a large sum of money. Both the case and its contents belong to me now, I guess.

It is growing dark, and the sky is leaden. It will snow again later. I will watch it alone. By then I hope to be far from here. I don't know where I'm going.

I never have.

They're already inside . . .

"BRILLIANT." *Newark Star-Ledger*

"TERRIFYING." *USA Today*

"EXCELLENT." *Baltimore Sun*

"SPOOKY." *New York Times*

"ENGROSSING." *Pittsburgh Post-Gazette*

"CHILLING." *New Orleans Times-Picayune*

"A STORY THAT WILL NOT LET YOU GO."
Arizona Republic